TABLE OF CONTENTS

THE SPIDER CHRONICLES

Edited by Joe Gentile, Garrett J. Anderson and Lori Gentile
Art Direction by Dave Ulanski
Production Design by Erik Enervold/Simian Brothers Creative
Cover Art by Doug Klauba
Interior Art by Tom Floyd

Moonstone would like to thank our SPIDER consultant Rich Harvey
And a special thanks to Tim Lasiuta and Martin Powell.

More just than the law,
more dangerous than the Underworld...
hated, feared, and wanted by both.

One cloaked, fanged, border-line crazy
denizen of the dark force-feeding hard justice
with a pair of 45s!

Moonstone is proud to present 19 new, short stories of
SEARING WHITE HOT PROSE
starring pulpdoms most violent and ruthless crime fighter ever:

THE MASTER OF MEN!
SPIDER.

INTRODUCTION

Step right this way, into our Metaphysical Reality Inversion Chamber, where we throw a switch and...*kzorp!* through the wonders of pseudo science you are inhabiting the body of your own great grandpa.

You're in a drugstore, standing in front of a magazine rack, scanning the dozens bright covers arrayed in front of you, looking for your favorite. You know a new issue should be out, but where is it? Ah, *there*, between the latest numbers of *Wild West Weekly* and *Jungle Stories*. *The Spider, Master of Men*. Your favorite magazine, your favorite hero. Oh, you can enjoy a Shadow adventure, and Doc Savage can always be counted on for an exciting read, but nobody beats The Spider when it comes to getting your blood racing. You give the nice old guy behind the counter a dime and slip your new treasure between the fold of a newspaper you got earlier. You have to take a street car home and, well...you might run into the parson and he wouldn't approve of your reading what church folks call "trash."

Well, maybe it *is* trash, but doggone it, a fella's got to have some entertainment and he can't go to the movies more than once a week or so, and sure, there are stories on the radio, but you don't think they're very exciting and anyway, any time the weather's bad and sometimes when it isn't the broadcast is full of static—sounds more like grocery bags being crumpled than anything a fella'd want to listen to. Maybe you could read books, but the only bookstore in the city is way downtown and what's in the musty-smelling public libraries is obviously intended for folks who've gone to college, or at least finished high school.

Sitting on the wooden seat, swaying with the motion of the street car, you suddenly hear a voice in your head. You wonder if you're going nuts. Stop worrying. It's only me, speaking to you from seventy three years in the future. So stop wondering and listen:

What you have there, that novel cheaply printed on cheap paper, that time-waster, is an example of a publishing phenomonon that began in 1896 with a publication called *Argosy*. There are hundreds of them and they will eventually be known as *pulps*, if they aren't already. The sad news is, they'll be as extinct as dinosaurs by the mid-1950s, giving them a life span of just about 58 years, give or take.

Of course, dinosaurs, though officially long gone from the Earth, are still around in the form of birds. They evolved. And so did pulps. Their most apparent descendants will be comic books and, in fact, some of the people who began as pulp publishers will among the first comics publishers by the end of the 1930s. They'll also be a big influence on movies, radio shows, and the radio-with-pictures thing called *television*. Some of them may even be studied in universities! The parson would have to gulp hard to swallow *that*.

Here's another fact the parson might have trouble with. In the Twenty First century, after men have actually walked on the moon, when an airplane ride from New York to Los Angeles take only six hours, when just about every house in the country has at least one of those television gadgets and a lot of them have their own electronic brains, when wristwatches are operated by batteries and incorporate alarms and calendars and other stuff, when music lovers can store thousands of songs in something the size of a pack of gum and listen to them through tiny ear buttons…when the world is awash in technological wizardry, folks will still remember The Spider, Master of Men. What's more, writers will still want to write Spider stories, and they will, and some of those new Spider yarns will be collected in a book, which your great grand child will read and enjoy just as much as you'll enjoy the Spider magazine you just bought.

Pretty amazing, huh?

Here's your stop. Time to get off the street car, walk home, hurry through dinner and get to your reading.

- Dennis O'Neil
Nyack, N.Y - July, 2006

illustration by Tom Floyd

Chapter One

CITY OF THE MELTING DEAD

by MARTIN POWELL

Human vermin swarmed out of a rain-slick alley, creeping like rats toward a rust-crusted manhole, melding with the midnight shadows. Their movements were precise and exact, resembling well-oiled soulless automatons. One by one, the gang labored with their weighted burden of ominous black metal boxes from the hidden supply truck, their booted feet ringing hollow chimes as they climbed down into the murk and slime of the sewer below.

A tall skeleton of a man descended last, the flickering of sputtering flares betraying the feverish madness in his eyes. His goons had worked rapidly in the fetid semi-darkness. The devices had been reconstructed even more quickly than during the hundred rehearsals of before. All was in readiness. Commissioner Kirkpatrick and the Mayor had been stubborn to the end. The million dollar ransom remained unpaid. Now New York City was to pay a very different, devastating price.

"Masks," he hissed.

The order was obeyed instantly with fidgeting fingers fumbling leather straps, and eleven pairs of yellow goggled eyes glowered from behind the gasmasks in anticipation of the next command. The cadaverous dictator secured his own protective respirator with a practiced ease. He cocked his head toward the leering lieutenants.

"They had their chance," his voice, never quite normal, droned all the more weirdly through the muffling gasmask. "Do it quickly."

They scuffled off, well-trained in exactly where to strategically plant the infernal gas bombs within the sewer system to filter their poison fog throughout the entire metropolis. No chances left. No mercy. Thousands would perish. Next time that damnable Kirkpatrick would have to give in. Yes, next time.

But wait. Where was Skaggs? He was to bring up the rear then turn east in the tunnel ahead toward upper Manhattan. Skaggs was nowhere to be seen.

Supremely confident mere moments before, the skeletal commander felt an icy sweat crawl down his spine. He turned to bark an order to McQuade, and shuddered upon realizing he too had vanished. Something was very wrong.

"Oh Gawd!" a minion squawked around a curve in the tunnel.

The commander splashed recklessly toward the cry, losing all stealth, his steely nerves melting like wax. The others gathered, drawn from their mission to the grotesque scene set before them deep in the arched underbelly of the city. For a full minute none said a word, not even their chief. They just stood there, knee deep in the filthy swill, staring at the horror suspended above.

Skaggs had been snagged and hanged by the neck, swaying like a puppet from an almost invisible silken cord. The crimson brand of a bristle-legged arachnid wetly embossed Skaggs' forehead.

Each man moved as one, all drawing guns. Eyes bulged and throats grew dry. Outside the range of the sulfur-spattering flares the shadows themselves pulsed like something alive. Then, worse of all, came the laughter, a low mirthless reverberation that seemed to originate from everywhere.

"The *Spider*!" one of the gang cried fearfully.

"Shut up!" the skeletal commander barked. "*Spider* or not, he's only one man."

Instantly thunder erupted in the cavernous tunnel, the innumerable blasts echoing a deafening clamor as half the gang keeled and slumped into the reeking sewage. Six hardened killers were dead in less than as many heartbeats, each unerringly shot between the eyes.

Blind panic seized the surviving thugs. Rounds were fired as fast as triggers could be squeezed. More blasts answered from the blackness, finely tuned and finding their mark. Almost as abruptly as it had begun, it was over. Only the gaunt and ghastly commander was still standing, his fist wetly melding with the pistol in his grip. He hadn't yet felt the three forty-five caliber slugs that had ripped through his guts.

The faint wisp of a noise captured his gaze as a figure on a silken line floated like an inky ghost. From the flicker of the flares the descending creature appeared to possess multiple writhing arms, an illusion cast by the flapping of a billowing black cloak. A venomous, fanged mouth again uttered its hideous cackle.

"You were smarter than most."

Oh God! The monster spoke!

The commander was more corpse-like than ever, his life pouring out in ruby driblets. The revolver weighed a ton, but still he tried to aim as the terrible hunched stalker crept nearer.

"Not smart enough to escape my web," the cloaked thing laughed again.

Two big guns in each black-gloved fist bucked twice, exploding the silence. The Poison Fog was to menace the city no more.

The *Spider* surveyed his territory, satisfied with the scene before him. Human scum sprawled dead at his feet, each of them guilty of a dozen unsolved murders, each of them now with his eight-legged scarlet seal emblazoned on what was left of their foreheads. The last Crime Ring. Finally. It was over. Kirkpatrick and his policemen could handle the petty crooks now.

At last, the *Spider* could rest.

Bill Henry had a deadline.

The crusty old crime reporter, nowadays known as "Bourbon Bill", had seen better days, but this story was special. This story would make all the difference. It was a fluke really, not at all like the way he did things in the old days. He just happened to be in the right place to overhear the right thing. Most people hardly noticed the derelict sleeping it off in dark alleyways where darker deeds dare to be discussed. But Bourbon Bill wasn't sleeping this time.

Scientist missing. No word of ransom, so a kidnapping was not taken seriously. Sometimes eccentric egg-heads just disappear, the authorities said. But Bill knew better. He'd heard things right this time.

This was something big.

The grizzled journalist glanced around his shabby apartment, normally a depressing place, but then he smiled his jack o'lantern grin. Everything would change once he turned in this story. The city beat would be his again, that was a cinch. And he could afford good whisky again, not that bathtub gin he'd resorted to. Maybe Linda would even take him back. Yes, sir, what a story. Award-winning stuff, no doubt about it.

Bourbon Bill lifted the bottle to his dry, chapped lips. Maybe he should stop drinking? Yes, perhaps he should. Tomorrow he would stop for good. Everything would be different. Tomorrow.

In celebration, he sucked in a short swig from the bottle and promptly, painfully, spat it out with a hiss. The liquor was scalding hot, actually sizzling on his blistering tongue. That didn't make sense. Mesmerized, he stared at the bottle as the liquid inside actually began to boil.

No…oh no.

They'd found out. They'd found him. Too late. Same old Bill Henry luck…bad as always.

His body was suddenly seized with thick sweat, wracked by a weird agony. They knew that he knew. And he didn't have much time. Bourbon Bill felt his flesh dissolving, dripping away like candle wax. No. Not yet. Desperately, with his last effort, he clacked away at his typewriter, his fleshy finger-tips sticking to the keys leaving raw red-pink blobs. Had to leave a warning. He was the only one who could.

That done, a glorious leap out the window seemed the best solution to the torture. The cold wind whipped across his oozing face all the dizzying way down, and Bourbon Bill was at peace even before he hit the pavement, confident that his hastily typed warning would be heeded, and satisfied that the pain would stop at the swift end of his ten story fall.

Bourbon Bill Henry had made his deadline, after all.

"Hard to believe you're finally serious," Police Commission Kirkpatrick said bluntly, easing back in an overstuffed chair.

Richard Wentworth laughed, handing his old friend an Irish whisky and soda.

"You'll never change," Wentworth chided back. "Suspicious of me till the end."

"With good reason," Kirkpatrick smiled, the ends of his mustache curling upward. "The news that Richard Wentworth, famed criminologist, is deciding to retire, get married and finally settle down, is going to raise a lot of eyebrows in this city."

Wentworth shrugged good-naturedly.

"Well, according to you, Kirk, the *Spider's* elimination of the Poison Fog Gang ends the last of New York's great crime-rings. Seems like things will be getting pretty dull around here from now on."

There was a long moment of silence as each man studied the other, many years of mysteries and mayhem shared between them. Each had risked his life for the other, many times. They hadn't always agreed, but both men were dedicated soldiers in the same war. Few men were closer than these two.

"And so I take it that the *Spider* will also be retiring, then?" Kirkpatrick sipped his drink with a smirk.

Wentworth refilled his own glass, his expression seemingly devoid of interest.

"Well, how on earth would I know what the *Spider* is planning? It's not like we share gossip during social functions, you know."

Kirkpatrick nodded, but noted that his old friend never quite looked him in the eye whenever discussion of the notorious vigilante came up between them.

"True enough, Dick," the Police Commissioner replied with narrowed eyes. "I'd like to think that you have very little in common with that murdering lunatic...and yet—"

The sudden clamor of the telephone interrupted Kirkpatrick's familiar accusation. Wentworth sardonically shook his head, his grey eyes glinting with amusement.

"As I've said many times before, I think you've got the *Spider* all wrong," his handsome face was almost boyish in its innocence. "You might not approve of his methods, but he definitely gets results that your official policemen frequently fail to achieve. Ah, what is it, Jenkins?"

The butler stood with formal dignity in the doorway, ignoring Kirkpatrick's obvious agitation.

"Miss Van Sloan phoned, sir. The Daimler has unfortunately broken down, stranding her in the Garment District. A faulty fan belt. I suggested that Mr. Jackson meet her with another vehicle, but she insisted the subway would be faster. She begs your pardon, sir, and should be here within half an hour."

Wentworth frowned slightly, then brightened.

"Well, Nita and I have waited this long," he sighed. "Another thirty minutes can hardly matter. Care for another drink, Kirk, ol'boy?"

The Commissioner waved him away.

"As I was saying, Dick, while it is true that I have, upon occasion, openly suspected you of being the *Spider*, there always existed an alibi to absolve you. Rather convenient alibis, too, I might add."

Wentworth smiled openly with a frank, honest expression. There was no denying the man's charm.

"Leave it up to you to reopen that old chestnut!" he casually clicked ice into his glass. "Well—what is it, then? Am I innocent...or am I guilty?"

The telephone again interrupted, slicing the sudden silence.

Kirkpatrick faintly grinned, and winked at his friend.

"Let's just say I wish you a happy retirement," he raised the glass, then drained the last swallow.

Both men noticed Jenkins again standing in the doorway, his normally aloof demeanor seeming noticeably pale.

"Your pardon, sir..." the butler nearly stammered. "It...it's the station for Commissioner Kirkpatrick. There's been an accident...a subway train has just wrecked in the tunnel near 94th and Broadway...there appears to be very few survivors, sir."

Kirkpatrick got instantly to his feet. Wentworth was already at the door, flinging on his heavy overcoat. His steely eyes shone with a terrible intensity as the suspected horror cut deep into his heart.

"My God! Nita—!" he breathed.

Suddenly, the ever-waiting shadows surged back into the soul of Richard Wentworth.

Imminent scientist Doctor Emerick Berg had done what was commanded of him. With deep regret he'd performed the test upon that old prying reporter in the tenement, where the range and precision of his machine had worked only too well. It had exceeded his theories, truly fantastic and terrible in its wake.

He peered down again at what remained of his hands, remembering the fine artistic extensions they had once been. Now only two digits remained, a thumb and a forefinger. He'd been generously allowed to keep these, so he could more deftly demonstrate the operation of his hellish mechanism. The other fingers had been wrenched out by the roots, a more than sufficient persuader in divulging all his confessed secrets.

Now, alone in his cell, Dr. Berg awaited the dreadful news of the subway. It was not long in coming.

"We are triumphant, Doctor...your destiny is fulfilled."

The being who called himself the Crucible lumbered his great amorphous mass into the chamber, the fragile dwarfish creature who was his brother followed helplessly behind him.

Berg's own deep sense of guilt wouldn't allow himself to look into the hate-seethed eyes of the roaring giant. The pained and tragic gaze of the brother, however, screamed volumes into his tormented conscience. Wretched as he was at that instant, the scientist still felt pity for the wizened little man in the shadow of the monster, knowing full well that he was, in many ways, just as much a prisoner of the Crucible as he himself.

The dwarf frantically clasped the other's massive shoulder.

"Please, brother," he pleaded with horror. "This madness must stop... be merciful—"

The Crucible savagely struck him.

"Was anyone ever merciful to us?" he scoffed. "You always were the weak one. It is ludicrous that we share the same blood."

The giant drew a heavy revolver from his ponderous robes. Berg sighed, and stopped his shuddering. A gun. Good. This would be quick, not like what the fiend had done to his hands with the rusty pliers.

"Your place in history is assured, Dr. Berg," the Crucible nodded as a loud report ended what was left of the scientist's brilliant mind, bursting it onto cracked plaster walls and rotten wooden rafters.

"He served his higher purpose," the Crucible rumbled. "I'm satisfied that I can successfully operate his machine alone. The subway was merely an experiment. The Crucible's masterpiece awaits."

Doctor Emerick Berg's slavery had abruptly ended, but to the terrified dwarf, the bondage was as complete as ever. Worse still, he knew full well of his brother's hideous scheme. Hot, seething Hell was coming to countless unsuspecting thousands. There seemed no chance of stopping it now.

New York was already doomed. The city just didn't know it yet.

Beneath the pavement of 94th and Broadway, chaos ran wild amid the dead and the dying. Tough, seasoned cops had gone down into the subway tunnel only to stagger out again in stupefied horror just as the entrance collapsed behind them. It could be hours before rescue crews might reach the dozens of casualties who remained trapped below. Although there were survivors, it all seemed quite hopeless.

Richard Wentworth clambered over the rubble and wreckage of the tunnel with the soundless stealth of an alley cat. Nita. Sweet, loving, ever-loyal Nita. Her bright intelligent eyes and warm luxuriant lips burned in his mind, and in his gut. No matter the risk, he would never abandon Nita.

It had been a simple matter to slip away from Kirkpatrick during the panic and confusion at the subway entrance above. Steadily Wentworth made his way toward the disaster, sometimes crawling, sometimes burrowing, heart pounding and throat tightening with each foot of painful progress. He didn't know how long he had been at it. It didn't matter.

Then, almost miraculously, Wentworth penetrated the tunnel. It took a long moment before his eyes could adjust to the sudden change of illumination. He stared, unblinking, taking it all in. The scene could almost have been a stanza out of Dante. Flinching emergency lights flashed a lightning storm the color of blood over the carnage, and thin ribbons of grey smoke snaked through the narrow claustrophobic passage carrying a thick, greasy stench throughout the underground. It was the odor of death.

The subway had jumped the track, that much was apparent, crashing into the coiling tunnel with its cars twisting and welding together from the awful impact. The two front cars still appeared to have living people inside, although there was an indescribable wrongness about them as seen at first glance through the shattered windows.

But, Wentworth had no time to dwell upon that for outside the train, there in the tunnel, terrified, once normal people, were dying and killing each other. The screams reminded him of the Great War, and being again in the trenches. The entire crowd of perhaps half a hundred survivors frantically, hopelessly, sought escape no matter the cost. Makeshift clubs raised and fell, bursting flesh and crushing bone.

In a growing rage, Wentworth watched as a small child was trampled. An elderly woman was struck and flung bodily like a broken doll above the splintered tracks. The crowd leapt and swarmed, and a surrounded man, already grievous injured, was torn to pieces.

He had seen enough. If this breeding fear were to be controlled, then it must been mastered by something even more fearsome.

Wentworth's sudden motion was deliberate and uncanny as his reversible topcoat unfurled into a full dark cloak draped about his shoulders and swinging down to his heels. He quickly molded his black hat into a slouch that pulled low over a lank dead wig concealed in its crown. A black silk mask and snarling ivory fangs came from a secret pocket, and were deftly donned to a more than sinister effect.

There was no more Richard Wentworth. Instead, a crouching, burning eyed monster stood in his place, seething with menace and revulsion. The maddened mob would recognize him instantly, and the sight of him would shock them with a fresh terror.

Big black guns slid from their hidden holsters, exploding thunder through the confines of the tunnel. The violence stopped instantly, replaced with utter silence.

Then, the *Spider* laughed.

"You all know who I am," he grimaced, the sharp teeth gleaming in the fading, pulsing electric light. "I will kill the next man who strikes a blow."

A low murmur followed, he heard his awesome name uttered by a few with hushed reverberations. The aggression was over.

The *Spider* indicated the makeshift tunnel with a wave of his gun-hand.

"Quietly now," he hissed, more creature than man. "You can all escape through here. Anyone who can still walk will take up the injured and carry them to safety."

After a brief moment of stillness, the mastered mob obeyed and, puppet-like, removed the wounded and themselves through the narrow tunnel to safety.

The *Spider* glided with his infamous lurching gait among the tracks. The fanged mouth suddenly lost most of its menace, becoming a grim straight line. Something had caught his eye.

He bent, snatched the thing up. It was a green high-heeled shoe.

The steely ferocity left his gaze, growing moist. Wentworth read the label visible on the inner sole, but he was already certain of its owner:

Made Expressly for Miss Nita Van Sloan

His gut had been right, as always. Nita was on the train.

Somewhere behind the hollow eye-slits of the mask and gnashing fangs, Richard Wentworth buried the creature deep inside him again. Instantly he began the agonized search for Nita…or for what remained of her. The engine and first two passenger cars of the train—he remembered that there'd been some ominous movement inside, behind the broken windows.

"Nita…" fighting back the choking sob in his throat, Wentworth made for there first.

The crumpled wreck looked unearthly in the pulsing glow of the dying emergency lights, haunted and forbidden. Wentworth's jaw muscles flexed and he scrambled inside a misshapen, jagged window. A pocket lantern came from his clothing and he sprayed its yellow light over the destroyed interior. He barely recognized the gasp of horror that escaped his own lips.

There, engulfing the space of the center aisle of the train car, was a loathsome mass of putrefied flesh—a semi-congealed heap of human beings fused together in a fleshy tangle of writhing death!

What once were arms and hands reached wetly out toward him, boney, dripping fingers losing skin like melting candles. Black mouths split and gaped in gurgling, pleading agony as eyes long dissolved stared with hollow sockets in outrage and despair. Wentworth could barely believe it, never had he seen such an abomination.

He gazed in sickened awe at the phantasmagoric things before him, the grimly distracted Wentworth nearly failed to notice the sodden, hulking entity that came lurking from behind. Abruptly he spun, his long cloak swirling in mid-air like an exploding ink drop. For an instant the fearsome form of the *Spider* seemed to become one with the shadows. His automatic whipped up cocked and ready, but the moist misshapen blobs that once were human hands were already at his throat.

"P-pleasssssssssssse..." the thing garbled from the liquefied gullet.

Possessed of a wild strength fueled by its death agonies, the Spider barely wrenched himself free from the desperate grip of the melting man. Once out of the gruesome clutches he watched in helpless pity as the form diminished before his eyes, drowning in its own tissues. Finally, slumping down to what remained of its knees, the last remaining mass poured from its clothing spilling onto the floor.

Wentworth stood utterly still over the hideous tragedy sprawled in a quickening puddle at his feet, his head bowed in mourning as the other awful liquescent vestiges also became silent and moved no more. A quick study of the engine found the train's doomed operator in an identical death, the oozing flesh of his forearm bubbling down the brake stick like a burnt out useless wick.

The oppressive sight was so frightful even the battle-hardened Wentworth had to shut his eyes. It was the glacial orbs of the *Spider* that reopened, seething again with their cold steel fire. These miserable souls would be avenged.

A muffled groan snapped Wentworth back from his deliberation. His heart quickened, his ears straining in a tense effort to detect the origin of the sound. Again, he heard the tormented wail. This was a fully human voice, weak but unfettered from the gurgling rasp of the victims he'd already encountered.

The low moan had come from the last passenger car. It was less damaged than the others, and from his earlier observation of the car's empty windows Wentworth had suspected it to be lifeless. It was not.

Using a broken section of track, he pried opened the doors. From within a pair of lovely violet eyes regarded him intimately, as if he'd been faithfully expected.

"Quick—I need something for another tourniquet," she said, her pale face bruised, begrimed, and beautiful. "If we can't stop the bleeding this mug's a goner."

Nita—! She was alive!

Wentworth's throat tightened and for an instant his tear ducts brimmed, then the *Spider* responded to the crisis.

"I've just the thing," he bent down over the grievously wounded man tended by Nita, observing several badly bleeding bone fractures.

Stout, slender rubber tubing snaked from a pocket in his cloak and the black-gloved hands expertly stemmed the hemorrhage. Satisfied that the victim was no longer in imminent danger, the *Spider* swiftly surveyed the remaining perimeter within the passenger car. Others were there, also injured, and had been capably treated by Nita. Tightly rolled newspapers had become improvised splints, while strips of her own clothing served as bandages, with her expensive silk stockings providing effective life-saving tourniquets.

Nita Van Sloan, black and blue herself, had done all she could, and that had been considerable. The weight of the last couple hours showed for a mere moment in her wide, haunted eyes. Nita wanted so very badly to fall into Wentworth's arms, hold him close, and breathe him in. Instead, she resumed her highly trained sense of calm.

"Dick, I saw inside the front cars. What…what could have done this?" she stammered only slightly.

The slouch-brimmed head shook slowly, clearly in restrained astonishment.

"Some kind of electromagnetic beam," he mused. "An unknown highly advanced technique for rebounding and refocusing pure sound waves, aimed at the front of the train. It's incredible, but it's the only explanation."

"My God," Nita breathed, her face suddenly losing more color. "Then this could have been so much worse…!"

The implications were staggering.

"We can't let Kirk and his policemen find us down here," the *Spider* offered her his hand. "If you can walk—"

"I can do better than that," Nita attempted a smile, rising quickly to her bare feet.

Her bruised toes stumbled painfully on a bit of debris, and in a blurring swoop, Wentworth swept her up in his arms. For a long, delicious moment their eyes were locked in a fervent gaze, and then their lips found each other.

"It's unbelievable…unthinkable," Stanley Kirkpatrick shook his head, his broad shoulders stooped and weighted from the tragedy. "All those people gone, so suddenly. In the past two days more than a dozen of the rescued passengers have also died from their injuries."

Richard Wentworth refilled the Commissioner's glass, and returned to Nita on the sofa.

"It's a terrible business all right, Kirk," Wentworth curled an affectionately protective arm around Nita's shoulders, mindful of her arm's sling. "You say there are still no leads?"

Kirkpatrick gratefully sipped his whisky and soda.

"None. Those who have survived, who owe their lives to Miss Van Sloan here, aren't talking. From the shock of it all, I'll wager."

"I don't blame them," Nita visibly trembled.

At that, observing her distress, Kirkpatrick promptly wished Nita a good evening, and a speedy recovery, as Wentworth walked him to the door.

"How's she doing, Dick? I mean, aside from the sprained arm and the cracked ribs. I hope my visit hasn't upset her more," Kirkpatrick whispered, chancing a fretful fatherly glance back over his shoulder.

"Nita's a scrapper," Wentworth shrugged. "She's as hungry for clues to this mystery as the rest of us."

The older man frowned and paused in the doorway.

"I wish I could provide one, but I only have this," he drew an envelope from his breast pocket.

Wentworth examined the inner contents, a single ragged sheet of cheap paper. There were five brief words boldly typed in all capitals:

SPIDER…BEWARE THE MELTING DEATH

"It's from the rusty typewriter of a suicide who took a ten story dive the day before the disaster," Kirkpatrick put on his hat. "A washed-up old crime reporter named Bill Henry. Seemed like a nutcase at first, but in light of what I saw on that train, not to mention the coroner's bizarre description of Henry's corpse…and, it could have been the alley rats like he said…but, well, now I'm not so sure."

Wentworth handed back the scrap.

"You could be on to something, Kirk. Let me know what turns up," he shook his old friend firmly by the hand.

Once the door was closed and locked, Wentworth's mind was in a sudden cyclone. The jumbling of a dozen facts that had been unfathomable mysteries moments before seemed almost magically to fall into place. A weird, low, chuckling laugh escaped his lips. It was startling, even menacing, in the sudden silence of the room.

"We know that sound, Major," Ronald Jackson, Wentworth's tall, wide-shouldered chauffeur and trusted aide, stated anxiously from across the room.

Ram Singh, another fiercely devoted disciple in Wentworth's war against criminals, regarded his master with grim resolution, nodding his proudly turbaned head.

"Indeed, sahib," the Sikh warrior responded, ominously stroking his bearded chin. "How may we serve you?"

Wentworth whirled around to find all eyes strained upon him. Nita's haunted gaze was especially troubled. For a moment he was perplexed at the sudden tension he had caused, then—seeing himself across the room in the mirror—Wentworth realized the alarming reason. Standing there, in his expensive tailored suit, within his familiar penthouse suite, Wentworth hardly recognized his own reflection. Not only his face, but his whole physique had unconsciously altered.

It was the *Spider* who stared back at him.

"Dick…are you all right?" Nita lightly touched his arm, startled by the coiling sinews tensing beneath his coat.

Wentworth paled a moment, then gave her a quiet reassuring smile.

"We've just become privy to an essential clue that the official police have missed," his voice was pitched with excitement. "I knew…or, rather, the *Spider* was very well acquainted with the late Bill Henry. The enemy has finally committed a fatal error."

The *Spider* tightened his web around the throat of the underworld. The darkened tenement hideouts were made blacker still by the invasion of his long, twisted shadow. None could escape him. No one could deny him. Small-time hoods and back alley predators literally wept in terror before the merciless onslaught of the Master of Men.

Nita, Jackson, and Ram Singh would remain vigilant, prepared for future catastrophes should Wentworth fail to return. This time the threat was different, far-reaching and devastating in its aimless goal of terror. He couldn't put them at risk. Not until the *Spider* gave his all, alone.

The trail itself had been elementary.

The deceased William Patrick Henry provided the light to show the way. Before falling upon such wicked days, "Bourbon Bill", was a first class crime reporter and an excellent covert contact to the underworld. The *Spider* had often gleaned invaluable information from the hard-drinking journalist that had ended the career of many a criminal mastermind.

Wentworth further knew that Bourbon Bill hadn't staggered more than ten blocks from his low-rent flophouse in over three years. Just a few weeks prior, the black-balled newsman had raised a stink over witnessing the kidnapping of the imminent scientist Doctor Emerick Berg. His former editors had merely laughed, assured of a pathetic ruse by the rummy to reclaim a byline.

It suddenly all made a kind of grotesque sense. The still-missing Dr. Berg's area of expertise had been the advanced application of electromagnetism. Wentworth had read many of the scientist's monographs, and they were brilliant.

Berg himself was once originally from the same neighborhood, which had since decayed into the bowery. Bourbon Bill, sober or not, could well have seen him there, perhaps he'd even observed his abduction. No one had seen Berg after that. Someone must be holding him, somewhere within those ten blocks, forcing the scientist into building some kind of terrible weapon. Berg might even be dead already, his temporary value fulfilled.

Lastly, there was something that even Commissioner Kirkpatrick had failed to notice. On that scrap of typing paper there had been a faint thumb print. Vague as it was, Wentworth immediately detected the faint scent of scorched skin coming from the paper. Once a man encountered the stench of burnt human flesh, as Wentworth had in many haunting circumstances, it was impossible to ever forget it.

If only someone had taken Henry's claims about the scientist seriously, but just the week before he'd made a fuss over seeing sea serpents under the Brooklyn Bridge.

Even Wentworth hadn't listened, then…but now the *Spider* had no choice.

One by one, using methods the official police force could not dare, the *Spider* got what he demanded. The petty thugs and gutter gangsters eagerly, sometimes literally, spilled their guts to the snarling masked man-monster. Finally, he learned of dim rumors of a reclusive megalomaniac called the Crucible, a fearsomely fitting name. Then, he got a location. Justice was closing in.

The *Spider*'s web was inescapable.

The dwarf waited. It was all he could do.

Rain splashing on the high windows of the abandoned warehouse diffused the street lights, streaking shadows like a barred cage across the floor. It was a prison, all right. But, being the dwarf beside the giant, he had truly never known anything else.

A corroded window latch gave way, falling almost noiselessly to the filthy floor. The dwarf smiled faintly as the *Spider* masterfully infested the chamber, gliding wraithlike down a silken rope with a heavy automatic in the other hand. Had the dwarf not been expecting him, doubtlessly the entrance of the slouched black figure would have been virtually invisible among the shadows.

The dwarf shuddered as the *Spider*'s piercing eyes regarded him with bitter hatred. Another gun had appeared in the other hand, thumbs cocked hammers, barrels unerringly aimed at the little man and at the still, silent monstrosity heaped beside him.

"The Crucible is dead," the little man breathed. "I murdered him two days ago."

Wentworth's quick eyes detected a blood-crusted claw hammer laying some distance from the victim and his confessed killer. He also observed the smashed remains of a weird cannon-like machine composed of coiling copper wires, shattered vacuum tubes, and fitted with a machinegun tripod.

"You found us sooner than I expected," the dwarf continued. "The *Spider* deserves his formidable reputation."

Awe saturated the diminutive voice, although, strangely, there was no hint of fear. Wentworth advanced, his savage fangs gritted.

"Who are you?" he furiously hissed.

The dwarf glanced sympathetically to the giant mass beside him.

"Just two brothers, cruelly used by this world," he sighed with a sob. "I did love him, you know, even through all his torment and torture. He was all I had."

Wentworth took in the strange sight of the withered dwarf protectively clumped next to the grey festering corpse of the giant. At last, he saw everything clearly and his rage diminished.

The Crucible had been an ogre, indeed, with the arms of a gorilla and the chest of a buffalo. Most of the brutish skull had been smashed into pulp. The little man breathed with a shuddering effort. He, too, Wentworth observed, was dying. It was inevitable. The reek of decay hung heavy in the air.

"The whole scheme was his...the kidnapping...the machine...the murders..." the dwarf confessed, wracked with emotion. "My brother had a cruel, peculiar genius for such things. He was...what the world had made of him."

Guns slid soundlessly back into concealed holsters, and Wentworth knelt at the dwarf's side.

"Yet, you had the courage to stop him," it was Wentworth's soft voice, not the *Spider*'s ugly rasp, which now issued from the fanged lips.

Tears streamed down the little man's doll-like cheeks.

"He was going to…aim that damnable machine at the whole skyline. I couldn't stand it anymore. Maybe I finally went mad, too. No one…will ever understand."

Wentworth clasped the small trembling hand held out to him. The mottled greyish flesh felt more dead than alive.

"I think I do," his tone was comforting.

The dwarf attempted a smile, though his weakness prevented it. Wentworth could hear the rattle in the little man's lungs. He was fading fast.

"P-please…" the small, tormented eyes implored. "…please don't let them find us like this…don't…don't let them…"

Wentworth nodded, and the little man was gone.

Kerosene and a lighted match fulfilled the final wish of the Crucible's last victim. No one would stare at them. No one would gawk. No awful exhibition. No one would ever know.

Wentworth watched mournfully as the flames consumed the secrets of the giant and the dwarf. The brothers passed from the world as they'd been born into it, together…as Siamese twins fused at the spine, bound forever in their prison of flesh and blood.

Their life-long internal conflict was over. Wentworth envied them.

The *Spider* could never rest.

illustration by Tom Floyd

Chapter Two

KING OF THE CITY

by C.J. HENDERSON

"Twixt kings and tyrants there's this difference known;
Kings seek their subjects' good: tyrants their own."
- Robert Herrick

"Leave me!" The woman screamed the words loud enough for the world to hear, her voice filled with the pain of love. "Leave me behind! You'll never make it carrying me. Stop being so damn noble!"

"Sorry, Nita," answered the man in the black hat and cloak, the one racing down the street with the woman in his arms, "can't hear you over all the gunfire."

Oddly enough, the man in black was laughing, as if his words had formed the funniest comment possible. And, under the circumstances, it was something of an amusing retort at that, for the man was the *Spider*, the mysterious vigilante who had made it his relentless mission to scrub the city free of criminals. In his arms, there apparently because of a gunshot wound in her leg, was his daring partner in that mission, the beautiful Nita Van Sloan.

As the pair moved with blinding speed, all around them gunfire continued uninterrupted, so loud that it was amazing he had heard her comment at all. The bullets, although fired in plenty, struck no where near the fleeing couple, however. So far the *Spider* had managed to easily outdistance their foes. Indeed, in any normal foot race against a band of the city's common criminal element he would have already disappeared, leaving them utterly baffled. But this was no normal contest; this was a matter of vengeance, one well-planned and thoroughly organized. This was a night where one of the most powerful men in the entire world had taken all the chips at his disposal, covered every single number on the table, and then rolled the dice hard, certain of victory.

"Duck your head!"

Giving the command, the *Spider* folded Nita close against himself and then dove straight forward into the large plate-glass window of a restaurant to his left. The move threw off those in pursuit—it was too random, too spectacular. They could not conceive of anyone who could move with such agility, who could be traveling at such astounding speed, and then simply step sideways and hurl himself, while carrying another person, with force enough to not only break the glass of the window, but to then move sufficiently past it not to be cut to pieces.

But, of course, this was no ordinary man. This was the legendary *Spider*. He had trained long and terribly hard for such moments, effort that allowed him now to make the impossible seem merely routine for him. Landing on his feet neatly in between two tables filled with diners, his gloved hands and their passenger less than an inch from the shard-covered floor, he forced his body erect and then launched it and his companion quickly for the back exit of the building without a second thought.

Those in pursuit did not despair losing their quarry, however. For them this was but a temporary setback, one gaining the *Spider* mere seconds. In fact, it must be said that many of those in the party closing in upon the *Spider* nodded to each other, chuckling at the sight, their feeling being that the longer their prey made things last, the better.

No, they snickered to one another with sinister assurance, this—this was their night. This was the night the thieves and murderers, the rapists and robbers and punks of all stripes, be they the lowest street hoodlums or the most insulated master string-pullers, were prepared to rejoice. And the reason was simple—finally, the *Spider*, the menace they feared worse than the police or the government, or even God Himself, had gone too far. He had enraged the most powerful crime lord in all the Americas beyond the brink of reason, outward to the point where all that mattered was vengeance. As far as those who thrived in the darkness were concerned, this was it.

This was the night the *Spider* would die.

It had begun almost two weeks earlier. For the members of the DiVico organization in the car outside the warehouse on 13th Street, quietly running their motor, it was a special night. This was the night young Joseph DiVico was to make his bones. He was home at last from his years in college, his head stuffed with the business and social skills he would need to take his family's operations ahead into the new world being promised every other day by Hoover and Roosevelt on the radio. That night, however, he was in a different type of training—the kind that would allow him to know what his troops in the field would be feeling when he sent them out to procure and steal and abuse and murder.

For the DiVico family fortunes had been acquired in one of the oldest fashions civilization had to offer. The DiVicos were in the business of distributing pleasure and good times, of offering hope and extortion with steel fists covered by the thinnest of velvet gloves. The first DiVicos had arrived just before the turn of the century from Italy, and during their time in the Americas, they had gone from immigrant status to that of the landed gentry. But they had done it over the bodies of the poor and the foolish, the weak and the innocent. Their hands were always found to be clean, and their fingers well manicured, but the slightest trace of blood always lingered under their polished nails.

As for Joseph, he was no naive waif being pulled down into a shameful life. He had been raised to be the king of the city, to ascend to his father's throne at the right time, and from the first he had relished the idea. Father and son were cut from the same cloth, alike in mind and deed in every way.

This did not mean young Joseph had been pampered. On the contrary, his father had watched over him in his ivy league school, making certain his instructors were as tough on him as possible. The master of the DiVico's wanted a genius returned to him for his investment, a hard-thinking, sharp-brained tactician who could lead his troops with more than just old world ferocity. DiVico senior had donated two buildings to his son's Alma Mater, not to pave the boy's way, but to ensure that he would be given not the slightest millimeter of slack.

And, when Joseph had graduated at the top of his class, the old man had cried openly. There in his seat, in front of his sister, in front of the men positioned around him, colleagues and bodyguards, men who feared him as they feared the inevitable reach of the grave and the promise of Hellfire beyond, he had freely wept tears of joy and pride.

Joseph DiVico, son of Ernesto DiVico, had made his father as proud as possible. For weeks after his graduation, a man could gain a favor or sometimes even mercy from Ernesto simply by complimenting the old man on his wonderful son. The parties celebrating his graduation had been lavish. Few returning offspring had ever seen so many fatted calves slaughtered in their honor.

But, even for a chest as swelled as that of the senior DiVico, the time for business finally returned. And thus, the boy had been sent to oversee his first operation in the streets. It had been a simple thing, a bit of hands-on work to give him the smell of sweat and fear in his nostrils. He had to know what it meant to face alarms and guards, and the police, among others.

Of course, Ernesto was no fool. He had chosen a quick in-and-out, the robbery of a warehouse filled with time pieces freshly arrived from Switzerland. High end items, easy to move, hard to trace. His son would be exposed to risk for no more than twenty minutes, and minimal risk at that. Indeed, the boy had no sooner left with his team when the old man had busied himself in his grand, dark wood office, setting out cigars and selecting his best brandy. In a practical moment, the back of his mind asked if he was not rushing things. The elder DiVico scoffed at the notion, daring the wrath of the gods by cavalierly asking the air around him:

"Paffff, what could go wrong?"

The self-proclaimed king of the city was soon to find out just how horribly things could go wrong.

"That way; he went that way. You bunch—after him!"

The man giving orders split the forces under his command, sending half of them into the building the *Spider* had entered. The other half he directed to the nearest corner, ordering them to the back alley as quickly as possible. They needed no barking to lend speed to their feet. If anything, most of them were around the corner before their boss had finished giving his orders.

Inside, before the restaurant patrons initially disturbed by the *Spider*'s hurried passing through could get over the remarkable sight, before they had even started brushing the bits of glass with which they were covered from their persons, the eight thugs sent in after the *Spider* burst through the door, searching high and low for the black-garbed crime fighter. Women screamed; fathers shoved their children under tables. Four of the men headed straight for the doors to the kitchen. The others tore the dining area apart, making certain their quarry had not attempted to hide somewhere inside. They were destined to find nothing.

"Richard," gasped Nita breathlessly. "Are you certain you can make it?"

Dashing through the kitchen, the *Spider* danced his way through waiters and busboys, assistant cooks, dishwashers and chefs, whisking himself and his passenger in between the tightly tangled assembly practically before any of the white-garbed workers could take note of him. His answer to Nita was, of course, one flippant almost to the point of juvenility, but she was the one person he could not fool. The *Spider* had every reason to be confident. He was supremely trained, master of a score of fighting skills, expert with countless weapons.

But, even the *Spider* could handle only so many men at a time. Even the *Spider*, powerful and cunning and as daring as any hero of legend, even he could not stop an entire army by himself. And that was what was on his trail at that moment, closing in on him from all sides, an entire army of killers, one spurred on by a reward most of them had never dreamed they might possess. The *Spider* was in the greatest trap of his life, one only minutes from closing about him entirely—and one entirely of his own making!

Hitting the door to the alley behind the restaurant with his shoulder, the *Spider* managed to stop himself just in time as a veritable hail of bullets either buried themselves inside the door or whizzed around it. He did not bother to attempt to look outside. He could tell from the way the door splintered, the way the shattered fragments flew through the air that the gunfire had come from every possible direction. His foes had already reached both ends of the alleyway and had caged him between their forces.

Spinning around without wasting a moment, the *Spider* kicked out with his left leg and knocked over a stand near the now open, broken door. The contents of its three shelves all struck the floor, most of them shattering, covering the area in front of the door with a variety of liquids, including cooking oil. The *Spider* did not waste time looking to see if the entire area had been covered. He dare not. Already those in pursuit of him were getting far ahead of where he felt they should be.

"This might actually get serious," the crime-fighter thought. When first passing through the kitchen, he had noted that the only exit was through the back. That gave him two choices, to either go out into the alley or return the way he came. Making his decision almost instantaneously, he commanded:

"Nita, hold on!"

Then, with blinding speed, he ducked his one shoulder low and threw his opposite hip forward, flipping the woman in his arms through the air so that, her arms still around his neck, she was now hanging down his back. His hands suddenly free, he pulled two .45s from beneath his cloak just as the first of the thugs sent through the restaurant's dining area hit the kitchen.

There are some members of the press, those whose words might have more properly belonged between the covers of pulp magazines rather than on the front pages of great newspapers, who often times would credit the *Spider* with making pithy comments when engaging his enemies. These were men who had never held a gun, never pointed one at another human being, never taken a life—men who believed, in their innocence, that lead was best sent sliding through human flesh accompanied by slogans. The *Spider* was not of their number.

As the first of his pursuers came through the door to the dining room, the *Spider* sent a blob of lead through the man's forehead. The back of the thug's head exploded outward, spraying the next three men behind him with blood, gray matter, bone fragments and hair. While they sputtered and blinked, the *Spider* wasted no time. Again he fired, and again and again. Each shot fired tore through either a man's brain or his heart. In under three seconds the *Spider* had slain half those coming through the dining room.

"Not good enough," he growled as his slain enemies flopped to the ground. Throwing himself forward over the heaped thugs, he risked exposing himself, hitting the door at full speed. As his body flew through the air, almost as if the woman hanging onto him weighed nothing at all, his arms snapped out, fanning in opposite directions, desperate to find their targets and then take them down without endangering the eatery's patrons any more than they already had been.

This is not the way it was supposed to work; a voice from the back of his mind reminded him. *The idea is to protect the helpless, not make their dangers greater.*

The thought stung the *Spider*, reminding him once more that the danger he was in that night, into which Nita and all others who knew him had been dragged, was a danger of his own making. It was not a pleasant thought, but it was also not one upon which he could turn his back.

All right, he sighed, *then let's get on with protecting them.*

His mind clear, the *Spider* concentrated on destroying those coming after him. Despite the pressure on his neck from the weight of his passenger, in spite of the confused flurry of screaming, scrambling diners, he leveled the .45 in his left hand and squeezed off two rounds. The first of his pursuers was spun around violently, his head exploding in a scarlet blossom.

"Perfect."

The *Spider* laughed at the sight, the sound of it sinister—metallic. Louder than his laughter, however, was the echoing thunder of gunfire as his trigger finger closed—once, twice—reducing two more of his foes to gruesome slaughter. He chose the head shots for maximum blood—maximum show. They caused more screams from those he would defend and more fear in those he would destroy. Again he fired, and another of those coming for him flopped helplessly, then fell to the ground, two more of his number following him to the beyond before his lifeless head could slam against the carpet.

The *Spider* brought up his right arm, sighting out the few remaining targets even as his keen ears picked up a disturbance in the kitchen. Half deaf from the gunfire there in the dining room, both his own and the multiple shots he had already dodged, still he could tell he was soon to have another wave of enemies with which to deal.

"No," he whispered to the world, gunning down two more of his foes as he did so, "this is not the way I thought this would go at all."

Then, as the *Spider* threw himself into eliminating the last of those in the dining room standing between himself and freedom, his mind danced back to how he had brought such wrath down upon himself. It played within his brain in rapid flashes. He saw again the warehouse on 13th Street, heard his voice recommending to the thieves he had found there that they surrender, letting them know how much he would prefer they did not.

Of course they had rushed him, desperate to protect DiVico the younger. The *Spider*, knowing of DiVico senior's plans to show his son what the business was like, had shown up at the petty break-in almost as a lark. What fun, he had thought, to capture the youngster and send him off for a night in lock-up. Let him have a real taste of his father's business.

But like any man, the *Spider* could make a mistake. He had under-estimated Joseph DiVico, thought him soft, over-educated. The boy proved him wrong. Instead of staying hidden within the car from where he was monitoring the operation, he grabbed a pistol and joined his men in firing upon the *Spider*. It was something a competent boss would have never done. A seasoned man would have surrendered, traded a moment of jail time for a lifetime to make someone pay for it.

But the young DiVico was too proud, too desperate to please his father—to repay, to justify the old man's faith in him. To Joseph, the chance to do what no man had done, to kill the *Spider*, to remove the threat of the hated vigilante had proved too great. And so, the heir to the DiVico throne had rolled the dice, and he had come up snake eyes. Never expecting such foolhardiness, the *Spider* had done as he always did, he returned fire, rained leaden death down upon his enemies until they were all bleeding in the street, breathing their last.

When he realized that Joseph DiVico was among the dead, he did not pause. Bending over him as he did the others, the *Spider* marked the forehead of the golden child with his blood red mark, letting the world know that once they embraced the mantle of dishonesty, none were safe as far as he was concerned. It was a thing he had done hundreds of times. Perhaps thousands. But, never before had it had the effect it would that night.

When Ernesto DiVico was informed of his son's death, he became inconsolable. Before he knew what he was doing, his hands seized the china plate he had been awarded by the Sons of Italy and smashed it against the wall. His inlaid mahogany cigar box was next, followed by a vase of flowers, blooms he had cut himself that morning. A statuette given to him by New York City's previous cardinal, a depiction of the Virgin Mother brought back from the Holy Land fared no better than anything else that came into the old man's hands.

Chairs and small tables were flung through windows and against walls. None dared stop the senior DiVico. None could think of a word to say to him. How many other men had the *Spider* slain? How many good sons and fathers, uncles and brothers had the black-clad monster of the night robbed from the world of the living? He was a hated thing for all of them for he made no sense. He was not so much a mystery as he was an absurdity.

Don Ernesto could understand a policeman firing upon his men. It was a policeman's duty. It was his job; he was paid to do so. But the *Spider*—the *Spider*.

"Son of a bitch," the old man screamed as he tore down the curtains behind his desk. "What does he think, who does he think he is? Why—*why* does he plague us? Why is there no end to him?!"

His lieutenants and his servants pleaded as far as they dared, but Ernesto DiVico was beyond hearing their words, beyond rationality, beyond the touch of any part of the real world, bereft with grief and consumed with hatred, which is why, without any part of his mind realizing what he was doing, the Don grabbed up the urn on his desk and flung it as hard as he could against the bricks of his fireplace.

"Anna!"

His recognition of what he had done came the instant the gold-flecked blue china piece left his fingers. He snapped them closed, desperate to halt the urn, but it was too late. The delicate old piece of handsome hand-crafted work shattered into a storm of shards, and the ashes of Anna DiVico, Ernesto's wife, were sent in every direction.

Unlike the moment of joy which had prompted the old man to tears only weeks earlier, this accident did not. This sight, on top of the news of his son's death, his boy's murder at the hands of the cursed *Spider*, his heir's beautiful face disfigured with the monster's scarlet sign above his eyes, this was all the old man could take. With a roar the boss of bosses, the man known across the land as the King of the City, called for representatives from all the various wings of his organization to gather at his mansion immediately.

Within an hour, some two-hundred and fifty-seven men had gathered at the home of Ernesto DiVico. The Don made his statement to them as short and simple as possible. After telling them of the death of his boy, he cut off their responses of sympathy, snarling out his next words;

"Let me tell you all something here and now, this time, this bastard, this whoreson, this time, he goes too far. This *Spider*, he thinks he can play with us. That he can laugh at us. And I'll tell you why—because no one is ever willing to do enough." He let them think about his words for several seconds, then continued.

"But I'm an old man, with nothing left to live for." Obligatory protests attempted to interrupt, but Don Ernesto roared fire, melting them away as he bellowed:

"Nothing! After Anna, it was only my Joey. What do I care now? The skies can turn green and piss blood and drown everything for all I care. If there was a button I could push, one that would end the world right here and now, I'd push it, just so I could know as I breathed my last that I was taking the damned *Spider* with me."

As the Don caught his breath the entire room, frozen in dread, remained as quiet as possible. All sat as reverently as they could, looking only at their lord, keeping everything from their breathing to their blinking to a minimum.

"And that is why I have made the following decision. I have no son now. No heir. What good, I ask you, is this organization of mine, if I have no one to leave it to? So this is what I intend on doing. I am going to liquidate everything I have if necessary, to see to it that the *Spider* dies!" Not yet under-standing, those in attendance merely listened as DiVico continued"

"I will spend whatever it takes to destroy him, to crush him, to hurt and humiliate him, to rob him of all he holds dear. I want him dead, and I will bankrupt myself to do it." The old man ran his tongue over his upper plate, pursed his lips, and then added the kicker, the sentence which would be known to the entire underworld from coast to coast in less than twenty minutes time.

"And, I make this pledge right now, to the man who can do this thing, who can kill the *Spider*, be he one of my most trusted lieutenants, or the lowest, newest legman in all the city, the one who kills the *Spider*, that man will take my place as head of the DiVico operation. For the price of one bullet, buried deep enough in the proper head, I offer my world."

The announcement stunned the assembly. None had suspected the elder DiVico was prepared to make such a move. Those closest to him, those few remaining old timers who had come up through the ranks with him, watched his back as he clawed his way to the very top of the heap, they understood the never-ending depths of his sorrow. As others in the room looked to them to question the Don, they disappointed the pragmatic by standing by their friend. There would be no discussions, no robbing the blood of its juice so that emotion could be weakened into practicality.

And thus it began. Within hours of the announcement that the king's throne was up for grabs, armed men prowled every corner of the city searching for the *Spider*. Indeed, so tempting was the Don's offer that crime actually took a vacation as a majority of its practitioners forgot about their normal small hauls as they dreamed of making the biggest score possible, taking over the DiVico crime syndicate.

The police's holiday ended after only a few days, however, as the city's criminal element slowly realized that if they were not committing crimes, the *Spider* would not appear. That epiphany lead to an overnight skyrocketing of both misdemeanors and felonies as those hoping for a chance at the city's defender went on a reckless rampage, pulling crime after crime, hoping to force the *Spider* out of the shadows and into an arena where they might have a chance at him. And, of course, the *Spider* had been more than happy to oblige their wishes.

Although the police were not helpless, they were overwhelmed by the monstrous wave of naked crime which suddenly engulfed the citizens they were sworn to protect. Overtime was assigned in quantities never before known, but there were no questions asked by city hall's battery of accountants. There was no doubt every patrolman, every squad car, and every detective no matter how old, how sickly, or how inexperienced was needed, and needed desperately.

Of course, the *Spider* made himself available for his hunters. Indeed, once he discovered through a bit of questioning the reason for the increase in criminal activity, he was almost delighted. It brought him no pleasure to think of those innocents being robbed or molested in any way merely because the city's hoodlum population was seeking him, but on the other hand he could not help but enjoy the notion that those he was sworn to destroy were lining up to give him the opportunity to do so.

In the beginning, the *Spider* felt slightly embarrassed over the fact he was actually having a wonderful time dispatching the various felons, gangsters and just plain thugs out to win Don DiVico's throne. For several weeks he spent nearly every waking hour scouring the city, tangling with groups of two and three gunmen hoping to murder him, with out-of-town hit men, entire gangs, sometimes two or three gangs banded together, dispatching them all, killing scores of them, sending the more fortunate to the hospital as well as the waiting arms of the law by the hundreds.

As time went by, however, the black-clad avenger began to feel the strain of his battles. Richard Wentworth was a supremely trained athlete; his powers of endurance went beyond the phenomenal, seemingly to the superhuman. In the end, however, he was only a man, and men can only accomplish so much. As days turned into weeks, as the *Spider* forced himself to go longer and longer without sleep, without food, he found himself losing his edge—needing two punches, or two shots, where one would have served in the past.

Ignoring the initial warning signs, the man sworn to keep the city safe turned to pharmaceuticals. Knowing full well the risks, still he knew what it would mean for the innocent if the *Spider* was not seen in the city. Those eager to flush him out, men driven by greed and their lust for power, if they thought their prey was not to be found they would fall on the good citizens of the city like the wolves they were, staining the streets with blood until they got what they wanted.

For an extra eleven days the *Spider* continued to push himself, striking back endlessly at the forces of evil on less and less sleep, until finally the night came when he simply could not move. It was only a momentary hesitation, but for that instant after he said he was leaving, he could not. His mind, ever-alert, ever-ready, was momentarily shocked when his body did not respond instantly to the simple command to rise. Catching the look of surprise in his eyes, his man servant, Ram Singh, growled at him:

"Forgive me, but I must protest. You are no fool, *Sahib*, this I know all too well, and so I offer you a riddle. What would you call a man who tries to do something he knows he cannot?"

"Determined?"

"Please," the great Sikh cried out, "listen to me. You have taken yourself to the edge. You are teetering over the endless abyss. You must stop this. You cannot win this way." When his master did not answer, the servant added:

"You are already losing, and you know it. That is why you keep destroying yourself along with your enemies."

"Ram Singh is right."

The softer, but equally determined voice belonged to Nita van Sloan. As she approached the two men, she added:

"Richard, the innocent are always at the mercy of evil. Even when you do go out, how many can you stop in one night? Somewhere else, at the same time, there are others doing their best to draw your attention. Others are being hurt, being robbed—others that you will never reach." Focusing her deep-violet eyes on those of the man she loved, Nita said:

"We're not asking you to give up on them, to quit. We know you could never do that. But DiVico, he's pulled you into a game you can never win. He can just keep buying more and more men, filling the city with death and madness until finally you have to succumb. We're not asking you to stop fighting him. But we're begging you, stop fighting him on his own terms."

Prepared to have to argue with the pair, Wentworth was left speechless by their words. Struggling to think clearly for a moment, blinking his way past the lack of sleep that had begun to devour his good sense, cloud his mind, he realized every word Nita had just spoken was true. And, in that moment, Richard Wentworth put the *Spider* to the back of his mind and slumped in his chair, allowing his fatigue to finally overwhelm him.

"Richard!" So suddenly did his collapse come that Nita feared it was something beyond his control. Chuckling, he told her:

"Don't worry. I know this might be hard for you to believe, but... I'm taking your advice." As the exhausted crimefighter caught his breath, he said quietly:

"Ram Singh, if you would be so good as to fetch me some sort of meal, please, nothing heavy ... I am going to sleep after I've eaten ..."

"At once, *Sahib*."

"And Nita, if you could hand me the private phone, and the *Spider*'s address book ..."

Richard Wentworth by necessity thought of the *Spider* as another person. Each had their own lives, their own things. This kept both of his personas separate, and helped make certain he did not make mistakes in conversation, talking about something of the *Spider*'s as if it were his own. As he thumbed through the thick, black booklet, he said:

"Actually, I've been thinking of a plan for some time. The concern you've shown me tonight forces me to admit it is time to set that plan into motion..."

And so, using the phone within his study which he only utilized to conduct business concerning the *Spider*, the city's last hope made several calls. Then he ate the broth and steamed vegetables Ram Singh brought him, took a long, very hot shower, and went to bed. His amazingly keen subconscious had seen the truth long before the rest of his mind, and begun working out the details of the plan which finally he had set into operation.

No, that night the *Spider* would not prowl the city. But he would do so two nights hence, and then it would be himself against the forces of the self-proclaimed king of the city—and the winner would take all!

Two night hence, however, it did not seem as if the *Spider*'s plan had been very well lain. A tip had been given to Ernesto DiVico. Into his ear, Leonardo Nardi, the head of the second largest family organization in the city had whispered a notion. Often, it seemed, the *Spider* had come to the rescue of the famed socialite Miss Nita van Sloan. She was destined to attend the opening of the opera season that week. If Ernesto was to gather his forces, surrounded the area, attack van Sloan—

DiVico had smiled in a way one would think the muscles of a human face could not achieve. There was no love lost between himself and Nardi, of course, but they had an understanding. And one thing men of their brotherhood shared implicitly was a hatred of the *Spider*. DiVico could see Nardi's plan—it profited the crime boss greatly to have the number one organization in town crippled. It was, however, a blessing from God if at the same time the DiVico family was hobbled the *Spider* was destroyed.

No, Ernesto DiVico knew why his rival was being so helpful. But, he did not care. Instantly he set his organization to sharpening the steel teeth of his trap. The correct opera house was located, the box seat reservations for van Sloan were confirmed. Maps of the streets were obtained and studied. When the correct night arrived, van Sloan would be nabbed, there in the middle of the opera, with as much show and noise as possible.

The *Spider*, DiVico knew, would arrive to rescue her. And in place all about the opera house, would be his forces. All of them. Every man he could afford. A veritable army of crime. They would be stationed on every street corner, in every storefront that could be rented. His men would have the radios used by the army. They would have the best weapons. And they would, finally, once and for all destroy the *Spider*!

And, as the King of the City had predicted, when the first night of the opera season arrived, the *Spider* did indeed enter his trap. He seemed to arrive almost as soon as DiVico's men closed in on van Sloan, whisking her into the backstage area before any of the thugs could react. But, his advantage of surprising speed did not last him long.

Luck seemed to favor DiVico and his minions. When the *Spider* was first spotted in the streets, fleeing with van Sloan, the gang lord's men reported that she appeared to be wounded, blood flowing down one of her legs. This, of course, made DiVico howl with glee. Finally his foe had made a wrong move. Hampered by the wounded van Sloan, the *Spider* would never be able to avoid his ever-tightening circle of death.

And sadly, despite all the master avenger's planning, it seemed that DiVico was to have his way. No matter which way the *Spider* turned, death appeared. Each time he dispatched another set of the elder mobster's men, a legion of fresh, well-armed warriors arrived to tear at him. He had noted their radio communications early on, and had seen no way to stop its use. Now, standing in the middle of the restaurant, men pouring in from the front door and from the kitchen, the end seemed to have arrived for the *Spider*.

Nita still clinging to his neck, his hands emptied of his .45s, DiVico's men rushed forward. As they raised their weapons, however, several noted that although the *Spider* was no longing holding his automatics, he did have some-thing in his black-gloved hands. As they watched, gun hands still closing on the hated form before them, the *Spider*'s thumbs flicked, and from each hand a glass vial was thrown with force. Each struck the chest of one of the approaching thugs and shattered into a hundred pieces.

A dozen of the gangsters fired simultaneously at the spot where the *Spider* had been. But, the black-cloaked figure and his passenger were already in motion, and their slugs ploughed through empty air. Nor did any of them get the chance for a second shot, because dense, opaque clouds of *Spider* Gas were rising in such thick, billowing waves that the dining area was completely filled with the all-masking smoke screen.

Under the cover of darkness, the *Spider* smashed his way to the street, exiting through the same window through which he had entered. Racing forward, he drove himself to his top speed, desperate to make a far-away corner before the rain of lead could come after him once more. He did manage to out-run the pursing army's guns, but not their eyes. Spotted turning onto Chestnut St., it was only a matter of seconds before the radios of the king of the city directed his men after the *Spider* once more.

"This is it," roared DiVico. Shouting for his driver to take him to Chestnut, he screamed into his transmitter to all his lieutenants. "This is what we've been waiting for. It's too good to be true."

DiVico was not wrong. Finally, the *Spider* had made what none could argue was not a fatal mistake. In his haste to protect Nita, he had mistakenly run down the one street in all the city he should not have taken. The *Spider* had entered a neighborhood on the city's lower East side that had been emptied of all life. His wrong turn had taken him into a series of blocks condemned for demolition. Everywhere he looked, the doors had been welded and barred shut—the windows boarded over.

The *Spider* had entered a cul de sac. Cackling with delight, DiVico ordered that his enemy be contained, not slain unless it was absolutely necessary. He wanted to be there to see the monster's death. He had to be there. Out of respect, or fear, all those under him knew they had to stay their hand. The *Spider* would be dead soon enough, and what remained of the DiVico organization would be theirs.

And in only a matter of minutes, all seemed to have fallen in place for the elder DiVico. As his car moved slowly through the masses of his men, he could see his foe trapped before him. Framed in the glow of the mob boss's headlights, the only illumination on the condemned street, DiVico could see the *Spider* with his back to the wall. The old man chuckled to see his enemy brought low by a woman, one who still needed to be held up by one of his powerful arms to keep her from falling to the ground.

"How does it feel, *Spider*, to know there is no hope?"

DiVico roared his words as he exited from his car. A machine gun in his hand, he walked forward slowly, shouting;

"How does it feel, to know you can't protect someone you care about anymore?"

As the black-garbed avenger remained silent, the mob boss stopped but ten yards from the *Spider*, and asked him plainly:

"What is it like, to know you've finally made a mistake? The mistake that will cost you everything?"

And then, in place of any kind of answer from the *Spider*, himself, suddenly, all around the gathered mobsters, the sound of scores of machine guns being cocked could be heard.

"Didn't you know, DiVico," the man in black said with a menacing tone, "the *Spider* never makes mistakes."

As the gang lord and his men looked upward, they saw the muzzles of automatic weapons being leveled at them from every window. Instantly DiVico understood that the *Spider* had entered the cul-de-sac on purpose. And, as he stared upward, he spotted one face which explained everything to him.

"Nardi," he screamed. "You bastard!"

"Now, now, Ernesto, it's just business," called down the rival gangster. "When my good friend here the *Spider* contacted me, offering to bring you and your entire organization to me on a silver platter... well now, really, how could I refuse? If you look hard, you'll see the Garintinos, the Cerasinis, all the other families are here to say 'goodbye' to you and yours tonight."

Seconds went by in infinitely long drags as DiVico tried to comprehend everything happening at that moment. As he watched, Nita van Sloan suddenly stood erect, her wound now seen as a bit of theatrics, nothing more than a part of the *Spider*'s plan to make his helplessness seem believable.

At the same time, the *Spider* moved his hand across the woman's back for some unknown reason, then his own. And in the same moment, Nardi's voice called out:

"Thank you, *Spider*, for setting this wonderful trap for my friend, Ernesto. I'm certain you can see that compared to the DiVicos, the Nardi family is much more reasonable. I'm thinking that you and I can get along. What do you think, *Spider*?"

"You fool," called out the city's champion. "You and yours are filth. You are nothing, nothing more than maggots beneath my booted heel. In seconds you will slaughter DiVico, and then you will fight among yourselves and tear each other to pieces and I will wash the last bloody dregs of you away myself." Stunned, Nardi shouted in anger;

"We had a truce, *Spider*."

Yes," the black-garbed avenger agreed, "we had a truce. And now it's over. Think for a moment, Nardi, when I arranged to bring the DiVicos here, I brought you here as well."

And, at that moment, with a hand-signal given to Ram Singh stationed on the rooftop above, the pre-positioned *spider*'s web which he had attached to the harness Nita had been wearing all evening jerked her skyward, just as the one he had attached to himself did the same.

"Kill them!"

DiVico's order came a split-second too late. As the powerful winches raced Nita and the *Spider* up out of the glare of the crime lord's headlights, they disappeared completely. Bullets tore the front of the building apart where they had been standing, but it was too late. They were gone, as were Ernesto DiVico's chances for revenge.

And everywhere, up and down the street, from every window, hands filled with weapons, triggers were pulled by the hundreds and a never-ending barrage of lead rained relentless death. As a mocking metallic laughter echoed above the canyons of the city, guns blazed in all directions. In mere seconds thousands of rounds were fired, bullets tore through flesh, blood splattered, and evil men died by the hundreds.

All at the hands of Richard Wentworth; the relentless, the ruthless, the *Spider*—the true King of the City.

The Master of Men.

illustration by Tom Floyd

Chapter Three

DEATH FROM A
BLOOD RED SKY

by ELIZABETH MASSIE

The air was as hot and still as a dead bum in an East Side alley in August. Wealthy, sweating men in gray suits and limp hats sat side by side on the wooden bleachers of Glaze Air Field, staring heavenward as aircraft after aircraft cut patterns in the sky, attempting to draw the rich men's awe, appreciation, and investments. Reporters buzzed about with cameras and notepads. Executives of the varied aircraft companies sat on the bleachers among the onlookers, gazing with controlled yet anxious hope between their flying creations and those who might fork over the cold hard cash to keep them in business. American flags snapped at occasional, dusty breezes. A loudspeaker broadcast the glory of each new craft as it taxied, took off, then performed in mid-air. Light racers climbed, dove, and rolled. Tri-motored passenger liners, freighters, and flying boats all vied for attention with their powerful engines and streamlined designs. Between flights and announcements, patriotic music was pumped into the crowd. Rich children of the rich men hopped up and down the bleachers. Rich wives of the rich men fanned themselves with handkerchiefs and patted their faces to hide their boredom.

On the back bleacher sat Richard Wentworth, his hat pulled low over his eyes to cut the glare, his arms crossed over his loosened tie. He'd driven the forty minutes from the city to the New Jersey airfield out of curiosity, and had sat through the first few hours of flight demonstrations not quite patiently, waiting for the only craft in which he was interested – the first in a line of new rigid airships, the *Aeolus Commander*.

Next to Wentworth sat Steven Thompson, a man a head shorter than Wentworth, with thinning sandy hair and a prominent scar on his neck. Thompson and Wentworth had served together as young lieutenants during the

Great War. Once they returned to the states, however, their roles had diverged significantly. Thompson remained in the military until 1927, when he assumed the position of advertising blimp pilot and then rose in the business to become co-owner of the blimp company. Wentworth had gone into business and with shrewd investments, had become one of the wealthiest men in the country.

"Our pride and joy is up soon," said Thompson, nodding toward the mooring mast on the far side of the field. Wentworth gazed out at the graceful silver airship hovering above the ground. "You'll like what you see, Richard. You're going to want to get in on it."

Wentworth held up his hand. "Steve, you don't need to woo me on this. I know you're sitting next to me not just because we're friends, but because you want to make sure I get all the facts and figures from the man in charge."

Thompson grinned and rubbed his chin.

"But I've done my research," said Wentworth. "I know what I'm getting ready to see, I just need to see it."

"Well, I'll look enthusiastic to keep up the ruse, so when members of the board glance back they can see I'm doing my duty. But we can talk about whatever you'd like, or nothing at all."

Wentworth nodded and went silent. He preferred nothing at all, though if Thompson wanted to pass the time with light banter about his wife, his five children, or even the weather, he would let it be, and would even toss in an occasional question to appear interested. Thompson was a good man with ordinary concerns and a simple, honest view of the world.

The hulking, luxurious passenger plane that had taken its turn on the ethereal stage came in for a landing, striking the runway with a rubber and metallic grunt then rolling to a stop. The onlookers applauded and a number of men scribbled notes into leather-bound journals. Then a man on the lowest bleacher hopped up, pushed through the gate of the fencing that separated the viewers from the field, and snatched the microphone from the announcer. The man was bald, rotund, and nervous.

"Hello, there!" he called out, his voice raspy through the speakers. "My name is Arnold Kittinger. As president of Vista Aircraft Manufacturers, I'd like to thank each and every one of you fine gentlemen for spending time viewing our products today. As you know, Vista is one of the largest companies in the business, and we are proud of what we've been able to accomplish in the last ten years. You've seen several of our craft thus far, but up next is one that will amaze even the most jaded."

"They've got a stratosphere plane," said Thompson. "It's really quite something, can fly at 35,000 feet. It's..."

"Hey!" shouted a little blond boy on the steps near Thompson and Wentworth. "Look-a that!" Wentworth and Thompson looked. On the horizon over the trees to the east was a red dot, darting back and forth as it approached, looking much like an irate dragonfly.

"Our engineers have worked long and hard on our next exhibit," continued Kittinger. "We've kept the details under wraps until now and..."

"Look!" shouted several children with the blond boy, pointing at the red craft heading their way.

"Look!" cried several of the women on a lower tier of the bleachers, rising up to wag fingers toward the east. The unusual craft was more visible now, sporting wings, top rotors, and a front propeller. Wentworth could hear the droning, throaty rumble of the engine as it approached.

"What is that?" came the murmurs in the crowd.

Kittinger hesitated, and looked where the rich men and their wives and children were looking.

"I like that!" said a young woman near Wentworth. "I would buy one of those and learn to fly. I'd spin circles around the homes of my friends. Charming."

"Is that a Vista plane?" asked another woman. "Is that the surprise Mr. Kittinger is talking about?"

The red aircraft reached the edge of the runway and made a wide circle.

That's an autogiro, thought Wentworth the very moment Thompson said, "Why, that's an autogiro." The little blond boy on the steps, on hearing Thompson, starting chanting, "Autogiro, autogiro!"

Kittinger stamped his foot and began waving the microphone over his head, as if to shoo the autogiro away. Clearly it was not one of his company's crafts and it was interfering with the show.

The autogiro was indeed red, with two distinct yellow stripes around its tail section. In the open cockpit sat the pilot, dressed in leather jacket, helmet, and goggles. The single seat vehicle swooped, rose, and circled, as if judging the other craft beneath it. Then it headed straight toward the bleachers. Someone in the crowd shouted, "Hey, that pilot's a woman!"

"A woman?" said Thompson.

"It is a woman!" said a rich wife one row down. "A red-haired woman!"

It was then that Wentworth saw the harpoon gun mounted beneath the body of the autogiro. The pilot angled the craft toward Kittinger.

"No!" Wentworth leapt to his feet but it was already too late. The pilot fired. The harpoon hurtled through the air, trailing a heavy cable. It cut into Kittinger's back and came to a stop with a half-foot, barbed protuberance out his chest. The microphone broadcast Kittinger's screech just before it fell from his grasp.

The autogiro flew upward again, pulling Kittinger like a hooked fish into the air. The man kicked and screamed, though his screams were drowned out by those of the horrified onlookers. As the autogiro reached a height of about 150 feet, Wentworth saw the pilot position a tommy gun over the side. There was a moment of silence, as if the crowd and Kittinger had taken a collective breath to pray or to hope or to hold back the inevitable. Then a spray of bullets slammed into the head of the dangling executive. He twitched then went still. The harpoon cable was released from the autogiro and he fell into a broken heap on the runway tarmac.

The autogiro made a small, triumphant circle, and flew off.

Rich men hugged their rich wives. Rich children of the rich men huddled together, whispering and giggling nervously. Reporters swarmed the body of the crushed and bloody Vista president as a trembling airfield manager shouted into the microphone, "Someone bring a car! Help us get this man to a hospital!" Not that it could matter. The man was dead. Then a brown-suited reporter snatched the microphone and wheezed enthusiastically to any who cared to hear him, "A woman did this! A deadly red-haired woman in a red aircraft, a Scarlet Stinger out for blood! Read all about it, and any new developments, in tomorrow's edition of *The Daily Record-Leader*! Don't miss it!"

Wentworth watched as the red dot vanished in the distance. He could feel his own red blood boiling beneath his skin. Fury pumped from him with each breath, like foul air through bellows.

Thompson said, "Who the hell was she? Why did she do that?"

Wentworth said nothing, but only looked at his friend with cold, narrowed eyes.

Argosy Towers stood tall and proud in the city, a behemoth of brick and mortar that held numerous businesses owned by Richard Wentworth. Wentworth often roamed the floors, keeping tabs on his managers and underlings, making sure that honesty prevailed and money rolled in. Yet he spent late Monday afternoon in his grand office, hands pressed against the windowsill, staring out at the ragged metropolitan skyline, planning, watching.

The Scarlet Stinger, so dubbed by the reporter at the airfield, was no casual killer, no fly-by-day vigilante. Since the harpooning on Saturday, two days earlier, she had killed twice more. Both happened in the city yesterday – Sunday – just as citizens and tourists were pouring into the streets and parks for afternoon strolls and picnics. The first victim was a man named Barney Charles, vice president of another local aircraft production company, Americraft. The second was George Addison, board member of Aeolus Airships.

The moment Wentworth saw the leather-clad woman spear Kittinger from her autogiro, he had suspected she was not just out for sport. She had not killed on a lark. There was too much fanfare, too much intelligence and design put into the dramatic attack. And now, with the death of Charles and Addison, it was clear this woman had a vendetta against aircraft companies or the men in charge of them.

There was a tap on the office door. Wentworth turned from the window. "Come in."

The door opened and a uniformed police officer and plainclothes man entered.

"What do you know so far?" Wentworth asked simply.

"Well, Mr. Wentworth," said the plainclothes man, a detective named Samson. "We have little information. Witnesses of the Charles murder saw the red auto… auto…"

"Giro," offered the uniformed cop.

"Yes, fine. The autogiro flew in from above the Crandall Building, just four blocks south of here. At first the witnesses thought it was some sort of advertising, like those blimps that bear signs and float above the city, but this one had no sign. The craft descended to just above the street light, and before anyone realized what was happening, shot a tethered harpoon through the back of Barney Charles as he was lighting a cigar outside Danver's Diner, his favorite lunch spot. The craft then flew nearly straight up, dragging the victim with it. At that point the pilot fired several rounds into Charles' head, released the tether, and the man dropped into the street where a car ran over him. Another car ran into that one. Both drivers were injured. Then, of course, folks started connecting this execution with the one out at Glaze Airfield Saturday."

Wentworth nodded. "In which direction did the autogiro leave the scene?"

The detective scratched at his chin. "Most witnesses say she went straight up into the cloud cover. A couple said she headed south. Someone else said north. Most people didn't watch her exit. They were too riveted on the carnage on the street."

"Indeed."

"The second killing," chimed in the uniformed cop, "was in Central Park, at 3:42 in the afternoon. George Addison was with his family and a friend who is another Aeolus board member. They were feeding ducks when the autogiro appeared over the trees and the harpoon fired. After he was hauled up and shot, he was dumped right into the water, killing two mallards. She left the city flying east, or so say witnesses. It seems she likes an audience for her crimes but then wants to run off and hide."

"Have you interviewed the families to find out if they have an enemy in common?" asked Wentworth.

"We're getting ready to do that," said Samson.

"Soon," said the cop.

Wentworth had expected as much. They couldn't drag their feet any more if they had size 20 shoes.

"We appreciate your concerns, Mr. Wentworth," said Samson. "Several other businesses are also up in arms about this…Scarlet Stinger. She's got folks saying they aren't keen on being downtown with the danger this poses. But we'll stop her, you can count on us."

"Will you? After how many more die?"

"More?" piped up the uniformed cop. "Why do you think there'll be more, Mr. Wentworth?"

"Determination, an almost careless bravado. This woman is on a mission. She is out for blood, the blood of those who own and control the aircraft companies."

The detective and officer considered this, their faces solemn. Wentworth let out a silent sigh. How many times had Wentworth, as his alter ego, been forced to take matters into his own hands because those with the badges and the authority were unable to?

"Well, gentlemen, thank you for stopping by," Wentworth continued. "Keep me updated with what your investigations turn up."

Samson and the uniformed cop left the office.

Wentworth was used to incompetence from many of the city's police. If it weren't for his friend Kirkpatrick and a few other smart men on the payroll, there might as well not be a force at all. Most were like dogs in uniform snarling over a pile of old bones, while scurrying around near them, just out of reach in the shadows, was fresh meat on the hoof. It was their frequent incompetence and their lack of imagination that infuriated Wentworth almost as much as the dastardly crimes heaped upon the hapless and the innocent. And it was the destruction of the hapless and the innocent that drove him to rage.

Unfortunately, Kirkpatrick was temporarily out of the city on family business. Wentworth would have to do what the cops and detectives wouldn't do, yet again. And he would do it with a vengeance and until it was finished.

He could already taste the blood.

Wentworth was on the phone, calling all the aircraft companies that had factories within a two hundred mile radius to find out who, if any, produced autogiros, when Nita Van Sloan ushered herself into his Sutton Place penthouse. She had a key and never knocked. She would rattle open the door, straighten out the front hall runner that was inevitably rumpled, toss her set of keys onto the Wedgwood dish atop the hall stand, and announce herself.

"Dick?"

Wentworth put his hand over the receiver and called back, "Den."

It was nearly ten in the morning, and Wentworth was on the phone with the last of the four companies. None were into the development of autogiros, and all gave the same reason. Autogiros wouldn't bring in the money required to counterbalance their production. These companies focused on the bigger planes and the bigger dollar. They dismissed the practicality of building autogiros, with the vice president at Americraft claiming, "They are fine craft, but primarily experimental even today. They can take off and land in very short spaces, yet cannot carry very heavy payloads. As maneuverable as they are, they haven't found their niche. Some wealthy individuals may want to get one to impress their friends, buzz cattle, or attempt to top Amelia Earhart's Beech-Nut altitude record. But we don't build them." None could offer any suggestions as to where the Scarlet Stinger got her wings. Her craft was of no known design.

Wentworth turned from his desk as Nita entered. She took off her satin cap and placed it next to the phone, then ran her fingers through the tight curls of her chestnut brown hair.

"You've heard of the autogiro slayings?" she asked.

Wentworth held up a finger, bid the Americraft vice-president good-bye, and put the receiver back in the cradle. Nita tucked her skirt beneath her, sat on one of the den's leather chairs, and lit a cigarette.

"Yes," said Wentworth. "The authorities don't seem to know how to begin and don't seem all that concerned. What are three dead airline executives to them when…"

"Four," corrected Nita.

"Four?"

"Another one, very early this morning. I witnessed the aftermath, just as I was coming up out of the subway on 42nd. Dreadful! I can't get the image of that man, dangling from a harpoon several stories above the road, out of my mind. And then his head blowing apart with the impact of the bullets, and him falling to the sidewalk. Oh!" Nita put one hand to her eyes then lowered it again.

"Who was he?"

"Chairman of the board of Aeolus Airships. He was on his way to work. I checked my watch. It wasn't quite seven."

Wentworth felt his jaw tighten. Damn, another Aeolus man. Thank God it hadn't been Thompson. "The Scarlet Stinger knows that the aircraft companies have their main headquarters here in the city, while their factories are in southern New York State and central New Jersey. She's out to get the men in charge. She wants to kill those who matter most to the companies."

"Why do you think, Dick?"

"I don't know yet. Which way did she leave the city?"

Nita let out a slow stream of smoke through her lips then flicked ash into a brass ash stand by the chair. "Southwest."

"She's likely coming in and going out in different directions each time to keep everyone confused."

"Yes."

Wentworth tapped his own cigarette from a silver case and leaned over to light it with Nita's. "I've contacted all the aircraft factories that have head-quarters in the city and are within a reasonable flying distance – Vista, Aeolus, Lavoisier, and Americraft. None manufacture autogiros. But I wonder about their employees? Is the Scarlet Stinger one of their employees? Is she a German agent, out to terrify and cripple the internal fabric of American aircraft companies to keep us in our place?"

"Could be," said Nita.

"Well, then we need to find out. Jackson can drive you out to Vista, and then the others. Tell them who you are, and that you're scouting for me and taking notes since I'm interested in investing. Insist on seeing each and every employee, tell them it's a quirk of mine, I want to feel comfortable about their staff, from mechanics to secretaries to janitors. Watch for a young woman with short red hair. You can do all four by tomorrow evening. I'll stay in the city and check the public records for female pilots in the area."

"And when do you suggest I leave for this mysterious investigative trip?"

"As soon as Jackson reports that the car is fueled."

"I suppose it doesn't matter that I had some other things planned today?"

For the first time that morning, Wentworth allowed a small grin to cross his face.

After Nita and Jackson left the penthouse, Wentworth donned his gray felt fedora, strolled the six blocks to City Hall. He rarely walked in the daylight; he much preferred the privacy of the limousine or the sporty comfort of the convertible. Today, however, Wentworth felt a need to be outside to look at the skies.

Beyond the thick, clumsy fingers of the high rise buildings, the sky was cloudless and near white. The summer air was heavy and damp as a baby's diaper. Pedestrians strolled more quickly than usual, glancing occasionally upward as if fearing a harpoon-bearing red autogiro might come for them.

If the Scarlet Stinger was employed by one of the companies, then she would not kill during her regular work hours. She would fly her craft back to wherever she housed it in time to clock in without raising suspicions. But still, it was an avenue that needed checking. He hoped Nita didn't mind the investigative jaunt, or if she did, she'd get over it quickly. She usually did.

The records room in City Hall was a vast, tiled space with tall windows, long tables, and countless hardwood shelves and drawered cabinets. What Wentworth sought was public record, and with prompt assistance from a lovely young clerk, he settled down with several years' worth of papers showing the licensing and registering of pilots in the city and surrounding counties.

The name, age, and gender of each registered pilot was typed neatly and enclosed in its own folder along with an occasional photograph. Wentworth flipped through countless folders, scanned the information and faces for that of a young woman with pale skin and short straight hair. On the wall, the heavy, rosewood pendulum clock registered 11 a.m, noon, 1 p.m., 2 p.m. At 2:32 he was done, and he sat back, frustrated. There were five female pilots in the greater metropolitan area, and none matched the Scarlet Stinger.

Wentworth shoved the files aside and flipped open the first of several log books in which area flight schools registered their instructors and students. He doubted he'd find much there, but couldn't leave without checking every possible clue.

He scanned name after name of instructors and their class lists from the previous year. Those who were graduated were duly noted. Those who dropped out were marked with a "W" – "withdrawn."

And then a name caught his attention.

"R. M. Lavoisier."

Lavoisier Aircraft Manufacturers was one of the four local companies. Its headquarters were on 54th Street. Was R.M. Lavoisier a relative of the company's owner? Why did R.M. take lessons and then quit?

Wentworth hailed a cab back to his apartment. As he came into the foyer, his personal assistant Ram Singh met him with a bow. The man was tall and misleadingly slight, for beneath the flowing shirt and trousers were muscles as strong and quick as those of a Bengal tiger. He wore a turban, long jacket, and dark mustache and beard.

"Master," said Singh in his soft Indian accent. "There has been another death, brought down from the sky by that flying devil woman."

Wentworth's hands clenched.

"It was not long ago, less than an hour I was told, outside the Americraft headquarters. The demon plane appeared in the sky between the buildings. People screamed and pointed, but she had her eye on one man in particular. An Americraft engineer, a man named Dickleman. How she should know this man and his whereabouts, I can't imagine, but then a demon has powers and knowledge we cannot have."

"How did you find out about this?"

"I was downstairs, getting the mail, and heard the chatter out on the sidewalk. Such fear on the faces."

"What else do you know?"

Ram Singh followed Wentworth to the kitchen, where Singh set a tea kettle on the stove. "It was as the others," he said, "a harpoon, a gun, and a very dead man on the walk."

"We can't have this," said Wentworth, and Singh nodded. Clearly, the man knew that Wentworth was not only talking of himself and of Singh, but of the man who would reveal himself at night, the dark figure who cast as much terror in the hearts of guilty, evil men as they cast in the hearts of the guiltless. Who often frightened even those who had never committed a crime, because of his appearance, his stealth, his cunning, and his merciless revenge.

"I must make a phone call," Wentworth said. "Tea can wait."

Singh bowed slightly. "Certainly."

In the den, Wentworth called the home office of Lavoisier Aircraft Manufacturers. As his finger pulled the dial around with each number, he realized, *Lavoisier is the only company thus far that hasn't lost a man to the Stinger. Lavoisier is also the only company that was not represented at the air show last weekend. Can this mean something?*

When the company's telephone operator answered, he disguised his voice to that of a mild mannered elderly man.

"Ma'am," he said simply, "I have found a book at the library and believe it belongs to someone at your company. It's a lovely book, with initials at the front. R.M. Lavoisier."

"Oh," said the operator, disarmed by Wentworth's vocal disguise. "That would belong to Mr. Lavoisier's daughter, Rose."

"Rose, all right," said Wentworth. "Sweet red-haired girl, is that right? I think I saw her leave the library, but didn't realize it was her book left behind."

"Yes, beautiful red-haired girl," said the operator.

"I can send it to her."

The woman took a moment to look up an address and then shared it with Wentworth. "Shall I tell her who called?" asked the woman. "I'm sure Rose would…"

But Wentworth hung up before she could finish.

Rose Lavoisier. R.M. Daughter to Philip Lavoisier. She could be the Scarlet Stinger.

But if so, why was she intent on harming her father's competition? What drove her to such hideous, cruel actions?

The *Spider* was going to find out.

He had hoped Nita would call that evening so he could tell her what he had unearthed. But as of nine, he had heard nothing from her. He had contacted all the aircraft factories, telling them to relay a message on her arrival, but the message had been forgotten or she had planned on calling him when she arrived at whatever hotel she chose as her stop over. Clearly, she was running late.

By 10:14 p.m., Wentworth was stealthily climbing the stairs to Rose Lavoisier's apartment, a rough tenement on a rough street on the lower East Side. The stairs creaked, and the electric light in the hall sputtered. Why a rich young woman would choose such a dingy home might cause some to wonder; Wentworth, on the other hand, had seen his share of spoiled grown children rebel and embrace the life of the bohemian. And if Rose Lavoisier was the Scarlet Stinger, not only had she embraced the living quarters of the poor and the crude, she had also decided, for some unknown reason, to adopt the evil that sometimes festered between water-stained walls, warped floors, and crumbling ceilings.

He found her door on the third floor, a simple sheet of heavy paper tacked to the wood reading "RML." Wentworth knocked on the door but no one answered. He pressed his ear to the door. There was no sound inside. Rose Lavoisier was not home yet.

Wentworth slid into the shadows beneath the stairs to the fourth floor and pressed himself against the wall. He wrapped his cape around him and tipped his head down, bringing the brim of his hat in line with his chin. He did not want to be seen but by those he wanted to see him. As the *Spider*, Wentworth was a terrifying demon in his own right.

Several drunken, cursing men stumbled up the stairs to be absorbed into their own flats. Several women shuffled up the stairs from their long days at the garment factories. Then, all was still until a heavy pair of feet walked with purpose up to the third floor, and a large man in suspenders and a white shirt with rolled sleeves jiggled a key into the lock on Rose Lavoisier's door.

The *Spider* sprang into action. Cape flying, he leapt from beneath the stairs and shoved the man in through the open door. The man tripped on the corner of a rug and nearly lost his balance, but grabbed a knife from a nearby table and turned to meet his attacker.

And he froze in place, the knife wavering in the air.

"God help me, help me, please!" the man screamed.

With a swift blow, the *Spider* knocked the knife from the man's hand. It spun like a lathe and imbedded itself into the wall at the far side of the room.

The man continued to stare. It was no surprise to the *Spider*. His appearance had made many men cry and go weak in the legs. Beneath his broad-brimmed cap was long straggly hair and red-rimmed eyes that alternatively narrowed and widened like those of some ancient, vicious bird of prey.

Then the man came to his senses, and lashed out with his fist. The *Spider* grabbed the fist, crushed it in his grasp, and drove the man to his knees. With his free hand he pulled one of his .45 automatics from his waist holster beneath his cape, and pressed the barrel to the man's temple.

"Now," whispered the *Spider*, for there was no need to yell. "Tell me about Rose Lavoisier."

"Who are…?" began the man, which was what the *Spider* expected. He flicked back the hammer. The sound of the click caused the man's mouth to snap shut.

"Have you ever heard," said the *Spider* quietly, showing the man the ring he wore, a ring on which the image of a lethal arachnid was engraved, "of the *Spider*?"

The man's head bobbed up and down obediently. His eyes were so wide it looked as though they would pop from his head and roll away.

"All right, then," said the *Spider*. "I have no reason to hurt you if you tell me everything I need to know about Rose Lavoisier."

"She's…she's old man Lavoisier's only daughter," sputtered the man. "I'm her bodyguard, he pays for me to keep tabs on her though she usually wants me out of her way."

"And…?" The *Spider* stepped back from the bodyguard but kept the gun trained on his forehead.

"And what? She's not here. She's out fine-tuning that damned autogiro of hers."

"So, she is the Scarlet Stinger."

"The what…oh, yes, in the papers. They call her that. She's the one, I tell you. I have nothing to do with it."

"Why is she killing?"

The bodyguard just stared.

"Why is she killing?"

The bodyguard's eyes showed a flicker of fury and hate. He said nothing.

The *Spider* flicked the barrel of the gun down a fraction and fired. A bullet shattered the bodyguard's foot. The bodyguard screamed.

"Talk," said the *Spider*.

The words came tumbling out amid wails and sobs. "Her father's company is headed for bankruptcy. It's been secretly squeezed out of government contracts by Vista, Americraft, and Aeolus. He's trying his best to keep up but it ain't happening. Rose is spoiled, but she's also brilliant and mad. As a child she used to hang around the engineers and mechanics, and learned a lot about planes and other aircraft. When she was thirteen, her daddy gave her a workshop of her own. It's on the Lavoisier property, part of the factory. She builds experimental aircraft in there, including that red thing she now flies. She doesn't have a license, though. Took lessons a couple times but then said the instructor couldn't teach her anything she couldn't learn herself. She has always cared about her father. She doesn't love anyone but him, him and..." The bodyguard hesitated, sputtered, and then continued. "She's hell bent on destroying her father's competition."

The *Spider* considered what the bodyguard had said. Was the man her lover? "Tell me, bodyguard. From where does she fly? Where does she keep the autogiro?"

"Her workshop is part of the Lavoisier factory complex, but don't know where she stashes her aircraft. She won't tell me. Close to the city somewhere, so she can get in, out, and back here in short order."

The *Spider*'s eyes narrowed considerably and he bent closer. He breathed hot breath into the man's face. "I said where...does...she...keep...the...craft?"

"Really," the man insisted. "I don't know!"

The *Spider* watched the bodyguard's face, and realizing the man had told the truth, straightened. "I'll wait for her outside," the *Spider* said. "And you are to stay put until then. Know that I can hear a window opening from a mile away. Do you understand?"

The man nodded vigorously and clutched at his bloody shoe.

"I said do you understand?" The *Spider* grinned then, widely, revealing long, pointed canine teeth that caught the glow of the ceiling light.

"Y-y-y-yes!"

The *Spider* backed toward the door, but the moment he glanced away and reached for the knob, the bodyguard flew up from the floor like a ghoul out of Hades, propelled by his one good foot. He dove into his nemesis, screaming, "You won't kill her!" The *Spider* was thrown against the door, and he lost his grip on his gun as the bodyguard grabbed him around the throat. The gun struck the floor and skidded several feet.

"Die, *Spider*!" screamed the bodyguard, but at that moment, the *Spider* took his second automatic from his holster, put it to the man's gut, and pulled the trigger. The man uttered a single grunt then fell backward in a heap on the rug. Blood ran down along his white shirt and pooled on the floor.

The *Spider* knelt beside the bodyguard and plucked the key to the apartment from the man's pocket. Then he balled his fist and with great force, crushed his ring against the dead man's forehead, cutting a brand into the flesh that marked him as a victim of the *Spider*.

Outside, beneath the stairs, along with several tiny *spider*s that had moved into the space, he waited for the return of Rose Lavoisier.

She did not come home that night. Furious, the *Spider* left his stakeout at 5:00 a.m., just before the sun made its appearance in the New York sky. At home, his disguise safely tucked into a briefcase, he paced, unable to sleep, waiting for the hour in which offices were open and men were awake.

He first called the landlord of Rose Lavoisier's tenement soon after six. He said he was a city inspector, and that he'd anonymously checked the building the day before, finding it worthy of nothing short of a police raid and a wrecking ball.

"The worst case is that Lavoisier woman," said Wentworth. "I understand she's been whoring and drugging with the worst elements, bringing them up to her flat. Neighbors have complained that she leaves her stove on, and tosses cigarettes into the stairwell. She'll have the place burned down before you know it."

"Pah!" came the scratchy voice.

"You are on the first floor. You will keep you eye on that front entrance. The moment she comes in, the very next time, I want you to give me a call so I can have her picked up."

"Well, good luck wi' that," said the landlord. "You a minute too late. She called not a half hour ago, said she was out of there for good. I ain't looked in her room yet but I'm sure she left a pile of shit for me to clean up!"

Damn! "Where did she say she was moving?"

"She didn't, and I don't care. Like you said, she was the worst case. Good riddance."

Wentworth slammed down the receiver. Rose Lavoisier had most likely heard the scuffle from out in the hall, and had disappeared. Where could she have gone? To daddy, perhaps? Wentworth and Ram Singh would have to watch the Lavoisier office building. Nita could pose as a reporter, perhaps catch the girl outside, play to her vanity as the daughter of a well-respected New York businessman, lure her away to chat inside a tea room, and right into Wentworth's grasp.

Next, Wentworth called the Vista factory. Had Nita Van Sloan visited? he asked the soft-spoken telephone operator. Yes, the operator said, yesterday morning, and a nice woman Miss Van Sloan was. Had the operator given Miss Van Sloan the message to call him? Oh, no, sorry, the operator had forgotten. "I'm sorry, things are so busy sometimes."

Wentworth then dialed the Aeolus factory. Had Nita visited? Yes, yesterday, quite late in the afternoon, and they hoped her visit was pleasant and informative. Had they given her Wentworth's message to call? They were sure they had, though it was very late when she left.

Nita had clearly not seen the request as important. She would call but would do it on her own time.

He dialed Americraft's factory.

"This is Richard Wentworth," he began. "I am calling to inquire about Nita Van Sloan. Has she...?"

"Oh, Mr. Wentworth, good morning and what timing!" replied the receptionist. "She just arrived, and is planning on taking a tour. Would you like to speak to her?"

"Yes, thank you."

There was a clack and clunk, and then Nita said, "Hi, Dick. How are things going?"

"You need to leave Americraft and go to the Lavoisier factory. It's just 30 miles south from where you are, near Lakehurst."

"But why?"

"The Scarlet Stinger is not an employee of any of these companies. Her name is Rose. She's the daughter of Philip Lavoisier. She has a workshop at the Lavoisier facility. Go there, look around, take notes. Find out where this workshop is located, exactly, but don't be too eager in your request to see each and every room and broom closet."

"Dick, you know I know how to do this kind of thing." The voice was slightly perturbed.

"Yes, I'm sorry. As soon as you know, call us, and then come right back to the city. We can get this woman, we can end her dastardly career and..."

There was a sudden roar on the other end of the line, and a scream into the phone. Then, the line went dead.

"Nita!" shouted Wentworth. "Nita, what happened?" He knew she couldn't hear him, but he had no idea what could have happened.

Nita was bandaged head to toe, and in great pain. She was propped up slightly in her hospital bed, breathing slowly and carefully, waiting for the latest pills the nurse had given her to take hold. It was clear to Wentworth when he got to her room that she had been crying, but she would have none of that while he was there.

"What...what happened?" she asked softly.

"It was the Scarlet Stinger," said Wentworth, barely able to contain his anger. "She was spotted by several employees outside the building, heading west in her autogiro. She aimed her harpoon at an aircraft fueling truck parked beside the front office. It blew up, caving in part of the office, killing five and wounding seven more. I'm quite sure the Stinger used an explosive on the harpoon head with all the damage it created."

"Oh, my God."

"You were knocked unconscious. Not burned, but cut..." he was going to say, "nearly to ribbons," but didn't have the heart. "You were cut pretty badly by flying glass. The doctor says you'll be all right with time. You'll need to stay here for a while."

Nita closed her eyes and Wentworth could see new tears roll down her cheeks.

"You were unconscious for nearly a day." He took her hand, the only one not enshrouded in white gauze, and gave it a tender squeeze.

"I heard the nurses talking in the hall," said Nita. "The Scarlet Stinger has killed twice since the explosion at the factory. Two more in the city again. One was an Americraft engineer and the other was Arnold Kittinger's son, just seventeen. Everyone is terrified, Dick!"

"But we know who she is now," said Wentworth. "We have her in our sights and will stop her. I promise you, I will stop her."

"Please...stop her," said Nita through butchered lips.

And suddenly, it dawned on Wentworth the best way to find the Stinger and end the airborne villain's ghastly rampage.

"If she's too difficult to track from below, I'll track her from above," Wentworth told Thompson as he climbed the ladder into the blimp's gondola behind his friend. "She enters and leaves the city in all different directions. She appears suddenly and catches everyone by surprise. Once she is spotted she disappears again behind another building. No one person or body of persons has been able to track her. With the blimp, however, if we spot her we can track her."

"Excellent idea, Richard," said Thompson. "Not only can you help the police department track the murderess, which is admirable, but you get to test out one of our airships first hand." He winked at Wentworth. "And of course, I'm sure you'll be favorably impressed with the blimp's performance."

Wentworth nodded. "I'm sure I will be." He had convinced Thompson to take him up with the promise that if suitably impressed by the blimp he might want to put his money into not only the new rigid ship but the continued operation of the company's non-rigids as well. It wasn't a lie, but that was far from being the first thing on his mind at the moment.

Thompson settled himself in the left-hand pilot's chair, propping his machine gun up between his chair and the wall. "I'm not going anywhere without some protection," he'd told Wentworth at the airfield when Wentworth had noted the weapon. "With airline executives dropping like flies, I'm not about to let myself be too vulnerable, on the ground or in the air." Thompson then donned his headphones, put his left hand on the throttle, his feet on the rudder pedals, and his right hand on the large elevator wheel beside his chair. Wentworth dropped into the co-pilot's chair to Thompson's right. He placed his polished leather briefcase on the floor by his feet.

The blimp rose sharply from Glaze Airfield, proudly displaying advertising signs for the Stout Scarab automobile on both sides, propelled by its throbbing outrigger engines, its hemp mooring lines drifting behind. When it reached altitude and leveled out, Thompson steered it east toward the city. The sun was high and hot today, and scattered clouds were blowing in from the sea, making soft pink splotches on the horizon.

Wentworth pulled binoculars from the briefcase and stood to study the cityscape below. He felt every nerve on edge, every muscle tightened and ready. They circled the city for several hours, Wentworth alternating between positions at the door and the various windows, willing the Scarlet Stinger to show herself.

"Richard, this may be a dead end," said Thompson, pulling off his sunglasses and wiping his brow.

But Wentworth shook his head and stared with even more concentration through the spyglasses. "She'll show up. She's not let a day go by without at least one killing. She has plenty more to go. I'll spot her."

Another hour passed. Thompson asked if Wentworth wanted to continue.

"I must," said Wentworth simply.

And then the Scarlet Stinger's autogiro came into view, skirting above the tallest buildings like a red herring gull seeking prey in a sea of concrete. Thompson brought the blimp around in a wide circle and they followed the aircraft, quietly gaining ground.

Suddenly the Scarlet Stinger made a sharp turn back around and up, clearly curious about the advertising blimp that seemed to have taken an interest in her. She flew to within mere yards of the blimp to have a closer look. Wentworth could see her short red hair batting the wind beneath her leather helmet, and the sneer on her lips as she clutched the controls.

The combined roars of the blimp and autogiro's engines were loud, but Wentworth could read the Scarlet Stinger's lips. "I see you, Steven Thompson! I know who you are!" Then she turned her craft away, circling down, around. She looked back over her shoulder and raised her Tommy gun.

"Thompson, move!" cried Wentworth. He dove for Thompson's machine gun, snatched it up, and then flung open the gondola's door.

Thompson pulled on the elevator wheel and the blimp's nose angled downward. The throttle kicked in, pushing the helium-filled giant forward and down. The Scarlet Stinger circled below the blimp, rolled her craft to clear the top rotor, and fired up through the gondola's floor. Wentworth leapt to the side and the bullets pierced the ceiling.

When the Scarlet Stinger rose to see the damage she'd done, Wentworth opened fire through the door with the machine gun. The windshield broke but the Scarlet Stinger ducked, and then steered sharply to the left and away, down into a cover of clouds.

There was a nothing for a moment, but then the autogiro popped back up from the clouds, heading straight for the blimp. "There she is again!"

Wentworth fired the heavy weapon, hitting the tail and a wheel. But then the gun went silent. The ammunition was spent.

"Thompson!" he shouted. "More ammo!"

"I didn't bring anymore! I thought thirty rounds would…"

The Scarlet Stinger turned her craft at a nearly impossible angle, revealing the loaded harpoon gun at the bottom. Wentworth yelled, "No!"

and jumped from the door, striking the floor on his side as the Scarlet Stinger fired. Startled, Thompson stood from his seat and turned to see what had happened. The metal lance cut the air and flew through the base of the open doorway. There was a thwack and a groan.

Wentworth rolled over and stared in disbelief. His friend was skewered through his abdomen but still standing, with the harpoon's tip embedded solidly in the control panel behind him and the cable trailing out the door. Thompson blinked several times and opened his mouth to speak, but only a bubbling pool of blood came out. Then his knees buckled but the harpoon kept him from falling.

"Steve!" cried Wentworth. He climbed over to his friend.

"She got me," gurgled Thompson. "She's won this round, looks like."

Wentworth clenched his teeth, ripped opened his briefcase and held up something for the dying Thompson to see. "No, she hasn't," he said. "The *Spider* will kill her, I promise!"

Thompson's eyes focused for just a moment in surprise, awe, and understanding, and then the consciousness was gone. His head dropped to his chest. Thompson was dead.

The Scarlet Stinger made a victory circle around the width of the blimp, the harpoon cable keeping the autogiro connected to the blimp like a puppy on a leash. But when she came back in line with the gondola door, it was not Wentworth she faced, but the *Spider*. He stood there, cape flapping, .45 pistols in a vice grip, aimed outward.

He would not let the next round go to the bell.

The *Spider* fired, empty brass shells flying around his head like angry hornets. Most of the bullets hit only air as the autogiro zipped back and forth, with one striking the aircraft's side.

The Scarlet Stinger fired a spray that struck the steel side of the gondola and several windows, punching through the former and shattering the latter. Then she flew off, the harpoon cable turning the blimp around and dragging it behind.

On my friend's name, I will see her die a terrible death!

The *Spider* braced his feet and knees against the frame around the open door, leaned forward slightly, and fired his .45s. A bullet bit her shoulder. Her head jerked up and back, and the *Spider* could see her face folded in pain. But then she sneered, shook her fist and turned the autogiro around, towing the blimp down.

The *Spider* pressed the .45's magazine release buttons. Before the empty magazines had even hit the floor, he had reloaded with fresh magazines from his pocket. He fired again and again toward the autogiro, striking the sides but not the girl. He tried to shoot the harpoon cable, but it was steel and the bullets were deflected. The autogiro played cat and mouse, darting back and forth and keeping away from the rain of lead. Down they went, through the clouds and back into the open.

It was then the *Spider* saw what the Scarlet Stinger had in mind.

There was a tall, stainless steel spire at the top of the nearby Chrysler Building. She aimed to pull the blimp onto it, to rip the envelope so it would lose its helium. It would then fall the 77 stories to the ground, taking the *Spider* with it.

The *Spider* loaded two more magazines into the .45s and continued firing at the Stinger. But her autogiro kept up its erratic movements, zooming back and forth, staying clear of most of the bullets. Then, she steered her craft upward slightly, unaware of the dangling mooring line in her path until it was too late. The top rotor tangled in the line. The rotor stopped short with a metallic crack, leaving the craft dangling from the blimp, unable to go farther.

The *Spider* heard the woman's furious scream. She stood in her craft and tugged at the hemp line, but then stopped as she realized it would do no good – she would plummet if released. She swung about, bracing her Tommy gun against her wounded shoulder, but before she could aim, the *Spider*, with his target in steady sight, fired it out of her hands.

It was at the same moment that the Scarlet Stinger and the *Spider* noticed that the blimp, weighted down by the lifeless autogiro, was still being pulled directly toward the spire. It would soon impale itself and, ripped asunder, let out its final breaths. Both would fall to their deaths. The *Spider* dashed over to Thompson, and with clenched jaw and strength born of rage, worked the harpoon and body back and forth until they came loose from the control panel. Then he heaved the speared body out the door. It fell the length of the cable and then snapped up short, leaving Thompson dangling from the autogiro.

"Miss Lavoisier!" the *Spider* called from the gondola as she glanced between the tangled mooring line and the cable swaying from her craft, "look at me. Have a long, hard look. I am the *Spider*. And this face is the last you'll see before you enter the gates of hell!"

She looked. Their eyes locked for a moment and she raised her fist defiantly.

He held one .45 out arm's length, and trained the barrel at her head, but at the last second pointed it instead at the mooring line.

She'll die a more tormented death, plunging to Earth like her victims!

He pulled the trigger. The hemp line snapped. The autogiro plunged, whirling, between two skyscrapers and a thin layer of clouds. He could hear her screams fade like mist in the sun. And then, he could see her no more.

The *Spider* stumbled to the pilot's seat and steered the craft away from the spire, turning it westward toward Argosy Towers. He brought the throttle back, giving it more speed, and when it was steady, changed quickly out of his disguise. Though he'd watched Thompson at the pilot's controls, the *Spider* wasn't sure he could get the blimp back to Glaze Airfield and bring it down safely. However, Argosy Towers had a wide, flat roof. All he needed to do was to float over it, close enough to jump. Then he would pull the line to the rip panel and that would deflate the blimp almost instantly, leaving it an empty, flattened envelope draped over the top of the building.

Richard Wentworth stood at the window of his office, gazing out across the vast ocean of stone, brick, blacktop, and humanity. Nita would be released from the hospital in two days, much healed and ready for her next adventure. When he'd visited her that afternoon, she'd wanted to hear all about the gun battle over the city. But Wentworth could only say, "I destroyed her, Nita, the same way she destroyed so many others down." He could not share the details of Thompson's death. He could not tell her how he, himself, had felt skewered in that awful moment. And he could also not tell her that when he'd at last climbed down from Argosy Towers' roof and had found the crushed autogiro in an alleyway surrounded by police and morbidly curious passersby, the Scarlet Stinger was not there. Steve Thompson, bent, twisted, and broken, was still tethered to the harpoon and its cable. But the Scarlet Stinger was gone. By the time the first witness got to the scene, she had vanished. What had happened to the evil woman?

Wentworth couldn't know.

For the last two weeks there had been no more killings, so perhaps she had died and someone had spirited her body away. Or she had survived and escaped but without her aircraft could no longer kill in her chosen fashion. Detective Samson and his cronies had searched for her, "relentlessly" they said, but came up empty-handed.

The phone on the desk rang. The sound crawled up his back but he did not answer. Tonight he needed to be silent, to be still. He needed to speak of nothing and to think of nothing.

The phone continued to ring. Wentworth turned toward the desk. Then he let out a long breath he realized he'd been holding, and picked up the receiver. After all, it could be something important, something deadly. It could be something for the *Spider*. 🔫

illustration by Tom Floyd

Chapter Four

DEATH REIGN OF THE ZOMBIE QUEEN

by HOWARD HOPKINS

The Norvell Hotel was a modern masterwork of chrome, concrete and blood.

More accurately, it would be by the time Malalaia Cervantes finished with the men four floors above, men pompously feasting on a meal of lavish elegance bought by the toil and taxes of this city's workforce. Men who controlled industry; men who deemed themselves above the destitute and degraded. Men who at this very moment prepared to crown a new king, another wealthy, self-serving monarch no different from those who had ruled before.

Control. Power. They had it.

She craved it.

She strode into the hotel, her figure concealed by a hooded robe. Five robed figures, all larger, followed her lead, their gait shuffling, yet not clumsy.

She paused, bare feet sinking into the rich cream carpet. A chandelier splashed glittering gems of light across Art Deco moldings and chrome trim. The lobby was deserted except for a bantam cock of a manager who popped out from behind a black-walnut counter and strutted towards them.

Slipping back her hood, she revealed a face that radiated a dark island beauty, despite the viciousness glinting in her mahogany eyes. Her hair, done in tight ringlets, framed an exquisite, high-cheekboned face.

"We do not allow your type in here..." the little manager snipped as he reached her.

Her gaze ran up and down his ebony suit and crisp ivory shirt. "Now, what type might that be, *la*?" A Haitian Creole lilt graced her tone.

The man stiffened, his chin lifting with an arrogance she little cared for.

"I think you know what I mean. Please leave this hotel at once."

Darkness moved across her eyes. "*Wi*, I am afraid I *do* know. A pity for you."

In a heartbeat a memory flared from the depths of her mind: a moonlit island night, torches flashing amber and shadow across her naked glistening flesh. Three men, three *white* men, forcing her down, their hands exploring areas of her body they had no right to touch, their mouths pressed to hers, tasting like cold, rancid bacon grease. Their bodies invading her, each in turn, on a night that seemed endless.

Control. Power. They owned it that night.

Never again.

"I have business here..." Her gaze focused on the manager. "You will detain me no longer."

Her hand drifted up; a casual flick of her fingers. The five figures behind her slid their hoods from their heads in unison. All five were men, their features cast in rich ebony, their jaundiced eyes shot through with webs of scarlet.

The manager bristled. "You cannot burst in here and—"

She laughed, a sound at once mocking and damning. "Oh, but I can, *mon ami*. I can."

The arrogance melted from the manager's face, overridden by terror as the robed men started towards him.

Zombies descending upon him, the manager disappeared beneath a shroud of humanity. His screams pleased her. The sounds of tearing flesh and crunching bone brought an indescribable satisfaction to her soul. Blood soaked into the carpet, spreading nearly to her feet.

Her gaze drifted above the carnage to the dial above one of the elevators at the rear of the lobby. The lever had stopped at the fourth floor.

"She's arrived," Malalaia whispered. "How very fortunate."

Crystal and chrome embellished the Scarlet Room. The hotel reserved the space for its most illustrious—and affluent—customers, catered to their every whim. Crimson draperies adorned the walls around a stage complete with an orchestra pit. A dance floor covered half the room, and a crystal chandelier cast a thousand glittering stars across the walls and vaulted ceiling. Tonight a long dining table adorned with fine linen occupied most of the dance area.

Upon the table spread a feast befitting the five men and four women seated about it. Whipped potatoes with sherry and almond-cream asparagus complimented an enormous slab of rare roast beef, its carved slices running with blood, on a silver platter. Chilled champagne rested in ice-filled buckets.

The men gathered represented some of New York's most powerful, Senator Ralph Ralston and Mayor Walter Steager, District Attorney Thorenson and Judge Harrison Carter. The remaining man, a prominent businessman named Jack Hubbly, worked behind the scenes. The hotel had provided the women, one of its little-advertised services to the right individual at the right price. The men wore tuxedoes, the women sparkling gowns with plunging necklines. Expensive necklaces embedded with glittering jewels provided by their dates in return for favors to be rendered later in the evening adorned the alabaster silk of their throats.

Senator Ralston, a man who had seen perhaps too many such dinners, stood from his seat at the head of table. He tapped a silver spoon against his champagne glass, halting the murmuring and gay laughter.

Ralston cleared his throat. "Gentlemen, you all know why you were called here tonight. Mayor Steager will be retiring shortly. It's imperative we make certain our candidate for his seat has no chance of losing and every chance of supporting our, shall I say, *philosophy*, when it comes to ridding this city of its unsavory element."

A smaller man with a prominent Adam's apple sitting to Ralston's left clinked his fork on his plate. "You've become a trifle paranoid in your old age, Ralston."

The woman sitting next to him, a death-grip on her champagne glass, giggled. The emeralds in her necklace splashed shimmering green droplets across her throat and bosom.

Ralston's brow knotted. "You better than anyone should know what an idiotic statement that is, Carter. Poverty runs rampant in this city. It germinates crime. Have you walked the streets, seen the pitiful souls wallowing in squalor? Or don't you ever leave that lofty leather throne of yours behind the bench?"

"Now see here—" Judge Carter half-rose, hands grasping the edge of the table.

"Sit the devil down, Harrison!" Mayor Steager cast the smaller fellow an annoyed frown. "Too many times your lenient sentencing made us wonder just whose side you were on. Don't give us further reason to suspect you of anything untoward." Steager was a steely-haired man, just north of sixty, with haggard features.

"Dammit, Steager, I'm sick and tired of your aspersions!" Carter's chest jutted out and the woman beside him became overcome with a case of champagne giggles at the bickering. Carter eyed her, looking as if he might slap the laughter off her face.

Ralston shook his head, face grim. "Carter, I won't ask you again to keep quiet. Your membership in this little coterie is tenuous at best. Another outburst and we'll be discussing replacing you—and don't get the notion your position protects you. You know how we can alter the status quo."

Carter glared at Ralston, but lowered himself back onto his chair. The woman stopped giggling.

With a scowl, Ralston resumed his speech. "We don't want another Chicago here. We need someone tough on crime, someone who's not afraid to circumvent the law when the situation demands it. That man must also be someone of means, someone who can't be bought with underworld money."

Jack Hubbly, who contributed large sums to Ralston's campaigns in exchange for certain zoning nods, cleared his throat. "And you think that man is Richard Wentworth?"

Ralston nodded. "Why not? He's wealthy; he has every chance of winning."

"There are rumors about him..." District Attorney Thorenson said, then took a sip from his glass.

Ralston shrugged, a wry smile pulling at his lips. "There are rumors about everyone in this city. We can't base our decision on them."

Thorenson laughed. "You know damn well what I'm talking about. At the very least, he's unmarried, a playboy."

"He's also a master criminologist." Ralston's tone issued a challenge. "He's not afraid to aid the police, nor use his wealth against crime."

Thorenson squirmed. "I've met Wentworth. There's something in his eyes I can't pin down. A peculiar hunger, perhaps. A look that made me wonder if he's...well, entirely *rational*. We need someone completely stable in this position."

Ralston gave a sharp laugh. "Fortunately being rational's not amongst the criteria for anyone running for office in this country. In fact, in this city, it may work against a man warring on crime. Take that *Spider* fellow, for instance. He gets the job done, I'd say."

Harrison Carter's lips twisted into a grimace. He was having trouble holding his tongue and that secretly pleased Ralston.

Ralston's brow lifted. "You have an opinion, Carter?"

Carter's eyes narrowed. "I can't believe you'd condone the antics of that maniac. He's more of a menace than the criminals. If I ever discovered his identity I'd put him away for good. Besides, Wentworth's known to be a philanthropist. What kind of man gives away money?"

"A man who gives a damn, Carter." Ralston's gaze skipped back to the mayor. "We can win with him, Steager. And mark my word we'll have no worries about his stance against the underworld and his ability to confront their threat."

Steager frowned. "I'm inclined to agree. Still, how much do we really know about him and will he be amenable to our guidance?"

"If you mean, will he be a puppet? Never. But he will work *with* us, I am certain. And if there are skeletons in his closet I've got people at the *Times*."

"Things have a way of coming out, no matter how many friends you have in high places, Ralston," District Attorney Thorenson said. "We'd better make sure his hands are clean."

"Conceded." Ralston lowered himself back into his chair. "But consider this: Can we afford *not* to run him with Lucky Conner eyeing the seat? His underworld ties are guaranteed. Surely nothing in Wentworth's closet could be darker than what lurks within a mob boss's past..."

"All right..." Steager slapped a palm atop the table. "Say we do run Wentworth. Has anyone determined whether he *wants* the job?"

"That." Ralston smiled. "shall be answered shortly."

As if in response a tap came from the door. A moment later the door opened and the woman who stood on the threshold was enough to capture the breath of every man at the table and raise a jealous eyebrow on every woman.

She strode into the room, her gait confident and her carriage regal. Dressed in a black skirt and waistcoat with a crisp white blouse, hat titled at a jaunty angle atop her chestnut locks, she walked to the end of table opposite Ralston.

"Gentlemen" Her contralto voice was almost a whisper. Her violet eyes sparkled.

Ralston snapped out of his spell. "Gentlemen, may I present Miss Nita Van Sloan, liaison to Richard Wentworth."

A murmur went through the gathered, as they nodded their greeting. A small sound of disgust came from the woman beside Carter when she noticed him eyeing the woman with a lascivious glint.

"Good evening, gentlemen..." Nita's gaze swept across the face of each person. "And *ladies*." She said the last with a knowing smile that annoyed the woman next to Carter all the more. The woman scowled and downed the rest of her champagne.

"It was my understanding Mr. Wentworth would come himself, Miss Van Sloan." Ralston cocked an eyebrow. "Not that I'm entirely disappointed, you understand." He tried a smile that wasn't quite as warm as he hoped it would be. That Van Sloan had come in Wentworth's place boded ill for their little plan.

"I quite understand, Senator." Nita's gloved fingers absently traced the edge of the tablecloth. "But it couldn't be helped. Mr. Wentworth's *flattered* by your offer. In fact, more than flattered. Perhaps amazed would be a more appropriate word."

"Then he'll accept?" Ralston asked it without hope. He already knew the answer.

"I regret to say he must respectfully decline."

"But why?" asked Steager, face tightening.

Nita's attention went to the mayor. "Please understand, Mayor, Richard's wary of the limelight and does not wish to involve himself in the politics of this or any other city. He feels he's more useful in his current role as a consultant to Kirkpatrick."

"Bosh!" Carter gave a dismissing wave of his hand. "Call a spade a spade, Miss Van Sloan. He's gotten too damn rich and too damn lazy to bother serving the city. He'd rather throw money at the problem and proclaim himself some sort of savior to the poor."

"Carter, that's the last time—" Ralston stopped, face draining as his gaze locked on the doorway.

Nita Van Sloan's attention shifted to the doorway the moment she saw the look on Ralston's face. Her eyes narrowed as her violet gaze settled on the robed form of a woman stepping into the room, followed by five men wearing robes. Nita's heart beat a step faster at the sight of those men, with their dead faces, blood-webbed eyes and blood-smeared lips.

The woman drifted into the room with a lightness of tread that reminded Nita of a jungle cat. Predatory. Feral. The look on her face, hard, cunning, only strengthened that impression. Ralston saw it too, and perhaps he had some inkling as to the woman's identity, though that puzzled Nita. Dick had mentioned nothing of new threats to the city in recent days.

"Close it." The woman gave a causal flick of her hand. One of the robed men turned and eased the door shut.

The woman came to the table, glancing at Nita and giving her a ghost of a smile.

"Who the devil are you?" Judge Carter blurted, again half-lifting out of his chair.

Malalaia ignored the judge, gaze settling on Ralston. "Why, Mr. Ralston, you must have forgotten to send my invitation to your little gathering. I t'ought I made it clear who your new mayor was to be, *non?*"

"Do you know this woman, Senator Ralston?" Nita's voice carried an edge of confidence that covered any sense of fear she might have felt at the sight of the dead-faced men. She was used to threat, used to menace, had witnessed things no society woman would have dared gaze upon. She was a confidant of Richard Wentworth, after all, and the mistress of the *Spider.*

"Malalaia Cervantes," Ralston answered, voice low. "Self-styled 'Queen of the Zombies'. She's been sending letters the past few weeks proclaiming her intention to rule the city. We paid her no attention. We receive letters every so often from lunatics such as her."

Nita frowned. So that was why no news of this woman had reached the *Spider.* Her threats had been ignored, her letters disposed of. Commissioner Kirkpatrick had likely never even been notified. Nita had a feeling Ralston and the police had probably made a huge mistake preventing news of her existence from reaching Richard Wentworth.

"Oh, bosh!" Carter said, now standing, his rheumy eyes focused on Malalaia Cervantes. "Throw these lunatics out of here. They've no business here and I'm not about to listen to the prattle of a woman, especially an inky dink!"

The woman next to Carter appeared to sober suddenly, and cast the judge a glare.

Ralston's face washed pale. Nita knew the senator was now taking this woman seriously. He saw something in Malalaia Cervantes' eyes that told him a terrible mistake had been made and the consequences would prove dire.

"For your own safety, Carter," Ralston said under his breath, "shut the hell up."

Malalaia uttered a husky laugh that held no humor. "Why, Mr. Charlie, you should listen to the fine Senator, *la.*"

"Now see here—" Carter started towards the woman, but instantly stopped as the dead-faced man next to her grunted a threat. He appeared to think better of his actions but Ralston's face bleached bone-white with the knowledge Carter's slur had sealed his doom.

Malalaia made a slight motion with her head. The robed man closest to Carter shuffled forward. His hand snapped out, fingers locking about Carter's throat. Carter gasped and suddenly went weak in the knees. With desperate fingers, he pried at the hand clamped to his neck, unable to dislodge the grip. Spittle gathered at the corners of his mouth and his face bled to crimson. A moment later his eyes rolled upward and the robed man dropped him. Carter hit the floor with a lifeless thud and lay still, tongue flopping from his mouth.

His date shrieked, the sound more unnerving, if that were possible, than the sudden death of Harrison Carter. She bolted from her chair but the robed figure grabbed her.

Malalaia stepped up to the woman, her mahogany eyes locked on the emerald necklace. Reaching out, she gently caressed the jewels, then ripped the necklace from the woman's neck. With a flick of Malalaia's head, the dead-faced man wrapped both arms about the screaming woman's head and twisted.

The brittle snap made Nita's stomach turn. It happened so suddenly she could not even take a step towards the zombie; she doubted she could have saved the woman had she reached her in time and the thought galled her.

The zombie dropped the woman's body next to the judge's lifeless form.

None of the other men or women at the table moved. Tears shimmered in the women's eyes; fear glared like skulls in those of the men.

"You're a monster," Nita said, unable to stop herself. "You will pay dearly for this."

Malalaia's attention shifted to Nita and she walked toward her, dropping the emeralds into a pocket in her robe. "Such melodrama, Miss Van Sloan. But what do we expect from the mistress of the famous *Spider*, *wi*?"

Something sank in Nita's belly. Somehow this woman knew Dick was the *Spider!* "I'm sure I have no idea what you talking about."

Malalaia laughed again, this time the expression carrying a note of mockery. "Oh, come now, Missy, it is hardly a secret. In fact, that is why I am here, to deliver a message to your master."

"He's not my master," Nita said, tone defiant.

"But he is a man, *non*? Their kind feels dominion over all females. Is this not true? Much the same way these men gathered do." Her hand swept out, indicating the men present about the table. "They would be king makers, men who wish to hold onto whatever little power they delude themselves into thinking they have. But they have none. By their own arrogance they ignored my offers of opportunity. They could never cede control to a woman, especially an—what was the phrase our late friend used? Oh, yes, 'inky dink'. A pity."

"What do you want here?" Nita held her voice steady, challenging. She refused to back down in the face of danger. She did not belong to the *Spider*, they belonged together.

"I t'ought I made that plain, *non*? I want this city, perhaps this state, perhaps this country. And your *Spider* will aid me in that quest. He is the only one worthy enough to rule by my side. His money, his rage...this he shares with me."

Nita scoffed. "If you knew anything about him, you'd know he'd never join you in such a delusion."

"Oh, but he will..." Malalaia reached beneath her robe, brought out a small leather case. "Because I will hold your life in my hand."

It was Nita's turn to laugh. "I imagine a man such as the *Spider* would sacrifice me or anyone else for his mission."

"Is that true?" A flicker of derision crossed Malalaia's eyes. "We shall see, Missy. We shall see." Malalaia opened the case. A ruby liquid gleamed in a syringe resting in purple velvet.

Nita moved then. She had no idea what that liquid would do to her and no desire to find out.

She lunged for the woman but a robed figure stepped forward, blocking her.

She doubled her hand into a fist, swung, putting all her force behind the blow. Her knuckles bounced off the zombie's chin with a sound like a gunshot. The zombie's head rocked. She'd dropped men with that punch before. But he didn't go down. He grabbed her, fingers closing like a vice on each of her wrists.

Pain lanced her arms all the way to her shoulders. She kicked at the zombie's shins, tried to break his kneecaps, but he whirled her around, clamping her against his massive chest.

About the table the rest sat paralyzed with fear, none daring to chance Carter's fate.

Malalaia Cervantes' eyes narrowed on Nita. "I almost respect you. You are a black widow, are you not? You realize what they do to their mates?" Malalaia plucked the syringe from the case and plunged the needle into Nita's neck.

Burning. Liquid fire. Flame raced through her veins. Across her flesh capillaries throbbed, some bursting. Yellow washed across her eyes, streaked through with crimson. Her mind became a blur of ebony and crimson. Anger; raw, surging. And hunger, a craving for something she'd dared not think about—the taste of human flesh!

Returning the leather case to her robe, Malalaia peered at Nita, waiting another moment until a blank look invaded the young woman's eyes.

Malalaia grabbed a portion of Nita's crisp blouse and tore open the top buttons, revealing the upper swell of Nita's breasts.

"We cannot have you joining the *Spider* for dinner all prim and proper now, can we?" Her hand vanished beneath her robe again, bringing out a hat pin and a slip of paper. She folded the paper and jammed the hat pin through it, then eyed the flesh of Nita's chest. Squeezing a pinch of Nita's skin together, Malalaia inserted the hatpin through it, attaching the note to her body with very little bleeding.

"Go back to your *Spider*. Bring him my challenge."

Nita nodded, unable to resist. Within her the hunger grew. The zombie holding her let her go. She shuffled to the door, opened it, then staggered out into the hallway.

Within the room Malalaia Cervantes peered at the others around the table, all of whom sat in terrified silence.

She plucked a sliver of roast beef from the platter, then took a bite. Blood dribbled down her chin and fingers. She smiled. "*Bon appetite...*"

The zombies moved toward the guests, whose dying shrieks mixed with the sounds of tearing flesh and crunching bone...

He stood on the terrace overlooking the city, his prized Stradivarius nestled beneath his chin. Behind him the French doors lay open, leading into the drawing room of the fifteen-room duplex penthouse. The bow slipped over the strings like silk caressing a woman's soft skin and he grew lost in the strains of Mendelssohn's "Concerto in E Minor". His thoughts wandered dark alleys.

Fifteen stories below lay his city. But was he failing it? Was the disease of crime running through its veins, flooding its cells, so powerful no tonic could eradicate it? Even one as vigilant and brutal as the *Spider*?

Was there no end to the madness?

Richard Wentworth's eyes narrowed and the music guided him deeper into a mood that bordered on despair. Beyond the terrace the twinkling city lights faded, dark stars, and blood seeped from brick and glass, streamed along concrete and steel until the streets grew soaked with scarlet. Then a torrent of rushing bloodwater engulfed the city's humanity, whisking them to their doom. Their screams filled his ears, saturated his very soul. Faces pleading, lips beseeching, eyes damning.

"You let us die, *Spider*! You let the Evil triumph!"

Perhaps they were right. Perhaps the battle was all too much, Evil too powerful, even for a man who would be Savior.

The blood river rose and its torrential fingers clawed at the terrace, splashing over the rails, spattering his face and clothes, his violin. The melancholy Concerto grew muffled, the only notes that came from the instrument like the dying shrieks of innocent children.

Good God—why didn't I stop it?

He snapped from his reverie, sweat springing out on his brow, tension knotting his jaw muscles. The image of those tragic souls he had lost was nearly overwhelming. The pleas of the dead and dying haunted him sometimes; they plagued his nightmares, yet he saw no choice but to carry on his grim war. Evil would indeed triumph if he faltered now. Perhaps one day the *Spider* would fall, but to give up trying meant to relinquish hope.

The city needed a Savior, someone unafraid to confront the task at hand, no matter how bloody, no matter how many innocent lives were lost. The cause was greater than himself, was it not? The quest of the *Spider?*

He bowed at the strings harder, minor strains slipping away to a sprightlier Bach's "Minuet in G".

Richard Wentworth was given to these moods. They sometimes besieged him, as did moments some might consider paranoia. But that wasn't it. They were simply the price one paid to battle the disease of Evil to its eventual eradication.

Few understood. Those who sought to bring down the *Spider* were fools, unthinking that if they removed the balance, the disease would overrun all and destroy them. So he fought his battle in secret, in perpetuity. But he would never concede, never relent. Until the day Evil stopped his heart with a blade or bullet.

"*Sahib?*" The voice came from behind him and his bow halted in mid-glide.

Wentworth turned to see his Sikh servant, Ram Singh, standing behind him, his turbaned head slightly cocked, dark eyes curious, but used to his master's flights of fancy.

"Yes?" Wentworth stepped into the drawing room, placed the violin in its case, then peered at his servant.

Ram Singh went to the floor radio in the corner. "You should hear this, *Sahib.*" The dark-eyed man switched on the radio and turned the dial.

To repeat, police are on the scene at the Hotel Norvell where a gruesome mass murder of the city's highest officials occurred within the past hour. Reports are sketchy but indicate the bodies were half-devoured. We'll have more as it becomes available. Now back to Your Hit Parade *and* Chasing Shadows *after a word from Blue Coal...*

The Sikh switched off the radio and turned to Wentworth.

Wentworth's face had washed pale. "Good God...Nita was on her way to that meeting." A snake of fear slithered into Wentworth's belly. If anything had happened to Nita...

Ram Singh nodded, face grim. "I will ready the Daimler, *Sahib*."

Wentworth's eyes narrowed, fury overriding all other emotions. The city's leading potentates, all dead on the eve of their bid to enlist Wentworth's aid by running him for mayor. He wondered how this new threat had arisen, why he had received no inkling of it. Such a hideous display of depravation, completely unexpected by the *Spider*.

A noise tore him from his thoughts. A loud bang—the front door flying open and crashing into the wall, if he judged it right.

He saw her then, stopping in the doorway leading into the room. His lips parted slightly in shock. She was wild-eyed, her hat missing, her hair in disarray, blouse torn. He spotted the note pinned into her flesh.

"Nita, my God..." he muttered. She glared at him, with a look he'd never seen on another human being and one he hoped never to see again. And her eyes, her eyes were blood-red with carnivorous lust.

She let out a roaring shriek and plunged into the room, straight for him. Ram Singh moved to head her off but was too far away.

Nita flew at Wentworth, her gloved nails gouging and her teeth gnashing. It became immediately apparent she was trying to bite into the soft flesh of his throat. Grabbing her wrists, he tried to force her back, but her wild strength was incredible. He fought to swing her around as Ram Singh neared, but Nita jerked a wrist loose and did her damnedest to scratch his eyes out. Spittle flecked her lips and inarticulate sounds gurgled from her throat.

"I'm sorry, Nita, but I have to—" Wentworth snapped a punch to her chin and she stopped fighting. A blank look replaced the wild gaze in her eyes. She stared, as if seeing through him, then her knees buckled.

Wentworth caught her, then carried her to a chair beside a bookcase. He manipulated a catch behind a book and the case slid outward, revealing a small celled room. Plucking the key from a peg beside the cell, he opened the cage. Inside was only a small cot.

He lifted Nita and brought her into the cell, laying her on the cot. Carefully, he drew the needle from her skin and slid the note from it.

Backing from the cell, he closed the door, then passed the key to Ram Singh. After tossing the needle onto a small table against the wall, he opened the note, scanned the brief message.

"Curious Imports, Little Haiti..." He handed the note to Ram Singh.

"A trap, *sahib*."

Wentworth nodded. "Most certainly. But right now it's the only lead I have to finding out what happened to Nita and whether there's any chance of reversing it."

"If there is not, *sahib*?" The Sikh's dark eyes grew even darker.

Wentworth's face welded with grim determination. "Then I will put the bullet in her myself. She would want it that way."

"Will there be final instructions, *Sahib*?" the Sikh asked, as Wentworth headed for the door. "Perhaps I should accompany you." His hand drifted to the hilt of the knife sticking out of his waist sash.

"No, my friend. Stay here. Make sure she's taken care of...and mind your fingers when you feed her." No humor came with Wentworth's words, merely a bleak sarcasm that boded ill for whoever dared endanger the woman he loved. That foe would know no mercy from the *Spider*.

Snakes of mist slithered through the streets of Little Haiti. Dilapidated buildings and shanties lined the main street. A sodden breeze rustled scraps of paper and sent litter skittering as the Daimler slipped along the darkened throughway that was scarcely wider than an alley.

Behind the wheel hunched a figure from a nightmare. Couched in shadow, a being wearing a cape and a wig of long scraggly hair topped with a dark slouch hat hunched over the wheel. Alert eyes behind a domino mask scanned the street. Lips that were almost nonexistent parted, fangs showing in the dim light. Tense hands gripped the wheel.

For all intents millionaire Richard Wentworth no longer existed. He had become a creature feared by the unscrupulous, those who threatened the innocent and murdered without compunction. A creature feared by Evil itself.

Richard Wentworth had become the *Spider*.

Why were the streets empty?

A trap, as Ram Singh had voiced. The note-sender who controlled this section of the city had lured him here by turning Nita into an inhuman killing machine devoid of rational thought, possessed of an irrational hunger, and was now taunting him.

The schemer desired counsel with the *Spider*, and knew who hid behind the persona. Somewhere Wentworth had gotten sloppy, given away his identity. But that mattered little now. What mattered was punishing the monster responsible for the madness and finding a cure—if one indeed existed—for Nita.

As he eased back on the throttle the Daimler slowed. The *Spider's* nerves danced. Something was wrong here. Was the trap set even before he reached the schemer's lair? Had the unknown figure summoned Wentworth merely to kill the *Spider?* To test him?

As if in answer, movement came from beyond the windshield. Figures shambled from alleyways.

Like a vision from Hell the figures advanced, their faces pallets of lifelessness and insatiable hunger. All five were large black men, their clothing ragged, their shoes split. Their gait was shuffling yet not particularly clumsy, as if they retained full control of their coordination but not their will.

They came with purpose, congregating before the Daimler, as if convinced its driver would have to stop.

Two more came from an alley near a little shop twenty yards on and joined the others.

Dread surged through the *Spider* but a cackling laugh trickled through his gritted teeth. He realized the grim task now before him. Each moment that slipped by meant a fading chance Nita might recover and that whoever plotted against the city came closer to some unknown goal. He could stop the car, plunge from the vehicle and engage these dead-faced hulks, but given Nita's wild strength he knew he would have to put a bullet in precisely the right place to stop the zombies in their tracks. That meant more wasted time, perhaps complete failure.

He saw no choice. Stamping the accelerator, he sent the Daimler forward with a squeal of tires.

The zombies never altered course, their mindless advance and mission apparently the only thing driving them. No sense of self-preservation remained and Wentworth cursed the plotter behind this madness. What sort of demon sent men to their deaths in this manner? What sort of monster turned men into beasts who fed on the flesh of others?

The zombies pounded on the hood as the Daimler overtook them. Wentworth's eyes narrowed and bile surged into his throat, but duty and determination steeled him. He could not let the city fall under the reign of this hidden mastermind.

The blows had no effect. The car was bulletproof, even down to the tires. Wentworth twisted the wheel left, then right, and zombies fell before its path. Their groans rose in the night, staining the mist and his memory. Thuds came from beneath the tires and the front end rose and fell as he drove over their bodies. The sound of crushing bone came, but no screams. Those men met their doom with barely a whimper and the thought angered Wentworth all the more. A laugh came from his lips, a laugh laced with a grim promise for the mastermind who had forced his decision of death.

It was over in a moment, but it felt like an eternity. Stopping the car just beyond the carnage, he glanced back at the bodies. All but two of the zombies lay broken and bleeding on the pavement. The two who'd escaped the Daimler's wheels peered down at their fallen comrades, then knelt. What Wentworth saw next would play in his nightmares for the rest of his days.

He was out of the car in an instant, hands whipping beneath his cape and bringing out two automatics. With deliberate, precise aim he triggered two shots. Lead punched into the Zombie's backs, just over the heart. They paused from their gruesome task, stiffening, then toppled face forward.

The *Spider* wasted no time discerning whether they were dead. He spun, automatics returning beneath his cape.

His gaze focused on a small shop to his right. Above it hung a wooden sign with singed letters sporting the legend: *Curious Imports*.

As he moved towards the shop, a new urgency took him. He had passed the mastermind's test. Now it was time to confront this unholy schemer and deliver the *Spider's* wrath.

The door was unlocked; that did not surprise him. Whoever sent the note expected his presence, making it easy.

Once inside, he swung the door shut, giving his eyes a moment to adjust to the gloom. His nostrils twitched at a peculiar odor, one vaguely reminiscent of cinnamon and clove.

Shelves lined the shop, stocked with items that catered mostly to tourists. He saw charms and dolls, jars of herbs and roots. Incense burned in small dishes on the countertop. Bins held rosary beads and Virgin Mary statues. Close to the back, a shelf had been pulled forward, leaving a gap between the wall and an opening behind it. A glow shimmered along the gap. Wentworth moved towards it.

Whoever had summoned him was making the way obvious.

Reaching the shelf, he pulled it towards him. The unit swung back on some hidden mechanism, revealing a passageway lit by wall torches.

A click sounded.

On instinct, Wentworth twisted, jerked sideways. With a swish a pendulum dropped from the ceiling and cleaved a path through the opening. If not for his expert move the blade would have embedded itself in his back, ending the *Spider's* career permanently.

As it was, the razor-honed blade sliced through his cape and suit at the shoulder, and into his flesh. A welt of pain burned across his deltoid and blood ran from the wound.

Pressed against the wall until the pendulum rocked to a halt, he gripped his shoulder. A flesh wound, he saw, as he pried back flaps of material, but it bled liberally.

He had no time to dress the wound now, not while Nita's life and the lives of the entire city rested on his shoulders.

He slid into the passageway, leery of further traps. Old boards and empty liquor bottles littered the floor. The walls, which appeared made of stone, seeped moisture, and flame light jittered across them. The passage sloped sharply downward and he recalled whispers of unstable tunnels that occasionally collapsed beneath this section of New York. Rumors had it, entire buildings had vanished into pits below, only to have new structures built atop them.

The *Spider* hurried his pace as much as caution would allow. His nerves buzzed and the thought of Nita sent fury racing through his veins.

A hundred feet on, something shifted beneath his foot. With a clunk, the floor beneath him suddenly vanished.

He spun in mid-fall, body twisting three-quarters in a display of agility that would have amazed a seasoned aerialist. His underarms slammed into the lip of the floor, a panel having dropped out below him into a pit filled with water. The opening was only about five feet wide and water covered the tips of his shoes. He had no idea how deep it might be, but instinct warned him the water itself was the danger here, not the depth.

The water began to boil and something tugged at the tips of his shoes. A flash of pain spiked through his toes.

Jerking up his feet, he struggled to pull himself from the opening but his left arm was starting to weaken and blood had trickled down his arm to his fingertips, making his grip perilous. Fingers dug into the stone floor. Sweat beaded on his forehead.

Glancing downward, he saw the toes of his shoes had been partially eaten away. A small fish of some sort clung to a strip of leather. The creature was unlike any Wentworth had seen, rows of needle-sharp teeth evident as it clung to his shoe.

Slamming his foot against the side of the pit, he crushed the thing; it dropped into the boiling water. The pit must have held hundreds of the monstrosities, enough to reduce a man to bone in a few instants.

His grip slipping, he strained to pull himself up. He managed to get a leg onto the lip of the pit and heaved himself onto the floor, breath beating out, arm muscles shaking. Rising to his feet, he located a long board that leaned against the wall, then flung it across the pit, drawbridge-style.

He scuttled across and trudged onward, shoulder paining, toes bleeding, heart thudding.

A hundred yards on, the tunnel ended at a set of ornate wooden doors.

The doors opened onto a mezzanine balcony above a huge vaulted chamber.

Easing forward, he peered over the rail into what appeared to be an old theater whose seats were long removed. Walls draped in purple velvet surrounded the chamber and sconces held flaming torches. The structure must have been above ground at some point in the past, its carved banisters and moldings signifying a once luxurious establishment.

At the front of the theater, squatting before a wall of velvet drapes, sat a wooden throne. Carved heads of African gods adorned the throne and gild emblazoned its edges. Upon it sat a woman, glaring up at him, lips set in a peculiar smile. She wore a purple gown, slit at the sides to reveal expanses of rich brown skin.

The *Spider* reached beneath his cape, pulling free a silk cord, then securing it to the rail. He slid over the rail, descending slowly into the theater like his namesake. Upon reaching the floor, he moved toward the figure.

"Welcome to *my* lair, Mr. Wentworth."

Wentworth's hands whipped beneath his cape, bringing out his automatics. "Who are you?"

She smiled. "My name is Malalaia Cervantes."

"How do you know who I am?" He took another step forward.

"Is it a secret?" She laughed, the expression mocking. "Seriously, Mr. Wentworth, you must be more discreet. It was not difficult observing you for a few weeks and discovering your identity."

"What have you done to Nita?" His tone came harsh, demanding. His fingers itched to squeeze the triggers, but he needed to know if any hope existed for Nita.

The laugh came again and it grated along his spine. "She belongs to the Zombie Queen now. There is no hope for her."

His heart sank, and he readied to squeeze the trigger. If he couldn't save Nita he would end any future threat posed by this madwoman.

"Why have you summoned the *Spider*?" His voice lowered, a grating whisper.

She leaned forward, and the mahogany globes of her breasts glowed with torch light. "Control, Mr. Wentworth. I want this city, this nation. I want to take power from those men who possess it and show them what it is to have what matters most torn away. But I need someone worthy to rule by my side."

"You're nothing more than another deluded madman, seeking what all have found elusive when the *Spider* met their schemes. You sought to circumvent my justice by enlisting my aid."

"Perhaps, *mon ami*. But together we can drink from the cup of power. We work on the fringes of our societies, you and I. You are labeled a menace in the eyes of the police, a blight on the good name of this city. I was ostracized in my own country, for deeds forced upon me by white men who took what they did not deserve. Now it is time to repay old debts and impose the reign of the Zombie Queen."

"You've misjudged me, woman. The only power I crave is the power to destroy the evil that spawns your kind."

Her head lifted a fraction. "The only way you'll leave here alive, Mr. Wentworth, is to see reason."

A laugh came from his lips, a cackling, taunting thing that made Cervantes' eyes narrow and face pinch. "Reason plays no part in your deeds. You would consign millions to a most hideous death. The *Spider* consigns you to yours!" One of his guns began an upward swing.

The velvet draperies along the walls rustled as men suddenly came from behind them. More of the mindless zombies, at least twenty. Wentworth's head swung in all directions; he saw no retreat, no escape. The Zombie Queen's laugh ululated through the theater.

The zombies converged upon him. He had ten bullets left in his guns and he knew each had to be delivered precisely, stilling the heart of a killer. Reloading would prove impossible before they were upon him.

Although certain of his doom, he wasted no time triggering a barrage of lead. The thunder of his automatics roared through the room, pounding his eardrums. Men dropped before his fire, lead punching into their hearts.

Five down. Six. Still they shuffled relentlessly forward, heedless of their fallen ranks. Ten bullets fired; ten men dead. Then the zombies converged, hands tearing at his hat and cape, grasping for his throat.

He clubbed with his guns, bringing down another man by cracking his skull. But the cause was lost. Hope had died and Malalaia Cervantes, Queen of the Zombies, would go forward with her plans for dominance unimpeded. The path was clear and Nita would die.

The thought drove Wentworth to a great surge of power and rage. He swung relentlessly as teeth sank into his wounded shoulder. The sheer weight of the mindless killers pulled him down. In a moment it would be over, horribly over, as the zombies chewed into his flesh and bone.

. The Zombie Queen's laughter rose, insane and damning. Then it stopped. Suddenly. Completely. But Wentworth had no time to ponder why.

Another moment dragged past. Then the load upon him lightened. New hope flooded his mind.

Someone was dragging the creatures off of him. He saw a flashing blade and renewed power surged into his muscles. He came up, automatics clubbing, crashing into bone, his crescendoing cackle filling the arena.

"*Sahib*, the woman!" came the voice of Ram Singh. Ram Singh, his faithful servant, who had ignored orders and followed him here. The Sikh's knife streaked, plunged into flesh, then snapped free again, only to taste more blood an instant later. The zombies fell and an instant later Wentworth was fishing a clip from a pocket and jamming it into an automatic. The other gun went beneath his cape.

The zombies lay dead on the floor, Ram Singh standing above their corpses, panting, blood dripping from his blade. Malalaia Cervantes leaned forward, fury on her face—and for the first time a glint of fear.

Wentworth's gun came up.

"No!" she yelled, hand whipping to a spot on the throne arm. "If you fire I'll press this button. This theater was built on a series of caves. I have explosives wired all through them that can be activated by my touch. If you kill me, you kill yourself!" The triumphant look that spread across her face brought a cackling laugh from Wentworth.

"Again, you have misjudged me." He fired. The bullet drilled in the woman's forehead and her expression froze on her face. She toppled forward.

A series of rumbles deep below Wentworth's feet accompanied her fall. Finger death-spasming, she had depressed the button. Her boast was no lie.

"Get out!" Wentworth yelled at Ram Singh, who had jammed his knife into the sash at his waist.

"*Sahib*, no—"

Wentworth swung the gun to Ram Singh. "Leave!"

The servant bowed slightly, then headed to the dangling spider's web and climbed up to the balcony.

Wentworth stepped over to the fallen Zombie Queen and brought a platinum lighter from beneath his cape. He stooped, pressing the exposed bottom of the lighter to the dead woman's forehead. When he pulled it away, a vermillion spider blazed on her flesh.

Straightening, he pocketed the lighter, about to follow Ram Singh when a scream came from behind the throne.

He lunged for the draperies, hauling them back to reveal a door. A kick sent it crashing inward.

As he stepped into what appeared to be a makeshift lab, he spotted a long wooden table holding vials of red liquid and flaming burners. A small black man shackled to the floor leaned against the table. Horror played on his face as he saw the *Spider*.

The *Spider* motioned with his automatic. "Who are you?"

"I-I'm Malalaia's brother. I'm a prisoner here."

"You are responsible for this madness, this zombie drug?" Wentworth's teeth ached with fury. Here was the source of the malady affecting Nita.

The man nodded, the frightened look growing.

The *Spider's* gun came up. He would wipe out the last of the zombie threat before saving his own life.

"No! I have a cure for it!"

"Malalaia said none existed." He couldn't stop a small burst of hope from exploding within him. If this man were telling the truth...

"She lied. She forced me to make this stuff. She needed your money to mass produce it. She had only small amounts bought by her robberies, but I made sure there was a cure first in case she ever tried to turn me into one of *them*."

The *Spider's* gun blasted and the man screamed, covering his face with an arm. The *Spider* triggered five shots and the manacles at the man's feet shattered.

"If you're lying you'll wish to God I had left you in this room."

The man nodded and Wentworth shoved the automatic beneath his cape.

Around them the theater shook and the floor rumbled. Great cracks opened and chunks of masonry dropped into an abyss.

Wentworth grabbed the man's wrist and pulled him through the theater, at times yanking him from certain death as the floor fell away beneath him. Reaching the underside of the balcony, he snatched the silken cord. Ram Singh waited above, face anxious.

"Cling to my back and don't let go," said Wentworth. The man clutched onto him for dear life.

Up the *Spider* went, hand over hand, strength sapped, but will dominant.

Grip faltering, he dropped, then came to a jarring stop, as he reestablished his hold. Friction had burned through his gloves, seared flesh from his palms.

Cracks opened along the balcony; portions rained down with great rending crashes. Clouds of dust billowed around them.

"Hurry, *sahib!*" Ram Singh called from above. The Sikh had gripped the silken cord and was drawing it upward with all his strength.

Wentworth's fingers clutched the edge of the balcony and Ram Singh dropped the cord to grab handfuls of Wentworth's clothing and haul them over.

As the remainder of the balcony gave way, Wentworth and the two men hurtled out into the hallway. Behind them sounded a roaring boom as the entire room plunged into rubble in a pit created by the caves below.

Walls beyond the theater split, great fissures opening. The trio hurried their exit, the place dissolving behind them.

Dawn washed across the terrace of Richard Wentworth's penthouse. He drew the bow across the strings of his Stradivarius, his mood mellow, and thankful. Nita Van Sloan watched the sunrise glinting off the windows of the waking city, a smile on her face, both hands clutching the railing.

"It's lovely, isn't it?" she said, voice sultry. "So much horror last night and yet the sunrise washes it all clean."

Wentworth stopped bowing, gaze traveling outward. "Does it? Or will another evil arise to take its place?"

"You stopped her, *Dick*. That should be enough for now."

He had, and the woman's brother had not been lying about the cure. His only grief came for the men he had killed who might have been saved, but their demise had brought about the greater good. The *Spider's* work would go on.

He uttered a soft laugh. "By the emphasis you placed on my name, Nita, one would almost sense a hidden resentment for the *Spider's* work."

It was Nita's turn to utter a soft laugh, but she didn't turn towards him. She merely folded her arms about herself and let a wry smile dance on her lips.

Sometimes a woman's thoughts were better left unknown, he told himself and went back to his violin."

illustration by Tom Floyd

Chapter Five

MARCH OF THE MURDER MUMMY

by WILL MURRAY

All heads turned when Richard Wentworth made his appearance at the reception party held in honor of the Museum of Antiquities' new Egyptian exhibit.

Tall and erect of carriage, his handsome head held at an angle both noble and yet arrogant, the scion of the Wentworth millions drew instant attention as he removed his black Homburg. Under level brows, his frank blue-grey gaze quested over the assembled throng.

"Oh Dick. Over here!"

Hearing that familiar musical voice, Wentworth began moving through the close-packed room, aglitter with the well-to-do and the upper crust of Manhattan society. Even so, people made way, as if for a head of state. There was something magnetic and commanding in his firm stride, a quality of unmatched power in the self-assured manner in which the amateur criminologist and clubman flowed through the crowd.

For many things were whispered about this rare individual, Richard Wentworth. Not the least of which was that he was secretly...the *Spider*!

A chesnut-haired woman with hauntingly violet eyes rushed up to meet him.

"Oh, Dick," she said laughingly. "I was afraid you weren't coming after all!"

"I was unavoidably...detained," Wentworth returned in crisp tones.

His fiancee, Nita van Sloan, lowered her gaze and her voice. She fussed at the cornflower reposing in the buttoniere of his immaculate evening jacket.

"Oh, Dick. Not..."

"The underworld is again becoming restless, I'm afraid. By morning the police may find a few *Spider*-marked thugs scattered here and there about town." A gay smile erased his solemn demeanor. "But all that is in the past. I am here to celebrate the evening. Where, pray tell, is the man of the hour?"

"You mean Chela Bey? He was here a moment ago, regaling us with his adventures in far-off Egypt."

"Indeed. It is not every day that someone discovers a hitherto-unsuspected pharaonic tomb in Luxor, of all places. It was thought the Valley of Kings had been stripped bare ages ago."

Nita smiled. "The unveiling of the sarcophogus is scheduled for nine sharp. Dick, I'm so glad you could make it. Isn't it thrilling? The papers are saying that this mummy predates all others so far unearthed. That it may well be one of the very first kings of pre-Dynastic Egypt."

"Egypt," repeated Wentworth, a troubled shadow crossing his intelligent forehead.

"What is it, Dick?"

"Oh, nothing, Nita. I was just thinking that in times past, Egypt has stood for deviltry and destruction. But those old cults were long ago wiped out."

Nita nodded. "I know, for I remember who helped erase them from civilized society. It was none other than..." Her voice trailed off, but her tapered fingernails made a creeping across the back of Wentworth's elevated hand. It was their little code. For Nita van Sloan knew, where few others did, that her lover was truly the Master of Men otherwise known as the *Spider*!

In ancient times, one such as Richard Wentworth might have been a proud paladin or even a warrior prince. But in these modern days, with its semi-civilized laws and politically-tainted courts, the one who walked as the *Spider* must by neccesity operate outside the law, not capturing criminals and murderers, but hunting them down like the vermin that they really are. Hunting them down and...*executing* them.

For this, Richard Wentworth toiled in secrecy. And for this, the forces of both law and disorder sought his life. Ever it must be so, in the sacred service of mankind. It was the way of the *Spider*!

Festive talk buzzed about them as the reception grew more and more animated. They mixed with high officials, and others of their social set. But ever were they wary, for all knew of Richard Wentworth's dangerous work as a criminologist. Where he went, danger often struck.

Then came the appointed hour.

Stepping onto a stage, Chela Bey looked nothing like a intrepid explorer who had accomplished the unbelievable. He was a tall, thin Coptic Egyptian with a copper-bronze cast to his ascetic features. One sleeve of his coat—the right—was pinned up to remind the world that exploration into Earth's harsher corners did not come without...price.

"I understand he lost that arm to a crocodile of the Nile delta," Wentworth murmured.

Nita shuddered, her chestnut curls trembling. "He must be a very brave man."

"Or a careless one," Wentworth commented dryly.

The gilded sarcophogus was draped in black velvet interwoven with dazzling multi-hued silks. Its age-seamed lid sat firmly in place.

"Ladies and gentlemen," Chela Bey proclaimed, "all of you know of my exploits in my native country. I will not bore you with my tiresome stories. Know only this: That in my proudest hour, I stumbled across a tomb of such antiquity that some have suggested I found, not a resting place of one of the earliest pharaohs, but a royal tomb of Atlantis, which came before Egypt."

Gasps circled the room. Here was high drama indeed.

"But as a proud Egyptian," Chela Bey continued, "I dismiss all such poppycock. The mummy I am about to unveil is not of Atlantis, if such a place ever existed, but truly of mysterious Egypt. Long before the Pharaohs we read of in our history books held sway over the upper and lower Niles, there ruled a line of powerful kings of a golden age history has failed to record."

"Remarkable!" a voice gasped.

"Because we do not yet know this one's true name," said Chela Bey, "I have dubbed him Konshu, after the mummy-enwrapped Moon god. But know this and know it well: I, Chela Bey, shall not rest until I can lay before you not just his royal bones, but his true name and lineage."

"And now, without further ado, may I present the mighty pharaoh I call Konshu!"

Dramatically, the chandelier lights went out.

The voice of a museum official spoke up. "Fret not, ladies and gentlemen. Merely adding to the mystery!"

Darkness settled. The wait was prolonged, seemingly interminable. Then everything changed.

The sibilant hiss of dropping drapes came across the room. It was followed by a splintering as of old cypress wood, a frantic clatter followed by a harsh scream that was soon choked off.

The lights came up, dazzling all.

It was good that their combined gazes were truly dazzled. For had the group beheld the grisly sight stark before them, many would have fainted. Most would surely have fled. As matters stood, all hesitated as they batted their blinkered eyes back into proper working order.

The mummy stood revealed before them. Stood, to their utter dumfoundment, not in its sarcophogus at rest, but looming before them all—*lean, unfleshed and clutching in one bony funereal-wrapped arm the neck of a dead Chela Bey!*

But it was not the same man who had declaimed so powerfully moments before. This Chela Bay hung limp and unrecognizable in the clutches of his murderer—*an animated cadaver dead thousands of years!*

Cursing, a museum guard strode forward, drawing his service weapon. The mummy dropped its wilted victim. The right arm pivoted with snaky speed, pointing toward the oncoming guard, and its bony fingers hissed....

The guard recoiled. The mummy stepped forward. He seemed but to brush the hapless guard with a jointed forefinger, and the man froze in his tracks.

Shrieks and gasps emerged from fear-tight throats. And as all eyes stood transfixed, the Mummy from Hell seized the stricken guard and while slow seconds ticked by, the fluid seemed to evacuate his fast-shrinking body the way the juices of a fly exit into a black widow spider's thirsty abdomen. All the while, a serpentine vein in its forehead throbbed...throbbed...

When the guard fell to the ground, he was no more than a mummy himself!

Panic broke out then. There was a rush for the exits. The Mummy raked the panicked crowd with eyes like lambent flames.

And where he pointed, men and women stumbled, fell, their frightened faces shrinking and shriveling as if touched by the fabled curse of King Tut himself!

The malevolent Mummy moved among the afflicted, bent down with arthritic difficulty, and touched each in turn. Those whom he touched, gave a final convulsive shudder, and expired!

All others fled. All save one man. Richard Wentworth!

Throwing protective arms around his fiancee, he held his ground as fear-maddened people trampled all around them.

"Stand fast!" he urged. "This will pass soon enough!"

Nita cried, "Oh, Dick, What is it? What could it be?"

"Either a spawn of some Egyptian hell," gritted the man whom all the Underworld feared, "or a man-made monster. Whichever it proves to be, it will answer to the *Spider!*"

As the crowd cleared, Wentworth rushed Nita to the safety of an alcove. Then, he emerged with twin automatics flipping into his palms. His face had lost the proud smooth lines of Richard Wentworth. Now they were a fierce grimace, the blue-grey orbs blazing naked wrath.

"Carrion dog of Egypt," he challenged. "Turn and meet the Master of Men!"

The Mummy did as the *Spider* bid. From its dried lips, a harsh curse ran past peg-like yellow teeth. Hands extended like vulture claws, the Mummy charged.

Twin automatics began their dance of death.

The first bullet clipped a rag of funereal garment, tore it free. The second struck the Mummy squarely in the chest. It staggered, recoiled, struggled to move forward. A vicious snarl leapt from its throat. The snarl was answered by a metallic laugh that shook the tapestried surroundings.

A skeletal, linen-wrapped arm lifted in a threatening manner, its brown talon of a hand gestured menacingly.

The *Spider* trained his gun muzzles on that outstretched claw and resumed firing.

Bullet by bullet, the *Spider* exacted a toll. The withered hand was carried off, followed by the forearm which snapped like a twig. Mummy wrappings uncoiled like modern gauze bandages. A startled twitch overtook the sunken death's-head face whose skin resembled old papyrus.

Again the *Spider* laughed.

The Mummy drew back as if in mortal pain. Yet no blood spurted from exposed wrist. Uncanny, that, for Wentworth knew that the pharaohs of old were buried with all blood drained, their internal organs removed, bodies preserved with natron.

"See how you taste death," the *Spider* taunted.

But before he could unleash more mad hell, the Mummy used its sole surviving hand to snatch a jackel-headed canopic jar and fling it at the overhead lights.

They went out, again plunging the museum into darkness.

Nita's voice lifted anew. "Dick! Dick!"

The *Spider* blazed away at the spot where his foe was last seen. Nothing rewarded his efforts except ricochets that caromed dangerously around the room. A hand torch jumped into his hand and its white beam began racing around the chamber with its porphory urns and heathen busts of Bast and Isis.

No trace of the Mummy did he see.

Holstering his spent weapons in his tuxedo, Wentworth gathered up his precious Nita and urged her toward the main exit.

Outside, shocked revelers milled about in white-faced confusion. Autos were leaving the vicinity with alacrity. Beat patrolmen were pounding up, exercising their whistles.

A moment later, a powerful limousine drew to the curb. From it stepped Police Commissioner Stanley Kirkpatrick, bristling from the pointed tips of his waxed military mustaches to his polished black shoes. His saturnine features were grim, his tone brusque.

"Dick, I might have known I'd find you where trouble has broken out."

"No time for idle talk," Wentworth snapped. "By some Egyptian sorcery, the mummy that was about to be unveiled tonight has come to life. It apparently murdered Chela Bey and a guard before turning on the crowd. I had the good luck to blast off a hand, but it's still at large inside. Kirk, have the place surrounded by your finest men. That abomination from Egypt must not be allowed to roam the city at will."

"I'll see to it!" Kirkpatrick snapped back.

Orders were issued. Police radio patrol cars began arriving. Soon the Museum of Antiquities was surrounded by green and white radio machines and a tense army in blue.

"You say you shot off a hand?" Kirkpatrick undertoned to Wentworth, straightening the fresh gardenia in his lapel.

"Yes, and struck him in the chest. But the damnable thing would not go down. Nor did it bleed."

Kirkpatrick frowned. "Is it your belief that this mad monster can't be killed?"

"It is my belief," Wentworth said sharply, "that only the *Spider* can slay such a diabolical devil."

"If the *Spider* dares show his face tonight," Kirk snapped, "I will have him behind bars for capital murder!"

Wentworth said nothing. A tense silence passed between the two old friends. Friends, but secretly enemies. For the Police Commissioner knew no law but that of the book, while the *Spider* was no respecter of laws or men. Despite their deep friendship, both men knew that if the *Spider* were ever caught and unmasked as Richard Wentworth, no quarter would be given.

"Kirk," Wentworth said grimly, "we are going to have to flush him out."

"Agreed." His voice lifted. "Tear gas squad! Line up in formation!"

Donning regulation gas masks, a picked squad took up positions behind their radio patrol cars.

Riot guns began detonating. Tear gas canisters boomed through windows, breaking them.

Soon, acrid fumes started seeping from the museum. Eyes began to sting. A bitter silence hung in the suddenly-still night air.

Gently, Richard Wentworth drew his companion aside. "Nita, please return to the car. This is no place for you, my dear."

But Nita van Sloan bravely took Wentworth by the arm. "My place is always beside you, Dick."

"Not this time. I implore you. Go. Go now." He lowered his voice to a tense whisper. "For the *Spider* must be free to act, unhampered by concern for those he loves."

Nita shuddered briefly. Reluctantly, she departed, leaving behind a brave kiss on her fiance's stern cheek.

Wentworth rejoined the commissioner.

"If that gas doesn't bring him out," Kirkpatrick vowed, "I am going in personally."

"Brave words. But you did not see that creature turn two grown men into mummified remains fit only for...interment."

"And I will have to see it with my own eyes to believe it," retorted Kirkpatrick. "Such occult occurrences do not happen in modern-day New York."

The tear gas was growing thick. The police cordon began inching back to protect itself from wind-borne fumes.

Wentworth said, "I must have Jackson drive Miss van Sloan home for her own safety and protection, Kirk."

Kirkpatrick nodded brusquely.

Wentworth returned to his Hispano-Suiza town car. Once inside, he reached under the seat and touched a concealed button. A back-seat cushion came forward, and revolving in place, disclosed a complete wardrobe of closely-hung garments.

"I'm afraid Commissioner Kirkpatrick is bound and determined to blunder into death and disaster," he said, brittle-voiced.

Nita frowned. "That can mean only one...recourse."

"Yes," Wentworth said, throwing a black cloak over his shoulder. "The *Spider* walks again."

Working before a lighted makeup mirror, he began transforming his face. Soon, it was a harridan countenance comprised of a beak of a nose and a thin slash of a mouth. Celluloid fangs completed the *Spider*'s fearsome smile. A lank wig topped by a black felt hat threw his harsh predatory features into concealing shadow.

Finally, an angular domino mask completed the transformation.

As the Hispano-Suiza eased away from the curb, a half-open door clicked shut and into the shadows scuttled the hunched form that the underworld knew and feared as....the *Spider*!

No one spotted the *Spider* as he scuttled from wan pools of streetlamps to concealing shadows. No eye measured his hunched form, his becloaked progress. For the *Spider* was as silent as his deadly namesake. And like his namesake, he drew from a cape pocket a stout silken line, his *Spider*'s Web.

Forming a loose loop, the *Spider* scaled this until it caught the projecting cornice of the unguarded stone church beside which he stood. Going hand over hand, like a monstrous arachnid, he worked his way up to a bell-tower alcove.

Then, reclaiming the loop, the *Spider* twirled it three times and cast it across the dark space that separated his coign of vantage from the Museum of Antiquities.

The loop failed the first time. On the second try, it captured a balustrade. The *Spider* drew the line taut and tied it fast to his position.

Then, balancing like a circus aerialist, he began walking his Web.

All eyes were upon the doors and windows of the museum. No one noticed the stealthy approach of the most feared man in Manhattan. No one saw the twisted shadow cast upon the ground. No one suspected the *Spider*'s coming.

Until—not six feet from the balustrade, a police car's searchlight threw its roving purple eye about the building front and captured—the *Spider*!

A hoarse shout rang out:

"*Spider*! It's the *Spider*! Get him!"

Police Positives were raised. Sharp shots snapped out.

The bullets, miraculously, nipped and plucked at Wentworth's trailing cape, but found not flesh nor bone.

With a leap, he cleared the last intervening space. One foot touched the granite rail—and slipped on fog-deposited moisture!

The Spider tumbled, caught himself.

Granite chips began flying all about him. Rock dust sprayed into his masked face. A lucky slug pierced the high crown of his hat, but it held in place. Wentworth felt a sullen burn that told that his scalp had been creased....

Desperately, the *Spider* clung to safety. Madly, he scrambled for better purchase. Then he choked back a vehement curse.

A metallic clatter told that he had lost one automatic from an underarm holster. It struck far below, carrying with it a precious ammunition clip— *ammunition the Spider would sorely need in the minutes ahead!*

For even with shells raining all about him, even with death snapping at his heels, the Master of Men held but one thought in his dedicated brain: his hunt for the Murder Mummy!

Over the railing, the *Spider* tumbled. Crawling like his namesake, he sought the French doors that led to a gallery crammed with Egyptian antiquities.

Lights blazed up here. That was good. One hand snaked inside his coat to unlimber his surviving automatic.

"Beware, Mummy from Hell, " the *Spider* whispered as he stole into the railed gallery. "Beware the coming of the *Spider....*"

Every quivering sense was alert as he picked his silent way through shattered basalt columns and other brick-a-brack of a storied past. His heels clicked faintly on the polished stone floor. His scalp throbbed. He paid the pain no heed.

Up here, the odor of gas was weak. Like all such noxious fumes, tear gas tended to settle. That meant relative safety high up in the gallery.

It might also mean that the Mummy had sought refuge up in these close confines as well.

If, that is, the Murder Mummy breathed air....

It was madness to think that a mummified pharaoh had reanimated over five thousand years after burial. But strange things happened in Egypt, where ancient wizards had practiced forgotten sorcery. And New York was not entirely immune to such strangeness, when transplanted to its shores. Wentworth had battled such fiendishness before....

And so warily, yet determinedly, the *Spider* advanced.

Out of the tail of his eye, he detected movement. Wentworth checked his stride.

Something stirring? The *Spider* trained his gun muzzle on that patch of murk. It was still. A trick of the senses? Or a skulking foe?

The *Spider* pretended to decide the former. Turning from that spot, he started to make for a marble stairway.

A warning hiss of air separating caused the *Spider* to execute a split-second dive. Over his head flashed something silent and sinister. An emphatic *thuck* told him that something sharp had found a target.

A ceremonial dagger, old as time, impaled a sarcophagus face. The gilded hilt quivered in the dried cypress wood.

All this Richard Wentworth took in over mere instance. Already, he was pivoting. Instantly, he threw a single shot into that patch of shadow that had disturbed him before.

The bullet broke something dry and fragile. A porcelain clatter rang out.

"Show yourself, Mummy!" the *Spider* challenged. "Show me that you do not fear my steel."

But no response came.

Interesting. A mummy that feared mortal lead....

The *Spider* held his position, poised to strike. His eyes sought the cobwebby shadows. Nothing moved in them. Nothing stirred.

Then—a flutter followed by a wild movement near the ceiling!

Wentworth's aim was unerring. His gun bucked once. A squeak and a squeal came back.

Plunging into the shadows, he discovered on the floor a bat threshing in its death agonies, one leathery wing broken.

The grisly sight registered for but an instant when the *Spider* became aware of a rustling behind him.

Whirling, he aimed at the stealthy sound. A dark shape began resolving.

The Murder Mummy!

It strode out of the shadows, tall and lean as a cadaver. Withered as death itself, and yet its hollow eye-pits held a bituminous sparkle. Its fleshless jaw yawned.

"Death..." it hissed. "Death to the *Spider*...."

"Death to you, foul thing!" Wentworth returned hotly.

He shot for the golden breastplate. The bullet bounced off. Literally. It clipped a overhead light on the ricochet, producing a sizzling blue electrical spark.

The Mummy staggered back. Clutching with its lone hand for support, then came on, half-lurching, half stumbling.

It was an awesome sight. Dead and yet alive. Wounded but also indestructable, the Murder Mummy reached towards him, ungainly, awkward—yet relentless in its maniacal fury!

The broken arm flailed upward, and flopped back down. The Mummy seized the lifeless wrist firm in his still-functioning left hand and lifted the stump with its exposed ulnar bones toward its foe, pointing it like a sword.

An eerie hissing sound issued forth.

Abruptly, Richard Wentworth felt his mouth go dry. His tongue seemed to turn into a desiccated sponge.

A strange weakness overcame him. And yet, he resisted. Not for nothing did others call him...Master of Men!

"Die, *Spider*!"

"The *Spider* will never die!" he choked back. But the words in his fast-shriveling throat were thin, failing.

Wentworth possessed strength sufficient to squeeze out a fast flurry of shots. They went wild. He could not aim for certain. Lead smashed and broke statuary he could not see.

Then...the *Spider* crumpled.

A protracted silence overtook the Egyptian gallery. Richard Wentworth lay insensate for he knew not how long.

At length, he stirred. The first sounds to reach his eyes were of a dull commotion. Raising himself on one elbow, he took stock of his gloomy surroundings.

There was no sign of the Murder Mummy. No sign of anyone. Odd...

He went to the balustrade. Down below, people milled about ambulances. A shrouded form on a gurney was being thrust into one. Of the police cordon and its machines, there was little evidence. But desperate meaning could be read into the tableau.

"Good Lord!" Wentworth gasped out. "The Murder Mummy has escaped into the city!"

Quickly, he found a washroom and there slaked his thirst. Wetting his cloak, he drew it before his face. One portion of the fabric was thinner than the rest. It afforded him the ability to see through the weave.

His mouth and nose half-protected by heavy wet cloth, Wentworth stole into the chamber below.

He found the corpse of the slain guard. It was as if all the fluids had been leached from his living body. His lips were drawn back from dull yellow teeth. His eyes were like shriveled raisins in sunken sockets.

The body of Chela Bey was no more appealing. Kneeling, trying to choke back the revulsion rising in him, Wentworth unbuttoned the dead man's coat and drew it off.

Exposed lay the raw stump of the missing arm.

Laughing softly, the *Spider* drew himself up to his full commanding height.

Off came his cape, his mask, the celluloid fangs-everything that marked him as the *Spider*. These he crammed into a compact ball, and thrust into the dead man's coat pockets.

By the time the police found them, it would not matter.

Wentworth slipped to a side exit that led it into an alley where refuse was stored until the sanitation department hauled it away.

Amid full ash cans and other rubbish, he lay down and waited. After a while, he let out an audible groan.

Presently, searching police discovered him.

"Mr. Wentworth! What happened to you?"

Pretending to be roused by their shakings, Wentworth picked himself up and dusted off his now-rumpled and torn evening jacket.

"I...I believe that I ventured too close—overcome by gas fumes," he gasped out. "Have you caught that marauding mummy?"

"No, sir. He came busting out the front door in a cloud of that infernal gas. Three men fell dead at his withering glance."

"Surely you shot him dead?" Wentworth demanded.

"He was too nimble, sir. He stole a radio car."

"He—what?"

"Stole one of our cars. Half of the force gave chase, but he drove it off a pier and into the Hudson River. They're dragging it now."

"Mark my words," Wentworth said flintily. "That murderous tatterde-malion will return to haunt us before another night falls."

"If you say so, sir."

"I promise it," Wentworth bit out.

"You'd best stand back. We're about to go in after the *Spider*."

Wentworth assumed a shocked expression. "Is he present as well?"

"We suspect that he's in league with that mummy. And the tear gas has thinned, so we can finally root him out."

"I would ordinarily join you," Wentworth said shakily, "but I fear I'm momentarily disadvantaged. Hello? Is that my car and driver across the way?"

"Yes sir. They showed up not long after the *Spider* was spotted."

"Very good. Inform Commissioner Kirkpatrick I will communicate with him later."

Jackson spun the Lancia sedan smartly out into traffic, Richard Wentworth comfortably ensconced inside.

"No further reports of the Murder Mummy?" Wentworth demanded.

"No, Major. Went into the river and never came out again."

Richard Wentworth's face and voice were stiff when he said, "We have not seen the last of him. And he has not seen the last of...The *Spider.*"

Dawn found Richard Wentworth pacing his Fifth Avenue apartment, black coffee laced with Brandy fueling his impatience.

The bulldog edition of the *Press* was full of large black scareheads.

MARAUDING MUMMY IN MUSEUM MASSACRE!
POLICE BAFFLED!

The death toll was nearly two dozen victims. The authorities were promising swift action. But otherwise they offered no explanation for the night's terrible events.

"The Devil!" Wentworth was saying. "There must be some meaning, some purpose to these infernal depredations."

Bodies had been found scattered throughout lower Manhattan, dried up like figs, depleted of all life and moisture. The killings appeared to be random. It was as if the Mummy had embarked on a murder spree to no purpose.

"But there is a purpose," Wentworth muttered to himself. "If only I might divine it."

A gong sounded.

Entering, Ram Singh, Wentworth's faithful Sikh servant announced, "Commissioner *sahib* requests admittance."

"Permit him to enter."

From the blunted tips of his mustaches to the wilted gardenia in his coat lapel, Stanley Kirkpatrick looked spent, defeated. His face was dark with repressed rage. His squared shoulders sagged.

"Dick, I am at my wit's end," he admitted.

"As am I," Wentworth said dryly. "Beastly long night, wasn't it?"

"The dead are stacking up in the city morgue like so much cordword. Have you any clue to the motives behind this murder rampage?"

"One thing, Kirk. I believe when he is brought to book, the Murder Mummy will prove not to be what he seems."

"What do you mean?"

"Has it occurred to you how *peculiar* it was that a freshly-disinterred pharoah possessed the wit to steal a police machine and evidently knowledge enough to drive it?"

"Yes. Of course. Most puzzling."

Wentworth changed the subject. "Has the body of Chela Bey been autopsied?"

"It will be by noon."

"Let me suggest that the medical examiner look very closely at that missing right arm."

"For what?"

Wentworth smiled. "Why, for a clue, of course."

"Confound it, Dick! Do not play with me."

Abruptly, Commissioner Kirkpatrick produced a big automatic from within his jacket. Stone-faced, he leveled it at his oldest friend.

"Am I under arrest?" Wentworth asked coolly.

"This," said Kirkpatrick, "was discovered on the sidewalk near the museum. Are you missing a pistol, Dick?"

Wentworth made a pretense of patting his silk smoking jacket. "I seem to be unarmed."

"It is registered to you."

"Fancy that. I must have lost it in all the excitement."

"It was found near the spot where the *Spider* was shot at."

"Did they find the blighter's body, by chance?"

"No. But his habiliments were discovered in Chela Bey's pockets."

Wentworth smiled mockingly. "Chela Bey? Don't tell me that he was really the *Spider*."

"I doubt it. But for the moment, that is where matters stand. Nothing can be proved either way."

The two men faced each other. Between them a deadly secret that would doom one to the electric chair and the other to bitter eternal remorse hovered. But neither man spoke. Only a silence preserved their friendship—and their lives.

Quietly, Kirkpatrick laid the weapon on a table. "Dick, you had a good look at that infernal mummy. What is your frank opinion?"

"My frank opinion is that the Mummy intends...something sinister. I do not yet know what. But murder without profit profits no one. Mark my words, Kirk: the Murder Mummy's true motives will come out."

A phone rang. Jenkyns, the white-haired family butler, announced, "For the commissioner, Master Dick."

"Thank you, Jenkyns."

Kirkpatrick took the call. "Yes? What! Are you certain? Very well."

Hanging up, he faced his old adversary. "An inventory of the Museum of Antiquities shows conclusively that it has been looted."

"Looted!" Wentworth smacked a meaty fist into his palm. "That is the Mummy's motive. Plunder, not murder."

"But why?"

"Gold. The Mummy is after gold. I'll wager that most of what is missing is gold."

"Correct. But why gold? Many of the museum's artifacts are priceless, whether gold or not."

Wentworth shrugged negligently. "Gold can be melted down into... disposable ingots. Quickly, Kirk. If you were the Murder Mummy, where would you strike next if you lusted for gold?"

"Diffiny's, the Fifth Avenue jeweler."

"Exactly. I suggest we lay a trap."

The phone rang again. Kirkpatrick snapped it up, unthinkng. "Kirkpatrick here. Yes? Damn! Dick, the Mummy has already stuck Diffiny's. Six are no more. Two persons who have been...withered are not expected to live. By God, how does he do it?"

"That too will come out in time," Wentworth promised thinly.

Kirkpatrick's icy blue eyes narrowed. "Dick, what are you keeping from me?"

"Oh, nothing," Wentworth said distractedly. "I was just thinking..."

"Thinking what?"

"I wounded the Mummy rather frightfully in the right arm. If you were seeking a culprit among the teeming millions, look for a man who favors a shattered right arm!"

"Bah!" Kirkpatrick roared, taking his leave.

The day passed as if in agony. No more depredations were reported. Repairing to his music room, Wentworth worried his Stradavarius for long hours, then stood on the balcony overlooking Fifth Avenue, and seemed to be marshalling his powers for another difficult night.

He placed a call to Nita van Sloan.

"How are you, my dear?"

"Sleepless with worry," she confessed. "But not any more. Dick, was it...real?"

"The police are baffled as usual. And as usual, the *Spider* has seen through the cobwebs of crime and penetrated to the truth."

Nita laughed her relief. "Is it any wonder that I love you?"

"I will call upon you when this matter is settled, dearest." Wentworth rang off and resumed his feverish pacing. The *Spider* was restless..so restless. And he would not—*could* not—sleep until the Murder Mumnmy was no more!

Eventually, darkness came. Quietly Wentworth again donned the sacred garments of humanity's lone defender.

Stuffing fresh shells into spare clips, he charged his automatics. A fresh Web was coiled into a cape pocket. Other implements, as well. The *Spider* never went forth to battle unprepared.

"Ram Singh, I have need of you."

The doughty manservant cupped palms to his turbanned forehead and bowed respectfully. "*Han, Sahib.*"

They took the Lancia Augusta sedan. Wentworth sat in back while the ferocious Sikh drove. They wended their way through the night streets, ears alert to police radio calls.

"Gold," muttered Wentworth in the darkness of the sumptuous cushions. "Gold. Where would a marauding mummy go to seek gold?"

"Where he plundered before," said the Sikh, white teeth flashing.

"What's that, Ram Singh?"

"*Wah!* It is sometimes written that criminals return to the scene of their first crime. Would a robber from a tomb not behave so, as well?"

Wentworth's keen eyes narrowed. "Brilliant, Ram Singh. Doubtless what was plundered last night was only a fraction of the museum's valuables. Unquestionably the museum is still guarded, but guarded lightly. For who would guard a prison cell from which a convict had successfully escaped?"

"No one, *Sahib*," growled the Sikh.

The Lancia abruptly changed direction and, its powerful motor throbbing under its long hood, arrowed for the part of town where the Museum of Antiquities stood on its granite foundations.

Foundations that were about to be shaken again—if Richard Wentworth had anything to say about it!

A police machine turned onto Sixth Avenue, and continued moving quietly and with doused headlamps in the same direction. Wentworth noticed it as they cut across a transverse street.

His eyes went warily to the skulking vehicle—then narrowed.

"Ram Singh!" he hissed.

"*Han, sahib?*"

"Take note of that vehicle. Police officer at the wheel."

"I see no police *sahib*...."

"But I see something else. Creep up on that car, O brave one. Carefully. Draw abreast so that I can confirm what my eyes believed they beheld."

The faithful Sikh trod the accelerator and wrung more power out of the long hood. The sedan slithered forward, pacing the police machine in intermittent traffic. Car horns set up a fitful background tumult as the pacing sedan pressed closer, ever closer....

From an underarm holster, Richard Wentworth drew forth a single automatic and thumbed the safety off. He did not war on the minions of the law, although its myrmidons held no such compunctions about warring upon the *Spider*. But this, this might be different....

When the Lancia was running nose to nose with the police machine, Wentworth parted a window curtain to peer at the driver.

The profile under the blue police cap was gaunt, staring—unholy. Only one grisly hand clutched the steering wheel. The left. It was as rough and brown as a coconut shell.

As if by some telepathic impulse, the driver seemed to sense the *Spider*'s keen eyes upon it.

The wizened face turned. Fiery eyes grew round, then knife-slit thin in its cadaverous sockets. A fleshless jaw dropped in furious surprise.

And on the brown forehead, a single bloated vein pulsed once in mounting fury.

"Ram Singh! *Cut off that police car!*"

Wentworth threw down the window with furious cranks of his hand. He pointed his weapon out and began blasting!

A cannonade of drumfire erupted from the weapon. He ran home fresh clips, firing anew.

The police machine lurched, jounced over the curb stone and slammed into a fruitier's storefront, bringing down a shower of deadly glass shards.

"Brake, Ram Singh!"

Shimmying, the Lancia swerved to a screeching halt.

Cape belling like black wings, the *Spider* burst out of the back, both guns held before him.

Out of the wrecked police vehicle lurched a monstrous half-human form. It hissed in defiant venom. Something else hissed too. That outstretched stump of a wrist....

Wentworth felt again the punishing waves of dry...heat...energy....he knew not what.

No matter. His twin guns began blasting, blasting, blasting....

More glass shattered. Pedestrian screams erupted. Lost in the din, smoking cartridges clinked and bounced on rain-washed concrete.

And amazingly, from within the police radio car the Murder Mummy produced a Tommy-gun! It set up a snarling chatter.

Wentworth dodged, weaved, rolled away from the stuttering hose of fierce, biting lead.

Snap-rolling, he got off a single shot. But the machine-gun proved too formidable. The Mummy shook violently with its convulsions, its linens unraveling here and there.

Leaping into an alley, the *Spider* again recharged his weapons.

The Tommy-gun fell silent. The silence was eerie...unquiet. More menace lay in its continuance than had accompanied the machine-gun's vicious racket.

When he reemerged into the night, the *Spider* beheld the unbelievable.

Ram Singh had moved in on the marauding mummy, was about to knife him with his deadly blade.

Stealthy as a cat, the Sikh prepared to pounce. But the Mummy possessed hearing even if he had no ears.

He swung his entire body, the Tommy-gun swung with him.

Ram Singh stuck. A blade went into the shoulder of the breastplate that had before turned .45 caliber bullets.

It proved impervious to naked steel too.

Ram Singh stepped back. The Tommy-gun muzzle came in line with his exposed body and Wentworth swirled out of the alley like a thing possessed of the fury of Hell itself.

Guns blazing, he struck.

"Turn about, Murder Mummy!" he cried. "Turn and confront the *Spider!*"

The Murder Mummy swung back to protect its back. Ram Singh went for its exposed neck, thin and brittle as a turkey's neck.

But no sooner had he laid hands upon the foul neck than the brave Sikh suddenly clutched at his own throat, gasping and coughing.

Wentworth full well knew the cause. Murderous Mummy magic!

"Die!" he cried, firing again.

The Tommy-gun cackled ghoulishly. Bullets went wild. The *Spider* twisted and ducked anew, his cloak turning to rags.

No shell sped true. Everywhere about them, brick and glass complained in snapping, snarling voices. A bullet-fractured fire hydrant was gushing water. Nothing mortal was penetrated, however.

Miraculously unhurt and unscathed, the Murder Mummy leapt behind the wheel of Wentworth's own sedan!

Rocketing off, it drilled through parting traffic.

The *Spider* flung a challenging laugh after it. If the laugh was heard, it was not heeded.

Seeing to Ram Singh, Wentworth forced city water down his throat.

Between greedy gulps, the Sikh gasped out, "*Sahib*... forgive... this unworthy... "

"Say nothing, thou warrior. There is nothing to forgive. You acquitted yourself well. Remain here while the *Spider* finishes what you only began."

"Slay him terribly, Sahib," Ram Singh croaked out.

"Terribly," vowed the *Spider*, "and thoroughly. This night the Murder Mummy will die again!"

Stalking off, he claimed an abandoned taxi, got it in gear. The tumultuous night soon swallowed him.

Wentworth was not surprised to discover his Lancia idling outside the Museum of Antiquities' broad entrance mere minutes later.

"How kind of you to leave it parked with the motor running," he murmured to himself. "How considerate, *Monsieur Konshu*. It is too bad that I am prevented from returning your thoughtfulness in kind..."

Twin automatics out and searching, the *Spider* mounted the broad steps to the Museum of Antiquities two at a time.

Guards had been placed inside. Unfortunately, even though the edifice was officially closed to the public, they had responded to their macabre visitor. Had he...knocked? Curious.

In any event, they had paid for their carelessness with their lives. Both men lay sprawled and supine inside, dry as discarded corn husks.

The *Spider* pushed inward.

Upstairs in the Egyptian gallery, he could hear a clattery rattle. The air still smelled acrid from the lingering tear gas of the prior night. Wentworth held the hem of his black cloak to mouth and nose, his eyes smarting. But his fevered brain burned with a controlled fury.

All this mad murder. And for what? Gold! Was there no end to the gold-lust of mortal men? Would there be no surcease to the *Spider*'s endless war with crime?

But the man who was the *Spider* shoved these despairing thoughts into his innermost mental recesses. Tomorrow, time enough to consider these bitter questions. Tonight, the *Spider* stalked his prey.

Gold drinking vessals were being lifted off shelves and thrown into a rough burlap sack.

From an alcove rich in history, the *Spider* watched. The Murder Mummy was quick, yet methodical in his plunderings. He grasped every item of gold that caught his avaricious eye and flung it one-handed into the sack. Nothing of value was spared.

When the sack was at last full, the Mummy seemed to pause.

Wentworth saw him clearly in the light, noticed again the slow pulse of a forehead vein, a telltale that would tell the tale of doom for the Murder Mummy!

Stepping forth, with both elbows he flung back his ebony cloak and proclaimed: "I suggest you throw up whatever remains of your arms, else I will have to finish shooting them to pieces like so much driftwood!"

The Mummy whirled. Hissing, he lifted the broken right arm. It failed to complete the motion.

"Good enough to cradle a Tommy-gun, but not good enough to send death to the *Spider*. No?" taunted Wentworth.

A hissing came from the Mummy. It seemed to emanate from the broken bone shards sticking out of its gaping right wrist.

"I know your secret, murderer!" the *Spider* spat.

"My secret is as old as time..." it retorted in its strange accents.

"Your secret is a sham. For you are no undead thing of the tomb, but a twentieth-century man like myself. But unlike myself, you are....evil."

"Prepare to die, *Spider*!"

"Ready yourself to taste death again, Mummy!"

The Mummy lifted its withered stump. The gesture was more of a upward flip. But it was enough to send waves of arid dryness beating in Richard Wentworth's direction.

Abruptly, he felt the cool night sweat evaporate off his exposed face. Then his eyes seemed to smart, not from tear gas but due to a sudden uncanny lack of moisture. It was as if, through some supernatural means, the raw, torrid equatorial sun of ancient Egypt was beating invisibly down upon him.

The Mummy croaked, "Taste the dust of the tomb!"

"Taste lead!" snarled the *Spider*.

He fired twice. Both weapons bucked in his hands. This time, he fired not at the gold breastplate, or the maimed forearm that seemed to draw the life out of so many victims, but right at that thready, pulsing forehead vein.

The Mummy's head snapped back. The neck could be heard to snap as the suddenly-split skull was driven back by a thousand foot-pounds of striking lead.

The Murder Mummy collapsed in a lifeless heap.

Confidently, the *Spider* strode over to the withered form. He knelt. From a pocket, he removed a platinum cigarette lighter. Pressing it to the shattered forehead, he planted a crimson seal beside the single bullet hole created by the *Spider*'s unerring aim.

Two bullets. *But one hole!*

The Murder Mummy was dead, on its blood-splashed brow sprawled a crimson seal of hairy legs and poison fangs—*the seal of the Spider!*

And yet...

Wentworth felt strange, woozy. As if... as if the very life were still being sucked out of him.

Suddenly, he realized his peril. The shattered right arm, with its pro-truding forearm bones, was still pointing toward him. Even in death, the diabolical touch of death lay upon him as if the Murder Mummy sought one final victim from the Great Beyond....

Staggering backward, the *Spider* put distance between that still-hissing limb and himself.

When he could stagger no more, he dropped to one knee and sighted carefully. Holstering one automatic, he cut loose with the other. The quiet shattered. Emaciated flesh and bone splattered and shattered along the entire length of that gnarled forearm.

The gun ran empty, slipped from nerveless fingers.

Wentworth collapsed. Slowly, painfully, he crawled toward a wash room. With a grim effort, he pulled himself up to wash basin and turned on the water full force. He drank. He did more than drink. He devoured the cool water that gushed out from the faucet, let it it cool his stiff face, rill joyously down the dry tunnel that was his parched throat.

Life! He was drinking life! And because of the life-giving water, the *Spider* lived!

Soon, Commissioner Kirkpatrick showed up, military mustaches bristling. Ram Singh was at his side, looking gaunt and unnaturally pale under his colorful turban.

Kirkpatrick rushed to his side. "Dick! Are you all right?"

Wentworth stood propped against a gilded mummy case, no trace of the Spider's sinister raiment about him. "The Murder Mummy, Kirk. He's back in there. The devil nearly did for me, even in...death."

Kirkpatrick stepped over to the desiccated corpse.

Casually, Wentworth took from a pocket a platinum cigarette lighter—the same one he had used to brand his kill but minutes before. It was typical of the *Spider* to risk all by imprinting a vanquished foe even when it meant incrim-inating his other self...Richard Wentworth. But then, his intimates sometimes believed that the *Spider* was an avenging demon who at times *possessed* the true Wentworth.

An eternity seemed to go by while Kirkpatrick examined the remains.

"If you strip away his mask and mummy wrappings," Wentworth cooly suggested, "you'll discover the features of...Chela Bey!"

Kirkpatrick's head swiveled sharply. "What? Impossible! Chela Bey was murdered by—"

"Himself?" Wentworth shook his head. "No, Kirk. Chela Bey was very clever. And quite mad. My theory is that he was driven mad by the loss of his arm to a Nile crocodile. And sought compensatory wealth in his madness."

"But the body in the morgue..."

"Some poor Egyptian lackey of Bey's," shrugged Wentworth. "He no doubt strangled the poor devil, and chopped off his arm. Under the cover of doused lights, he performed an expert substitution, then put on a macabre show by draining the corpse of all natural liquids in front of the reception party. My guess is Bey's first victim had been secreted in the sealed sarcophogus, dressed in identical clothing. For his part, Chela Bey had merely to doff his evening attire and don mummy mask and linen-wrapped gloves to effect his grisly transformation."

"But how—why?" Kirkpatrick sputtered.

"The body in the morgue—the Chela Bey who was mummified—had a fresh forearm stump. This wretch's stump will prove to be completely healed, I will wager."

Kirkpatrick nudged the broken stump with one shoe. A faint greyish exhalation seemed to waft from it.

"Be careful with that," Wentworth warned. "That is the device with which the Murder Mummy dealt death."

"What is it?"

"A machine of some sort. Grisly thing. Chela Bey cunningly attached it to his elbow stump. I think when examined by accredited scientists, it will prove to contain two mechanisms—a paralysing poison no doubt delivered by an injecting needle concealed in one false fingernail, and something else I shall call a dehydrator. Those ulnar 'bones' are actually tubes for drawing the life out of a victim. By some modern miracle, they leached all moisture from its hapless victims with astonishing speed. I felt its adder's bite twice. Ram Singh nearly succumbed, as well."

Wentworth allowed himself a tight-lipped smile of supreme satisfaction. "But its author instead perished. By a stroke of good fortune, I damaged the mechanism in my first encounter with the Murder Mummy, when I blew off its right hand. The dehydration device never worked properly after that, hence I survived its attempts to....mummify me."

Wentworth's voice trailed off into eternity. The moment of truth had come. Would Kirkpatrick discern....?

Abruptly, Stanley Kirkpatrick stripped off the bloody mask and head wrappings, seeming not to notice the scarlet many-legged blot that might be mistaken for a blood stain were it not such an instantly-recognizable symbol. He stared down at the coppery face of...Chela Bey.

"If you examine his pockets," Wentworth said dryly, "I would not be very astonished if you were to again find the *Spider's*...personal effects."

Rising to his feet, Kirkpatrick said hoarsely, "The city can't thank you enough, Dick."

Wentworth shrugged casually, and drew a cork-tipped cigarette from a monogrammed case. He started to snap flame to his lighter.

"Think nothing of it, Kirk," he drawled. Examining the unlit cigarette, he suddenly hesitated.

"What is it?" Kirkpatrick demanded.

"This cigarette," Wentworth muttered darkly, brows knitting together.

"Out with it, man."

"It's...Egyptian."

Then Richard Wentworth laughed, a warm, full-bodied laugh that was nothing at all like the harsh metallic untterances of the *Spider*!

illustration by Tom Floyd

Chapter Six

REGRETS ONLY

by CHUCK DIXON

It was always the social event of the season.

An invitation to the all-night bash at Ronnie Tilton's near-palatial penthouse atop the Condor Tower was coveted by all of Manhattan's elite. A glittering mix of the city's idle millionaires and Broadway's brightest stars mixed and mingled in celebration of Ronnie's latest musical opus. *Sisters in Arms* had opened at the Orpheum Pantages earlier that evening; opened to tepid applause. It was certain to receive savage reviews. All of which did little to dampen the mood at the long open bar packed three deep with well-wishers and revelers.

Out on the balcony, an attractive young couple had escaped the lights and heat of the main room where the party was in full swing.

"He's slipping, you know," Brice Severn confided to Nita.

"Slipping? Who?" Nita Van Sloan pulled her ermine stole tighter about her shoulders against the brisk October air ripping across the broad terrace. The lights of 34th Street below led down to the deep blackness of the river three blocks west. A wind funneled between the buildings carrying the Hudson's autumn chill with it.

"Ronnie, I mean. He hasn't had a success since *Paradise for Two*," Brice swirled his drink for emphasis. "Three years without a hit is an *age* on Broadway. The only reason he could gather the finances for *this* show is his reputation. And *that* will be in rags by morning when the papers come in."

"It wasn't his strongest effort," Nita offered.

"It was dreadful," Brice snorted. "Making it to act three was a chore, I tell you. I saw more than a few of our fellow partygoers slipping away for the lobby long before then."

Nita could not repress a smile at Brice's indignation.

"It wasn't **so** bad," she laughed.

It was Brice's turn to guffaw.

"That hospital number, what was it?" his eyes rolled in thought and he began to hum and then sing.

> *You're my panacea*
> *My vaccine too*
> *There's no remedy*
> *There's no cure for me*
> *I'm in love with only you*

"You're terrible, Brice," she gave him a playful shove.

"Really, I don't know how he'll come back from *this* calamity," Brice shook his head. "What financier will touch him now?"

"He seems unaffected by it all," Nita turned to look back through the portico to where Ronnie Tilton himself was seated at the grand piano, surrounded by pretty men and women. He was playing lightly on the keys and speaking with a lazy smile, a cigarette dangling from the corner of his thin lips. The smoldering gasper juxtaposed to a baby face that was now beginning to show his age. A natural charmer. He did not appear troubled in the slightest by the buzz circling about him. He'd gone cold. The luster was gone. The magic touch that turned every show into a blockbuster was a thing of the past. Though you'd never know it by the carefree way he joshed his admirers and tickled the ivories.

Nita drifted back into the warmth of the penthouse's main room, casually handing her wrap to the attending Brice as a way of dismissing him. Her fine, bare shoulders were exposed now above a sleek, floor-length bottle-green dress that set off her violet eyes. Matching evening gloves rose up over her elbows to frame her elegant décolletage. A stratum of cigarette smoke hung in the air and the tinkle of ice against glass punctuated the music of laughter in the high-ceilinged, brightly-lit room. In addition to the fact that she was chilled, she wanted to hear Ronnie play and sing. He was crooning one of his own, earlier, compositions with his roaming alto. What he lacked in singing talent he more than made up for in charisma. And what a rare treat to hear the composer perform his own work.

> *Your smile, your style*
> *It always leaves me weak*
> *Excuse me if it's a while*
> *Before I'm able to speak*

But yours is the face
That leaves my tongue tied
You bring me to that place
Where my élan is tried.

These show types were shallow and fickle and their parties a dumb show of egos and excess. But Nita looked forward to Ronnie's soirees for their eclectic mix from all levels of society. She saw an oil magnate, an auto maker, an heiress with nearly as many lovers as she had real estate holdings. Seasoning this crowd of hoi polloi were motion picture starlets, chorus boys, stage magicians, jazz musicians and gigolos; all at Ronnie's invitation and meticulously chosen to interest, engage and outrage.

But even knowing Ronnie's idea of an amusing guest list, Nita was taken aback by a tall dark man standing in the dim light at the far end of the full bar stocked for the party. The man's tuxedo was perfectly tailored and yet still looked like an unwelcome disguise. His features were sharp and his jowls were bluish with a five o'clock shadow that was several hours old as midnight neared. Dark eyes scanned the room and eyed the guests as if they were numbers on a balance sheet rather than living souls. This man was a predator and Nita wondered why he was here. He didn't fit Ronnie's usual sense of fun.

The song drifted to a close to a patter of applause and Ronnie glanced up at his admirers. A blue-eyed blonde starlet who'd been gracing the covers of the movie slicks for months was gazing into Ronnie's eyes with open invitation. But he was looking past her to lock eyes with an attractive boy singer who boldly returned the older man's attention. None of this was lost on Gregory Del Prado, Ronnie's longtime "roommate" who sidled up to the piano next to the blonde as if unaware that he had broken the eye contact of Ronnie and the singer.

"Play the song you wrote for *me*, Ronnie," Gregory cooed with the barely disguised heat behind his eyes betraying his smile. If he noticed the glare of the miffed actress he'd shouldered aside he did not show it. He slid onto the stool beside Ronnie until their arms touched. Ronnie regarded him with bland amusement and, without looking, began to coax the opening bars of *My Man's the Man For Me* from the keys.

This was precisely the kind of wicked by-play that drew Nita to Ronnie's parties. For her, gatherings like this were normally social obligations with a capital "O". They were necessities for someone at her station in society and she'd thrown a number of these tiresome pantomimes herself. But Ronnie Tilton's she-bangs were the only ones she looked forward to. If only he were still as expert at assembling a song and dance show as he was at these salons.

Nita looked around to find the dark man again but he was no longer holding up the end of the bar. She noticed his drink left on the bar top and that it remained full to the brim. She was scanning the packed room of partiers for him when Mrs. Alicia Monkmorton sailed into her line of vision.

"And where is Richard tonight?" Alicia was a dowager with more money left her from a newspaper fortune than she could ever spend in a lifetime. Although, to her credit, she was giving it the old college try.

"He's otherwise engaged, though I'm expecting him to show up later to take me home," Nita returned Mrs. Monkmorton's smile with all of the false sincerity that the other woman had mustered. In fact, her beau, the millionaire philanthropist Richard Wentworth, was following a hot lead about a home burglary on Long Island. Even now, cloaked in a dark cape, his face hidden in the shadow of a slouch hat, Richard was most probably stalking a gang of vicious thugs as his alter ego, the *Spider*. Nita hoped he could wrap that up early enough to join her here. But she was understanding of, and even a participant in, his never-ending war on the city's gangland parasites.

"Of course, you are," Mrs. Monkmorton said with a tone that implied the opposite. "Though, in the absence of Richard, I'm certain you can find any one of these young men to squire you this evening."

"If I could tear them away from each other," Nita allowed herself a wry smile.

Mrs. Monkmorton hooted with a laugh that surprised even herself and she planted a light, playful slap on Nita's bare white shoulder.

"You're so bad, Nita," Mrs. Monkmorton moved away toward the cold buffet just as Brice rejoined Nita. Brice was pouting. They'd known each other at school and he always acted proprietarily around her. They associated in much the same social circles and so she was forever running into him at fetes and charity balls and openings. And he was eternally trying to kindle more than a friendship between them.

"Quite unfair of you to consign me to valet service," he said standing too close at her side as they watched Ronnie run through a playful version of his and "Gregory's" song.

"You *know* I treasure that stole, Brice," she said and allowed him to hold her arm. "I wanted it out of the way where nothing could happen to it."

"I suppose *he* gave it to you?" Brice muttered bitterly.

"What of it?" she said and gently removed his hand. "Richard is generous and enjoys seeing me in fine things."

"Not enough to marry you," he dared and flinched even as she turned, ready for the slap that never came.

Ronnie brought his song to a crashing finish that had everyone laughing and applauding. Gregory sensed he was being mocked by the barrelhouse way in which Ronnie built the song and sat forcing a weak smile even as his eyes betrayed his anger.

Standing up from the piano, Ronnie clapped his hands for attention. He was paying for the victuals and drinks so the crowd hushed and turned to him. Those in other rooms drifted closer in response to his calls of "Everyone! Everyone!"

Nita saw the dark man with the reptilian eyes again. He was sidling through the ring of partygoers behind Ronnie who now stood on the piano stool and quieted the crowd. Moving closer through the throng, the man's size could be appreciated. He was tall, broad shouldered and glided with the easy assurance of one who felt secure that he was the lord of his jungle. A wolf among sheep with the sheep all unawares. A thrill, not of fear, of warning coursed up Nita's spine and she slipped away from Brice to move cautiously backward; distancing herself from…from *what*?

"Tonight saw the opening of my latest stage production," Ronnie began, a knowing smile on his face. A smattering of applause greeted this and he held his hands out to quell it.

"Applause? Where were you when I needed you?" Nervous titters from a few in the circle.

"From the deafening silence at the Pantages," Ronnie's smile took on a sickly quality. "I'm certain that I have penned another disaster. The bloom is off the lily and the dew off the rose to borrow a cliché."

There were murmurs of denial but they were more to preserve decorum than any sincere gainsaying of Ronnie's confession.

"Oh, and I *needed* a moneymaker, friends and relations," Ronnie went on, ignoring the contradictions of well-wishers. "I have a little secret. I'm a bit of a hedonist." Honest laughter from the revelers. "And that's an expensive hobby for a boy to have. The drink, the clothes, the gambling. It all adds up to the national debt of Bulgaria, I tell you."

"You're not going to touch us all for a loan, are you, old man?" called out Hardy St Vincent, the novelist of the moment who fancied himself a wit. Chuckles all around.

"In a way, that's precisely what I plan to do, brothers and sisters," Ronnie's smile was more forced. Nita could see the sheen of sweat on his upper lip even as she drew away toward the doors leading to the back bedrooms of the suite. She glanced at the dark man who regarded the circle of guests crowded about with a cold appraisal.

Ronnie continued on, speaking faster as he went. "The ponies especially were my downfall. I sunk quite a bit on their precious little heads and proved a positive genius at picking the darling who would come in dead last every time." Appreciative laughter and catcalls.

"Which brings me to the reason for this clambake. You see, I wound up with more month at the end of my money when the rent-man came to call, I had to borrow and borrow big. And the men I borrowed from were not patrons of the arts and they charge a heftier percentage than any bank."

Nita was almost to the broad double doors of the master bedroom and, more specifically, the pretty little German automatic pistol snugly seated in her clutch purse resting atop a chest of drawers within. The doors opened behind her as she was reaching back for the pull. Four men that she had not seen before emerged from the back rooms. Rough men with calloused hands, scarred faces and eyes that were so lacking in human emotion they might have been placed there by a taxidermist.

A frisson of nervous tension swept the party people as more men emerged from side rooms. The tension escalated to fear as two of the men were seen holding sub-machine guns glistening black in their fists. A woman screamed only to be hushed by the man escorting her.

Ronnie Tilton relaxed now as though a threshold had been crossed; a point of no return had been breached.

"These men, were they not repaid in the green stuff, would seek repayment in suffering," Ronnie stepped down from the stool and regained his audience's attention. "*My* suffering, specifically. And I was not anxious to live the rest of my life in a wheelchair digesting only liquids for my supper. But I had nothing, no collateral, to offer these men in exchange for their loan."

"Nothing, that is, except *you*, dear friends."

Aurora Grant, an heiress to a railroad or three, stepped forward angrily.

"Do you mean to say that we're kidnapped?" she demanded. "Right here on Tenth Avenue?"

Ronnie began to explain and the dark man shoved him aside, drawing a big black automatic as he did so. He grabbed the stunned Aurora by the hair and pressed the barrel of the Colt to her temple; his face a mask of cold rage.

"We don't have time for this," his voice a reptilian hiss.

Ronnie stepped forward timidly as the crowd melted back in horror.

"Sipes, you promised me it wouldn't go like this," Ronnie pleaded. Sipes' eyes bored into Aurora's and she was frozen in fear, terrified to break his gaze should it anger him further.

Nita's mind raced. Antonin Sipes. The Clipper. A ganglord who specialized in extortion and loan-sharking and who commanded a small army of the city's most bloody- minded criminals. He was as unexpected and out of place here as a coiled rattlesnake might be in a nursery. The scheme came together in Nita's mind even as Sipes released the weeping Aurora and addressed the crowd.

"This ain't a kidnapping no how," Sipes began and lowered the automatic in his fist to his side. "It's plain and simple. The only way any of you swells is leaving this joint in the morning is if you *pay* for your lives."

The crowd was uncomprehending which only compounded their fear.

"You all got goods in your homes and apartments. In safes or vaults or hidden in grandma's jam jar," Sipes' lips curled slightly in appreciation of his own jest. He was warming to the task of keeping this captive audience snake-charmed.

"I got gangs all over the five boroughs," he returned to the subject at hand. "You tell me where your cash, your jewels, your bonds are squirreled away and my boys go get 'em. If there's no tricks or funny stuff and I'm happy with the take then you get to walk outta here when the sun comes up."

The impending burglary at the Waldman Estate out in Glen Cove, Nita thought in sudden flash of insight. The *Spider* was waiting there for soldiers from the very gang that Sipes was directing from this penthouse. The intelligence that he and Ram Singh had been gathering all week was, in truth, but a hint of the grander scheme that was coming to horrible fruition in this room. Nita looked about her and found Guy Waldman and his wife Patricia standing close in fear at the edge of the gathering. Without knowing, the *Spider* would doom this couple were he to thwart the robbery soon to take place at their home out on the island.

"Maybe some of you need convincing," Sipes swept the room with his heartless gaze. "And it ain't like I got a lot of time to put the strongarm on alla you."

He turned to Ronnie who stood goggling.

"A demonstration?" Ronnie offered timidly.

"You know this bunch," Sipes gestured with the automatic so casually gripped in his fist. "I need a patsy that ain't got so much cash value."

Ronnie turned to Gregory still seated on the piano stool uncertain of precisely what was going on here but acting as more of an observer than a participant.

"My sweet," Ronnie shrugged as a way of apology and looked away.

Gregory was still uncomprehending as he was roughly snatched to his feet by two of the thugs. Nervous laughter turned to hoarse declarations of his love for Ronnie as Gregory was led toward where two more thugs pried open the doors of the express elevator.

Ronnie was the only one not watching as Gregory, now emitting shrill shrieks for mercy, was pitched into the open shaft.

All in attendance held their breath in silent anticipation as the echoing screams died away to end abruptly forty two floors below in a sickening sound that none who heard it would ever forget though they spent a lifetime trying.

As everyone's attention was on the nightmare playing out before them, Nita slipped slowly from the peripheral vision of the captors closest to her. They were too involved in the vicarious thrill of watching a human being fall to his death. She backed against the table that held the buffet. Her eyes fixed on Sipes and Ronnie, Nita's hands searched blindly behind her until she found the wooden handle of the carving knife set by a cutting board that held a cold roast. Hands working at the small of her back, she slid the six inch blade into one of her evening gloves. The movement, though calculated and smooth, caught the attention of one of the lowlifes holding a sub-machine gun on the crowd. He turned to her, hefting the heavy tommygun in the crook of one arm and slid a calloused hand to the flesh at the small of her bare back. Without a word beyond a guttural growl, he shoved her back in place among her fellows. Nita was careful to keep her arm bent to secure the carving knife inside the sheer glove on her left arm.

Sipes was commanding Ronnie to choose another victim. "Someone heeled." Everyone in the broad room tensed and, with eyes wide, watched as Ronnie made his choice.

"Reynold Hughes," Ronnie said and pointed out a distinguished gentlemen with graying temples and pince-nez eyeglasses. The man's suave demeanor melted as two heavies grabbed him by the elbows and shifted him closer to Sipes who now sat at an occasional table upon which was placed a telephone.

"What's his bona fides, Tilton?" Sipes snapped at Ronnie.

"A trust fund and interests in some South American mining concerns," Ronnie stammered.

Sipes looked up at the trembling gentleman from under dark brows.

"I hope I don't have to go to South America to see a payout, pal,"

Hughes quickly offered the combination to his home safe as well as helpful suggestions for entry into his Park Avenue apartment. Sipes wrote on a pad of paper the numbers and directions as well as what might be expected to be found within the safe. Hughes was then shoved to the side of the room where the doors opened on the balcony.

Sipes dialed a number from a leather bound notebook he had set by the phone. He spoke in hushed tones and relayed the information given him by the terrified millionaire. Nita pictured a criminal comrade of Sipes stationed by a payphone in a drug store or on a street corner near the Hughes apartment. Sipes finished his directions and hung up.

"Let's have another one while we wait," Sipes said and Ronnie turned to his miserable company of guests. He next chose Mrs. Monkmorton who surrendered the location of her jewelcase and a file box of bearer bonds hidden beneath a stairwell in her brownstone on East 72nd.

A fourth victim had been coerced into revealing hiding places and bolt-holes and lock combinations when the phone rang suddenly at Sipes' elbow. Sipes picked up and listened a moment. He replaced the receiver and smiled without humor toward where Reynold Hughes stood in a huddle with the others who came after him.

"Good news, Hughsie," Sipes chuckled darkly. "The swag was where you said it was. Every dime and every diamond. In the morning, you get to go down in the elevator the slow way."

Hughes was visibly relieved and mopped sweat from his temple with a handkerchief as another victim was muscled before Sipes.

Nita, standing with Brice among those not yet called, looked upon a grim tableau. A line now formed before the table where Sipes sat taking notes and making and answering calls. Across the room, closer to the terrace windows were those who had already revealed their secrets and were cast aside. All were watched over by gunsels keeping an eye on their charges.

Here they stood like frightened children in a column before their tormentor. Some of the city's most admired and envied citizens, darlings of the society page, bargaining for their lives; lips white with tension and hands trembling. Nita felt shame for them. All of their privilege and influence melted away before the dire threats of a dozen thugs with guns.

Was she now seeing the true nature of the jungle they all lived in? Were the creatures of the gutter, in the end, superior to those who were often considered their betters? Stripped of the power that their wealth provided, were all of society's elite indeed craven weaklings?

She reminded herself that this pampered crowd of first nighters was made up of the children and grandchildren of the men who'd made their fortunes. They had inherited their largesse and not struggled up from the streets and fields and mines for it. A few of the others, playwrights and actresses and songsmiths, had come by their cash in a windfall as their work caught on with the public. They could never be described as working their knuckles to the bone for their successes.

She could barely stand to watch Karl Rumstetter, heir to steel and timber millions, holding back tears as he awaited his turn before Sipes. She could not imagine his father, Theobald Rumstetter, behaving in this manner. The old man would have *acted*, would have resisted these animals and fought until his last drop of blood had been spilt. It was not money that corrupted the souls before her. It was the placid and sedentary life of a trust fund baby that had turned these children of lions into lambs.

Ronnie Tilton sat alone at the piano and poured himself glass after glass from a cut crystal decanter of gin. He played tuneless fragments of songs providing a sort of twisted background music to the proceedings.

Silly Brice was trying to play at the protector and insisted on standing close to Nita. She had to keep shifting as he placed her arm about her. It would not do to have him touch the long-bladed carving knife concealed in her glove.

The line thinned and Sipes turned to Ronnie to "pick another pigeon." Ronnie didn't even bother to stand up from the piano and called out as he teased the ivories with a snippet of a dirge as though to underscore his next utterance.

"Waldman," Ronnie slurred. "He's flush with the stuff."

Nita started slightly as Guy Waldman was taken from his pleading spouse and manhandled into line before Sipes.

"You're the one with the big pile of bricks out on Glen Cove, right?" Sipes sneered. He was becoming intoxicated with the power he held over the lives in this room. Some of the most powerful people in America were his to do with whatever he wished.

"I have a home there," Waldman offered, shoulders squared, trying to maintain what was left of his dignity.

At a nod from Sipes, the thug by Waldman's side slapped the tycoon across the face with the back of a hand.

"Stow the wisecracks and just give me the goods, pally," Sipes smiled with pen poised above the paper pad already crowded with his crabbed handwriting.

Holding a hand to his bleeding ear, Waldman began describing a floor safe concealed beneath a Persian carpet in the master bedroom of his home. Nita had slipped from Brice's attentions and moved closer to the table to listen in. She pictured the *Spider* crouched in the darkness of the Waldman home in anticipation of the home-breakers soon to arrive. He would be watchful with a .45 held in each of his gloved fists ready to spit death at the first sign of intruders.

Sipes dialed the phone and spoke briefly to someone on the other end. He then had Waldman shoved aside and motioned for another victim to approach and make their bid for life.

Nita sank back on a settee and paid scant attention to the portly gentlemen nervously listing hidden assets in his home. She could think only of what would happen when the burglars assigned to loot the Glen Cove home did not call back. Would Sipes imagine that perhaps they had simply run off with the treasures they uncovered? He could not be so naïve as to believe in honor among thieves. Or would he suspect that something had interfered with their plundering of the Waldman manor? Might he not simply kill Guy and his wife out of suspicion or spite?

She could not shake the image of Richard, in the guise of the *Spider*, standing over the bloody remains of the sneak thieves in a haze of acrid gunsmoke with not the slightest idea that he had sealed the fate of two innocents. Or that the events on Long Island were directly tied to the fate of herself in a penthouse high above the streets of Manhattan.

She was startled from her thoughts by shouts and cries of dismay. Thugs were dragging poor Barney Braymoor from the crowd of those who had already surrendered their fortunes. Braymoor, a spindly young man with jug ears and a stammer, was brought struggling before a livid Sipes who came around the table and savagely gut-punched the hapless Barney. Sipes growled a string of profanities as Barney folded over the blow and sank to the floor gasping for air.

"My boys found nothing' Nothin!" Sipes crouched by Barney and held his head up by the hair. "No strongbox. No securities. No bullion!"

Barney could only move his mouth and gasp for air. His eyelids fluttered as he fought to maintain consciousness.

Sipes stood and jerked his automatic from his waistband as he rose. The gasps and shrieks of the captives could be heard as a *leitmotif* to the boom of the .45 as Sipes pumped three heavy slugs into Barney from pointblank range. The hood tossed the hot rod to the tabletop by the phone and dabbed at the spots of blood on his tuxedo lapel with his fingertips. Barney's limp form was dragged to the open elevator doors and tossed down to join Gregory at the shaft's bottom. The heels of his alligator dress shoes left twin furrows in the carpet as the only reminder Barney Braymoor had ever existed; that and the black pool of blood seeping into the broadloom before the telephone table.

The room was silent now but for the heavy breathing of Sipes leaning on the occasional table and the gurgle of gin splashing into Ronnie's tumbler where he sat at the piano.

All in the room were startled by the ring of the phone.

It sounded louder, in the wake of those few seconds of quiet, than the roar of the pistol shots had been.

Nita strained to hear as Sipes lifted the receiver. The triple explosions of the big .45 had left her ears ringing and she relied on her ability to lip read to determine what Sipes was saying into the mouthpiece. Those thin, bloodless lips curled into a snarl and he spit words rather than spoke them. She stiffened as she recognized the words "Glen Cove" being formed by his mouth. She prepared herself for what might come next.

Sipes slammed the receiver down and stood gesturing to Waldman.

"You weren't feedin' me no lines, Waldman," Sipes grinned. "My boys hauled a truckload of loot out of that barn of yours."

Guy Waldman's shoulders relaxed as he appeared to exhale for the first time in hours.

"Boys, take Mrs. Waldman over to her old man," Sipes made a sweeping gesture. "They're both oh-kay in my books." A shaken Patricia Waldman was escorted across the room to her husband who embraced her protectively.

Nita's mind was awhirl. How had the burglars successfully taken off the Waldman valuables from a house protected by the *Spider*? Is it possible that she was mistaken about which home Richard planned to lay low in tonight? No, she remembered clearly it was to be the Waldman home in Glen Cove. He even asked Nita if she knew the couple and had she ever visited their home. She dismissed the notion that common thieves might have bested the *Spider*. Had that imponderable contingency occurred then Sipes would be bragging about it even now. There was a third possibility but Nita drove it from her mind. Hope was one thing. But *false* hope was only cruel self-delusion.

The mention of her own name dragged her back from her reverie. She turned to see Ronnie gazing drunkenly at her from over the top of the piano. Was he speaking to her?

Hands took her by the elbows and lifted her from the settee. She'd been chosen. She was to join the others in the sad parade of those expected to barter for their lives with their personal fortunes. Brice had stepped in as her paladin but was easily brushed aside by the thugs handling Nita. His further protests were rewarded with a stroke across the back of the neck from the butt of a tommygun held in a third crook's fists.

She was shoved before Sipes who looked her up and down with rude appraisal from where he sat leaning over the phone. He was about to say something she was certain would prove to be obscene when the jangle of the phone turned his attention away.

He smiled as the thief on the other end reported in. This time it was Oscar Bonaventure's gallery in the Village. From his end of the conversation, Nita could tell that Sipes was pleased with the removal of many valuable original oils and watercolors from the gallery's fortified storeroom. Sipes snapped his fingers and a weeping Oscar was taken to stand with those who had won their lives in exchange for swag.

"So, what you got that I *can't* see, sugar?" Sipes returned his gaze to Nita. The hoods at her side snickered.

She mustered all the contempt she had for this piece of human filth and aimed it at him from her violet eyes.

He got the message and his face flushed scarlet as he stood and took her by the wrist to pull her closer. Sipes' hand closed on the handle of the knife and he recoiled. He regained his composure and stepped close to her, tearing the glove from her arm. The sheer fabric parted easily and the wooden-handled meat knife with its heavy blade fell to the carpet. His face contracted like a fist and he snarled showing yellowed teeth.

Sipes backhanded Nita and she stumbled back against the chest of the nearest hood.

"You're used to traveling far on your looks, ain't you, sugar?" he took her chin in his hand and smeared the blood from the corner of her lip with his thumb. Nita was not cowed and returned his frank gaze with a glare of frosty rage. He placed his thumb between his lips to taste her blood and smiled broadly.

"Take her over to the bar and keep an eye on her," Sipes snarled to the pair of thugs gripping Nita's arms. "Things might wrap up early and I'll have some time to kill."

She was hauled past poor Brice standing with fisted hands and eyes filled with impotent fantasies of rescue and retribution. She made a mew of her lips and cautioned him with a gentle shake of her head. There was only one man capable of getting her out of a corner like this and she had no idea where he might be.

Perched on an upholstered stool and watched hungrily by one of the tommy-gun-wielding goons, Nita witnessed the procession to the table where Sipes kept his tally and monitored the progress of his gangs as they prowled the city on their assigned missions. At her elbow was the highball abandoned earlier by Sipes when she saw him standing at this exact spot at the end of the long marble-topped bar. She cupped the heavy, lead-glass tumbler in her hands and mimicked taking cautious sips from it.

The line before the table was shrinking as the crowd of those who had been fleeced grew larger. A few of the chorus boys pleaded poverty and Ronnie's lazy nod gave them amnesty to join the others. The thugs shared knowing glances and demeaning remarks as the pretty young men were herded to the terrace foyer and disregarded as harmless. The only further disruption was from Raleigh Graves who made a feeble attempt at claiming that he was "cash poor" with all of his funds tied up in annuities and commercial property. After he was held down and three of his fingers were snapped like dry twigs, Raleigh gave up the location of a house he owned in Hyde Park with currency reserves hidden behind a secret panel in the wine cellar. This was all confirmed via telephone and Raleigh, sniffing back tears and cradling his ruined hand, was taken to join the rest of the company of victims.

Finally, the last two swells made their generous bids for the opportunity to die in bed and their claims of hidden wealth were validated by Sipes' roving thieves.

Ronnie staggered to Sipes' side as the ganglord flipped over the dozens of pages of notes he'd made on the pad.

"Are we square, Antonin?" Ronnie said with a thick tongue. He touched Sipes' shoulder in an attempt at camaraderie, a gesture that the hood shrugged off in irritation.

"You're in the clear, Tilton," Sipes stood and straightened his tuxedo jacket. "At least with *me*. But you better make tracks outta the country and quick."

"I've made plans too," Ronnie said and stumbled away from the table toward the clutch of guests regarding him with naked loathing. "I've just enough mad money to whisk me away to southern climes where I will dine out upon this evening until I am old and gray."

Dolores Calborn, recognized as a paragon of manners and etiquette in the highest social strata, spat noisily at Ronnie's feet.

"Well, never let it be said that Ronnie Tilton doesn't know when he's wanted," and he tipsily made his way toward the rear bedrooms. He had his back to the room when Sipes gestured for one of his gunsels to hand over a submachine gun. Ronnie's shoulders hunched as he heard the clack of the big lever being slapped back and released. He had no time to turn as Sipes crouched and let off a long burst of slugs that lifted the little man from his feet and sent him in a nearly graceful, stumbling series of skips to slam against the doors of the master bedroom in a shower of blood.

"Paid in full, you little fruit," Sipes announced to the room as he handed off the smoking tommy to his grinning cohort.

Nita knew now that none of them were leaving this penthouse alive. Sipes had his lucre but had no intention of going on the lam as he must were he to leave dozens of the country's most influential citizens alive as witnesses. There was nothing to lose now as they were all most certainly doomed never to see the sun rise over the Hudson.

Clutching the heavy tumbler in her right hand, Nita swung for the jaw of the pre-occupied hood tasked as her watchdog. She connected solidly and the tumbler exploded in a thousand shards. Through the shattering glass she felt something break beneath the blow. Teeth were mixed in the spray of glass and spirits as the hood keeled over, the Thompson falling from nerveless fingers.

Cries of anger ringing in her ears, Nita snatched up the submachine gun and rolled over the bartop as the first shots shattered bottles and glassware stacked in the orderly shelves behind the bar. Lying on her back beneath the shower of glass and liquor, Nita worked the bolt of the gun back and released it. The situation was hopeless and she knew that she was cornered with not a prayer of escape. She'd take down as many of Sipes' gang as she could before the end. Heavy slugs pounded a relentless tattoo on the Italian marble bar front that sheltered her as she tore at the hem of her dress. If she was going to make this a fight she'd need freedom of movement. She ripped a ragged tear up the seam of the Paris original to above her garter. She kicked off her matching slingback heels and crouched with the Tommy ready.

A series of shouts and the shooting stopped. The silence that followed was broken by the sibilant hiss of Sipes.

"Don't be that way, sugar," he fairly cooed. "Toss out the burp gun and all's forgiven, okay?"

Her response was a stream of slugs fired at the ceiling from concealment behind the bar. She knew she hadn't struck any of them. But the crash of furniture and roar of obscenities that came on the heels of the deafening roar of her fusillade told her that they'd understood her answer.

"Bring that whore to me!" Sipes roared. "I'll make her *beg* me to kill her!"

Nita was steeling herself for their assault and prepared to make them pay for blood with blood when suddenly the room was plunged in darkness. She heard stumbling and the thud of a chair falling over, all magnified in the absolute blackness that had fallen over everyone.

Then she heard laughter.

A hard, bitter laugh that rose from a deep rumble to a malicious cackle.

Even in the stygian gloom she could tell the source of that nightmarish sound. It was echoing up from the throat of the open elevator shaft.

The *Spider!*

From the first moment of their capture, Nita had taken the opportunity to look about and memorize as much of the penthouse's main room as she could. This precaution allowed her to move sightless from behind the bar to get closer to the terrace where the shorn victims of this hellish evening cowered. Her eyes were already adjusting to the faint glow of moonlight throwing shadows across the room. She was going to serve as a shield for the unfortunate partygoers for as long as she was able. She took up a position using a heavy Chesterfield wingchair as a makeshift bunker and hefted the submachine gun onto her bent knee with the muzzle pointed to the darkness between her and the elevator doors.

Sipes was trying to cull order from chaos as he gang milled about the room blindly.

"The elevator!" he called and began using the automatic in his fist as a flail to knock his men into some sort of organized defense. "He's in the shaft!"

"Who's in the shaft?" whispered back a twice-convicted murderer with all the quavering fear of a child frightened by a lightning storm.

"You know damn well who!" Sipes snapped back just as a fresh torrent of laughter, much closer this time, exploded from the shaft.

One hood stood up in a panic and let off some wild shots in the direction of the elevator. The muzzle flashes from his revolver silhouetted him for an instant. Enough illumination for Nita's stream of tracers to find him and throw him tumbling to the floor spraying hot blood over many of his fellows. This touched off a cacophony of gunfire as the shaken thugs tried to throw up a screen of hot lead in all directions. Nita called over the roar to the screaming hostages to find cover and lay low. She then added to the maddened confusion of the criminals by loosing a spray of .45s into their midst from the juddering Tommy in her manicured hands. With some satisfaction she heard groans and shrieks followed by meaty impacts upon the carpet.

Kapok and horsehair showered over her as a storm of slugs tore through the upholstery of her adopted rampart. She flattened on the floor and blazed away through the legs of the chair and heard muffled curses and a deep gasp of agony from the dark.

She rolled from her cover through a litter of her own empty shellcasings while hugging the hot weapon close to her. She came up against a davenport and crouched listening to the sounds from the room beyond. The sobbing of the hostages. The gurgling moans of a dying hood. A voice she believed to be Sipes' hissing commands to his men. Beneath it all a low, bass chuckle traveled across the room like dry leaves cast by a chill October wind.

Gunfire erupted again in every direction shattering glass and tearing into furniture and walls. Taking advantage of a few seconds lull, Nita sprang to her feet and let fly with a sweeping burst from the Tommy. She aimed low, more as a diversion than anything else. In the dying muzzle flash from the bucking chopper in her hands she saw a dark shape moving swiftly from the elevator opening. Twin flashes of flame lit the room and above the staccato glow of their deadly incandescence she could see, floating in the darkness like a wraith, the contorted features of the *Spider*.

Shapes rose up and returned fire even as they backed away from the laughing figure throwing leaden death into their tightly packed ranks. Nita braced herself against an armoire and opened up on the backs of the retreating thugs. Trapped between two hails of lead the hoods either sought cover or danced spasmodically in a whirling tarantella; caught helpless in the deadly crosscurrent of slugs.

Nita walked forward to meet the *Spider*, spraying lead at the crawling and creeping shapes at her feet. The *Spider* moved forward as well, firing one .45 and then the other at any available target he saw slithering for momentary cover beneath a table or behind a sofa, narrowing the gap between them until they were but a few paces apart in the center of the bloody slaughter they'd created. A fog of gun smoke hung thick in the air.

A wet gasp followed by a strangled curse alerted them to a survivor among the hoods. Nita overturned the bullet-riddled occasional table to find Sipes concealed beneath it. His tuxedo was in crimson tatters as he dragged himself over the carpet sodden with the blood of himself and his cohorts. Nita raised the Tommy to her shoulder and aimed squarely at his back.

"What's you life worth to you, Antonin?" she whispered hoarsely, an icy edge in her voice.

She depressed the trigger and was rewarded only with a dry clicking sound.

"If I may be of assistance," the *Spider* chuckled at her discomfiture and offered one of his own black handguns.

Nita smiled sardonically as she tossed aside the empty Tommy and brushed a stray strand of her chestnut brown hair from her forehead.

"You always know what a woman wants," she smiled as she took the warm pistol from his gloved hand.

The big Colt bucked twice in her slim fingers and then silence.

Seated in the rear of a speeding black Daimler sedan gliding east along 34th through the retreating darkness of dawn, Nita accepted the splash of bourbon offered her by Richard Wentworth. In the driver's seat, loyal Ram Singh expertly navigated the early-morning traffic of milk trucks and taxis.

"A man should never be allowed to see a girl like this," she smiled and gestured with her one bare hand at the tear in her gunpowder-dusted dress.

"You've never been lovelier, Nita," Richard smiled easily in stark contrast to the horrifying visage he'd presented less than an hour before. "Those people owe you their lives."

She dismissed that with a gesture and leaned back against him, cupping the tumbler in her hands.

"Where *did* you come from, Richard? How could you have known what was going on at Tilton's?"

Richard chuckled deep in his throat, a vestige of his other persona revealing itself to her.

"The hoods at Waldman's house. As I lay for them they made mention of Sipes. Curiosity trumped justice for a moment and I allowed one of them to live long enough to describe this grand scheme to me."

"So it was *you* on the telephone with Sipes," she laughed prettily at this.

"I did a fair enough mimic to fool him," Richard grinned. "No trick at all when you're telling someone what they want to hear."

"You *did* say that you would join me at the party if you could get away," she turned her head to roll her eyes up at him lovingly.

"You know how I enjoy a good wingding," he smirked, returning her gaze with equal heat. 🔫

illustration by Tom Floyd

Chapter Seven

THE MARCHING MADMEN

by BILL CRIDER

The political power of New York was gathered in the banquet room of the best hotel on South Park Avenue to honor Dr. Martin Riley for his contributions to the city's hospitals. His tireless devotion to the sick and needy was legend. He had given freely of his time and expertise for years, and to honor him, the mayor, the governor, two congressmen, and a senator were present.

So, too, were Stanley Kirkpatrick, the city's Police Commissioner, and his good friend, the wealthy entrepreneur Richard Wentworth, accompanied by the lovely Nita Van Sloan. Food, wine, and the appearance of good cheer were present as well, but underneath the air of apparent conviviality there was a covert fear that tightened the nerves and slid behind the eyes.

The crowd listened with feigned attention as the mayor opened the speeches with an encomium devoted to Dr. Riley's lengthy list of charitable accomplishments, but everyone there had something else in mind.

All had received or seen a copy of the latest letter written by Dr. Dionysus, a clever madman who had threatened the entire city. If his ransom demands were not met, he said, all the city's leaders would die. And after them, the state's leaders would begin to perish.

Already the fire chief had been horribly killed as an example to all the rest, his neck broken by the brute strength of a maniac who had simply taken the chief's head in his huge hands and popped his spine like a rotten stick.

The killer died laughing as police bullets tore into his body, leaving no one in doubt of the powers of Dr. Dionysus, who boasted that he had the ability to free people from the material world and send them to the realm of spiritual ecstasy. However, in their new state of ecstatic intoxication they served the purpose of Dr. Dionysus, and his purpose was death.

It was little wonder that terror lurked beneath the glamorous surface of the evening's supposed celebration.

As the mayor continued his speech, Wentworth and Nita excused themselves from their table.

"I'm sorry to leave, but I have another engagement," Wentworth said to his friend Kirkpatrick.

The Police Commissioner gave him a skeptical look. "And what would that be?"

"I'm meeting someone," Wentworth replied with a thin smile, as he picked up a small leather satchel that rested on the floor by his chair.

"But I'll be back," Nita said. "I'll just see Richard out."

They left the table, and Kirkpatrick watched them go with suspicion plain on his face.

When they reached the lobby, Nita pulled Wentworth aside.

"Must you leave?" she said. "Wouldn't it be better if you stayed here?"

"You know how well-guarded this place is," Wentworth answered, and indeed it was true. Nita was well aware that even the bellmen in the lobby were armed policemen in disguise. "I'm needed elsewhere."

"But where?" Nita said. "Do you really put so much credence in the threats of this Dr. Dionysus?"

Wentworth gave a curt nod. "I do. You know what he is capable of."

"And do you think he would dare to strike tonight? He must know that he could never enter this building, or, if he did, he could never leave alive."

"Every powerful person in the city is here, and several from the state and national governments. This is the perfect place for him to strike."

"But Dr. Dionysus isn't here."

"Perhaps. But even if he isn't, I believe he might send others to do his bidding," Wentworth said. "That is what we must be wary of. You stay with Kirkpatrick. He may need your help."

Wentworth knew that the Police Commissioner could take care of himself, but in certain circumstances, he might need assistance-the kind that Nita was quite capable of providing.

"Do you have your pistol?" he asked.

"Yes. And you?"

Wentworth merely smiled.

"And I have mine, of course," Nita said. "Though I hope nothing happens that will require me to use it."

"So do I," Wentworth replied, and then, without further comment, he left her.

There was much that he would have said, and done, had he been free to do so, but until the world had been set right, he could never do as he wished. Nita understood, though it pained her as much as it did him. She waited until he had left the building, and then she returned to the banquet hall.

Wentworth drifted into the darkened streets that were chilled by the wind from the East River, a wind that moaned around the buildings and stirred the trash in the alleys.

With the satchel dangling from his right hand, Wentworth might have been a physician on the way to make a house call. He took the satchel with him into one of the alleys, where he concealed himself in a doorway. There, he opened the bag, and his hands worked with the speed and skill of long practice as he used the make-up from the bag's interior to give his skin an unhealthy grayish-yellow hue. He pulled on a wig of lank black hair and fitted into his mouth the sharp, vampire-like incisors.

He then removed a cape and black slouch hat, and when he put them on, even his posture subtly changed so that he no longer resembled the man who had entered the alley.

When he emerged from the doorway, he was no longer Richard Wentworth. He was – the *Spider*!

Madmen on the March

At the mouth of the alley, the *Spider* paused and listened to the sounds of the city. Because of a police cordon at the ends of the block, the street and sidewalks were deserted. The *Spider* heard the distant hum of traffic and the whine of the wind that flapped his cape. He wondered how Dr. Dionysus could possibly mount an attack, but he was almost certain that he would.

Standing in the shadows where he was virtually invisible, the *Spider* scanned the buildings where a few scattered lights burned. There was no other sign of life aside from the doorman at the hotel across the street, and that doorman was a cop.

Suddenly the *Spider* turned back to the alley. His keen ears had picked up a noise from no more than two blocks away, the sound of a scream.

It was a scream of terror, and it was followed by another scream that ripped through the night with a terrible glee: the scream of a madman!

The *Spider* ducked into the alley and swiftly ran toward the opposite end. As he ran, he considered what lay in the direction of the river. Only blocks from the hotel was Bellevue Hospital.

Bellevue, the *Spider* thought. The notorious "bug ward," as the psychiatric unit was called by the city's less elegant denizens. The *Spider* wondered why he hadn't made the connection sooner.

What if some of the madmen and women there were already adherents of Dr. Dionysus. What if all of them were? And what if they had now been unleashed upon the city?

As the *Spider* increased his pace, a chill that had nothing to do with the wind from the river passed over him. Before he reached the end of the alley, he heard police sirens. More screams erupted into the night.

He rounded the corner of the alley and saw a sight from a nightmare. Down each side of the street the madmen marched, antic and terrible under the street lamps, all of them wearing masks that concealed their features while making them even more grotesque, giving them the faces of harlequins and clowns, satyrs and witches, ghosts and devils.

They were still several blocks away, too far away for the *Spider* to act. He estimated that there must be at least fifty of the bizarre individuals. From some of them came screams and from others insane laughter as they trudged along with no regard for anyone or anything in their path. In their wake more than one mutilated body lay on the sidewalk or in the street, killed by nothing more than the bare hands of the marchers.

A newsvendor saw them approach his stand as he stood paralyzed with fear. The flimsy newsstand was no obstacle to the madmen. It was overwhelmed, ripped apart, and scattered. Boards flew through the air, colorful pulp magazines flopped like wounded exotic birds, and sheets of newspaper floated away on the wind.

The vendor didn't have a chance. Like the newsstand, he was torn to pieces before the *Spider*'s eyes. The madmen were no more concerned with the vendor than if he had been a rag doll. They tossed his arms and legs aside, blood flying, and marched on, laughing.

The beat cop stepped out of a doorway where he had concealed himself as they approached. His service revolver hammered out five shots, but they had no effect that the *Spider* could see. The cop had the presence of mind to withdraw into the doorway to hide, thus being spared the fate of the newsvendor.

The *Spider* drew his automatics from the shoulder holsters where they had been concealed. He was certain that the marchers were headed for the hotel where the banquet was being held. It might be that no one could stop them, but the *Spider* would have to try.

A police car screamed around the corner on two wheels. The cops were not known to be friends of the *Spider*. He withdrew into the shadows as the car screeched to a stop.

Four cops jumped out of the car armed with Tommy-guns, and with the furious sound of a machine-gun opera the choppers sent lead flying.

The cops were nervous, perhaps frightened, and their singing lead wasn't always directed accurately. Some of the heavy slugs chipped the bricks of buildings, and others smashed windows. A few even plowed into their intended targets.

The madmen were hardly slowed by the fusillade of fire, except for one who managed to catch a bullet directly in the mask that covered his face. His head exploded in a haze of blood and brain matter.

The marchers paid no heed to him and surged over the police car like a living wave. They ripped off the car doors as if they were made of clay and flung them along the street, striking sparks from the pavement. They tore the Tommy-guns from the hands of the police and threw them away as well, as if the weapons were no more than a child's toys. They struck the policemen down and left them where they fell. It was impossible to tell if they were dead or alive.

The *Spider* stepped from the shadows. His twin automatics spit bullets and flame, but while the bullets hit their targets, the madmen hardly slowed.

Another police car arrived, siren howling, and more armed cops poured out. The *Spider* thought they would have no more luck than the first group, and he was right. In less than a minute, the marchers swept over and around the car, dismantling it from bumper to bumper and brushing aside the cops like a few pesky insects.

The shrieks and laughter increased with each encounter. The madmen literally shook with jollity and glee, just happy pedestrians out for a casual stroll in the cold of the evening.

The *Spider* knew the police in the cordons near the hotel would meet the threat, but he had no confidence that they were a match for the outlandish crew that had been unleashed from the bug ward.

How could even the *Spider* stand against them? They seemed almost invulnerable. Machine-gun bullets and slugs from his own automatics hardly slowed them. They seemed insensible to pain. The *Spider* knew that there were certain drugs which could increase the degree of someone's madness, increase it so much that pain and suffering meant nothing. Some such drug must have been administered to the pack that moved in his direction. But who had done it? Who would have had the opportunity?

As the mob drew nearer, the *Spider* saw that several of the men were bleeding from wounds to their arms and torsos, but it was as if the wounds had never happened as far as the men bearing them were concerned. Perhaps they would drop eventually from loss of blood, but what havoc would they wreak before that happened? The thought was enough to chill even the blood of the *Spider*.

The *Spider* did not have time to consider it at length, however, because the ever-moving crowd had now almost reached the entrance to the alley, and even as he moved backward into the darkness, the leaders turned the corner and headed straight for him.

He knew that he could stop a few of them with head shots as the police had done by accident, but that would hardly slow the others, and not even the *Spider* could fight such a vast number of lunatics bent on destruction.

The leaders spotted him in the dark, and they walked faster, their cackling laughter echoed off the walls of the alley as they reached out their arms to destroy him.

The *Spider* could have run. He could have lunged for the lower rungs of a nearby fire escape. But neither of those alternatives guaranteed his escape.

The marchers were almost upon him. Their leader, a hulking brute well over six feet tall, was only a few feet away. His mask was that of a laughing demon, and he reached toward the *Spider* with hands the size of fielders' mitts. He could snap a man's spine like a child would snap a twig.

And the spine he intended to snap was that of the *Spider!*

A Celebration Ended

There was only one chance, and the *Spider* took it.

Wasn't his face as outlandish as any mask? Wasn't his form as grotesquely twisted as that of any wounded man? The answers were *yes* and *yes*, and so instead of running, the *Spider* joined the hideous throng, madman among madmen. He capered in front of the others, laughing and shrieking like the rest.

The leader never faltered in his forward motion, but he dropped his hands to his sides. He and all the others accepted the *Spider* as one of their demented band. And so they went together through the alley, toward South Park Avenue, raving maniacs whose frenzy was only beginning, making their way to the hotel where their intended victims waited.

"And in conclusion," the mayor said, much to the relief of many of those in attendance, some of whom were beginning to suspect that their earlier misgivings had been baseless. After all, nothing had happened, and the banquet was almost over.

"In conclusion, let me say that no one has given more selflessly to our city than Dr. Martin Riley. For all his efforts he has asked for no reward other than our thanks, and tonight we honor him for that, and for the lives that he has saved in our hospitals and medical institutions."

The mayor gestured to Dr. Riley, who sat at the head table on his right. There was prolonged applause, and Riley, a short, hirsute man, stood and nodded his thanks. The mayor took a seat, and Riley made his way to the podium.

"I would like to thank you for your kindness," he said by way of beginning. He looked out over the audience and smiled. "I know that you would have repaid me many times over, had I asked, but, as you know, I never did. But money has never been my desire. My service was enough reward."

Nita Van Sloan heard the words, but somehow she doubted their sincerity. Dr. Riley's smile seemed counterfeit to her, and his eyes were shifty. It appeared that he might be looking for something or someone. Perhaps he was just nervous, like everyone else there, she thought, thanks to the threats of Dr. Dionysus.

"My wife, were she here tonight, would also thank you," Riley continued.

Everyone knew that Dr. Riley's wife, also a doctor, was so devoted to her work that she had refused to take time off for the banquet. Perhaps it was she that Riley was looking for, hoping that she might show up to share some of the honor with him.

Some people whispered that she was jealous of the honor that was his instead of hers, but others dismissed such comments as nothing more than gossip.

While Nita was thinking about this, a uniformed policeman burst into the room through the back door. His head swiveled as he looked rapidly around the room. His gaze landed on Kirkpatrick, and he ran to the table where the commissioner sat with Nita. The man's eyes were wide, and sweat beaded his forehead.

"Commissioner," he said. "I . . . ."

He stopped and looked at Nita.

"Go on," Kirkpatrick told him. "Say whatever you came to say."

"Sir," he began, but he paused a second time, and Nita realized that the room around them had grown absolutely silent. Riley had stopped speaking, and there was not so much as a single clink of silverware or rattle of ice. The policeman lowered his voice. "It's the madmen, Sir. They're coming."

"What madmen?" Kirkpatrick demanded. "What are you talking about?"

"The ones that are coming here, Sir."

Kirkpatrick pushed back his chair and stood up.

"The ones being led by . . . the *Spider*."

Kirkpatrick looked at Nita. She knew he suspected that Richard Wentworth was the *Spider*. She felt her heartbeat accelerate, but she let nothing show on her face.

"We'll get ready," Kirkpatrick told the cop. "You go join the others outside."

The policeman left, and Kirkpatrick, with one more look at Nita, strode toward the front of the room.

"Good Lord," Frank Stern said, his finger tightening on the trigger of his Tommy-gun as the fantastical parade emerged from the alley. "Look at them."

"I thought Halloween was last month," Larry Parker said. "And look who's in the lead!"

"It's the *Spider*!" Stern said. "We'll get him this time for sure!"

It was a byword among the police that the *Spider* was a criminal, and not just any criminal but one of the worst, a killer who had so far been too clever for them to catch but who would sooner or later make a mistake that would lead to his arrest. Or to his death.

"We can stop that mob for sure if we gun him down!" Parker said. "And the way we got this place surrounded, we can't miss!"

When the alarm had gone out about the deaths near Bellevue, the cordon around the hotel had drawn inward. The cops had come from blocks around to form phalanxes in front of the entrances.

"When do we start shooting?" Stern said.

"Jackson went in to get the Commissioner." Parker wiped his brow with his left hand. "He'll be out here with his orders any second."

"He'd better hurry," Stern said. "It won't be much longer than that until they get here."

"If he don't come pretty quick, I'm pulling the trigger," Parker said. "And the first one I'll be taking down will be the *Spider*!"

A Desperate Dilemma

As the *Spider* cavorted in front of the lunatic rabble, he knew that he had never been in greater danger than he was at that moment. The police lined the sidewalk in front of the hotel, and all of them had eyes only for him.

If he continued on his present course, he would be the target of hundreds of rounds of ammunition. If he tried to turn back, the madmen would sense that he was not one of them and tear him to pieces.

He doubted that the cops, even with their Tommy-guns could stop the madmen, certainly not all of them. Some would survive to get inside the hotel.

The *Spider* had only seconds to make his decision.

After going to the podium and asking for calm, Kirkpatrick told everyone in the banquet room to go to the hotel stairways and begin heading for the top of the building. He reasoned that if madmen were marching on the hotel, they would try to get inside through the doorways and then into the hall where their targets were gathered. So Kirkpatrick would move the targets elsewhere and trust his cops to do the rest.

As soon as an orderly evacuation had begun, he headed for the front of the building. Going out the door he saw his men lined along the curb, while across the street was the weirdest assemblage he'd ever seen, a gibbering crew of loonies with the *Spider* right in front.

Kirkpatrick, no matter what he might have thought of the *Spider* in the past, would never have imagined him the leader of such a mad horde.

Several of the cops glanced back over their shoulders, as if to ask Kirkpatrick what he wanted them to do. The Commissioner considered his options. Surely, he thought, the *Spider* would be there only if he had thrown in his lot with Dr. Dionysus. For that matter, it was not inconceivable that the *Spider* and the mysterious Dr. Dionysus were one and the same. Whatever the case, it was Kirkpatrick's job to protect the people in the hotel.

But before he could make up his mind, the decision was taken out of his hands. The madmen, who had paused for a moment to take in the situation, suddenly surged forward all together, as if responding to some unspoken signal.

When that occurred, Kirkpatrick really had no choice.

"Fire!" he said.

Before the mob began to move, the *Spider* noticed that the leader had made a hand motion. Clearly he had some sort of control over them. The *Spider* threw himself to the pavement. The stumbling feet battered him for a moment, and then the mob was past. He heard the blasts of the choppers along with shrieks and demonic laughter as he stood up.

In front of him the heavy bullets struck the madmen, tearing off fingers and hands. One man's foot was shot to bits, yet he shambled forward on the bloody stump. Some of them, however, escaped any damage at all.

Now that the *Spider* was behind them, he was much safer, though he did not pause to consider that. He raced instead to the end of the line and then around it, looking for the alley that ran alongside the hotel.

A couple of the cops saw him, and thinking that he was trying to escape, they turned their artillery in his direction. Bullets chewed up chunks of pavement, whipped through the air around him, even tore ragged holes through his swirling cape, but they never touched the *Spider*. He flung himself into the dark mouth of the alley and leapt up to grab the lower rung of the fire escape.

The fire escape rattled rustily downward, and the *Spider* started to scramble up before it touched the ground. The cops hurtled into the alley and began firing at him. Bullets whanged off the iron rungs and railings as the *Spider* shoved open the fire door and barged through it.

He hit the floor of the hallway on his shoulder and somersaulted to his feet. He hurried down the hallway to the banquet room and found it deserted, the overturned tables and chairs indicating a hasty departure. After taking in the scene and giving it a moment's thought, the *Spider* ran back to the lobby and through the door to stand behind Kirkpatrick.

"Commissioner," he said. "Don't turn around yet. This is the *Spider*."

"I know your voice," Kirkpatrick said. "Have you come to kill me?"

The machine guns blasted away, holding the madmen at bay, but only for the moment. Some had taken cover behind parked cars, but others still lumbered forward, oblivious to their wounds.

"Tell your men to stop firing," the *Spider* said.

"Never," Kirkpatrick replied.

"I'm trying to help you, Commissioner," the *Spider* told him. "Let the madmen into the hotel. They've no doubt been told to go to the banquet room, which is now empty. When they're inside, bar the doors on the outside and use teargas. It will stop them, and you won't have to kill them."

Kirkpatrick knew that the *Spider* had helped him before, and he saw the wisdom of the plan immediately. He gave the order to stop firing and to let the lunatics through the cordon. The cops didn't like it, but they obeyed.

The *Spider* stepped back inside, and Kirkpatrick called one of his lieutenants over. He explained the plan and rejoined the *Spider*.

"It's taken care of," Kirkpatrick said. "Now what?"

"Come with me," the *Spider* said, and Kirkpatrick followed him toward the stairs. "Where are the others?"

"I sent them to the upper floors," Kirkpatrick said. "I thought they'd be safer there. I told them not to use the elevators and dismissed the operators."

"No doubt you were right to send them higher. Unless someone else discovers them there."

"Someone else?"

"Dr. Dionysus."

"Dr. Dionysus? Do you know who he is?"

"I have an idea," the *Spider* said.

They reached the stairs, and the *Spider* started up with Kirkpatrick close behind him.

"Who is it?" he said.

"I'm not certain yet. I need to talk to Dr. Riley."

"Surely you don't think that he could be behind this awful affair."

The *Spider* didn't answer. He simply proceeded upward. Kirkpatrick asked no further questions. He saved his breath for the climb.

They came out onto the roof where all the banquet guests were now assembled. Nita Van Sloan stood facing the roof door with a pistol in her hand. Her finger tightened on the trigger, but she relaxed it when she saw the *Spider*, who was followed closely by Kirkpatrick.

Some of the guests recoiled at the sight of the *Spider*, though no one commented on his presence. The look of relief on Nita's face when she saw him might have given something away had anyone noticed, but no one did. She put the pistol back into her purse.

"Where is Dr. Riley?" Kirkpatrick said.

"He's right here," Nita said, but he was not.

People glanced around, but no one saw him. Dr. Riley had disappeared.

Dionysus Revealed

"It would have been easy for Dr. Riley to stop off on one of the lower floors," Nita Van Sloan said. "No one was keeping track of anyone else."

"But why would he do that?" asked the mayor, a stout, self-important man. "He knew we were to stay together."

"We'll find him," the *Spider* said, and he went back down the stairs, Kirkpatrick close on his heels.

They did not pause until they had reached the mezzanine, where the banquet room was located. The hallways swarmed with policemen, some of them wearing gas masks. They had already barred the doors of the big room. From inside it came a chorus of frustrated cries. One cop was preparing to remove the bar from a doorway so that four others could toss in teargas grenades.

The men opened the door, and the grenades flew in one after another until about twenty had been thrown. Then the men shoved the door closed before anyone inside could escape, though some of the acrid gas had gotten into the hallway.

"If that doesn't do the job, use more," Kirkpatrick said, coughing.

"What about him?" a cop asked, pointing at the *Spider*.

Kirkpatrick cleared his throat. "He's with me. Has anyone here seen Dr. Martin Riley?"

"Haven't seen anybody except the people in that room," the cop said.

"He's here somewhere," the *Spider* said. "We have to find him."

"Where do we start?" Kirkpatrick asked.

The *Spider* thought he might know. "Where's the service entrance?"

"I'll show you," Kirkpatrick said.

He led the *Spider* down the hall and to the stair. When they had descended to street level, the *Spider* said, "Let's go outside. We can come in through the service entrance rather than approach from inside."

They did as he suggested and found themselves in a large, dark room with several doors leading out.

"We'll have to check each one," the *Spider* said.

Kirkpatrick took the first, which opened into the kitchen. Several workers and cooks crouched below the long worktables. Kirkpatrick reassured them and closed the door.

The *Spider* opened the second door, which proved to be the entrance to a storeroom. The light was on, and the *Spider* saw two shadows move at one end. He drew his automatics and stepped into the room, moving silently down a row of boxes. He heard low voices as he approached the shadows.

"You were a fool," one said. "You always have been."

"But this," a second voice replied. "This is madness."

"Madness, indeed!"

There was laughter then, mad laughter, and the *Spider* stepped around the boxes, aiming the automatics at the two figures standing there.

One of them was Dr. Riley. The other was a madman, wearing the mask of a clown with a wide red smile.

"Remove her mask, Dr. Riley," the *Spider* said.

The two turned to him in surprise.

"Do as I said."

Martin Riley hesitated, and the *Spider* motioned toward him with his pistols.

"The bulletproof vest she's undoubtedly wearing will protect her upper body, but not her head," the *Spider* said. "She won't harm you."

Riley took hold of the mask and pulled, revealing the face of a woman. His wife.

"You might not have resented the lack of financial reward for all you've done," the *Spider* said to Riley, "but your wife did. Working at Bellevue, she had access to the patients on the psychiatric ward and to the drugs needed to increase their madness. She was able to control them, and she planned to use them to extort money or to have her revenge. I'm sure either would have been fine with her."

The woman laughed, a mad shriek, and jumped for the *Spider*.

The automatics barked. One bullet struck her in the chest. One took out her knee, and she toppled to the floor.

"She'll have plenty of time to recover in prison," Kirkpatrick said from behind the *Spider*. "The question is, how much of this scheme did you know about, Dr. Riley?"

"None of it, I swear."

"We'll see about that," Kirkpatrick said, and then he noticed that the *Spider* was gone like a puff of wind, as if he'd never been there at all.

As he changed out of the *Spider*'s costume and stuffed the clothing back into the leather bag in the alley, Wentworth wondered if Kirkpatrick would ever acknowledge his help. Not that it mattered. His only regret was that he hadn't finished eating at the banquet. Perhaps, he thought, Nita would like to go out for a nightcap

illustration by Tom Floyd

Chapter Eight

FEAR ITSELF

by JOEL FRIEMAN & C.J. HENDERSON

"Let me assert my firm belief that the only thing we have to fear is fear itself."
-*Franklin D. Roosevelt*

"Oh, Stanley, you simply say the wittiest things."

The woman's words were meant as flattery, and despite the enormous stretch of the imagination it would take for anyone who knew Stanley Kirkpatrick to think of him as one who might actually string together a witty sentence, they had their effect. The commissioner of New York City's police was beside himself with hearing them. But then, there were few men who could resist the effects of such a woman as—

"Nita van Sloan," the commissioner said, "if I was just a few years younger and a few million dollars richer ..."

"You'd be far too much competition for that annoyingly late boor we're waiting for," the woman across from Kirkpatrick said in a sultry voice. She was a dazzling beauty, a woman perfect in form and features, one blessed with a brain that thought three steps ahead of most and eyes that could inflame any man or freeze a leopard in its tracks. Glancing at her watch, she feigned annoyance as she said;

"Honestly, whatever could be keeping that man?"

"To be fair to poor Richard," the commissioner offered, "this professor fellow isn't here, either."

"Yes, but I don't care about him. I want Richard here to adore me. I've had such an absolutely dreadful day, and I need some male with grace and a roguish snap to him to charm me out of my doldrums." Then, putting a finger to her temple as if she had just had a flash of inspiration, the most sought-after socialite on all of Manhattan Island clapped her hands, announcing:

"You can do it, Stanley. Women are putty in your hands. You shall dazzle me with your attentions, and I shall delight in them. Start now, Stanley dear—make me forget all about that dullard Richard Wentworth."

Nita certainly did not mean any of what she was saying, and Stanley Kirkpatrick had not risen to the command of the NYC police force by being easily manipulated. Still, Nita and Richard were his friends, and he had no reason not to indulge in a bit of innocent flirting with one of high society's most dazzling stars. If she was bored enough to be that playful, who was he not to come to her rescue with a few well-chosen bon mots?

Of course, Nita van Sloan was not actually bored. She was what she always was when the man she loved did not appear when he said he would. She was worried. For Richard Wentworth was a notoriously punctual man. Indeed, there was only one thing she could think of that could make him late for their meeting that evening, and that was a need somewhere for his legendary alter ego, the *Spider*. And, Nita told herself, if that was the case, then it was her duty to keep Kirkpatrick as distracted as possible.

The commissioner had long suspected his close friend Wentworth might possibly be his great nemesis, but had never been able to prove it. If he was actually operating somewhere in the city at that moment as the *Spider*, Nita needed to keep Kirkpatrick's mind off his absence, as his well-trained police-man's mind would certainly put the facts that Wentworth did not show up on time for something during a period during which the *Spider* was operating within the city. It was not any kind of proof except circumstantial, but Wentworth and Nita both knew the commissioner had a long memory, and a fat file devoted toward putting the *Spider* behind bars.

Of course, Wentworth was a master of covering his tracks and, Nita told herself, if any evening was ideal for a man to miss without arousing suspicion, this one was it. For all the enthusiasm being poured into their evening, it was still merely the opening of a new hotel. The Riverview, erected on the Hudson side of lower Manhattan's financial district, was intended to be a palace for the world's investors. The entire idea of the place was for those international bankers, deal makers and other potentates of the ledger to be able to disembark from their liners and be only minutes away from the luxury to which they were accustomed. So far, the place was a rousing success.

No expense had been spared. The art deco look, long suspected as being on the way out, had been given a new lease on life due to the innovative and refreshingly new ways it had been incorporated into the Riverview's design. The place had a style and glamour all its own, one that flowed from the carpeting upward to the chandeliers, affecting everything in between. A laundry list of special features could be made about any part of the hotel, but there was only one of which everyone spoke, and that was the reason for the gathering in the high rise's terrace ballroom that night.

A newly discovered ruin found deep within the jungles of Central America had been transported to the place as its show piece. There in the center of the terrace, where it could be viewed from every angle, sat a massive Olmec head, one like no one in the modern world had ever before beheld.

Ancient it was, a colossal gray single slab of stone which had been carved into the shape of a massive head, but one with hundreds of faces upon it. And, a fierce and terrifying collection of visages they were, too. Although some seemed human enough, in that ancient stylized way of depicting the human face, most were anything but. The grand majority of the heads were stark and horrific things, more reptilian than human, visages with fanged mouths and forked tongues, slit eyes and flattened nostrils.

The find was a thing of major anthropological importance, and those bank-rolling the Riverview seized on the opportunity to make their hotel the most unique rest stop on the face of the planet. Securing the head was only the first step in their plan. To assuage those who would protest that such an important discovery should be in a museum, the owners had made much of the fact they not only intended to allow the piece to be studied, but that they would finance those scientific investigations.

The great Olmec head would be poured over by a team assembled from the best Manhattan's Museum of Natural History had to offer, as well as members of the Smithsonian's Anthropological Division. And, these teams would work at all hours, meaning that when diners came to the splendid surroundings of the Riverview's terrace ballroom, they would be able to watch the scientific researchers in action.

It was all piffle, and Nita knew it. She suspected even Kirkpatrick realized it was a silly notion. Men in long white coats staring at a colossal head for hours on end did not really contain much entertainment value for the layman. It was a dodge much on the level of the story of *The Emperor's New Clothes*. Saying that having dinner while the scientists worked was a fabulous night out kept one from looking like a fool for paying the Riverview's outrageous prices. And the more of the rich and famous who said it, the greater would grow the hotel's reputation.

"Is that why you've stranded me here tonight, Richard," wondered Nita aloud to the amusement of her companion, her agile mind searching for reasons to explain Wentworth's absence. "Just to avoid the tedium?"

She knew that was not the reason, of course. Richard Wentworth knew the value of social appearance, and went out of his way to maintain his role as one of high society's leading businessmen. For him, attending such a function was all part of keeping up appearances, something very important to a man like Wentworth, considering the large section of his life he was trying to keep from appearing.

But if that was the case then, where was he? It was a question both Nita and the commissioner were wondering. Where was this Professor Guicet, the scholar who was supposed to dine with them, explaining all that was known about the head—a thrill, thought Kirkpatrick, to be certain—and where was Richard Wentworth?

If either of the pair had even suspected where their missing dinner companions were at that moment, they would have thought themselves mad. Ironically enough, if they had but been paying more attention to things going on within the range of their own eyes, they would have had all the answers they needed. Their only problem would have been with believing them.

It was, indeed, a supreme irony that in a direct line from the spacious window next to which Nita and the commissioner were sitting was a magnificent view of the Hudson River. If one were to narrow that view, however, they would see a sight most bizarre and amazing. On a lonely tramp steamer slowly piloting the waterway, two cowled, monk-like figures sat in the rear of a rowboat ready for lowering. Situated in front of the pair was a large, ornate incense burner, tendrils of a thick white smoke laced with ribbons of purple and green emanating upward and outward.

"I'll be needing more money than this."

The speaker was the captain of the steamer, a shabby and disreputable looking human being. His need was directed at a third cowled figure still standing on the deck. In a hissing voice, the monk answered:

"You will get your payment when delivery is made to the Riverview pier. Do not fail in your duties, Captain Garza. You would not want to displease us."

To anyone else the seaman would have at the very least hurled a round of bluster, to keep face before his crew if nothing else. But, Garza said nothing, and his men understood his hesitation. To a man they were happy to have the monks off their boat, all of them breathing an unconscious sigh of relief as the third cowled figure stepped into the rowboat. As the smaller craft sped along toward the pier, the men on board uncovered the hatch to the hold, the first mate saying:

"God save a mackerel, it's good to have those hissin' bastards and their stinkin' smoke off and gone."

"Amen," answered the bosun. As the man checked the anchors, preparing for docking with the Riverside pier, he added, "Those three put an itch in my backbone a porcupine couldn't scratch."

The crew laughed, all of them adding jibes one after another now that their strange passengers had disembarked. Their comedy was vulgar and raucous, which was to their detriment, for their good-natured noise covered more sinister sounds coming from the hold. Down below, the crates to be off-loaded on the pier began to tremble. Throughout the voyage to New York, the hold had reeked of the monk's incense. The sailors had detested its fumes, often complaining that it made them drowsy and left them coughing. But now, the oddly colored clouds were gone, and something inside the crates was reacting to their absence. This activity was finally noticed by the crewman trying to prepare the first of the crates for transfer to the deck.

"Hey, this damn thing is moving."

"There can't be that much shift," responded the first mate, "the captain's got us on as even a drift as ever we've sailed."

"N-Nooooo," answered the sailor with uncomprehending concern. "I mean, I, I think something inside the crate—"

A sharp cracking noise interrupted the man's words, stopping them altogether. Curious, the first mate stepped forward to the hold opening and thrust his head into the darkness, calling out:

"Jason, what in hell goes on?"

Those were his last words. As the rest of the crew watched, the first mate's body shook violently, then fell backwards, slapping against the deck with a wet thud.

"Neptune's beard," bellowed one of the sailors. "Where's his head?"

As all stared, a different type of head rose from below the hatch level. Hairless it was, hard and leathery, large as a watermelon. With vicious, bulbous eyes on either side of its head, and a mouth filled with blood-stained razors, the thing let out a terrible howl, then threw itself upward onto the deck. With fantastic speed, it threw itself at the bosun, even as another of its kind came up behind it. And another. And another.

And another.

Minutes later, the steamer crashed into the Riverside pier. Its decks were empty of human life, its weathered planks holding only the savaged remains of the crew and a small herd of the terrible things which had smashed their way out of their crates. Freed from the influence of the monk's vapors, the horrors had replenished themselves, tearing apart the crew, gobbling down great slabs of meat and blood.

Now, gorged on the seamen's lives, the monsters tossed their horrid snouts in one direction, then the next, searching for any whiff upon the air that might lead them to their next destination. Catching a familiar, beloved aroma, the largest of them threw itself over the ship's railing, landing on the pier below. Catching the same trigger in their flaring nostrils, the others followed, racing across the pier to the trio of monks who stood waiting with their billowing incense. In mere seconds the horrors were docile once more, falling easily into line with but the merest breath of the monk's potent incense.

Hand gestures were made between the three, and in moments the robed figures were leading their monstrosities down the darkened pier toward the truck delivery bay of the Riverview. As the monks lured their small parade toward the skyscraper's over-sized delivery elevator, however, none of them realized they were being watched.

"By Vishnu's beard," said the large Sikh sitting behind the driver's wheel of a sleek, black Daimler roadster, "what wonders assail my eyes now?"

"Ahhh, Ram Singh," answered the man in the back seat, "you know New York, if it's not one thing in this town, it's another!"

The turbaned driver stared at the parade of monks and monsters, his mind reeling from the sight. The things following the monks, the smallest of them bigger than any man, all built with fantastically strong legs, short but powerful arms, both sporting massive claws which looked to be able to tear any man in half with but the merest gesture, caught his attention as nothing in his life ever had. Their tiny yellow eyes revealed no trace of intelligence except the meanest, most primitive sort.

They were impossible creatures, horrors resembling nothing less than dinosaurs. But they were not extinct, they were alive. Living, snarling, drooling engines of destruction, being lead into the most glittering palace within which the privileged rich of the city had gathered to play.

"Mr. Wentworth, sir," said the Sikh softly, "they mean to ascend. Miss Nita is up there."

"Yes, quite," answered the man in the back. Oddly enough, his voice had actually changed in timbre to the point where someone listening in on the conversation in the car would swear there must be three people within the vehicle. And, to all intents and purposes, they would have been correct for the first person to whom the driver had spoken had effectively disappeared— transformed from playboy Richard Wentworth into the mysterious entity known as the *Spider*!

"Best I do something about that, don't you think?"

Several days earlier, Wentworth had received a most disturbing letter, disturbing because it was not meant for him, or at least for his persona of a dashing financier and entrepreneur, but for his true self—the *Spider*. It had warned him that something terrible might happen at the Riverview, something of unimaginable, apocalyptic proportions. Never one to take chances, the city's defender had positioned men on rooftops around the area, and on the ground as well, to watch for anything untoward which might approach the hotel that evening. He had taken the watch position in the garage for the letter had made a final warning that if evil did approach, that it would do so from below.

In truth, the *Spider* should have been more concerned about the fact that someone seemed to have pierced his most important secret, but such a thought scarcely entered his mind. Instead, from the first moment his hands had touched the letter, his only thought had been to prepare for the suggested threat. Somehow, the mere event of his eyes scanning the hand-written page had urged him to immediate action. Something about the missive, the feel of the paper, the shape of the letters upon it—something had convinced him at once that it was genuine in all its aspects.

The first thing he had done was to invite his friend police commissioner Kirkpatrick to join his party at the soiree being held to unveil the Olmec head and christen the Riverview. The official's presence would mean heightened police security. Next he arranged for a battery of his own men to be in place. At that point, making certain some fifty to sixty armed and trained professionals would be watching for the slightest hint of trouble would be enough for most men—but not the *Spider*.

Throwing himself to work in his hidden design shop, he worked feverishly to make certain all his weapons were in perfect working order. His favorite .45 automatics were broken down, cleaned and oiled. New springs were fit into all his spare clips. His *Spider* Web, the gossamer line with the strength of a ship's hawser was tested to the breaking point, as if the fate of the world might depend upon it. Even his rarely used pistol, the Weblee, was brought forth, stripped apart, rethought, retinkered, until even it was far superior to its former self.

During the days between the arrival of the letter and the evening when the Olmec head would be unveiled, the *Spider* worked at a fever pitch, honing both his weapons and his body to previously unheard of levels. Both his beautiful fiancée and his faithful man servant worried over his sudden zeal, as well as his complete ignoring of the letter which had set off his sudden regiment of refurbishing and self-improvement. Finally, when confronted by the pair of them while working out on the heavy bag in his private gymnasium, the defender of the city stopped for a moment, telling them:

"Nita, Ram Singh, please don't think I'm not touched by your loyal concern. But, if ever you have trusted my instincts, I'm asking you to do so now. I can't explain this feeling in my gut, but something tells me I'm in for the greatest fight of my life, something beyond all understanding. Tell me you can do that, that I can count on you both as I always have."

Of course both of them said they would do anything they could to help him. In those troubled times, many cities had men and women who had stepped forward to protect the weak and the unsuspecting, but none had found themselves a champion, a hero, like the *Spider*. He had, for years, often been the only thing standing between the innocent and the forces of overwhelming villainy. If that special sense of his which told him danger was coming was warning him once again that evil was afoot, then they had no choice but to believe him, and to stand by him as they always had.

When he had asked them to do so, however, the *Spider* had not considered the possibility that what they would be facing would be demonic horrors that for all he knew might have stepped outward through the gates of Hell to threaten his city. Sitting in the back seat of his roadster, gloved hand on the door release, he hesitated for an instant, his eyes staring outward. The small part of his mind that still reacted as any man's would, screamed within his brain pointing out the obvious.

You idiot, those are monsters. Do you understand? Monsters! You've fought bad men of all types—bad men—but this is something different. Something beyond you. How can you expect to beat something like that?

And then, for a moment, it was Richard Wentworth staring out from behind the *Spider's* mask, Richard Wentworth looking out upon the sight of a swarming horde of gigantic lizard-like horrors, and his blood ran cold. He had thrown himself against entire armies of men, men armed with every possible weapon, and he had always emerged victorious. But this, this was something beyond any man's ability to combat. This was no human foe, perhaps not even an earthly one. How was one man supposed to deal with anything like that which he saw before him?

And, just as quickly as the alien thought had entered his mind, it was banished. The mere man known as Richard Wentworth was shoved back into the safety of the recesses within his mind, and the *Spider* threw open the Daimler's door. With calculated abandon, he leaped out of the roadster and strode across the massive freight delivery bay, heading straight for the monks and their creatures.

There was nothing subtle or strategic about his approach. Reaching a halfway point between himself and his targets, knowing the elevator would have to arrive soon, the *Spider* pulled forth one of his .45's in one hand, his Weblee in the other, and then stopped, threw back his head, and laughed.

It was a harsh, metallic, damning laughter, and it caught the attention of all three of the monks instantly. As the figures wheeled about, the *Spider* leveled his .45 and emptied it into the head of the closest of their monsters. The thing went down hard, its meaty head slamming against the ground hard enough to crack its skull. The masked avenger smiled, relieved to see that his lead could find blood and dispatch even the terrible foes before him. As one of the other reptiles began to turn in his direction, he let loose a barrage from his Weblee. The newly retooled weapon released a length of his chemically treated Web, the mass of it encircling the head and one of the arms of the second beast.

The *Spider* pulled forth a second .45 and targeted the head of a third monster even as the elevator door finally opened. Firing, he screamed out his challenge to the monks:

"Face me, you fiends. You'll not reach whatever it is you desire, for my desires trump yours—my desire to see you in Hell!"

A third of the dinosaur-like creatures crashed to the concrete floor, bleeding and thrashing and screaming its pain in a terrible voice. For their part, the monks seemed to ignore the *Spider*, coolly concentrating on their work, instead. With astonishing indifference, they herded the majority of their monsters inside the elevator, leaving three behind. Then, taking their hand-held incense burners inside with them, the trio made to leave the loading bay.

Rapidly jamming another round into his Weblee, the *Spider* fired, not at one of their beasts, but at one of the monks. With his typical skill, he caught the robed figure mid-torso, gluing it to the wall next to the elevator. Leveling his reloaded .45, he made to shoot the other two, but they stepped behind their beasts, allowing the massive flesh of the monsters to absorb the lead meant for them. And then, the elevator door closed, leaving the *Spider* alone with the trio of slavering creatures.

And, as on the steamer, released from proximity to the monks' incense, the reptiles began to rapidly come back to their more natural state. As the *Spider* rapidly emptied a clip into the head of one of the creatures, the other two came back to their senses and charged forward. The *Spider*, realizing he would be able to stop one of them, but in doing so leave himself exposed to the other, threw himself into the depths of the loading bay, racing for the area where the night's guests had parked their vehicles.

Running in between the rows of pricey sports cars and limousines, the *Spider* hoped a quick turn would lose his far more ponderous opponents. Sadly, despite their great size and weight, the creatures proved to be incredibly agile, making a following turn with ease. The masked avenger continued to use the tactic, however, noting that although the maneuver did not allow him to lose the monsters, still it did slow them a bit each time he used it. The creatures also could not follow him in between the cars, but rather had to race over the tops of them.

With each step the *Spider* began to gain ground as the horrors' claws dug into the hoods, trunks and roofs of the vehicles over which they traveled. Each time one did, the seconds it took for the monsters to extract their tangled limb gave the *Spider* another moment's breathing time. His disadvantage was the relatively small area of the parking space within the bay. His advantage, however, was that of surprise. Making a full circle, the Master of Men reached the open area of the bay and then stood his ground, waiting for the monsters to catch up to him.

The demonic reptiles came charging across the tops of the last cars, sliding and stumbling in their haste to reach the *Spider*. His weapons held at his sides, the masked avenger waited grimly, his eyes staring straight ahead, watching the creatures' progress. He made no motion to defend himself, instead simply standing and waiting, luring the monsters back into the open area of the bay. For their part, the creatures were most obliging, charging down over the hoods of the last vehicles, racing straight for the *Spider*, until suddenly a piercing bellow caught their attention.

As the horrors turned their massive heads, from the sidelines came Richard Wentworth's sleek roadster, horn blaring non-stop. Without pause or delay, Ram Singh drove the Daimler directly into the creatures, shattering it against the legs of the first. His head slamming against the steering wheel, the Sikh was knocked momentarily unconscious. Unfortunately, his valiant effort had only accomplished half of what it was meant to do.

Much to the *Spider*'s surprise, the second reptile had gone completely untouched. Also, it recovered its senses with an amazing speed, and without hesitation charged forward once more. The *Spider* raised his .45 and drove bullet after bullet into the creature's closing body, but he could not do enough damage to slay, or even slow the colossal beast. Out of ammunition, he made to throw himself to the side, but even as he began the move, he sensed the terrible thing had somehow read his intentions and was following him, its taloned arms reaching, closing on him—

And then, at that moment, a great explosion of light and heat went off seemingly throughout the entire bay. The *Spider* was thrown by the blast, as was the beast straining to catch him. The two were slammed one against the other, both rolling to a stop on the cold concrete floor. The *Spider*, stunned but otherwise unharmed, found himself encumbered by the body of the monster. He frantically pushed at it, straining his great shoulders to roll the thing off his leg, until he noted that the beast's head had been completely sheered away.

But, even as relief flooded his body, his mind still working to calm itself after the unbelievable things it had witnessed, his ears caught hint of something else moving within the loading bay. Instantly the avenger realized he was hearing unhurried footsteps headed in his direction. Swiftly, he thrust his hand beneath his cloak and fished out another clip. Jamming it into the .45 in his hand, he got it lined up on the figure approaching him, even as a voice said:

"I've seen to your man. Glad to see you got my note, Mr. Wentworth."

It was only moments later that the *Spider* and Professor Guicet found themselves riding the service elevator upward in a desperate attempt to over-take the monks and their monsters. With some sixty floors still to go, the *Spider* demanded:

"I'm grateful for your assistance, but you'll understand if I'm insistent—tell me now; how did you know how to find me?"

"I also watch over this city," answered the professor gravely. "And a great deal more. But the menaces I've been charged to safeguard humanity from are of a different sort than you've chosen to battle."

"Indeed?"

"Oh, yes; quite so," responded Guicet. "The supernatural is my domain. The weird, the bizarre, the occult. And just as the city rarely learns the whole truth of how much the *Spider* does for it, so too does it serve me best they not learn of my work."

"Still, you haven't answered me—how did you learn what you did of me?"

"I had to," came the older man's response. "When the discovery of the Olmec head was brought to my attention, of its being brought to America, to this very city, I knew I could not defend it alone—no; not by myself ...," the older man's voice trailed off for a moment, a sound like fear whispering in along the sides of his voice as he added:

"Not from the cult of Set."

At that moment the elevator stopped at the fortieth floor, the highest to which it rose. Immediately the pair exited to switch to a second car, one designed to take passengers the rest of the way to the top of the building. Their hope, of course, was to catch up to the freight elevator and its passengers before they could complete their own transfer. But, the pair of avengers were too late, seeing the others' door closing just as theirs was opening. Rushing into the hall, instantly depressing the call button for their elevator, the *Spider*'s mind divided itself.

On the one hand, his simple, surface attention was grateful the Riverside had been built with the latest in elevator features, push button controls which left the cars pilot-free. That had certainly saved at least two lives which would have been lost in the freight elevators. Beyond that, the part of him that was classically trained recognized the reference to the cult of Set, a faction which dated back to the days of ancient Egypt and beyond. Still another part of his mind told him to cease badgering Guicet about the particulars of learning his identity, and to concentrate of what was about to happen. Every part of him felt a supreme confidence that the professor was a man to be trusted. There was simply something about him that radiated his good intentions.

Besides, thought the *Spider, if he means me some sort of harm, he certainly has a strange way of bringing it to me.*

"Millions of years ago, long before the time of the dinosaurs, the serpent men of Set walked the Earth."

"Serpent men," exclaimed the *Spider.* "You mean those lizards?"

"No, I mean their masters. In the robes, those aren't any kind of monks you've ever known. They aren't human at all, but a species of bipedal reptiles. At one time they controlled a vast empire which spanned across Europe and most of Africa."

As the new elevator came in response to their call, the two men quickly entered it and pressed for the ballroom floor, their conversation never lapsing for a moment.

"Some great calamity fell over them, however, and their great kingdom was thrown into ruin. There are those that say the dinosaurs are creatures which evolved from the serpent men themselves. Be that as it may, you must understand them. On the one hand they have little use for our machinery or technology, which gives us some advantage, but on the other, they are a race of supremely skilled magicians and poisoners. Capable of remaining hidden from humanity for millennia at a time, they only come forth when the timing is right for them to attempt once more to reach their ultimate goal."

"Which is ..."

"The subjugation of humanity. The extermination or at least the enslavement of our entire race."

The floors were passing one after another. On one level, the *Spider* felt their ascension was disastrously slow. On the other, however, a part of him feared they were dreadfully rapid. Even his perfect mind was having trouble comprehending everything he was being asked to accept and he was beginning to lose grip of his mental balance. It had only been a handful of minutes, actually, since he had first watched the procession of the monks and their creatures cross the freight bay. Now, as Guicet spoke, it was just beginning to dawn on him what he had seen. What he had fought. What had almost taken his head from its shoulders with its terrible jaws.

"I've been able to divine that there is something sinisterly supernatural about the antique ruin on display above us, but it wasn't until I learned of the serpent men's interest in it that I became truly worried. I knew any attempt to seize the head would be launched on two levels—within the physical world and the one beyond. Hoping I could handle the latter, I made to enlist your aid in halting their progress through the former."

The ideas put before him staggered the *Spider*. A vast conspiracy of inhuman monsters, poised to take over the world with some artifact from beyond. Rational, thinking creatures whose existence predated the dinosaurs, that built continent spanning kingdoms before man was even a whisper in the image of life, it was a staggering notion. But, not one more shocking than the idea that these creatures still lived, still controlled actual magic, and that they were about to use such sorceries to attempt to cleanse the world of mankind.

"Spider," asked Guicet, "are you all right?"

He was being asked to combat living dinosaurs and their reptilian, magician masters. But, his mind asked him, what exactly could he do against *magic?*

"Wentworth, we're almost to the ballroom."

Time splitting itself down into micro-seconds, the *Spider* looked out over the world if he did not fight, if he did not triumph. All he knew, swept away. All the great works of man, all his progress, all his noble aspirations—gone. Overnight.

Yes, he thought, man was no perfect creature. The *Spider* had known far too many men, and women, who deserved to be swept into the ashbin of history, but not everyone. For every tyrant there was a saint, for every opium den there stood a house of worship, for every gangster an honest cop.

"It's not a perfect world," answered the *Spider* finally, the elevator a single floor from the ballroom, "but it's ours. Let's make certain we get to keep it."

And with those words, the steel door slid open on a nightmare of chaos. The freight elevator had already disgorged its occupants who were racing through the ballroom, heading straight for the Olmec head.

"Concentrate on the serpent men," shouted Guicet over the cacophony of noise crashing against them. "Nothing else matters!"

Beyond the elevator all was madness. The great creatures of the monks had poured out into the ballroom and were causing a hideous carnage. Released from the calming effects of the vapors, they charged about wildly, attacking anything that moved. Tuxedoed arms and bejeweled heads were torn loose at random.

The police, both uniformed and plainclothes, stationed about not only because of the commissioner's presence but also because of the "who's who" guest list of the rich and famous in attendance, were stunned for a moment, but soon found their weapons and began firing upon the monsters. Most of their shots struck the dinosaurs in the body, however, doing minimal damage to the primitive creatures. The monks were ignored by the officers, barely noticed considering the more immediate threat, which the *Spider* knew had to be the robed figures' plan all along.

Assessing the entire scene in but a moment, the Master of Men followed Guicet out of the elevator and into the fray. Part of his brain knew, of course, that any of the police officers might take notice of him and turn their weapons on him, but it was a chance he had to take. There was no telling what kind of sinister power the Olmec head held, but he knew it was his duty to make certain it did not fall into the wrong hands.

Racing across the ballroom, the *Spider* moved up onto the table tops, using the clear field to make his way through the strangle of people jamming up against each other in their mindless panic. Again, at least a part of his mind knew he was exposing himself to greater risk, but he was not the sort of man who worried about such things. He had only one goal, to stop the fiends in the brown robes.

Almost finding himself with a clear shot at one of them, he was suddenly interrupted as one of the towering reptiles leaped upward onto the tables next in front of him and cut off his forward assault. In a blinding motion the horror swung its great head around, snapping for the *Spider*'s. With equal speed, however, the masked avenger brought both his .45s around and fired directly into the creature's mouth, blowing what little brains it had out the back of its head.

At the same moment, a blinding white and blue flash like the one which had saved him in the basement went off, and the *Spider* saw one of the berobed figures blaze out of existence. Guicet had stopped one of their main targets. As the dinosaur he had just slain fell backwards, smashing into a massive, bamboo bird cage, releasing a flock of mixed birds into the room, the *Spider* noted a second monk only some twenty feet in front of him.

Ignoring everything else, the avenger leaped from the table he was on to the next and then the next, throwing himself through the air in a desperate bid to tackle the figure. His maneuver worked, and he slammed into the monk with force enough to knock over any living thing short of a rhinoceros. He was amazed to discover that it was just barely enough to knock down his target. That was not the end of his amazement.

As he leapt to his feet, his gloved hand caught hold of his foe's robe and pulled. It was an automatic gesture, an unconscious desire to see the menace beneath with his own eyes. What he saw froze the *Spider* momentarily in his tracks. Supple was the thing he found, hairless and covered with scales and cold to the touch. Its ophidian head stared at him, its eyes and nostrils, slithering tongue and great slit mouth all reptilian and frightening in a way that seized the *Spider* in a manner he had never known.

"Human filth," the thing hissed, its voice filled with a loathsome disgust, "you dare touch *me*?"

The thing's words tore through the *Spider*'s brain, dragging him back through the ages, reaching the part of his soul still in touch with his very first ancestors. As he saw the serpent man's hand reaching for him, taloned hand glistening, dripping with what had to be poison, his moment of hesitation was that brought on by countless millions of years of instinct, to avoid these terrible creatures, to fear the reptile world and all its minions, to freeze and hide and run when the hissing terrors showed themselves—

But, it was only a moment.

"The *Spider* dares *anything*."

With calculated deliberation, the masked avenger pulled the triggers of both his weapons, sending twin shots through the mouth of the serpent man and into its brain just as he had the dinosaur seconds earlier. His perfect mind rejecting the fearful instinct of another time, he followed up those shots with two more to the chest, and then two more to the gut. The creature jerked wildly with each contact, finally flopping onto the ground.

But that was the end of the avenger's triumph. Suddenly, all around the ballroom, the noise level quickly began to drop. People stopped screaming, stopped running. Their eyes shrank from wide stares to their normal range. Those severely wounded stopped resisting the call of death and slipped away quietly. Those less severely injured simply sat down in a chair or on the floor and allowed their blood to flow freely.

"There," came a terrible hissing voice, sounding more within the *Spider*'s head than his ears, "that's better."

Straining his eyes in every direction, the *Spider* spotted Guicet, closer to the Olmec head than himself, but no longer making his way toward it. In fact, he seemed like everyone else, not moving, standing in place, all of them seeming as if they were awaiting orders from somebody else.

"I can almost stand your hideous race this way."

And then, the *Spider* suddenly realized that he was not moving, was standing in place, almost as if he too were awaiting orders from somebody else. Moving his eyes once more, he scanned the room in the direction of what little of the hissing voice he was actually hearing with his ears, and then he saw it.

Tall it was, naked with its lashing tail exposed for all to see. It walked forward lithely, sinuously erect on its pre-mammalian members, their harsh nails making a terrible sound as they struck the marble floor.

And then the *Spider* revised his assessment. The thing was not completely naked, for on its head it wore a somewhat conical crown of gold, a thing wrought in the shape of a serpent and encrusted with diamonds. At once the *Spider* knew that the headdress had been that which Guicet had felt was hidden within the Olmec head. How the thing had gotten there, from a civilization on the other side of the world that had vanished millions of years before man arrived on the scene did not matter. How the serpent man had recovered it so quickly, after human experts had failed to find the slightest evidence of anything concealed within the head whatsoever. Nothing mattered, except for the fact that the thing before him had its prize, and that its influence had been immediate and all-powerful.

The *Spider* made to bring his guns to play, but he could not move his arms. Forgetting his left arm, he poured all his force of will into moving his right alone. To just bring it to bear, to turn it at all—a foot, an inch ...

"Where is this ape that defies me so?"

The *Spider* knew the hissing voice meant him, could feel it in his mind as the monster's question raced throughout the minds it was controlling, seeking the only one struggling against it. It's flat head tilted at a comical angle, what appeared to be a serpentine gesture meant to replace a smile, it strolled toward the *Spider*, whispering to the rest of the room:

"Sleep."

The command was obeyed instantaneously. Men and women across the ballroom fell into deep, snoring comas, the remaining few dinosaurs strolling among them, grazing where they liked. As the creature closed the distance between himself and the *Spider*, it said:

"There are always some like you, aren't there? From the halls of the ancients, unto this very day, always some ..."

The thing tilted its head further, its tongue slithering in and out of its mouth as it thought its comments directly into the *Spider*'s head.

"But that ends now. I am the greatest sorcerer my people have ever known, and I have planned this day too carefully." The *Spider* continued to struggle, but to no avail. Horribly, he realized that any plan he might conceive, the serpent man would hear him put together.

"Far too often my kind have gone against yours too early, too quickly. They would not wait until they had learned all they needed to know. I have not made that mistake."

What can I do, wondered the *Spider*, his thoughts tinged with despair. *I have to keep my guns.*

"I have studied and practiced and watched, you cannot believe how many centuries I have extended my existence, waiting for the cobra crown to be discovered once more. Struggle all you want, ape; I rule now. And, if you are having trouble believing me ... well, allow me to show you."

Have to resist, thought the *Spider* desperately. *Can't let this thing take my guns.*

Even as the *Spider* struggled, the serpent man reached out into the city, touching the minds of every single resident of the city. Allowing the *Spider* to join him within those millions of minds, to see through their eyes, the thing commanded them all:

"All of you, walk to the nearest river, throw yourselves in. Do not bother to swim. Simply die."

Instantly, across the city, people began to walk from their homes, leave their cars, swarm up out of the subways, all of them headed for the nearest of the city's rivers. Those driving across the great metropolis' many bridges stopped their cars, walked directly to the edges and flung themselves into the water without hesitation. In horrible dark comedy, the young helped the elderly struggle up over the higher railings. Husbands held babies while their wives made the passage, then returned their children to their mothers so they could leap into the dark water together. Within his mind, the *Spider* saw and heard and felt it all.

Have to do something, he told himself over and over. *Can't let this thing take my guns.*

The serpent man hissed in what the *Spider* could feel through their mind link was a joyous fashion. As they both felt the deaths of those drowning, first by the dozens, soon by the hundreds, the masked avenger actually shook with rage, so great was his concentration, but it availed him nothing. He could not move, could not resist the amplified mind of the monster before him.

His fear of losing his weapons amused the serpent man greatly. So strongly had the *Spider*'s terror built the image of him being stripped of his guns within his mind that the creature could see it clearly, its taloned hands reaching forward, jerking the .45s out of his hands, striking him with them, killing him with them. Tilting its head once more, the serpent man hissed:

"Actually, I believe you have the right idea. Too often in the past the plans of my people have been stopped by things like you. It would be the worse kind of hubris to let you live. That's something only the villains in your pulp novels do, isn't it. Well, *Spider*," the reptile sneered, its tail lashing back and forth:

"This is no pulp novel, *hero*. This is the moment of your death."

Outside, thousands upon thousands walked off of docks, threw themselves from bridges, millions more following. Its mind drunk with the endless steam of human misery, lungs filling with water, water-logged clothing dragging bodies under, the serpent man reached out and grabbed the *Spider*'s weapons just as he had seen within his foe's mind, jerked them sharply, forcing the masked avenger's clenched trigger fingers to close and fire both automatics.

As the serpent man reeled from the two gut shots, the *Spider* immediately dropped the two .45s, reaching for the spares hanging from the back of his belt. He knew those were empty for he always kept track of how many rounds he had fired. He also knew it would take him far less time to bring forth his extra set rather than try to reload those he was holding.

Without hesitation or comment, he brought the twin weapons to bear with lightning speed and fired again, then again and again and again. Bullet after bullet tore through the reptile, splattering organs, tearing muscle, driving gold and diamonds through the serpent man's brain. Taking no chances, the *Spider* emptied his weapons into the monster, then reloaded and emptied those clips as well. By the time he was finished, the cobra crown was a twisted ruin, and the head upon which it had sat had ceased to exist.

By the time the panting, wild-eyed *Spider* ceased firing, many within the ballroom had begun to stir once more. Looking up, he found Guicet approaching him at a run.

"I've instructed a competent looking sergeant to aim for the dinosaur's heads," he said. "I believe it might be a good time for us to take our leave."

The pair headed back to the service elevator, the broken remains of the crown in Guicet's hands. He assured the *Spider* he could dispose of the shattered remains safely enough, and the avenger trusted his words. Quickly the two descended to the basement, readying themselves to simply slide within Wentworth's crumpled Daimler with the recovering Ram Singh. Claiming to be afraid to leave the car with dinosaurs about seemed a convincing enough way to explain their absence. As they exited the elevator and crossed the garage, Guicet said:

"Because of my own studies, I did not fall asleep when the others did, and was able to conceal the fact from the serpent man. But that was all I could do. I must compliment you; your strategy was brilliant."

"It wasn't that much," a now tuxedoed Richard Wentworth told the professor. "You said they didn't like or understand our machines much. The back of my mind reasoned out that they might not know about triggers, or at least not think about them." Opening the door to the rear of the vehicle for Guicet, he added:

"I was counting on its arrogance to allow me to get away with it. I thought I had a reasonably good chance. Knowing it could read my mind, my hope was that while reading so many minds at once, that it would only be worrying about what was on the surface of mine. I gave it what it wanted to find—fear. And that was enough for it." As the two men popped into the back seat, Wentworth added:

"Like Ram Singh here, using the car to plow down that dinosaur, I used the only tool I had at my disposal."

"I am relieved to hear that you understand I had to do what I did, sahib." The *Spider* turned to his man servant, answering:

"Of course, warrior."

"That is good, for I would very much not enjoy having you take the damages out of my salary."

The two men in the back seat stared at each other for a moment, then looked into the Sikh's grinning face and burst into laughter. The merriment was something they needed, and they howled until tears formed in their eyes, and the memory of the last moments of the drowning thousands finally began to fade from within their minds.

illustration by Tom Floyd

Chapter Nine

BLAZING BARRELS
AT THE REICH HOUSE

by JAMES ANTHONY KUHORIC

Blam! Blam! Blam! Blam!

The *Spider*'s twin blazing barrels roared to life. Tiny comets of lead tore through the air like miniature meteor fragments lighting the atmosphere afire with the friction of cosmic re-entry. Their impacts left golf ball sized holes in the concrete wall of the bank in a wide arcing pattern directly over the heads of two ghoulish figures hunched in the shadows.

"Cripes, Vinny! It's him, it's da *Spider*!" the smaller of the two hoods cried out with a wavering high pitched voice. Dropping a small snub nosed pistol to the ground, the thug threw his hands up in the universal sign for surrender.

His partner in crime, a bullish figure with a balding crown that resembled a caveman more than a petty thief, wasn't as frightened of the specter stalking them. Roaring a sub-human cry he whirled toward the source of the oncoming gunfire raising a large drum machine gun in two beefy hands. The gun bucked with a life of its own, saturating the air with hot lead and raining a hail of destructive fire through the bank lobby.

Shell casings refracted in the night, sparking like fat water droplets loosed from a lazy hose stream. One lazy casing rolled to a stop at the *Spider*'s boot. He stared at it for a moment as the oaf with the tumbler fired this final salvo into the banker's office. The *Spider* sneered with palpable revulsion, revealing a hint of the vampiric fangs he used to inspire such fear in his prey. These two would be easy work, a warm up before the evening's real festivities would begin. With that thought he began to laugh loudly into the night. A deep raspy roar devoid of humor and full of righteous anger. It was the laugh of the *Spider*.

His breath coming in deep rasps, Vincent "Vinny" Ancehnzo held the trigger of his machine gun depressed for long seconds after the ammunition was depleted. His face was pale, drawn, like someone that had just seen a vision of their own impending doom. The laughter that he heard was like something from beyond the grave. A harbinger of an otherworldly apparition that had targeted his soul to feed upon. It made his knees weak and drained the strength from his simian arms. He'd never felt this powerless in a lifetime of bullying and petty crime. Until now.

From the darkness in the bank lobby he saw a solitary shadow move. Slowly at first. Carefully. With practiced precision, he crept forward, looking like an apparition born from the very maws of hell. As the *Spider* materialized in front of the terror-stricken eyes of the two criminals they could only cower. On the right hand of the approaching phantasm a small pinpoint of red light glowed ominously. It was the mark of the *Spider*, the last thing they'd see before the twin 45s would send a dozen fiery shards fatally ripping through them.

Police sirens wailed in the distance. "Right on time," the *Spider* chuckled as he ducked into the waiting car. "Quickly, Ram Singh, we must collect Ms. Van Sloan and arrive at our appointment with the President."

"As you wish, Sahib," Ram virtually sang in his deeply Indian accented baritone. In a few short minutes they were in route to the biggest celebration of the century. A private party at the White House for the movers and shakers of industry thrown to celebrate the end of World War II only a few short days ago. Millionaire entrepreneur Richard Wentworth was on the short invitation-only list and he intended to be on time.

Far above the unsuspecting vehicle, circling at virtually orbital altitudes, two dozen futuristically metal-clad storm troopers shifted anxiously in their flight harnesses aboard the stealth zeppelin, Iron Eagle. The ship was regal as airships went, with a steel colored exterior and the characteristic streamline of German engineered flying machines. Her hull was deep red and sported an intimidating swastika that seemed to add weight to the already substantial mass of the ship. Those crooked cross bars had come to symbolize evil every bit as much as the very devil himself, only this villain was ever present and in every home as a weary nation watched, worried, and listened. Satan made tangible in millions of homes every night on the radio. As each trooper double and triple checked the bulky alien looking gear they wore aboard the Eagle, they scowled at the incoming radio transmissions. The world was celebrating the death of Hitler and the downfall of the Third Reich. It seemed that the Americans believed their "just cause" was rewarded and that their Yankee cowboy attitudes would influence and shape the entire old world. They may have won a victory but the war was hardly over. The Nazi Sky Troopers would soon see to that.

Inside the palatial White House ballroom Wentworth strode with his head high and a hundred dollar shine on his perfectly manicured smile. And why not smile? He had the lovely Ms. Nita Van Sloan on his right arm. Nita always was the pearl among a sea of petty baubles wherever she went. Her slim figure radiated sensuality like heat from a star beneath the trappings of a low necked crimson gown. Every male eye in the room was drawn to her like a moth to a flame greedily seeking to make her light their own. She took it in with a grace that few could manage and even fewer could pull off.

As the two were seated centrally to the large Presidential podium in the northern annex of the room, the catering crew began to distribute glasses and champagne for the inevitable victory toast to come. Wentworth's spine tingled as a glass was set in front of him and the foodstuffs employee moved to the next table. Something about the waiter wasn't right but he couldn't quite put his finger on it. The man seemed normal enough on the exterior. He was European with stark blonde hair that was meticulously groomed. Wearing a white suit jacket with red lapel and scarf, he seemed a normal picture of the modern Maitre'D. But still…there was something gnawing at him, something the *Spider* would sense and react to. Yes, something was very wrong. He was sure of it.

As the last of the guests were seated, a deep hush fell over the assembled men and women of privilege as the lights were dimmed to virtually subterranean levels. The gloom was short lived as spotlights illuminated the pedestal where President Truman would soon appear to kick off the festivities. As a hundred pairs of eager eyes watched, a white clad caterer walked stiffly toward the illuminated podium. He must be the head or owner of the foodstuffs company to have the honor of introducing the president. For though he wore a similar white coat and red scarf of the serving men, he also had a large white fedora with a red band that enveloped his head and hid his features beneath a wide brim pulled low. Only the glint of his waxy jaw line with a steely straight pair of lips and a strong chin were clearly visible from below the expanse of the hat. His footfalls echoed off the floor with a metallic resonance that seemed out of place on the polished hard wood floors of the ballroom. The strange stiff legged march ended just a few feet short of the podium where he made a series of strange hand gestures to the crowd before leaning in to the microphone.

President Truman was ready for his entrance and began his trip toward the podium. Two burly marines flanked him as he made his way across the pre-arranged route to the podium where he would address the collected heads of industry. Stepping in front of the President, his two personal guards looked perplexed by the unforeseen appearance of the man at the podium. Knowing this was not part of the scheduled plans they signaled to the sentries at the exits who quickly secured the doors and turned back for orders. They raised their rifles tentatively from beneath perplexed glances hoping they were not making a mistake and fast tracking their upcoming duties to the mess hall instead of the cushy Presidential defense detail. But what could one unarmed caterer hope to accomplish by waylaying the President's speech?

Leaning in close to Nita's ear, Wentworth made his move. "Something's wrong," Wentworth whispered urgently. "This is a good time to take a trip to the lady's lavatory." Nita didn't like that "suggestion" one bit. She was a dame of action and if there was going to be trouble she wanted to be there to dish out a little of her own brand of justice. Turning to express her dissatisfaction with the idea, Wentworth silenced her with the intensity of his glare. This was the part of Richard "Dick" Wentworth she secretly loved. The fierce inner fire and underlying fervor was exhilarating and, quite frankly, a little frightening. In one graceful move she rose and quickly started across the floor in the midst of the unfolding drama.

Wentworth only watched for a moment then turned his attention back to the strange events in the banquet hall. With Nita safe for the moment, he could focus on the events unfolding and making his move.

Without warning, a woman screamed. The sound electrified the room like the harsh blare of a police siren slicing through the silence of the night. As she did, chaos erupted in the dining hall. Tables were abruptly overturned, sending fine silver and expensive china plates into the air momentarily and then crashing to the ground in a glass storm of destruction. The caterers, as if responding to the will of the strange leader, tore large metal tubular objects from the cart frames. Pointing them ominously toward the ranks of soldiers, the roar of gunfire erupted, sending a spray of bullets into the stunned men. Somehow these intruders had designed machine guns into the very skeleton of the serving trays they manned. Abruptly guests dove for cover like pin balls violently launched from a spring, and a deadly barrage of gunfire struck down the men in uniform at the exits. With equal precision, the President's guards pushed the leader of the free world to the floor clear of the zinging bullets and unloaded their own weapons into the attackers. In the cacophony of violence Wentworth struck, his fist hammering the nearest Maitre'D with a pile-driving blow that snapped the thug's arm at the elbow sending his weapon flying uselessly to the ground. With relentless ferocity he struck again, and again, and again, until the man was an unmoving bloody pulp. Had anyone been watching him in the melee they would have seen the soul of the *Spider* laid bare before them. Wiping the speckled blood from his face, Wentworth reflected momentarily on how lucky he had been to have this slip of his "other face" overlooked by the otherwise occupied presidential guests.

When the smoke cleared both the soldiers and imposter caterers lay dead or wounded amid a sea of frightened dignitaries. Wentworth's attention was focused on the strange waxen man at the podium stood stark still. Unmoving and statuesque, he watched the scene unfold.

Over the discord in the White House, the clouds broke momentarily revealing the presence of the Iron Eagle far above like a bird of prey waiting for the perfect moment to strike. From beneath the undercarriage of the mighty air beast came a procession of four large silver figures to earth like an unexpected spring sleet storm. Without warning, plumes of fire erupted from each of the plummeting bodies, suddenly changing their trajectory into tiny shooting stars dive-bombing with dark intent toward the capital below. Within seconds the first of the rocketing storm troopers hit the roof like a meteor and blasted a hole through it! Plaster, wood, and steel exploded into the banquet hall sending tuxedoed men and gowned women scattering like fish in a barrel. Flying down on a trail of fire like a demon from the netherworld, the first of three armored thugs landed among the frightened dignitaries.

As the first troopers broke through the ceiling, Wentworth was already in motion. He didn't know what was going on here, but it was obvious from the swastikas painted boldly on these alien robots that the war wasn't as over as everyone thought. Diving headfirst into an acrobatic roll he snatched a service pistol from a downed security guard. It was awkward compared to the perfectly weighted irons he toted as his underworld persona, but it would do. He had lamented leaving his own guns in the car, but security was tight and there was no satisfactory excuse to get firearms into the White House. Making a mental note, he decided that if he got out of this mess alive he'd have to investigate designing pistols that could be hidden in the frame of a briefcase. If Nazi infiltrators could engineer such a marvel, so could the *Spider*.

For now, there were simply too many people and potential bystanders here in the room. And where was the President? Things could get real ugly quickly if he didn't act. For the moment, he had to get clear of this mess if the *Spider* was going to be able to do anything. Scrambling through the coat room doors while the commotion was at its peak, he found just what he was looking for. Amidst the classy wraps and coats of the movers and shakers he found his full length black overcoat and hat. Reaching into a large hidden interior pocket he pulled the mask, wig, and sharp teeth, trademarks of the *Spider*, and put them on. The *Spider* would soon be making an appearance in this madhouse. Now he just needed to find an edge.

In the women's lavatory Nita Van Sloan was battered by the concussion of the exploding roof of the restroom. The fourth of the Nazi sky troopers, apparently off course from the main banquet hall, obliterated the ceiling and left a four foot crater where the leftmost toilet had been only minutes before. Water pattered down from busted overhead pipes and sent a fine mist of spray over the destruction like a cleansing rain after a deep dry spell. Being around Dick, she was used to seeing crazy things – murderous thugs, spectral minions, and even mad scientists seemed common place in her life. But now one of those insane visions was here in front of her and he was off playing Peter Pan, leaving Wendy left to face Captain Hook alone in high heels and an evening gown. Typical…just typical.

The armored sky soldier seemed momentarily disoriented, stunned from his explosive entrance to the women's lavatory. Part of his strange flight pack was sparking and sending up a small trail of smoke. Nita's hand closed over a thick copper pipe that had been severed from the overhead destruction – it felt good in her hand, heavy, substantial and cool in her hot palm. It was a reassuring weight in the face of an insane situation.

The trooper was getting his bearings now and seemed to realize where his trajectory error had been. On his feet and waddling toward the exit like a six foot tall metal cased penguin bristling with weapons, he was taken by surprise when a copper pipe whistled through the air and connected with his chin just under the strap that kept his helmet secured. With a sickening thunk that sounded like a meat tenderizer pounding out the gristle of a tough steak, the makeshift cudgel knocked the trooper senseless sending several capped teeth flying out to scatter upon the polished pearl. Nita had a vividly morbid vision of an exuberant child playing a game of jacks with molars and bicuspids at the sight of the uprooted teeth. With a loud clank he hit the ground face-first, unconscious. Nita stepped back and brushed a stray lock of hair from her face as she stared at the alien contraption encasing the fallen Nazi in front of her. "Well...that'll teach you for peeking in on a gal in the powder room."

From his position just inside the vast hall of the presidential coatroom, The *Spider* bristled, his anger growing into the fire that fueled the violent justice the Spider would soon unleash. Two of the sky soldiers helped the awkwardly moving man behind the podium while the third kept the dignitaries pinned down with a particularly wicked looking high caliber machine gun. On the stage, the wide brimmed hat worn by the caterer was suddenly thrown back to reveal a familiar ghostly waxen face staring blindly forward. This was a face every theatre visiting man, woman, and child recognized from the Saturday matinees where newsreels of the horrors unfolding across Europe were brought into their daily lives. It was the unmistakable face of Adolf Hitler!

But how could that be? Hitler was dead. The war was over. Wasn't it?

The *Spider* knew something was unbelievably surreal about this entire scenario. Everything about it was wrong. Hitler wasn't that tall or bulky and he had behavior ticks that everyone knew. This man displayed none of them. And the face...the face was so rigid and molded. Like something from a sideshow museum not real life.

As he watched, the figure stiffly moved forward speaking toward the microphone on the podium. But the voice emanating from the figure didn't seem to reach the mike quite right. It seemed to be coming from his chest, not the unmoving lips from the etched steel mouth. And something else. His lips were not moving at all. Now that the *Spider* watched more closely, he realized the man's eyes were unblinking too. The face was a frozen mockery of life.

"You thought that the war was over, that you had defeated the Fatherland," the odd Hitler effigy said, his voice muted from beneath the microphone. He paused then, building the tension in the room to the point of explosion. "You were wrong!" he screamed. The force of his statement buffeted people from their prone positions on the floor as if his will had a tangible force of its own. The waxen face seemed to deepen in ominous shadow as he leaned forward. Displaced hair fell over his eyes and the flickering light deepened the hallow beneath his lip where the distinctive mustache furled. "I have learned from your examples in Nagasaki and Hiroshima and have brought that very example to your shores. A single blow must destroy our enemies without regard for losses. A gigantic all destroying blow…like this. The President and White House are ours as is all of America!" he bellowed with his whole body convulsing from the effort of the exclamation.

The *Spider* had seen enough. This mockery could not exist, not if he had anything to say about it. Lifting his borrowed service revolver, he carefully aimed at his targets. Seven bogies and eight bullets. Very little margin for error. But he didn't need much. Looking again to the sky through the shattered remnants of the ceiling he saw the looming zeppelin blocking out the moonlight on this deep velvet overcast night. The blackness of the sky comforted him. The *Spider* worked best in the dark and this would buy him the edge he needed.

Firing in rapid succession, hot lead annihilated the only remaining light fixtures in the room, obliterating them like a hail of shrapnel from an exploding grenade. The *Spider* kept firing until the last light exploded sending the room into pitch blackness. The last bullet hit something in the dark with a sickening muddy "twack" and then frightened screaming began. All at once the terrified party guests let out howls of fear and frustration. Before the first note had registered, the *Spider* was on the move grabbing up a huge kitchen kukri from the wreckage as he plunged into the darkness of the room. Pouncing upon the first Nazi Sky Trooper he struck. The slow moving armored soldier was exactly where he remembered, and the knife sank deep into the flesh of its target. Three large clear tubes that protruded from the shoulder harness of the flight pack erupted sending a spray of rocket fuel down the armored torso of the stunned trooper. Before anyone could react, the *Spider* was on the pair of Nazi sky soldiers near the podium slicing and cutting the fuel tubes on the two remaining villains.

As the *Spider* severed the last of the Advance Guard's fuel lines, the Iron Eagle cleared the moon sending a ray of clear illumination into the room, giving the first Nazi soldier a perfect line of sight through the ballroom directly to his location. Drawing up a bristling weapons array, the soldier sneered overconfidently as his eyes locked with the *Spider*. The Fuehrer would reward him well for this. With the pulling of the trigger he thought his place in the new world order was assured. He was wrong.

With a barely audible "click," the depression of the trigger doomed the Nazi soldiers. As the bullets sought the *Spider's* exposed flesh they lit the severed spewing fuel lines of his fellow Nazis jetpacks aflame creating an instant inferno that enveloped them completely. The two soldiers were engulfed in twin bright blazing fireballs that singed the *Spider's* cloak as he skidded out of harm's way. The shooter only had a fraction of a second to regret his action as a hot shell casing ignited his own spraying fuel supply, turning his dreams of reward into a blazing funeral pyre. He let out a brief scream before the fire stole the air from his lungs burning him externally and internally simultaneously.

The few dignitaries who dared raise their heads from the rubble-strewn floor shook in terror at the inhuman sight. As they watched the men die, it was both the horror of the burning figures and the haunting laughter that came from the podium where the *Spider* stood, his head thrown back in a primal screaming laugh that froze them in their spots. This was the fear that the under-world denizens knew all too well. The sheer terror induced by the inhuman laughter of an enemy sent straight from hell to dole out the devil's own justice, fire and brimstone style.

The *Spider* breathed heavily as the scenario played out. That couldn't have gone better. His plan was desperate but worked perfectly. As he scanned the room for the Hitler look alike, he started. High above a loud fwoosh of fire heralded the second phase of this unimaginable invasion. A line of sky troopers were just launching from the under belly of the Iron Eagle. This was what they planned all along. An advance guard to secure the room and then force the president to watch their display of power as a platoon of Sky troopers would parade into the White House and secure the capital with theatrical intimidation. It was the way the Nazis eroded the fighting spirit of their victims in Europe. It was Hitler's "all destroying blow" to the morale of the free world.

"*Spider*, take this!" a voice called from beneath a large slab of ceiling rubble. Turning toward the voice he saw President Truman partially buried in rubble and throwing something large in his direction. Twirling end over end, the service rifle landed smoothly in the *Spider*'s hands. In one fluid move, Wentworth turned the weapon skyward and took aim. The Sky soldiers numbered at least twenty now and their flight path was taking them directly toward the White House. With one ammunition clip he had no chance of taking out the entire parade of incoming soldiers. Unless...

His hatred boiling over like molten steel spewing from a foundry, the *Spider* opened fire, releasing a torrent of inhuman glee as the bullets erupted from the muzzle. High above the White House, the Iron Eagle stood out starkly silhouetted against the glowing trails of fire each Sky soldier emitted from their jetpacks. As the first of the slugs hit the giant hydrogen sky ship, the air in the room was collectively sucked out by a massive explosion high above. The Iron Eagle exploded with the force and concussion of a three ton bomb. Glowing like a miniature sun the Eagle plumed into a fireball the size of a skyscraper. Fire engulfed all of the flying Sky soldiers turning them into tiny screaming comets plummeting toward the ground.

Everyone in the ballroom was thrown to the floor by the force of the multiple explosions. The *Spider* was no exception. He felt the heat and smoke everywhere, making him question whether he was still alive or had died and gone to hell.

Movement caught his eye drawing him back to the here and now. Nearby on the ground he saw the Hitler automaton jerking spasmodically like a seizure patient from its prone position on the floor. Getting to his feet, the *Spider* examined the fallen figure closely. The waxen face was partially melted and a large round hole between the eyes marked the location of the *Spider*'s last pistol shot that began the melee. Sparking and burning bright, the internal mechanical systems of the robot were completely ruined. Whatever this thing was meant to be, it wasn't human and wasn't Hitler. At least not the real one.

Coming from the remnants of the women's lavatory, Nita Van Sloan walked shakily into the devastation of the ballroom. She was battered and bruised – flustered and befuddled. Still holding the metal pipe from the restroom she limped on one broken heel into the war ravaged room. Her eyes caught for a second on the form of the *Spider* as he planted his signature ring mark deeply into the wax head of the faux Fuehrer.

Wentworth, as the *Spider*, could feel the evening's events catching up with him. He only had a few minutes to make the *Spider* disappear before the White House guards burst into the room and would find a masked vigilante within reach of the President. It only took one over zealous soldier with an itchy trigger finger to put a dreadful end on this crazy night. President Truman was safe and the Nazi invaders were thwarted. It was time for the *Spider* to fade into the darkness. While the frightened guests watched the remnants of the Iron Eagle fall flaming to Earth, Wentworth slipped behind the still raging fire of the two downed Sky troopers and shed his coat, hat, and mask into the flames. With their incineration, the evidence of the *Spider* would be gone and Richard Wentworth could join the shell-shocked onlookers and make a clean get away.

When the marines burst through the door only moments later, they found Wentworth and Nita helping a battered President Truman out from beneath the rubble that had pinned him from the initial invasion. "Well…that was quite unexpected," the President said as he struggled to a sitting position. Staring deep into Wentworth's eyes he seemed to make a connection. There was a recognition there that took Dick by surprise. Did he know…?

"I didn't know which side the *Spider* was on until today, Mr. Wentworth. But if it wasn't for his quick action we may have been having dinner at the Reich House instead of the White House." With an enlightened smile he patted Wentworth on the shoulder and turned to address the frightened dignitaries.

Clearing his throat, President Truman spoke in a clear and decisive voice to the collected men and women. "Ladies and gentlemen, it seems that for the second time in as many weeks it is my pleasure to tell you that the war is over, once and for all. God bless America."

illustration by Tom Floyd

Chapter Ten

SEÑOR SUICIDE

by STEVE ENGLEHART

Suicide for the Spider!

Wentworth looked at the .45 automatic in his hand. It was his own pistol, fully loaded, and he knew its awesome power to deal death better than any man alive. If he didn't shoot himself with it, Santander would kill Nita. So he put the gun in his mouth and pulled the trigger!

When he awoke, he was lying in a pool of blood, agony rocketing around his head. Resolutely he forced his hand to move, to rise and feel his face. His left cheek was all but gone, and so were three teeth. At the last split-second, using his knowledge that other men seldom looked directly at death, he had twisted his aim, firing the shot through the side of his face instead of the base of his brain. The bullet had clipped the teeth and they'd joined it as projectiles mushrooming through the soft flesh. Undoubtedly, he'd fallen like a dead man, and Santander had taken him for such. But he was not a dead man. He was the living *Spider!*

He sat up, weakened from shock and loss of blood but calling once more on his fabled constitution. From the hidden pocket in his evening jacket he pulled a small kit. Inside its supple cover was the make-up Wentworth used to rebuild his face as the *Spider*. He took most of the wax he used to build the *Spider's* brow ridges and nose, and applied it to the hole in his cheek. He could pack the hole with it, to close off the screaming nerve endings, but he'd have to keep his jaw closed thereafter or risk it working free. Well, he didn't anticipate any soliloquies tonight. His gun had spoken first and it would continue the drama on its own.

When he stood, an outside observer would have beheld the *Spider*. Again, not wanting to look at death, that observer would have seen no difference in that dread figure. But one who knew him — like Nita! — would see the immobility of his jaw, the hooded agony in his eyes, and the indomitable will that held it all together.

The *Spider* stumbled from the murder room, into the vast proscenium of the *Castle* Theatre. It was dark and his footfalls echoed emptily. The audience had gone home, convinced they'd seen the greatest living actor of the American stage.

Wentworth and Nita had thought so, too. All of New York had thought so. Sergio Santander was the toast of Broadway, and the theatre district was packed nightly with wildly enthusiastic patrons of his hit show, *Don Juan*. He played the tormented Latin lover with the grandeur of a John Barrymore, the sensitivity of a Leslie Howard, the brash finesse of an Orson Welles. Hordes came from all across America to pay dearly for a scalped ticket and see the man everyone was talking about. Many came as skeptics; all left as believers.

But then a British cameraman, rebuffed in his attempt to film a scene of *Don Juan* for exhibit abroad, filmed it anyway, his camera hidden in the box seats by his evening jacket. He keenly felt the elation of being the man who could bring such artistry to the rest of the world. But when he sent his film to London on the *Queen Elizabeth*, London had replied with a severance notice. Which was not surprising when the theatre newsreels showed the film. It depicted a stooped, overweight, and rather ugly actor attempting to project Barrymore, Howard, and Welles, and producing Daffy Duck. It was pure ham, corn-fed glazed-in-apple ham, all overwrought gestures and plummy insincerity. It was the hit of the week in Britain, and the cameraman got his job back.

In New York, news of this was met with wry condescension. Those snooty Englishmen, having been surpassed on the stage, were having some sort of fit. The crowds continued to clamor for Santander. Richard Wentworth himself was looking forward to seeing *Don Juan* for the third time; it would be Nita's sixth. But Richard Wentworth was more than a Broadway Johnny.

So it was that after the thunderous applause died down, and the mighty stage beneath its looming masks of Comedy and Tragedy closed its scarlet curtain, Wentworth and Nita made their way to the dressing rooms. As she joined the adoring crowd surrounding Santander, Wentworth slipped unobtrusively into the shadows and began to explore the catacombs that made up the back of the ancient, elegant theatre. Nothing here appeared to have changed since the gaslight days - except for one room. Its door and lock were both new. It took all of four minutes for Wentworth to crack that lock and open that door.

Inside was a strange device, about four feet tall, rounded, with symmetrical bulbous protrusions. One protrusion collapsed inward at the tip, forming a sort of rounded mouth. Small gray-green lights dotted the circumference. It was like nothing Wentworth had ever seen before, and he'd seen plenty. But he felt the sudden desperate urge to look away — and he knew it was his own urge, long suppressed, long forgotten, not to look at death.

"Make no sudden moves," said the well-known voice of Santander behind him. Wentworth was shocked that he hadn't heard the man coming. Slowly, calmly, he turned, and saw the impossibly handsome actor with a gun in Nita's back. They moved into the room deliberately, and Santander reached behind himself to close and lock the door.

"What is it?" Wentworth asked, motioning toward the machine.

"I think you've guessed," answered the actor. "It controls minds. An old man in my native Ecuador devised it. He was one of those crazy old fellows who follows his own strange dream, far from the world. It was his life's work — literally, since I killed him when I took it — but no one but myself knew of it. And I saw how I could come to the greatest city in the world and make my fortune with it, following my own dream of being the world's greatest actor."

Nita stood bravely, though the exaggerated curve of her slender back showed how deeply Santander's gun was driven into her spine. She said, "I've told him, Dick, that you alerted Commissioner Kirkpatrick to what we found."

"Exactly," answered Wentworth. "Kirk sent us here to investigate, Santander, and I 'phoned him from the lobby while Nita kept you busy. So there's no point to this melodrama."

"You're wrong," said Santander. "You've destroyed my dream, so I have nothing left to live for. But I was a dream to you all, so you have nothing, either. I'll reset the switches on my machine, stage my last and greatest work, but you won't be around to see it. You certainly have a gun, so take it out, put it in your mouth, and pull the trigger, or I'll blow this lovely lady in two."

Suicide for the World!

The *Spider* hurtled from the theatre into hell.

Broadway and Fifty-Second Street was a mass of people, writhing, screaming. Fires were burning in every direction, north and south along the avenue, up and down along the faces of the massive buildings. As the *Spider* looked upward, he saw a body falling from the darkness above.

A woman clutched at him. "Kill me!" she screamed, spittle flying from her once-beautiful face, now twisted by grief and despair. "I'm not strong enough! I'm a weak, useless woman! Kill me!"

"And me!" bawled a fat man, grabbing the *Spider*'s arm like a vise. "I cheat, I lie! Kill me!"

Others began to surge toward them, seemingly drawn by the very idea that the *Spider* might put an end to their lives. The *Spider*, whose mouth was a fanged and lipless gash, and whose nose was a predatory beak. The *Spider*, whose sinister black fedora covered oily hair and whose black cape billowed from sinewy shoulders. This was the creature they took for a savior!

Suddenly, as the waves of pain from his cheek and jaw ebbed for a moment, the thought exploded in his mind: "Kill me! I've killed hundreds and hundreds of men!" A great wave of self-loathing broke over him, followed by the urgent desire to rid himself of all his pain.

He stood stock-still and realized what Santander had done.

"I'll reset the switches on my machine," the actor had said. "Stage my last and greatest work." The man who had caused all of New York to love him now caused them all to hate themselves. And the *Spider* was not immune.

But the *Spider* had trained himself to withstand pain, of any sort. Even while the highest, most human parts of his brain called out for self-destruction, the deepest, reptilian parts looked coldly out at hell and swore never to succumb.

He pried the fat man's hands off his arm, and thought "Kill me! I won't give him what he needs!" But he pried the fat hands off. He jerked the woman's hands from his coat and thought "Kill me! I can't treat women this way!" But he got clear of her, too.

Another body crashed down from above.

The *Spider* launched himself into the clamoring crowd. Some of them looked hopeful, thinking he would kill them after all. Others recoiled, their fear of death overwhelming their hatred of themselves. This last group gave the *Spider* leverage, momentum — he burst through the cluster. A panhandler nearby smashed his gin bottle and raked himself across the throat, spewing blood. A mother left her baby carriage and dived to grab the jagged glass before it fell and shattered. She caught it, sobbing in gratitude, and turned back toward her squalling baby. The *Spider* dropped her with a blow to the back of the head. But these were the symptoms of the disease which had struck New York this night, not the cause. He had to find Santander — and Nita!

Farther down Broadway, perhaps in Times Square, the fires were larger. Whole buildings were in flames, and a billboard, its bracing weakened by the fire, toppled slowly down into the street, picking up momentum as it fell. The *Spider* could clearly hear the shout of joy that greeted its impact. That was where he'd find his quarry.

But every inch of the street and sidewalk between here and there, a distance of seven blocks, was thronged with the mad and the doomed. The *Spider* could hardly keep his feet as he stood in front of the *Castle*, yet he had to cover those blocks.

Looking around, he saw a motorcycle lying on its side, next to its rider who had ridden it into a crowd, next to the rider's victims. The *Spider* ran to pick it up. The jolting of his feet on the asphalt caused the pain in his face to redouble itself. The wax he'd used to fill the hole gave structure but transmitted each impact. "Kill me!" he thought. "I can't do this! I don't deserve to do this! I am a criminal!" The face of the first man he'd ever killed, a Bosch in the Ardennes forest, burst over him. The man had tried to kill him, it was war, Wentworth had never regretted his action in the slightest, but now he saw the man turn to him, holding his stomach together, his eyes strangely bright before the light faded for all time and he pitched face-first into the snow. "Kill me!" shrieked the *Spider*'s mind. "I'm a murderer!" And then the face of the second man appeared.

The *Spider* picked up the fallen motorcycle and straddled it. There was no hope of riding on the street or the sidewalks; he wouldn't get ten yards. He revved the machine, a powerful Ariel, and shot forward. As he closed on the nearest automobile he jerked the front wheel upward. The machine climbed up the back of the auto and onto the roof. He accelerated and the Ariel rode forward down the windshield, over the hood and leapt to the trunk of the car in front of it. The ride was bumpy, up and down, and ever more violent as the *Spider* picked up speed, but it was the only way to move. Cars were parked in a solid line ahead of him; this was New York.

Another body fell from the heavens, crashing into a Daimler just in front of him. The auto's roof collapsed inward under the impact. The *Spider* swerved, drove off the side of the car, bounced off the sidewalk. He couldn't avoid the body of a drooling mailman sprawled across the curb. The combination of collisions threw the *Spider* forward, his bike's back wheel coming off the ground. He kept racing, riding on one tire, looking almost straight down at the concrete flashing by — then the rear wheel came down with a jolt that almost shattered the remaining teeth in his head. A typhoon of darkness swept over his consciousness. For a moment he was actually unconscious. But as his will somehow clawed its way back, he found that his luck had not failed him. He had continued in a straight line and not hit anyone or anything. Impossible, yet there he was, still upright on the Ariel. He twisted the handlebar left and rode back up the trunk of a Ford.

The haziness of his mind helped him now. Each jolt along the highway of car roofs that led down Broadway shook him, but they had little effect on him. He wondered if he were going back into shock, or if the loss of blood had caught up to him. He took his left hand off the handlebar and wiped it along his cheek. In the lurid light from the surrounding fires it came back dark with blood, but not too much blood. If there was one thing the *Spider* knew, it was the nature of wounds. He was nearer his limit than he'd like to be, but he could go on.

He came to the intersection of Broadway and Fifty-First Street. The highway of cars ended here but various autos were scattered ahead, at random angles, abandoned by their drivers. By gauging his speed he could leap from car to car, and in what seemed a split second he was onto the next row of parked vehicles, heading straight for Fiftieth.

Forty-Ninth, Forty-Eighth, the blocks vanished under his wheels. But as he neared Forty-Seventh he saw the cars ahead were covered with people, standing on the roofs, the hoods, the trunks, all craning to see further down the street, where the huge fires burned. Even if he'd wanted to, the *Spider* could not continue. He drove down into the intersection and squealed the Ariel to a halt beside a flaming newsstand. The faces of the men he'd killed continued to flow through his mind. For the first time, the faces began to appear with a blood-red mark on their foreheads — the sign of the *Spider*. It was the tiny outline of an ugly arachnid, and as the faces jumped out at him, the insect seemed to dance and writhe.

"The *Spider!*" On the corner, a crying policeman stared at him through his tears. He wiped his eyes with the back of one hand as he raised his service revolver with the other. The police of this city had standing orders to capture or kill the *Spider*. Whatever personal despair the policeman was going through, his duty had been drilled into him as strongly as the *Spider*'s into him. But the dictates of that duty were filtered through an unsound mind. The officer did not intend to capture the *Spider*. And the *Spider* did not fight the law, did not fire upon its minions. In his efforts to bring justice to many of those the police could not touch, he often went outside the law, but against the police, he was disarmed. Nothing could change that — not even his recognition of the fact that his death now would lead to the deaths of millions in Manhattan tonight.

He revved his bike one more time and kicked it into gear. The Ariel roared forward even as the *Spider* leapt from its seat. It struck the curb and rocketed upward, a massive hunk of metal falling back to the concrete and sliding sideways across it. The policeman fired but was already jumping out of the bike's way. His shot went wide. He looked for the *Spider* and saw him just vanishing into the tightly packed crowd — then saw a thin man wearing plus-fours waver, clutching his chest. The policeman realized he had shot an innocent bystander. The policeman shot himself.

The *Spider* shoved his way through the crowd, but it was slow going. At one point he took an elbow to the side of his face, and he felt the blood pour onto his collar. There were dead men everywhere he looked now, but the live ones were his problem. He could not continue down this way.

He fought his way back onto the sidewalk. The crowd was not as dense here, since whatever was going on farther south was invisible beyond the cars and the people atop them. The *Spider* plunged forward like the All-American halfback he'd been in college, fighting his way through the Yale line, and reached the door to the Page Building. It was a revolving door but it wasn't revolving now, having been locked in position after the last workers had left for the day. The *Spider*'s .45s spat lead and the glass in the door shattered. He dove inside.

Behind him, men on the sidewalk snatched up the jagged glass.

Before him, the night watchman hung from the multi-faceted chandelier. His twisting body threw long, angular shadows in all directions, painting the ceiling and walls with strands of shadow like a spider's web.

The *Spider* ran across the entryway, past the reception desk, to the elevator. If only the car were stopped on the ground floor — ! Yes! He wedged his fingers into the sliding doors, pulling them apart. Slowly but surely they opened. To his surprise, the elevator operator was crouched whimpering inside.

"Don't kill me," the man begged, scrabbling toward the back of the car. "I know I'm a bad man but I don't want to die!" To the *Spider*'s ears these were the sweetest words he'd heard in a long, long time. Inside his own brain, his own voice kept screaming, "Kill me!"

The *Spider* stepped into the car and threw the wall lever to close the doors, then the floor lever to begin the ascent. The Page had twenty floors, he knew, and they rose swiftly. He turned back toward the operator, even as a solid blow struck him in the back. He ducked, completed his turn, found the operator clawing at him in a paroxysm of fear. "Don't kill me!" he screamed, harsh and metallic in the cramped car. "Don't kill me, *Spider!*"

Even if the *Spider* had dared open his jaws to speak, there was nothing to say. The reputation of the *Spider* had been too carefully cultivated, was too widely known, for a man lost in the depths of mortal terror to believe that the *Spider* would not kill him. Why else did the *Spider* appear, but to kill? Instead, the *Spider* grabbed the operator by the shoulders and slammed his back against the elevator wall. The car shook.

This did nothing to calm the man. With the strength of a madman, he tore himself free of the *Spider's* grip and lunged past him, coming up with a wrench clutched in his trembling hand. He swung it at the *Spider's* head with all his might. Under normal circumstances the *Spider* would have evaded the blow easily, but now, hampered by pain both physical and mental, he barely escaped having his brains spread all over the car. He swung hard, connected on his assailant's jaw, but nothing would slow the man down. The man swung the wrench again, missing again but putting a deep crease in the elevator's wall. The *Spider* grabbed him from behind, trying to wrestle him into submission. The man shoved backward. The *Spider's* back struck the wall and the car rocked. The now familiar blackness burst up inside the *Spider's* brain like swamp gas. But he held on, and used the rocking of the car to throw them both forward again, driving the operator's face into the far wall. The car was rocking wildly now, and a quick glance at the numbers on the gauge showed they had but three floors to go before reaching the top of the building. If the *Spider* didn't bring them to halt they'd crash into the machinery at the top and the instability of the car even now didn't bode well for what would happen then. The *Spider* slammed the man sideways against a wall, then again used the natural reaction of the blow to help him put the man's head into the opposite wall.

The man sagged. The *Spider* dropped him and grabbed at the control lever. With a screech the car slowed abruptly…and came to a halt. The car swung a good six inches back and forth, back and forth. The *Spider* threw open the doors and found the floor marked "20" four feet below the bottom of the car. They could not have gone any higher.

He slid swiftly over the edge of the car and jumped to the building floor. In the instant he caught a glimpse of the elevator shaft yawning below him. There was fire down there. Ahead of him was a door marked "Roof." He approached it, saw that it was locked, blew it wide with his .45s.

He stepped out into a New York night he had never seen before. The air, instead of being the dark gray of a city seeped in its electrical lighting, was orange, flickering, suffused in the brilliance of the raging fires. They were all around now, buildings, even whole blocks in flames. Just ahead was what he'd come for, and it, too, was in flames. A covered walkway led from the Page to the Steeger Building across Forty-Sixth Street, but its structure was engulfed in a blaze shooting high in the thermal whirlwind sweeping up from the canyon below. The walkway cracked, sagged, swayed. The *Spider* ran straight for it, into its tunnel of fire. A horrid shriek ran through the dying metal, and the walkway lurched to the right. The *Spider*'s sleeve touched the wall and started to smolder. He smothered that against his side. He staggered on along the tilting passageway, each step threatening to bring everything down. At last he came out near the Steeger's water tower, also aflame. He ran along the block-long patch of softening asphalt leading toward Times Square, where the lights burned brightest of all. Behind him the walkway screamed one last time and crumpled into the street far below in an explosion of sparks.

Suddenly, under the thrumming in his head from the hole in his face, the thunder of the flames in all directions, and the growing gabble of human voices rising up from below, the *Spider* found another sound — the growling whine of a descending airplane. He threw himself flat just before an Eastern Airlines passenger ship sailed overhead. The backwash almost tore him from the roof and he drove his fingers into the hot asphalt to hold him on his perch. The airship sailed onward, a majestic bird, until the first skyscrapers tore its wings off. Then the fuselage turned over and dove without slowing into Broadway and Thirty-ninth, taking out the Metropolitan Opera House.

Even people flying *over* Manhattan were succumbing to Santander's suicide machine!

The *Spider* got back on his feet and finished his run to the front of the building. He came out twenty floors above Times Square, but his sharp eyes, perhaps rejuvenated by what he saw below, picked out the details clearly.

The great triangular intersection between Broadway, Seventh Avenue, and Forty-Fifth Street was awash with lurid light. Nearly every visible building was aflame; the *New York Times* complex which had given the area its name was a massive conflagration. The streets and sidewalks in all directions were packed with humanity, writhing, wailing. And in the center of it all was Santander, his infernal machine — and Nita!

Santander was holding a bullhorn, declaiming, gesticulating, "staging his last and greatest work." A hastily-lettered sign scrawled on the side of the so-far unburned Harvey Building proclaimed *DON JUAN IN HELL*, though the second word was almost illegible under the blood and brains of a suicide sprawled below it. With that intelligence, the *Spider* could begin to make out the words of Bernard Shaw's drama.

"Beware of the pursuit of the Superhuman: it leads to an indiscriminate contempt for the Human. To a man, horses and dogs and cats are mere species, outside the moral world. Well, to the Superman, men and women are a mere species too, also outside the moral world."

Santander was playing the Devil, of course.

"Nietzsche? It was he who raked up the Superman, who is as old as Prometheus; and the 20th century will run after this newest of the old crazes when it gets tired of the world, the flesh, and your humble servant."

He bowed, in what now seemed to the *Spider* an excessively bad parody of his former rôle of Latin lover, toward his Dona Ana — Nita, bound and gagged in a chair across from him. The men and women watching, however, shrieked in response to his every word. They were the shrieks of the damned, delaying their self-destruction only for the chance to see their great idol once more. In a world now filled with darkness, the sole light source was Santander, and Santander obviously knew it. His rhetoric was becoming more orotund, his gestures more insanely flamboyant.

Behind him squatted the suicide machine, gray-green lights flashing madly, red-orange reflections of the flaming city swirling over its polished surface and strange protrusions.

Just looking at it doubled and then redoubled the faces of the dead men crowding the *Spider*'s brain. For the first time, he felt his strength ebbing. His shirtfront was soaked through with blood, and the wax had come loose; the hot updrafts from Times Square battered his decimated cheek, and burned his tongue inside his mouth. He withdrew his *Spider* web from its place of concealment on his hip and attached the silken strand to one of the massive pipes which brought water to the building below his feet. He tested the line to make sure it was solid, then held his cape in his hand as he grabbed it, to act as a buffer. He leapt from the roof into the 20-story canyon.

Down and down he flew, one hand sliding along the line, the other holding his .45 at the ready. The cape was made from non-flammable material and his hands were gloved, but still the line grew almost unbearably hot in his iron grip. A low chuckle arose from his throat, pushing past his set jaws; he'd found something that hurt more than a gunshot to the face. But there was no way to lessen the burning in his hand without speeding his descent, and then he would die on arrival, his body shattering on the street. He kept sliding as fast as he dared and silently bore the pain, his eyes flicking from Nita's bound form to Santander's theatrics, both flying toward him.

At the last second he crushed the *Spider*'s web in his grip. He had braced for the momentum shift and still his arm felt wrenched from its socket. He slowed, let go, and landed hard beside Nita.

Santander stumbled backward at this sudden apparition of the *Spider*. Then his voice rose in what must have seemed the voice of God to his acolytes. "Kill him!" he roared. "Death to the *Spider!*"

Nita's bonds flew wide, slit by the *Spider*'s knife. She surged up off her chair and clutched at his arm. "Kill me!" she screamed. It was only the bonds which had kept her from joining the deluded mob. He took her by the shoulders, shook her, stared hard into her eyes. He spoke, and as he spoke, the last of the wax holding his face together fell away. "No, Nita," he gritted. "Kill *him!*" He knew it was what she needed now, as he handed her the knife. Her natural bravery would return to the surface; he was sure of it. She looked at his eyes — the eyes of the terrible *Spider* — the eyes of her lover. She took the knife, turned toward Santander.

The actor ran toward them, the very model of a stage hero, almost leaping. Hundreds of men, women, and children from the raging crowds surged after him, toward the lone woman standing poised and ready for them.

The *Spider* spun toward the suicide machine — but now, at last, even his iron will was overwhelmed. All the horrible things he had done, all the horrible things he had faced, the thousands of men he had killed, all exploded in his brain *at once!* His strength was failing. For one eternal moment he was staggered, the pit of undoing yawning before him!

Somewhere behind him rose the most realistic utterance Santander had ever made: a choked and horrified scream!

The *Spider* found himself again, deep inside an icy calm, deep inside the reptilian brain that had kept better men than he alive since the Paleozoic era. Though he had often tortured himself, asking himself if everything he had done was justified, he found in this moment of stark naked clarity that the answer had to be a resounding "Yes!" He could have no regrets, nothing for which to reproach himself. Everyone he had ever killed had deserved it, and the world was a better place because he was in it, end of story.

So he put the gun in the mouth of the machine and pulled the trigger! 🔫

illustration by Tom Floyd

Chapter Eleven

WHEELMAN FOR TERROR

by SHANNON ERIC DENTON & JOHN HELFERS

Leo Shmell was a small time crook in a big time city. He had worked his way up from errand boy to driver, which was still pretty much an errand boy, but at least now he had access to the men who made the decisions in this town. Not the honest, mayoral type of decision-making men, but the real kind. The kind of men that dealt in money and dames and, every now and then, maybe a little killing. Leo had hoped for a long time he would be that kind of man one day. And although he didn't know it yet, Leo was about to get his shot.

Leo drove the black limo up to the curb at exactly 10:30 p.m. He knew being punctual mattered. His bosses wouldn't want him there too early so as to give a would-be assassin the opportunity to strike, nor would they want him arriving too late. So Leo, lacking in most other things intellectual, made up for it by being punctual. He was pretty sure his boss, Tony "Thumbs" Malone, noticed.

"Nice evening, huh boss?" asked Leo, but the answering grunt of Tony Malone was about the only recognition he ever got. But Leo knew that Tony was a man of few words. Leo understood his boss. After all, they were the same kind of guy, well, except for the fact Tony was the boss and Leo had never had his thumbs chopped off in a knife fight.

Leo rolled the limo down 3rd Avenue towards Park Street through the back alleys. The gin joint they were heading to was owned by Tony's boss, Oliver "Maple" Moretti. Moretti was a pleasant sort of fella, leading many to erroneously believe he was called Maple either out of affection or due to his sweet nature. Maple, however, got his name after drowning a baker in a vat of syrup after catching said baker with his girl, who also happened to mysteriously drown in that very same vat. Therefore Leo had made a rule early on in his employment. Never look at any girl within fifty feet of Maple Moretti.

The limo pulled into the alley behind Maple's place and Leo relaxed only after Tony went inside. After all, he had delivered Tony exactly on time for the big meeting. Even so, he kept the engine running and made sure he was aware of the time. He knew any screw up could cost him a promotion, and a second one could cost him his life. Thus he tried to focus as well as he could on the task at hand, but Leo often wondered what went on inside these meetings. He was sure it was all very exciting and important stuff that he would no doubt be privy to one day. *Hopefully that day will be soon,* thought Leo. He couldn't wait to get inside with the others. He could almost see it—walking into a room like that in an expensive suit, the other gangsters rising to greet him with the respect he deserved, crowding around him, shaking his hand—

The explosion that blew the back wall off the gin joint also blasted Leo from his daydream as it hurled the limo across the alley. The car flipped over and smashed down on the ground in a crunch of steel and glass. Leo was pretty sure he was bleeding from somewhere, but he didn't feel any pain. He pulled himself free from the twisted metal that had been a shiny black car only a few seconds ago, and almost didn't notice Malone stumbling out of the giant hole that used to be the rear wall. Tony was firing back into the building with his wrist mounted .45s, a necessity for a man with no thumbs. Maple Moretti staggered out right after him, shooting a Tommy gun from the hip into the hole as well.

Tony screamed something at Leo, his open mouth revealing yellowed teeth, but no sound seemed to be coming out of his furious face.

"What?" Leo shouted, unable to hear anything but a high-pitched whine that seemed to echo through his skull.

Maple shouted, audible this time as the whining faded. "He said get us a freakin' car!"

For a moment, Leo wasn't sure what to do. He knew how to do his job, driving, and he did it well. Boosting cars wasn't his job. Well, Leo was going to show Tony and Maple he could make it his job. He could adapt. Leo would get them a car. He'd figure out what had happened and who they were shooting at later. *One thing at a time,* he thought as he ran towards the street.

The woman in a four-door Packard waiting for the light to change didn't even have time to scream as she was yanked out of her car and thrown to the ground. *So far, so good,* thought Leo, even though he felt uncomfortable about hurting a lady. He tried to kick her in the head gently, to make sure she wouldn't get up and try to get her car back or call for help. Leo was pretty sure he'd moved her far enough out of the way before gunning the car back down the alley. He was almost positive that the crunch he heard was probably just her foot, nothing vital. He knew that if he just could have explained how big an opportunity this was for him, she'd understand.

The yellow headlights lit the alley, and anything outside of their radius was swallowed by inky blackness. From within that shroud erupted the sound of gunfire exploding all around Tony, Maple, and whoever else had made it into the alley alive. Leo hit the gas, hoping to outrun any bullets that could end his chance at a promotion.

"Boss, I got the car!" Leo screamed, suddenly wondering if not making that comment plural was going to affect his job security. He hoped they didn't notice due to the bullets tearing holes through the two guys on either side of them.

Maple and Tony scrambled into the back seat, leaving their bleeding compatriots to fend for themselves. Leo saw this, but knew they wouldn't do the same to him. Unlike those other guys, he was important to his bosses.

"Take us to the Beltway!" screamed Maple, obviously still unable to hear himself.

Leo had just turned his head to answer, "I can do...."

"Look out!" screamed Tony.

Leo barely had time to register the cloaked figure illuminated in the alley-way directly in front of him. Barely had time to make out the obsidian lining of the figure's long cloak. Barely had time to react as the masked man's twin .45s shattered the car's headlights and once again plunged the world into darkness. Leo was blind save for the flashes of the two large pistols as they spit bullets at the three men. As much as he'd have loved to run over the guy shooting at them, Leo knew he was more likely to accelerate into the alley wall.

To his credit, he hit the brakes almost immediately, the car screeching to a stop in the blinding darkness. Otherwise he would have been responsible for totaling two cars in one night. Leo liked automobiles far too much to want that burden, and besides, this wasn't even his car. Leo knew that woman would want it back after she got out of the hospital, and he was hoping she might even reward his generosity. Leo always liked to plan for the future.

Despite his valiant efforts, the sedan's front end crunched into the wall. The damage looked minor, but a plume of steam from the radiator told Leo they weren't driving it anywhere else tonight. Tony and Maple staggered out of the car and immediately started shouting at each other.

"He's gonna kill us!" screamed Tony.

"Shut up," screamed Maple, then turned to Leo. "You! What's your name?"

"Leo. Leo Shmell," he replied proudly. He had just been asked his name and couldn't believe his luck.

Maple tossed Leo a snub-nosed .38 pistol. "Anything but us moves, kill it."

"You got it!" said Leo, awestruck at being trusted with such an important job. He didn't even have time to enjoy his good fortune as a bullet hit his shoulder, spinning him around hard. "Ow!" he screamed as he collapsed to the ground.

Maple and Tony stood back-to-back, firing in every direction. The darkness swallowed every bullet. "Show yourself!" screamed a sweating Tony, breathing hard as he scanned the night for their unseen assailant.

"Gladly," said a voice from everywhere and nowhere. To Leo, clutching his bleeding shoulder, the blackness simply appeared to reach out and pull the suddenly pale Tony into it before he could react. Two shots rang out, and in those flashes of gunfire Leo saw what looked like a huge cloaked figure, and then silence filled the alley again.

"You think that scares me? You come into my house and mess with my people and you think I'm scared of some clown who's too gutless to face me like a man?" screamed Maple. "I'm gonna kill you! I make my living killing little punks like you!"

"And I do it for fun," said the icy voice from directly behind Maple. Maple spun around. His gun was knocked loose from his hands, spinning into the darkness. With dread in his eyes, Maple saw the man who had killed a legion of his men for the first time. Maple saw ...the *Spider*.

The *Spider* hit Maple so hard fragments of teeth sprayed from his mouth. The second punch was no less powerful. Maple doubled over, blood spilling from his pulped lips. His head throbbed, and he saw the ground trying to rush up and meet him, but Maple was a tough man. And tough men don't go down easy.

Maple rolled with the next punch, no longer underestimating the slender, well tailored assassin that was battering his skull. This time Maple struck first, his meaty fist connecting with his attacker's jaw. The *Spider* reeled from the blow, staggering back a step.

"You think I'm a nancy?" shouted Maple.

The *Spider* looked up, a small trickle of blood flowing from his lip. But instead of concern, a wry smile revealed sharp fangs that Maple had no trouble seeing even in the darkness. The fangs sent a shiver down the gangster's spine. They'd all heard how the *Spider* was a cannibal who used those fangs to tear out the throats of the criminals he hunted.

"You don't get to be Maple Moretti without being able to take a punch or two," shouted Maple to bolster his confidence, unaware his confidence—and his life—would both be so very short.

"Good, because your punishment is just beginning, and the longer you take it, the more I'll enjoy it," hissed the night-cloaked assassin.

Maple Moretti had pictured all of the ways a man in his line of work could die. He often imagined it'd be a knife in the back, an assassin's gun, or maybe poison from a traitorous henchman. He'd also assumed it would be many years from now. Maple had never pictured this, however. The black-cloaked dervish tore into him like a lumberjack tore into a tree, his fists seeming to come from high, low, and everywhere in between. With every hammer-like blow, Maple's bones shattered faster than he could scream...though he tried his best to keep up.

Maple fell hard to the filthy alley floor. His skull was fractured, and the blood leaking from his pulverized face almost completely obscured his vision, but he could still hear that damned *Spider* calmly walking towards him. Maple wanted to spit a curse at this savage killer looming above him. It would serve as a good epitaph to an otherwise successful life. That was what Maple wanted to do, but his lack of teeth and fractured jaw prevented any such spitting or cursing.

"The city is free of your corruption, your greed. Goodbye, Oliver Moretti, and good riddance." The *Spider* pointed his .45 at Maple's head and began to pull the trigger.

That gunshot was loud, thought Maple, surprised that he was able to think anything at all. He was even more surprised when the *Spider* fell to his knees, clutching his chest. Blood poured from the *Spider*'s fingers. But what surprised Maple Moretti most of all was the sight of Leo Shmell, holding a smoking .38 snub-nose revolver.

"I got him!" screamed Leo, "I really got him!" The *Spider* started to rise, still clutching his chest. Leo Shmell obviously had no qualms about shooting a man in the back, and neither did Maple Moretti as he screamed, "Shoot him again!" Of course, all that came out of Maple's mouth was an inaudible jumble of noise, but Leo got the picture and fired several shots.

He hit the *Spider* three more times as the vigilante tried to stumble into the darkness. Leo couldn't see him anymore, but he knew he'd need to finish this guy off if he was going to get his promotion. His courage bolstered by the knowledge that he had already shot his prey four times in the back, Leo ran forward. He hadn't gone far when his foot hit something. He bent down and there at his feet lay the body of the man who had shot him in the shoulder, killed Thumbs Malone, and beat Maple Moretti to within an inch of his life only moments earlier. Leo was enjoying his victory right up until he noticed the ticking bomb in the dead man's hand. He had only a few seconds...

Leo grabbed Moretti and hoisted him onto his back, ignoring the stab of pain in his shoulder. He knew the hurt was temporary, but his success today would change his life forever. Leo also knew it did him no good unless Moretti lived to tell everyone how great a job he had done. And so Leo ran. He ran as fast as he could, knowing that in seconds the alley would be a fireball and any chance of him getting a promotion would be gone.

Leo had just rounded the corner of the alley when it erupted behind him in a huge fireball. He had made it. He'd get Moretti and himself to the doc, and then he'd enjoy his newfound success. They'd definitely reward this.

The Spider is dead, thought Leo, *and I, Leo Shmell, am the man that killed him!*

Leo knew it had only been a week since he had killed the *Spider*, but he was hoping to have received more recognition by now. Maple was still in the hospital. Leo's shoulder still hurt, but it was nothing he couldn't handle. This job didn't exactly come with benefits or paid vacations, so Leo had been hitting the pavement looking for someone to employ him. He had a list of potential employers from Maple. Unfortunately, most of his would-be employers were too busy killing each other or getting killed. This was the third interview Leo had shown up for only to find the outfit he was meeting with had been slaughtered.

Between the absence of Maple and the new sense of freedom that came with not being hunted by a notorious, gun-toting vigilante, the criminal element in the city had gone nuts. Everywhere, gangsters were killing gangsters in an attempt to seize absolute control. What's more, two names were rising to the top, The Mad Mudejar and The Octopus.

Leo knew The Mad Mudejar, who had previously gone by the moniker Crazy Tom. Tom had switched his name after seeing a psychic swami, who had told him he saw Tom's name on a headstone. The swami had told him that in order to change his fortune he needed to take a new identity and start over in order to find harmony within his life. Living up to the first part of his former name, Tom had murdered the psychic right then and there, and from that day forward lived life as Mudejar. Tom was always willing to take good advice, he just had a different version of harmony than most. The "Mad" part of his name had been bestowed by the other criminal gangs, since The Mudejar was still capable of killing anyone on a whim, and had done so on many occasions.

Leo was pretty sure The Mudejar had also killed this potential employer as well. The Mudejar believed the city should be his. After all, he had killed and stolen here longer than anyone, and while he'd taken his lumps from the *Spider*, he also had managed to avoid getting killed by the vigilante over the years, a feat that few others could claim. *Which is why he's got so many men following him now*, thought Leo.

With the *Spider* out of the way, The Mudejar had moved swiftly to install himself as the kingpin of the city. The new arrival in town, The Octopus, was just one more obstacle Leo knew The Mudejar would be anxious to be rid of.

But first The Mudejar was removing the rest of his competition. Though this killing was bloody, it didn't have any of the fancy flair The Octopus was quickly becoming known for. No men found mysteriously drowned in a dry room with an octopus covering their face, no men found floating face down in a bathtub full of ink in their own homes, and certainly nothing like the convoy of coffins that had floated down the Harbor River with the entire Coyle Street Gang dead inside of them.

No, The Mudejar didn't mess around with any of that. Despite The Octopus making some of The Mudejar's men nervous, Mudejar ruled with an iron fist and the more Leo thought about it, the more he decided to go with a sure thing. He was too far along in his career to take chances on newcomers, no matter how impressive they might seem at the moment. Leo would go straight to the top and see The Mudejar about his job. Leo was sure the Mudejar would be thrilled to meet the man who had done him such a huge favor.

"Who?!?" screamed The Mudejar from behind closed doors.

"It's that Shmell guy who whacked the *Spider*. He's from Maple's outfit," said another voice. Leo was pretty sure it was the guy who had thrown him against the wall and frisked him when he entered. *At least they're thorough here*, thought Leo. He liked thorough.

"Fine. Send him in, but keep it quick. My massage girl is coming up," screamed The Mudejar.

Leo was happy to be let in. He had removed his sling despite the pain, knowing this was his big chance and...

"I need a driver, so you're in luck." The Mudejar's voice blasted Leo's eardrums. "You'll make what Maple paid ya, and if I find out it's any more, you'll be missing the days when ya had knees. Now get out and send my massage girl in!"

Leo couldn't believe it. He was only in the office for a few seconds. In just under a minute Leo had a job working with one of the most powerful men in the city. *I really am blessed*, thought Leo as he worked his way past the guard who brushed past him with the beautiful massage girl. *I'm on the fast track now.*

A few nights later, Leo sat outside a warehouse on the docks in a parked delivery truck. While he had hoped he'd be driving a limo like he did for Maple, Leo knew The Mudejar had a plan, so it didn't really bother him too much... sitting in this uncomfortable truck...in a stinky harbor alley...on the hottest night of the summer. Leo was just doing his job, and he knew the rewards would be coming soon. He had to show Mudejar he was a good employee, even if it meant getting eaten by a few hundred mosquitoes to demonstrate his loyalty.

The Mudejar had spent the last week consolidating his burgeoning empire, either forcing other gang leaders to join him or completely eradicating any opposing gangs that tried to cross him. For a man who wore a turban and carried a scimitar, he commanded a lot of respect, mainly by whacking off the heads of the guys that didn't respect him. As a lackey, you didn't want to screw up anywhere in chopping distance of Mudejar.

With The Octopus moving in on their territory and drawing many of the remaining gangs to his cause, Leo knew the Mad Mudejar needed to be bold. Leo liked that word. "Bold," he muttered as he looked at himself in the cab mirror, careful not to take his eyes off the warehouse for very long. Leo also knew everything revolved around him getting things right tonight.

Yes, Leo liked this plan, despite the fact it made him an insect food source. *Mad Mudejar doesn't know what the Octopus has planned, but he certainly has something planned for the Octopus.* Mudejar had suffered the *Spider's* interference long enough, and now that the entire brass ring of the city was within his grasp, he had resolved that no interloper was going to take it from him, even if he had to kill everyone to get it. *Bold, definitely bold*, thought Leo.

Leo also couldn't believe that Mudejar had been able to convince every-one to a public meet. Well, as public as an assembly of armed gangsters could be. Down by the docks the cops usually stayed clear, and there were enough warehouses to hold everyone. The proposed plan was to see if they could all stop the bloodletting and carve up the city into territories for The Octopus's men and Mudejar's men.

Of course, Mudejar was planning a double cross. He would kill The Octopus himself, right in front of everyone, and thus take over his gangs, making him unstoppable. Leo knew this because Mudejar had said so, even if he had been saying it to someone else and hadn't planned for Leo to overhear. He was pretty sure Mudejar wanted the Spider-Killer in on things, but just didn't want to make the other guys jealous. Leo thought that was very thoughtful of Mudejar. He was glad he had joined Mudejar's gang and not the Octopus. That poor guy had it coming.

"He's not here. His men are here but he ain't," Mudejar shouted over the radio. "You see anything, Schmell?"

Leo had been positioned far enough away that he would be out of sight, but would still had a clear vantage point of the warehouse's only entrance. "No, boss," he replied, "Nothing out here but—" Leo screamed as a bloody man pounded on the truck door. Leo hoped he hadn't accidentally transmitted his girlish cry to The Mudejar. That was not how the Spider-Killer was supposed to sound.

"The double cross....The Octopus knows," hissed the dying man. "He's gonna kill Mudejar and everyone inside."

"How" asked Leo.

"He's already inside," said the dying thug, "disguised as one of his own henchmen."

Leo couldn't believe what he had just heard. How did this guy know of the double cross? He had to be one of Mudejar's men. *Only a trusted aide like myself*, thought Leo, *would know about that.*

"Boss, boss!" shouted Leo into the transmitter, but all he heard on the other end was static. Leo shoved the dying man away from the cab, knowing he'd understand Leo's need to relay the warning. After all, it's not like Leo was a doctor and could do anything to help the guy anyway.

Leo stomped on the accelerator, and the big delivery truck sped towards the warehouse. He'd save Mudejar, and then Maple wouldn't be the only powerful man to owe Leo Schmell.

The delivery truck plowed straight through the massive warehouse doors, smashing them to tiny pieces. Leo leaped out of the truck, "Boss, it's a trap!" he screamed, suddenly aware that every gun in the place was drawn and trained on him.

"Geez, Schmell! I told you to wait outside! Whaddya mean it's a trap?" yelled Mudejar.

"The Octopus is already here! He's disguised as one of his own boys," Leo said, pointing at the Octopus's men. Everyone had expected to see the dark-clothed figure who wore an emerald-green tie and had been reported to wear a mask and a cloak that was cut to resemble an octopuses' arms. No one ever really expected a gang boss to dress normally in this town.

The place erupted in an angry chatter that sounded like a thousand furious bees. Leo finally got within whispering distance of his boss. "He knew about the double cross, Boss. He was gonna whack you first. One of our boys just told me. I came to get you out of here." Leo knew this was what any boss would want to hear.

"You moron, I ain't going anywhere," Mudejar hissed. "If this guy wants to hide, I'm sticking around to find him...and then kill him!" Mudejar drew his scimitar and pointed it menacingly at the men gathered across from him.

"So one a youse is The Octopus, huh? We invite you here in peace, looking for some mutual brotherhood, and you plan a double cross? Well, why don't you step on out and save your boys an unnecessary bloodbath?" screamed Mudejar as pointed his sword down the line at the assembled gangsters, each looking innocently at the men next to them. Mudejar waited, growing more furious with every second that passed without anyone coming forward. "I said..."

The lights went out almost as fast as the gunshot that followed. What had already been a tense situation erupted into a full-blown war. Gang members shot at other gang members, the truck, the boxes in the warehouse, and anything else that looked even remotely threatening.

Leo did his best to stay out of the firefight. He had wanted Mudejar to get into the truck so they could leave. Mudejar, however, had other plans. Scimitar raised, he ran into the war zone, beheading everyone within chopping distance of his blade. *What's the point of having hired guns if yer not gonna use them,* thought Leo? He'd do things differently when he was in charge.

"I'll kill you all if I have to, so for the friggin' last time—which one of you is The friggin' Octopus!" screamed Mudejar, barely audible above the din of gunfire.

"I am," said the gravelly voice from behind him as the place suddenly lit up. Despite the noise, despite the slaughter, everyone seemed to hear this. What's more, the fighting and killing stopped immediately. Those left standing had turned, and instead of seeing The Octopus standing behind the man who asked the question, they only saw the *Spider*, lit from behind by the headlights of Leo's truck.

And then once again darkness reigned as the man known only as the *Spider* killed the lights and then proceeded to kill everyone else.

The *Spider*'s pistols blazed, his deadly bullets tearing into the gangsters.

They dropped two and three at a time, all blasted to pieces. Their momentary shock at not seeing the Octopus had been replaced with the shock of seeing the resurrected *Spider*. This shock was finally replaced with the realization they were being annihilated themselves. Mad Mudejar, less prone to distraction, had dived for cover behind a crate when the first shots had sounded.

"No," whispered Leo. "I killed him. I swear I killed him." He was petrified by the sight of the *Spider*, his black cloak swirling around him as he destroyed everything that moved. Not because he feared the spectral avenger had come to take them all across the river Styx, but because he wondered if the guy bleeding on the floor next to him would die thinking Leo was a liar. Leo knew that'd make getting a promotion really tough. He also knew somewhere in the dark, Mudejar still had his sword.

Leo decided it was time to check in on Maple at the hospital.

Unfortunately, as he rose to leave, he saw Mad Mudejar right next to him. Mudejar tossed his trademark scimitar at Leo and grabbed a Tommy gun off a nearby dead guy. Leo was happy Mudejar wasn't in a chopping mood at the moment. Leo had no interest in losing his head over this slight turn of events.

Leo set the scimitar on a crate next to him. He had no idea how to use it, and was about to say so as a shadow darted past them.

The Mudejar's roaring Tommy gun ripped through the wood crates in front of them, its blasting muzzle casting a strobe-like effect in the darkened warehouse. Leo thought he could almost make out a figure darting between the bullets that destroyed everything they hit, but that was impossible. *Just like it was impossible to get shot, blown up, and then come back from the dead*, thought Leo.

The gun clicked dry, its barrel smoking from the heat. "I think I nailed him," shouted Mudejar. Leo cringed as the darkness was disturbed by hideous, echoing laughter. He wanted to run, but he didn't know which direction to go, since the sound came from everywhere.

"Where are you?" screamed Mudejar.

"In the web, just like you, Mad Mudejar. You entered the web the moment you committed a crime in this city," said the gravelly voice from the darkness. "This town will never belong to the likes of you. You are a dead thing trapped in a web, and now—the *Spider* has come to feast."

"You ain't takin' me down that easy! Schmell, throw me my sword!" barked Mudejar.

Leo reached for the sword, but it wasn't there. He turned to tell Mudejar he didn't know where it was, but that would have been a lie. He saw where it was all too clearly...in the hands of the *Spider*.

Mudejar probably didn't feel a thing as his head was sliced clean off. He probably never heard Leo's girlish scream, his second in one night.

The *Spider* stood motionless in the darkness, the dead bodies of those caught in his web strewn all about him. Leo just stood there quivering, and then his blood ran cold when he heard from the mouth of the dark assassin: "Leo Schmell. You have done wrong."

Leo turned to run. He had wanted more than anything to be an important person. To do big, important things with his life. He realized he had done none of that. He was going to die. Leo Schmell had run out of good fortune.

Leo had only gone two steps when he felt an immense pain in his head and the world he knew faded into darkness.

"—so there we were, me and the *Spider*, in a warehouse fulla dead men. I raised my Tommy gun and was gonna splatter that louse all over the walls. But the dang gun jammed, and the *Spider* ran for it like the coward he is. Lucky he did, too, otherwise I'da finished what I'd started in that alley six months ago."

The other convicts encircling Leo in the prison yard muttered their admiration. Leo just nodded, flipping his collar up against the whistling winter air.

Five months earlier, he had woken up in the warehouse after running into a thick lead pipe—just in time for the cops to arrive. He had been arrested, booked, and jailed. Leo had confessed to all of the crimes he was accused of. He was sentenced to prison, and once there, "Lucky" Leo realized he had fifteen years to plan what he was going to do when he got out.

But inside the high stone walls, Leo had discovered, to his delight—he was finally somebody. He was the only man who had ever survived not one, but two encounters with the *Spider*. All of the cons had been talking about him ever since they'd heard he was coming to the big house, and once there, he was treated like gangland royalty. A cell all to himself, and everyone bowing and scraping as they tried to get on his good side.

Only Leo knew the truth, and he wasn't telling anyone else. He was lucky to be alive. At least, everyone else thought he was lucky.

A guard walked by, nightstick twirling around his wrist. "All right, break it up, you guys. Time to head back inside."

The knot of prisoners slowly dispersed around Leo, and he got up last, nonchalantly, like he didn't have a care in the world. Leo sauntered back into the main prison hall, his mind whirling with ideas. Ideas on how he was gonna change things once he got out.

He had seen the men running the gangs in the city, and it didn't look that hard. He was smarter than them—and luckier too. And now, with his reputation as the man who had twice faced the *Spider* and survived, there wouldn't be anyone in the city who could stand in his way. He would rule it all—

"Hey, Shmell." A guard's voice derailed Leo's train of thought. "You got a cellmate."

Leo scowled at the warden outside his cell. "Put an egg in your shoe and beat it, screw. You know I don't bunk with anybody."

The beefy guard shrugged, obviously enjoying Leo's discomfort. "Orders straight from the top, so ya better get used to it."

"We'll see who gets used to what," Leo snarled. This guard, Johnny Kentworth, was one of the few honest men in the joint, and Leo knew he'd have to do something about him one of these days. But that would come later. "First, I gotta see who I'm saddled with now."

Leo stepped into his dank cell to see a shadowy figure sitting on the bottom bunk—Leo's bunk. The man was hunched over, his head down, staring at the floor.

"I'll leave you two to get acquainted." Johnny said, slamming the steel cell door shut with a *clang*.

"Hey, new fish. You know whose bunk you're squattin' on?"

"This is the bunk of Leo Schmell." The other man didn't move a muscle as he spoke, and Leo had to strain to hear his voice. "The man who faced the *Spider* not once, but twice, and lived to tell about it."

Leo took a step forward. There was something about that voice that sounded familiar, but he couldn't quite put a finger on it—

But when the man raised his head to look at Leo, pinning him with his eyes—those bleak, icy, gray-blue eyes that stared at him like the gaze of the Grim Reaper himself! It was a gaze that still haunted Leo every night, coming to him in his nightmares...

Leo was frozen with terror. It was him! Leo was locked in a cell with the *Spider*! Fear fueled his muscles, and he whirled and leaped to the door, opening his mouth to scream for the guards, to plead for help, to beg for mercy—

But before even a squeak could spill from his lips, Leo sensed a presence behind him, and he was suddenly smashed against the cell door, his face flattened against the black bars of the small window.

"You've been telling stories that I don't like, Leo Shmell," the *Spider* hissed in that deadly, sinister voice. "But after today, you won't be telling anyone anything anymore."

And Leo didn't have time to say another word as he felt an incredible, crushing pressure on his neck. His vision swam, everything turning gray around him, and there was time for one last realization before the lights turned off forever:

I'm dead, thought Leo, *and the Spider was the man that killed me.*

illustration by Tom Floyd

Chapter Twelve

MORE SOULS FOR HELL

by C.J. HENDERSON

"In the following him, I follow but myself."
-Shakespeare

"Y ou are absolutely certain of this, Darell?"

"Yes, sir, Mr. Finetti, sir; a man'd have to be crazy to come to you with something like this and not be sure."

"No—" answered the older man behind the over-sized mahogany desk. Pretending to examine the papers in his hands further, wanting merely to think privately for a few additional seconds, Finetti muttered, "Some are just stupid. Some are just greedy."

The idea looked perfect—on paper. A stinking rich investment type and his society girlfriend out of the city on vacation. Photograph copies of bank drafts, carbons of contracts, stolen memos—more—all of it indicating that this particular money mover had left town with something close to three million dollars in bonds, Treasury Bills, international draft notes and just plain cash in his office safe.

Finetti first thought was that he must employ a private security force, but Darell had covered that angle as well. When the ganglord had questioned that aspect of the younger man's plan, the foot soldier had assured him the investor left his property in the hands of just two men, and one of those was his butler—old, an antique, useless.

"Oh," Darell had added, "when he goes out of town with his girlfriend, they leave her dog at his place for the butler and the other guy to watch."

Finetti studied the pages once more. It all came up sweet. And, there was one thing the gangster knew thanks to a contact at UPI. Police reports—just two hours old—confirmed the *Spider* was tearing things up in San Francisco at that very moment. That meant, even if the cursed vigilante departed the moment he was spotted, he could not be back in New York City for another half day. Antonio Finetti was known for studying a thing from all angles, then moving swiftly. He had analyzed Darell's plan for three days and found no holes within it.

And now, he thought, the *Spider*'s out of town?

"Get the Squad together," the ganglord said suddenly. "I want them here, armed and ready in one hour or they don't work for me no more!"

Finetti's lieutenants raced for their phones. There were over forty men in the Squad. They would have to work quickly to assemble them all.

My God, thought Darell, chuckling as he did so, those guys at that estate, they are about to become the deadest men in town.

Then, as the first number he dialed responded, the man put the idea from his head and threw all his concentration into preparing the Squad for the assault to come on the home of Richard Wentworth.

Ram Singh stood in the conservatory of his master's sprawling apartment. He did not like the way the intense summer heat was affecting the plants at that end of the complex. Several of the leafy crawlers especially were doing poorly—leaves crisping, tendrils curling to yellow, then black. It displeased the massive Sikh to have anything on the grounds not as Sahib Richard had left it. And, although he was no gardener by any stretch of the imagination, he stood in the corner of the room where the worst afflicted of the plants were, applying water, adding new soil, and trimming away dead foliage.

A clicking sound broke the silence in the room, but it caused no worry. Singh recognized the clawed footsteps of Apollo, the massive Harlequin Great Dane Master Richard had imported for missie Nita. They were alone in Sutton Place that evening, Wentworth's butler having decided to go to the cinema to see the new film "King Kong" everyone was raving about so.

Such distractions were not for Singh, however. The thought of leaving the apartment for even a moment while his master was away from the city was more than inconceivable to him—in many ways it was a notion closer to blasphemy. Stopping from ministering the failing plants for a moment, he bent down, one knee touching the floor, so he might greet his visitor.

"Ho, Apollo, you feel the restless need, too? Wah, but I understand. Without the master's presence, your fangs and my knife both grow dull from disuse."

The dog pushed against the large Sikh, rubbing his monstrous jaw against the man's briar of a beard. The action would have knocked most men over, as would the man's beard have scratched the flesh from most others. But dog and man were two of the same, and enjoyed each other's company. The great hound made a forlorn noise deep in its throat to which Singh answered;

"I understand, fierce one. Here we sit, these many days, with not the slightest morsel of battle to warm our blood." Taking Apollo's massive head within his own large hands, the Sikh confided to the dog;

"By Shiva, I do believe we are being tested. Shall we fail our master, or shall we remain steadfast?" The hound responded to the question by suddenly sitting erect and lifting it's great head to let forth a mighty howl. It stopped itself, however, as both dog and man heard a noise each knew was out of the ordinary. As the ears of both strained to hear more, Singh whispered;

"And then, perhaps our test is at an end."

The noise in question had been the forcing of the front door's main bolt. The Squad's members were somewhat surprised to find the owner had no alarms wired to his home. They could not know, of course, that the estate's owner had reasons why he did not want the police to suddenly have the right to invade his property. They did not worry about the detail, however. They had come across many strange quirks in the homes of the city's wealthy. This one just made their work easier.

"Let's go," ordered a large man standing in the center of the penthouse's main foyer. A submachine gun in one hand, he barked, "there's a safe somewhere in this dump and you've got one hour to find, crack, and empty it. Now—*move!*"

The Squad had come prepared. Every man was heavily armed. Each of them wore the same nondescript black uniform—boots, work pants and pullover, gloves and a face mask. Several wore back packs carrying burglary tools and explosives. The thugs showed obvious training as they moved forward into the lavish home. None of them spoke, as they broke off in pairs, all heading in separate, pre-determined directions. As he reached the second story landing, Ram Singh restrained Apollo, thinking;

By the prophet, they are everywhere—like locusts.

The back of the Sikh's mind contradicted him, pointing out that the men were searching only the first floor at that time. He sorely wished to send Apollo at the invaders, following the hound with blade drawn and a battle cry on his lips. But, he was too finely trained a warrior to charge uselessly into a hail of bullets. Nor would he sacrifice the Great Dane in such a manner. Instructing the massive Harlequin to await his signal, the dog followed Singh into a side room. While Apollo fell back on his haunches to wait, the Sikh slipped into what would appear to be a closet to any other and disappeared.

"Why are we searchin' da damn kitchen?"

"It's a room, ain't it?"

"Yeah, but—"

"And all the rooms hav'ta be searched, right?"

"I know, but—"

"And dis is where we were told to head first, ain't it?"

"I know, but the kitchen—"

"Is just the kinda place a smart guy would hide his safe, just because dull wits like you would never think to look there."

The second man sighed, tired of having to explain things to the newer team members. Mr. Finetti did his best to get the finest talent available, the man knew he did. But still, he thought, some of them could not grasp the simplest concepts.

The man pulled open the refrigerator, just to be able to say he had checked. He moved a few things around, made certain there were no hidden latches or trip switches anywhere. Satisfied there was nothing of interest within, he swung the door shut. His surprise to find Ram Singh behind the door was evident by the extra seconds it took him to raise his weapon. Just before his trigger finger could close, the blood arcing forcefully from his throat gave him pause, giving the Sikh time to pluck the automatic weapon from his hands.

As a third crimson spurt splashed against the wall, it caught the attention of the thug with so many questions. Spinning around at the wet and sloppy sound, his eyes almost focused on the large bearded form closing on him. His mouth began to form a word, but the sword already slicing through the air reached his neck and took his head away from his shoulders. Catching the thug's falling body with one hand, Singh wiped his weapon clean on the man's pullover, then cast the corpse aside, muttering;

"Well, jackal, did you enjoy the taste of my blade?"

Gliding across the kitchen, the Sikh cracked the door to the dining room. Inside he saw another two man team checking the walls, inspecting the larger pieces of furniture and so forth. Singh boiled to charge the pair, but he forced himself to caution. He himself had witnessed more than two score men entering his master's home. If he was to serve Sahib Wentworth well, he knew he must call upon all his training.

Remaining breathlessly still, he stood his ground watching the two men from his vantage point. As they swept the room, one drew close to Singh's position. Seeing his best opportunity coming swiftly, he reached with practiced silence down to retrieve one of the slender throwing blades secreted within his boot. Even as he did so, the man drawing near said;

"Where's this door go?"

"Open it and find out, ya moron."

Singh allowed the man to both open the door, and to take a step inside. Then, with a terrible blow he sliced away the man's forward hand, the one holding the machine gun. As the man screamed in pain, the Sikh stepped into him, smashing the bleeding man into the door jamb with his body as he launched his throwing knife across the room. The blade tore into the second man's throat, sending blood splashing across the room. Then, only a second after making contact with the first man, he reached up and grabbed hold of the thug's head, twisting his neck—killing him instantly.

The second man, unable to speak because of his injury, was stumbling for the hallway door. Throwing himself into the room, Ram Singh leaped up and slid across the great dining room table. His approach sent the crystal centerpiece and other decorations flying, but it also allowed him to cut off the thug's escape. Singh slammed into the man, his great booted feet crushing the other's rib cage. Standing quickly, quietly, the Sikh then leapt to the door to the hallway, putting his ear to the center panel. As the second man twitched on the floor, the warrior put all his attention to listening for evidence that he had been heard. Finally satisfied the scuffle had aroused no suspicion, he headed back for the kitchen.

Crossing the room, he was about to check the pantry on the other side of the room when its door suddenly opened. The Sikh ducked down behind the great butcher's block near the refrigerator. Just as his turban disappeared from sight, two more of Finetti's men entered the room. As they did, however, both spotted the slaughtered remains of their comrades.

"What the hell happened in here?"

"I did."

The pair turned at the sound of the voice to their side, but they were too late. The razor-sharp cleaver which always hung from the side of the cutting block slammed into the closest man's forehead before he could complete his turn. The slicing blade which always hung next to the cleaver caught the second man in the chest, carving a path neatly through his lung and out his back as if through cotton. Unfortunately, the man lived just long enough to fire his weapon.

"What was that?"

"Probably someone found the butler, or the dog—whatever."

"Whatever ain't good enough," snapped the thug in charge. Bellowing at the top of his lungs, he ordered, "Find out where that shot came from! Everybody—group up! Give me an answer—now, damnit!"

Hearing the orders, Ram Singh returned to the secret passage he had used to descend to the first floor and quickly scrambled back upstairs, then ran to the other end of the penthouse. Entering a second closet with a false back, he dropped down the hidden passage, his feet not even touching the rungs of the ladder. Then, while the thugs responded to their team leader's orders, the Sikh came out on the other end of the first floor, behind the force searching for him.

To move into the hallway would be suicide for most men, but the Hindu warrior was not a one to consider such trifles. Seizing what to one of his skill seemed an excellent opportunity, he came up behind two of the men and grabbed their heads in his terrible hands. With unbelievable speed, he smashed their skulls one against the other. They shattered with the sound of a sack of flour hitting a sidewalk. So violent had his blow been that bone shards tore through each man's mask, stabbing Singh in his palms.

Not noticing the pain, the Sikh stepped smoothly around the falling bodies and, before either of them touched the floor, he had reached the next closest of the thugs. Pulling his long-blade, he whirled the great knife and removed the man's head from his shoulders. The head went flying, bouncing off the nearest wall, making a sickening thud which more than one of the thugs heard.

Turning, two of them managed to actually focus on the sight of the long-blade as it tore them open, one across his neck, the other his abdomen. Blood spurting, guts spilling across the marble hallway, these two did more than manage to get out a word or two—they howled in mortal agony, attracting the attention of all the Squad.

"There's the son'va bitch! Kill him!"

A normal warrior, a well-trained soldier, a man of this century, any of them would have recognized that moment as the time to retreat. But Ram Singh was not any of those men. Knowing his duty, aching to feel the sting of battle, he did what no man would expect—he threw himself into the dense pack of men before him.

As he landed between the crowd, three of them fired wildly, actually taking out their own men. At the same time, the instant his feet touched the floor, his arms completed the swing he had begun in mid-air, his great blade carving its way completely through the bodies of two of the thugs! The sight so stunned the invaders that the Sihk was able to swing again and take the head of yet another man.

"For the love of Mike, you bastards," screamed the team leader, "he's just one man!"

Ram knew the moment to retreat was upon him, but he was deep within the blood lust, and his heart could not hear the sage council of his mind. Lashing out, he stuck another through the bowels and lifted him upon his blade, hurling him backward into the others. The screaming man knocked over three of his fellows, but it was not enough.

Those standing behind him fired. Several score bullets shattered the hallway, gouging terrible holes in the walls and ceiling, bringing down the delicate white glass chandeliers, destroying several paintings and one fine granite bust. They also found their real target. Ram Singh's large body was too great a target not to be discovered by such a hail of lead.

The first bullet tore through his shoulder, exiting out his back. The second lodged in his thigh against the bone, tripling the pain because of the contact. The third and fourth took him in the forearm and the chest, while a fifth slashed through his turban, singeing his hair and blooding his scalp.

Any of the wounds would have been enough to incapacitate a normal man. Indeed, most any other mortal would have been on their back, the best of them screaming, the rest of them dying from shock or already gone. But, Ram Singh was not any ordinary man.

The Sihk knew his foes would expect him to simply fall down and die. His body staggered by pain and shock, his blood flowing freely, he knew if he were to survive to protect his master's home, that he had to retreat. Dismissing the feelings of shame overwhelming him as the crutches of fools, Singh retreated into the room from which he had exited.

Knowing he would have a handful of extra seconds, that those coming behind him would not believe him capable of any more violence, he headed back upstairs via the hidden ladder, purposely leaving open the closet door behind him.

Each rung was a thing of agony. His leg screamed pain at him, his shoulder barked it. Every movement was a torment. Blood dribbling over his smiling lips, Ram fought off each shock of agony as it blistered through his body, praising Allah for allowing him this glorious chance to prove himself once more. He dragged himself up onto the second floor, then staggered off just as the men below reached the closet.

Knowing they were closing on their lone prey, the thugs below swarmed straight for the closet. As the first neared the top of the ladder, he sprayed the exit with several bursts, looking to force anyone waiting for him away from the entrance. The bullets tore through walls and the floor, letting the thug know that if anyone were waiting close by, they were no further threat. Pulling himself up to where he could enter the second floor, however, he had only long enough to look across the bedroom to note that his prey was waiting for him, leaning against the opposite door—throwing knife in hand.

The thug screamed as the blade tore open his face, then he went crashing down atop the man behind him. The slain crook's body slammed into the second thug, forcing his leg in between the rungs of the ladder, breaking it in two places. As the man howled in torturous agony, the Squad leader barked;

"Upstairs, go—_go_! Half the shares of the dead to the man who kills this bastard!"

Not even two thirds of them, thought Ram Singh, cursing himself for an old woman instead of a warrior. As two men approached the top of the main staircase, Singh hurled the chair he had grabbed just in case he might need it, striking the first and knocking him into the second. Both men fell backward into the others, one man toppling over the railing to the foyer below.

A terrible hail of lead screamed up from the stairs and the foyer, but none struck its target for the crippled Ram had somehow managed to reach the room to which he was headed by the time the others had taken note of him. Even as the leader of the Squad bellowed more orders, the Sikh was opening a hidden panel within his master's bedroom. Pulling a small device from within, he turned to Apollo, giving the monstrous hound a weak but sinister grin.

"Their numbers are close to half, but all our advantages are taken now, like dew in the morning. I think that which comes beyond life may reveal itself to us shortly. Are you ready?"

The dog pawed the ground, grinding his terrible fangs as he growled a low and evil note.

"Then, my good true friend, let us kill these mice who think they are men."

The bedroom door opened just as Ram Singh depressed the button on the control in his hand. The first thugs to enter saw just a glimpse of the Sikh as all the lights in the house were extinguished, as all the doors and windows were barred, as all the gates were closed fast. The suddenly fearful men fired their weapons wildly. All they did was give light to the blades and fangs seeking their lives.

Richard Wentworth was quite nonplussed to find workmen stretched from one end of his home to the other when he returned. A brief moment of explanation from his butler sent him instantly to the room of his manservant where the great Sikh and Apollo were recovering from their many wounds. As they walked, the butler swore he had insisted the dog be removed to a proper facility, but—

"I'm telling you, sir, he actually threatened me grievous injury if I removed the dog from his side."

"I'm surprised Apollo didn't try to bite you," answered Wentworth, hiding his amusement. He managed to do so for a moment, but had to smile when his old retainer answered;

"He did; that's the only reason I gave up."

Wentworth spent a moment calming the older man, then entered Ram Singh's room. The great Sikh was covered in bandages. His left leg was in a full cast, as was his right arm. His neck had been braced and one of his eyes was patched. The warrior's usually dark complexion had been drained to the point where his skin was nearly as white as the sheet upon which he rested.

A thousand notions entered the mind of the man known to the world as the *Spider*. He especially wanted to berate Singh for taking such awful risks merely to protect useless trifles like money. He knew, however, that the Sikh had not suffered such wounds to merely guard his valuables.

Singh was the greatest warrior Richard Wentworth had ever met. After the two had first fought side-by-side years earlier, the Sikh had pledged himself to follow his "master" to the ends of the Earth. The *Spider* knew he had not done so for any other reason than the fact that Singh had known to be near the *Spider* would be to be near the evil against which he so dearly loved to test himself. Looking down at the half-dead warrior, Wentworth said;

"You're looking pretty good."

"Forgive your servant, master," Singh answered weakly. "It is but a pin prick, but I somehow have not the will to rise."

"Forget it," said Wentworth softly, fiercely proud to have such a man feel so strongly about remaining worthy to stay by his side. Stroking the massive Harlequin Dane sprawled on the bed next to the Sikh, he added;

"Things are quiet now. You get a little rest. Something will pop up sooner or later to give you a reason to get out of bed."

"When it does," the Hindu said softly, straining to get out each word, "we will dispatch them together."

"Indeed," answered Wentworth. Rising, he headed back to the hall, adding just before he closed the door, "I don't see how I could do it without you."

His master gone, the Sikh smiled. The pain coursing through his broken, shattered body was as nothing. He had done well. So had Apollo, whose neck he scratched with his undamaged hand. The great hound murmured its appreciation. Soon, the pinpricks would be healed and they would be back at their master's side. And when the moment came, he and his master would comb the city for more fiends to combat, for more evil to thwart, for—

"More souls for Hell."

illustration by Tom Floyd

Chapter Thirteen

CAUGHT IN THE CROSSFIRE

by ANN NOCENTI

Miles McCrea is swell, the kind of muck who just needs a bone to chew. He doesn't care what bone. Women, horses, drink, dice.... Sometimes you can snatch a bone out of his jaw but he'll just pick up another one. Grab the bottle out of his hand before his liver explodes and he'll yank the nearest woman onto his lap, usually someone's wife. Steal the woman away before he gets a bellyful of angry husband buckshot, and he'll hop a bi-plane and do his best to crash it doing loop-de-loops flirting with mountaintops. His new jones is gambling, and he's been hitting the hottest games from Morocco to Mexico. Not that I judge a man for his appetites. Whatever wags your tail, I say. And Miles has been quick on the draw more than once, watching my back. If he's dead, I owe it to him to kill whoever ended his short happy life.

Last time anyone saw Miles, he was in the Bahamas, at a poker game in Delectable Bay, home of a buccaneer descendant of Blackbeard known only as Red Slash. Apparently this Red Slash gets his kicks laying wait outside big cash games, then he pounces, steals the winner's booty and leaves his trademark red slash across his mark's throat. If that's what Red Slash has done to Miles, it's only polite to return the courtesy.

Most days I'm Richard Wentworth, but for this jaunt I've jiggered it to Richard Worthington. I've stumbled on a curious notion: a man can't have too many names. You never know when you don't want to be who you are. Or when you'll want to leave yourself elsewhere. Or want your different selves in different cities. Why this time? Let's just say that back in New York City I got all worked up over a blonde. She wore her hair in pigtails and got a kick out of how she only came up to my hip. She would laugh and whisper in my ear, "I'm just a length of leg."

Anyway, that's another story, but one that left a three-block stretch of The Bowery a little messy. When I get worked up, my less tolerant persona, the *Spider*, has his merciless way with my prey: whoever happens to be irritating me at the moment. The city's garbage men, otherwise known as coppers, were washing blood off cobblestones and flushing it down gutters for days.

Which is why Wentworth has to stay in New York City, but Worthington can do whatever the hell he wants. This whole speech is a long way round to explaining why I'm on a slow steamer with Nita Van Sloan. We're headed south, slicing a fat wake through the thousands of isles that make up the West Indies. Cruise ship on charter from Miami to the Bahamas; the kind of idle excursion that amuses the affluent, but I'm finding a bit like a stretch in the big house. Like walking the yard, but with a cocktail.

At 28 knots, the *El Rey del Mar* is now cutting a swath through the endless cays and inlets that pepper the Bahamas. The all-negro band is having a fine time matching the ocean swells with some new sound called "swing" that involves a lot of brass. It swung all right, but too snappy happy for my taste. The litter of aristocrats lounging about on deck twiddling cocktails and squandering unearned money is comprised mostly of the worthless spawn of Morgans and Fords and Vanderbilts and Rockefellers. You could say I'm part of the same tribe, but it would be rude.

There's one slouch of youth skulking about who's clearly a have-not, but he's easy on the eyes enough to be along for the ride. A boy with the depth of a dime and a predator's instinct that proximity to money begets money. At the moment, his pretty face is having just such an effect on the bejeweled dowager at whose feet he sits.

It isn't the safest sea passage. Mob bootleggers, mostly Gambinos, run rum boats from Nassau to Miami, and while the legendary pirates Blackbeard and Anne Bonney are long dead, their cheaper, flashier knock-offs shark the seas for suckers. Not that it matters for a passenger ship like this; the few crusty gems draping the dowager's neck and dappling her fingers are hardly worth the effort of chasing down this beast of a ship, climbing ropes and getting shot at for your trouble.

I watched Nita as she walked my way. There isn't a man on deck that hasn't given Nita Van Sloan the all up and down. She wore a clingy slip of a dress the color of a good burgundy, made from a kind of flimsy silk that inspired a man to pray for a stiff sea breeze. She leaned casually against the railing and I made my way to her side.

"Enjoying the show?" I asked.

"What show," demurred Nita.

"The bevy of handsome young men of wealth and indistinction. And the attending muscle running the ship."

"Muscles? I hadn't noticed. You'll have to point one out to me."

"Heave ho," I replied.

She yanked the long end of my tie, and found an excuse to keep fiddling with it. Then she gave me her smallest smile, the one that came with a flash of violet. Nita's pale eyes were sometimes iridescent as a dragonfly's wing, and never failed to catch my breath.

"And the leggy thing?" she teased. "You're enjoying that, I assume?" There was quite a bit of leg showing on deck, as was last decade's style. Hemlines went back down after the crash, but not for the kind of sailing out-fits worn by rich women on cruisers. Besides Nita's eyes, I did have a weakness for leg, but she didn't need to know that.

"What legs? Are they serving chicken?"

She laughed. It was our game. "So, Richard," she began with dubious nonchalance, "Your friend Miles. Is he the one we visited in the sanitarium last year?"

"Oh, darling, don't focus on a man's darkest hour," I said, happy she hadn't stopped stroking my tie.

"Just wanting a bit of the lay of the land," she said, gazing out to sea.

I looked at her suspiciously. "Nita. You're not thinking of doing anything but getting out of the way, say, if…"

"…there's any fisticuffs or bullets spraying about?" she asked. "You know me, dear, first under the table."

"Only when we drink. But really, promise me…"

"Let's watch the game, shall we?" She tossed my tie so that it swung over my shoulder, cutting the fun short. There was no telling Nita Van Sloan what to do. Not that I'm a man that would want any woman I could control. And there are worse things in life than a woman with a habit of throwing herself into the fire for you.

The game she referred to was spread out on a table in the middle of the deck. The robber baron spawn that played it were fiddling with real estate deeds and toy houses. It was a prototype of a board game about to hit the market next month. "Monopoly" they called it; a tedious game of buying lots, building hotels and collecting rent. The players chattered inanely about dominating city blocks and monopolizing each other's empires, as if they had a clue how their grandfathers actually built their fortunes. They'd tossed the "play" money that came with the game aside, and were using real, large bills. Nothing smaller than a Franklin.

An elderly colored waiter moved silently among them, offering gin gimlets and old fashioneds and rum somethings, without inspiring a single thanks or tip. He'd perfected the art of subservient invisibility, his good nature barely visible after years of serving this ilk.

"You're a luck bucket!" The angry cry went up from a player as he landed on another player's high-rent Park Avenue. The loser then switched gears, laughing off his misfortune. "Good thing it's only money!" he said, tossing down a heap of smacks. The old waiter flinched. These were hard times for most. "The Depression" they were calling it. He carried his empty tray away.

I glanced at the game. I couldn't get past the fact that the so-called hotels you could build on the lots were only an inch high and made of chunks of cheap metal. This game, this Monopoly, it wasn't going to be much. Not as long as the real thing was up for grabs.

I turned my attention to the few suspect characters on board, drifting away from Nita to do a slow circle around the deck. At the game board was a squirrelly little fellow perched on the arm of a chaise. Gravity demanded the chair should topple, but it didn't. He had muscles like roots, but perhaps he was hollow-boned like a bird. And he had the edge of the undersized; small men, children, pygmies, monkeys, midgets… people tend to underestimate those of small stature, treat them like pets or dimwits or blocks of wood. I could see him using it to his advantage. He was watching them all for weakness, for tells, jockeying to control the board. He'd make naïve comments about building a cash stack before investing in land. Everyone would laugh nervously at such bad advice, but secretly follow it, allowing him to trump their missed chances and steal prime real estate. I liked his style.

Then there was a fireplug of a guy with a handlebar mustache twice as wide as his wide face, who claimed to be an entrepreneur but had the manners of somebody's hired grunt. I disliked him right off, mostly for the way his eyes tended to stay stuck somewhere on Nita. I'd seen his moves before; lugs like him lurk at the edge of every speakeasy, brothel and gameroom on the East Coast. The only entrepreneurship he knew was tossing drunks for cash and crunching skulls for the cheap rush. Far more curious to me was the high seas preacher, a Reverend Ezekiel Stump, who was ranting about the tent cities and Hoovervilles and how the whole middle of the country was turning to dust for the sins of short skirts and the dubiously Roaring Twenties. And watching over all this was the ship's Captain, a handsome but useless ruddy named Roddy, who hadn't spent a minute in the wheelhouse.

After I'd eyeballed everyone worth eyeballing, I drifted back over to Nita. We kept it unclear as to whether or not we were together, which was easy, because it also happened to be the truth. When you have as many enemies as I have, any woman you care about you'll keep on the long-arm. And working any game, it was best to let the guys think they had a shot at her. Something about the jut of her hip where she rested her cocktail, or maybe it was that thing she did with her lower lip when she was bored, but I noticed she was having an affect even on the good Reverend Stump, which made me doubt his commitment to the Lord.

We divvied up the watch.

"Who do you prefer?" I offered.

"The Preacher, for entertainment..." mused Nita. "And the Captain, for..."

"Muscle?"

"I hadn't noticed," she replied lightly.

"The sun *is* blinding today. All right, I'll take the dwarf and the handlebar mustache."

"Dwarf? How crude, darling."

"Midget?"

"Richard, please. So, just what am I fishing for?"

"Entrée. Someone who can get us a quick invite to an underground card game."

"It would help if I knew if a straight beat a flush."

We were interrupted by a roar bellowing out of Handlebar. "Dustbowl!? Never happen!" Nita took advantage of the distraction to drift closer to the fight.

"I've got my stock in the railroad and stakes in banks from New York to San Francisco," Handlebar yelled at the Preacher. "The middle of this country's going to be as lucrative as the coasts, mark my words."

"Money lenders out of the temple," the Preacher barked back. "The stock market crash? That was just God's opening gambit for vengeance. What about this thing called jazz? Mixing God's music with the devil's? Gospel is the voice of the Lord!" The Reverend Stump was working up the necessary froth for a sermon, belting it out for the entire deck to hear. "The heathen's music should never mix notes with God's voice! They're asking for it!" He held up a less-than-mighty fist and shook it. "You can't rouse heaven by raising hell!"

A few of the lounging Monopoly players raised an eyebrow, but most were too engrossed in the game to pay any mind.

"Take it to the pulpit," said Handlebar sourly, but his eyes were on Nita, with that dogged fix I didn't care for.

"That's the price of sin! Dust! He'll scorch the land till they beg for relief, and then he'll bless us with a flood!" Ezekiel Stump was winning an argument no one was listening to.

Nita returned to the rail, and I whispered in her ear. "Your take on

Handlebar?"

"More muscle than business. Not that I'd notice," teased Nita.

"And the Preacher? Seems no more a man of the cloth than Handlebar has a dime in the bank."

"Good call, darling. He happens to have a very hard muscle where there shouldn't be one."

I ran my eyes over Reverend Stump till I saw it, the bulge just under his knee. A gun; strapped, cloaked and protected by holy cloth.

"Things could get messy, darling," murmured Nita. "Remember your promise."

"This week, I am Richard and Richard only. A vacation from the *Spider*. My promise to you."

"That includes not *acting* like the *Spider*, hmm?

"Semantics, darling. Need we split hairs…" But I was distracted by the rising prattle of the Pretty Boy, who had shifted like a cat from the Dowager's feet to her lap.

"I don't see why they call these the jeweled isles," he said sullenly. "They look dull."

Captain Roddy paused from coiling rope, a chore usually bestowed on a swab. When he spoke, his tone had an ominous burn that Pretty Boy was oblivious to. "You've seen nothing till you've seen one of these isles in full Royal Poinciana bloom, a flaming scarlet glow above the clear blue sea…."

I wasn't one for pontificators, and now we had two preachers on deck.

The Captain's face darkened. "Islands that are now awash in a new shade of red, the sky and seas tinted pink from the glow of it, the blood trails of mobsters and pirates!"

"Pirates!" gasped the Dowager. "Oh, I adore that Errol Flynn!"

"Pirates?" Pretty Boy looked at the Captain with disdain. "You're confusing the movies with real life, old man. There's no pirates left."

Captain Roddy again paused from the rope and eyed Pretty Boy, a tiger deciding not *if* there would be a kill, but mulling over when. He continued his slow coil, handling the task as if each measure of rope were a potential noose or whip.

Collective moans from around the board game saved Pretty Boy the pounce. The players were shoving back their chairs as the little man gathered piles of cash, having taken everyone's money, one by one, and just now bankrupting the last. The faces of the losers were flush, as if freshly slapped. It was dawning on them that they, the progeny of some of the greatest businessmen of the era, had been suckered, trounced by a hip-high guy they'd been treating as a child.

Captain Roddy walked over to Pretty Boy and fixed his stare. "No pirates? Their lairs are everywhere, you stupid whelp. Hard Hill, Gun Point Island, Cripple Hill, Delectable Bay... the wretched seadogs lie in shallow inlet creeks and scrape barnacles off their hulls, wax the wood to give their pitiful skiffs the speed to overtake even a big ship like this one. They can outrun anyone, and when they catch you? They'd sooner cut your heart out still beating than spit on you."

"Oh dear!" The Dowager clutched for Pretty Boy's manicured hand.

"Yeah, I knew all that," lied Pretty Boy. "I heard of that Blackbeard."

"He's long dead," was Captain Roddy's curt reply.

The little man sauntered toward us, stuffing cash in his pockets. Nita flashed her dragonflies at me, drained her cocktail and went for another. She was aware of how her presence altered a conversation, and that a man could get more out of another man without those violets watching.

"Don't listen to that old salt," the little man said, nodding a polite good-bye to Nita. "There hasn't been a proper pirate around since 1750. The pirates he speaks of are just hoodlums with fast boats dressed in the dirty rags they fantasize their betters wore. Their knives are short and blunt and they've never even heard of a swashbuckler."

He extended his hand. "Jim Bolt," he said.

"Richard Worthington." I shook his hand, which was surprisingly calloused and strong.

Pretty Boy's whine rose across the deck. "Well, all this talk of pirates, these shabby islands... Why did I even come here?"

"Shabby!" bellowed the Captain. "These islands have history. Dignity! They're more than just baubles to amuse your stupid eyes, boy. See that island? That there's Rum Cay, home to the wreck of a 100-gun man-o-war, sunk in 1861. Served in the Crimean, she did. Didn't deserve to be raped as booty for pirates." He moved in close and spoke an inch from boy's face, "You don't rape the likes of her!" Then, quietly, glancing at the Dowager, "No offense, ma'am."

"None taken," she answered quickly, a flicker of confusion on her face.

Roddy turned to address the sea. "You have no idea the riches! The gulf-streams bring in monster schools of bonefish, tuna, wahoo, billfish.... Fish that need a man to catch..."

"I'd like to get me a big fish," said Pretty Boy brightly.

The Dowager looked tired as she patted his hand, her glow for the boy somewhat dimmed. "You will, don't worry."

"I see he already hooked his," said Bolt, and I smiled.

The old waiter approached with drinks. "I wouldn't mind another medicinal," said Bolt, as we both took fresh ones off his tray.

"Here's to international waters," Bolt said, and raised his glass. Three miles offshore, and a man left Prohibition behind him.

I shot my eyes at the Monopoly players and said to the waiter, "Thanks for the drink, and I apologize for the rudeness of the entertainment."

The old man smiled. "Thank you sir."

"What's your name?" asked Bolt.

"Jules, sir."

"Well, Jules, my winnings owe a lot to your service," he said, placing an enormous tip on the plate. The waiter's eyes widened slightly, but he remained composed. "Thank you, sir." He bowed and left.

"But what about Blackbeard?" Pretty Boy was whining. "How can we go fishing if *he's* out there?"

"His descendants, whelp," said Roddy, as he rummaged through a box of gear, pulling out hooks and weights. "You know the bloodlines here? Calico Jack Rackman, Black Bart, and yes, Blackbeard himself! They plundered more Spanish fools... Right here's where Anne Bonney was captured at twenty, spared the noose only because she was with child. Many a ship she plundered. There's rabbles of their spawn out there, even rumored to be a few female freebooters about." He turned and shook a fist at the sea, screaming into the wind, "Freebooters! Seadogs! Scum of the sea!" and walked off.

"Oh dear," said Bolt. "How dramatic. If I knew this cruise came with such cut-rate thespians I'd have booked cheaper passage."

I glanced at Nita, and she casually strolled after the Captain.

"I feel faint," said the Dowager. "I've heard pirates even eat babies and..."

"I'll protect you," insisted Pretty Boy stupidly. "From a score of rogues and scoundrels..."

"Quite the duet," Bolt deadpanned. He hopped up to perch on the rail; that gravity-defying trick of his again.

"I thought the pirates were all like Errol Flynn!" the Dowager pouted at Pretty Boy. "Handsome swashbucklers!" He took her jeweled hand in his. I counted seven big rocks.

"Pirates," said Bolt. "People like to romanticize these things. What's the life of a pirate? They rape, pillage, plunder and drink. A short merry life, ending with a shorter length of swinging rope."

Nita walked back to join us. Somewhere along the line she'd touched up her already plum ripe lips. "The Captain has gone fishing," she said softly.

"I prefer Miami," Pretty Boy was saying, as he startled the Dowager by caressing her dry hair and wrinkled cheek. I quickly looked to her hand and counted only four rocks. Three diamonds missing. He'd done a misdirect and a flourish. Shifted her attention to his caresses so that she wouldn't notice that the sudden lightness of her hand wasn't from the euphoria of new love.

I saw her hesitation. She was just old, not stupid. She was aware that Pretty Boy was forty years her junior. So she goes on a little fishing trip of her own. "Why, I've heard Juan Ponce de Leon found the Fountain of Youth here…" She looked expectantly into Pretty Boy's eyes.

"Who needs a fountain of youth?" he answered with the quickness and lack of grace of the baby grifter he was. "People age like wine, they get better, more beautiful, richer…."

I couldn't watch any more. I was saved this gruesome spectacle by a WHOMP!, as an enormous bloody fish hit the deck with the thrashing violence of its own imminent death. Captain Roddy had swung down his catch, a large tuna, to a spot purposefully marked to splatter Pretty Boy with fishblood. The boy screamed. Roddy grinned, pulled a huge knife, killed, butchered and thundered: "Still putting down our seas, boy? Look at this beauty!"

The flesh of the fish split, guts spilled, the thrashing finally stilled, eyes now murky and still, a slow pool of blood spreading.

"You know who our boisterous Captain reminds me of?" said Bolt. "That big game hunter with the new book out. Hemingway he's called. He likes to fish our seas and drink in our best Nassau joints. Writes like a schoolchild. Little words, blunt sentences, but full of meat. Captain Roddy here, he knows his kind is dying. He's hanging on with bluster, talking of the grand seas and the grand men that ride them." Bolt paused, and looked at me significantly before saying, "Hemingway thinks violence is at the heart of life. He speaks to men like this. You know what I mean, don't you, Richard?"

I could see the amusement gathering at the corners of Nita's eyes as she decided to answer for me; "Oh, he certainly does."

"Like our Captain Roddy," Bolt continued. "He's a dinosaur. So are the pirates. Men that don't know their time is past, lumbering off into the horizon. Men like these, they're singing their own death songs and they don't even know it. So is Hemingway, really. He's writing his own eulogy." Again he paused and stared at me.

"That's quite an essay," I replied as dryly as I could, trying not to look at the grin I knew to be spreading across Nita's face.

"You want to read something good," said Bolt, "Read Dale Carnegie's *How to Win Friends and Influence People*. Dale Carnegie's the future. It's not muscle but mind that will matter from now on." He paused, then added, "Why don't you two be my guests at Cable Beach tonight, I have a suite near the horsetrack. I'm in a few races tomorrow."

A jockey, not a midget. I should have known.

"May I ask why you're here?" asked Bolt.

I paused. Nita took this as her cue to take another constitutional round the deck.

"You're wondering whether or not to trust me?" said Bolt, reading my mind. "You know what they say of men of small stature… we have to develop in other ways to make up for it. So we've either got a grandiose sense of self, or we live by immense wit and discretion. Which do you think?"

I smile.

"So then, Richard Worthington. Not your real name, I presume?"

"If you juggle the letters a bit, it is."

Bolt's response was quick. "I'm a man who knows there are things I don't need to know."

"I had some complications in New York I'm avoiding," I tell him, leaving out the small detail of a significant amount of blood spilled and autographed by the *Spider*. "And I expect complications down here also. So I'd rather my world at large believe me to still be in New York."

"And to curtail any hasty recriminations on my part as to your character," said Bolt, pulling out a pack of smokes, "your complications in New York were inspired by…?"

"A blonde…."

"Ah."

"… who only came up to my hip. Hair in pigtails. Eight years old. They held her bound and gagged for three days. Wanted a half-million ransom. A blonde worth getting worked up for."

Bolt nodded and tapped out two fags, handing me one. "And what brings you south?"

"I lost a friend to a gambling den. I'm looking for a game. And his killer."

"I know of one or two," he said, leaning in to light my cigarette. "Games, not killers."

"I heard a rumor that pirates lie in wait, in hopes of picking off big winners."

"I've heard that too. But rumors flow around these islands with the tides. In and out."

"Well, assuming this one's accurate, I can play a bit. What if I got in a game and won big."

"You'd become a fly in a pirate's web," said Bolt. "I can arrange it, if you're so inclined."

We paused to enjoy our smoke. In the silence, I listened to the cries of distant sea gulls that sounded almost human. I glanced at the Captain. He, too, was listening to the gulls, with a curious expression. Bolt gestured at the lounging guests and said, "What do you make of this bunch?"

"We have a preacher protected by the Lord that's packing the extra insurance only a gun can give, and somebody's hired muscle doing a bad impression of a businessman," I said, with a nod at Handlebar. "And a Captain who isn't driving the ship, and has instead demoted himself to a deckhand's chores in order to stay close to the action."

"So," smiled Bolt, "We can expect some entertainment."

I heard Nita's high laugh from across deck, a signal for me to follow her gaze. Ezekiel Stump was scanning the horizon, as he checked a pocket watch that dangled, along with a large crucifix, off his rosary. The Captain, his fish knife still in hand, walked swiftly along the rail.

It's then that I felt the railing vibrate, as if something, somewhere had struck the hull of the boat. I slipped down starboard side and peered overboard. Boats. Pirates. Grappling lines tossed and hooked, hoisting rope ladders. Captain Roddy was slicing a rope, sending pirates shrieking back to the sea, but a score of others crawled aboard. I stepped up just in time to slam lead into the first pirate's chest. The shot was followed by screams on deck, and I realized they must have also crested portside. We were blindsided.

They were all over us like blackflies in July. They had necklaces made of teeth and hunks of dried meat hanging off embroidered and bejeweled sashes. Their hair was matted and braided with gems, their dress a mix of leather, burlap rags and satin belts. Bolt was right, like some fantasy they had of Blackbeard, who was probably an impeccable dresser. What seemed to be the top pirate had a bright red sash across his chest. The fabled Red Slash.

The pirates scrambled across the deck like crabs, slashing necks and dragging others to the rails, binding them by their wrists and hanging them off it. They reminded me less of warriors than of wasps swarming. I pointlessly tried to signal Nita to hide. She already had her Derringer out and flashing. Handlebar displayed his bravery by cowering behind the stack. The Preacher walked right into the fray, bullets miraculously missing him from all directions, not so much evidence of the Divine as proof he was in cahoots.

Between ducking and trading shots I noticed one pirate had some class, moving with stealth and intelligence, avoiding the crossfire and corralling a few of the best-dressed aristocrats. Another pretty boy, this pirate. Features so delicate they looked to be drawn on with brush and ink. Eyes smeared with coal. A thin mustache. A dandy? Red Slash and the dandy sidekick were clearly calling the shots. I emptied both my .45s into the sea dogs and Roddy crippled a few more, but not before they had tied up enough human collateral to gain an edge. I ducked back to reload. I had to find a way to dance between bullets and over to Nita, and pull her gorgeous but at the moment foolish self to safety.

I'd just slammed a new clip into my second automatic when I saw something I liked, Nita tucking herself safely away in the wheelhouse, and something I didn't like, the boss pirate Red Slash branding his trademark slice across the neck of Jules, the colored waiter, seemingly just for the sport of it. I marked Slash for death. I heard a shot come from behind the stack a second before I fired, and something slammed me and ruined my aim. I only managed to gimp Red Slash's leg. It was the Reverend that had fallen on me, and over his shoulder I saw that from out behind the stack slunk a smug Handlebar, gun smoking.

Ezekiel Stump clung to my jacket as he died, gazing into an other-worldly distance. When he turned back, his eyes were soft. "The light! It narrows… follow it! Follow it as I couldn't when chasing the Lord…" His eyes widened as he seemed to see something in the depths of mine. "But you! You *know*. You follow a narrow vision of light…." His eyes were swirling now, his voice sluggish. "But you know it's the wrong path… why do you follow it any-way?" He slipped a small Bible into the breast pocket of my jacket. "Thank you. You've shown me the way!"

"I didn't shoot you," I tell him. "I didn't show you anything." But he was beyond where human voice could travel.

He may have been a traitor, complicit with pirates, but perhaps he was a real preacher. His words had a strange resonance I was doomed to think about later. As he slid down my leg and into his Lord's arms, I glanced over just in time to see Pretty Boy take pirate lead in the neck. The Dowager crept over to the dying boy. I didn't expect tears, but was nonetheless surprised when, rather than comfort her beloved, she rifled his pockets and retrieved the diamond rings she must have felt slip off her fingers after all.

I dashed for the wheelhouse and ducked inside, taking Nita in my arms. "You all right?"

"I'm fine! I had a moment of courage," said Nita apologetically, "that slipped away rather quickly."

"I'll be back to retrieve you, darling. Now be a good girl and stay hidden!"

I went back out just in time to see Red Slash's minions, their scion captives cowering, guns to their heads, but Bolt now had a knife to the Dandy's throat and I leveled my pistol at Red Slash's temple. I had to hand it to both pirates: they simply ignored us. Red Slash roared: "We'll have that rum now!"

"There's a gun to your head and a knife to your second's throat," I reminded him.

"And a gun to every rich whelp on deck. A Mexican standoff, you agree?"

I glanced around at the number of guns aimed at various heads. "An Albanian stand-off more like it."

Red Slash just held his pinprick eyes on mine, while I noticed a slight smile twist the Dandy's lip. At least one of these pirates had a sense of humor. I turned to the Captain.

"What rum do they refer to?"

He shrugged. "Man's gotta make a buck," he said. "There's some gunny sacks in the hull. Crates inside. So much booze it'd take an hour to offload."

The Dandy ordered the few coloreds left that could still walk to start hauling the booty up from the hull. They disappeared obediently, and soon there was the sound of bottles rattling in crates.

"I'm not interested in the rum," I tell Red Slash. "You can take enough to sink your skiffs for all I care. I want to know about the poker games you plunder and the men you kill for their winnings."

I'm surprised that it's Red Slash's second, the Dandy, that answers. He spits in disgust. "Not our style. We don't kill our own kind." Perhaps he was telling the truth, but Red Slash's silence gave me another story. Besides, I owed Jules his payback blood, so I was in no mood to avoid more bloodshed, not just yet. I dug my .45 deeper into Red Slash's temple.

"Jump overboard, the lot of you, and swim to hell," I yelled, "Or I shoot your boss."

The pirates didn't budge. They looked rather unconcerned, almost bored. A lazy but pointed mutiny.

So I shot Red Slash, for Jules, and it felt good. The pirate got off a dying shot, shattering the deck. No one moved. I even detected a sly smirk on one pirate minion's face. Were they happy their boss was dead? Which meant all we'd done was trade worthless pawns. I nodded to Bolt. Time to threaten what I now realized was the real boss.

"How about that one, then?" I said, pointing at the Dandy. "Jump or he dies."

Bolt pushed the knife hard against the Dandy's fair throat. I had to hand it to him, the threat just made him smile. But as for the rest of the pirates, they scrambled, dashed and stumbled to the rails, ready to jump.

"Lower your guns," I ordered, and they did. "Jump and he lives." They did. Bolt dropped his arm and the freed Dandy paused. We eyed each other.

"I'll be playing poker tonight," I told him. "I expect I'll see you."

"You might," he answered. "But not for the reason you expect."

He leapt overboard, and I ran to the rail to watch them row off, loaded to the gunnels in rum, raising their sails, picking up speed.

"Why did you let them go?" Bolt was at my side.

"There's more to my friend's murder than I thought. If I find a game tonight, I'll know just who gets my next bullet."

A sudden silence, that on second listen was resonant with the moans and final twitches of the dead. The deck was half cleared of guests, most likely cowering in their rooms; the only signs of life were from the dying.

It was then I heard a scrape, a grunt, and the squeak of a rusted gear just far enough down starboard side that the source of these curious sounds were out of my line of sight. I remembered I hadn't seen the Captain in a while, nor Handlebar since he murdered the Preacher. I walked toward the prow and saw Captain Roddy letting down a good-sized sailboat.

I glanced at the wheelhouse and saw Nita emerging.

I turned to Bolt. "Don't the demands of sea law require the Captain to be last to leave ship?"

Bolt followed my gaze and nodded. Nita was upon us.

"I'm going to help the wounded," said Nita breathlessly, and she was off to the task.

"I'll help her," said Bolt, "and then we'll find you."

I sprinted portside aft to double back, and soon had my pistol poised at the backdoor to Roddy's heart. He didn't flinch.

"Welcome aboard," he quipped, with a conciliatory gesture at the escape boat.

"Why are you abandoning your own ship?"

"I'm done here."

Bolt and Nita were soon behind me. "By the way, Mister Worthington," said Bolt casually, "weren't you looking for a game?"

"Yes."

Bolt looked at the Captain and said, "Delectable Bay, thirteen miles north."

"Wind kicks us to seven knots," smiled Roddy, "we'll be there when she opens. I can sell off my stock, stake myself a seat."

I turned back to watch the guests untying and tending one another.

"Is everyone taken care of?" I asked, knowing we'd stay to help if needed.

"Luckily there's a nurse on board," said Nita. "She's on top of things."

At my feet a hunk of metal glistened with blood. I picked it up and wiped it off. A Monopoly hotel. I put it in my pocket.

Soon the four of us were under way, along with Handlebar shackled to an oarlock. We settled in to listen to Roddy's dirty little tale.

"I was a real Captain. Now I'm a Ness man."

"As in Eliot the Untouchable?"

"That's the ticket. Handlebar here is in my custody. He's a rummy for the mob. But Ness is a fish. He's spittin' in the wind with this Prohibition thing. I can't stand righteous prigs. Like that damn preacher. The Senate is ready for another liquor vote. They'll vote to repeal the 18th and the House will follow. Before the year's out, drink will be legal again. It'll be a free market. I'm working the game, but already got my stake in a shack in Florida. A beautiful bar. All I gotta do is bide my time, dig up the bottles and put them on the shelf."

"That's a fine little story," I said, "but I have another question. That boat up ahead. It's displaying a disregard for sea law. Isn't it our right of way? It's headed straight for us."

"Let's test their intent." The Captain gently turned the rudder to avoid a collision course, they corrected to put us back on one. "Our pirate friends," he smiled. "Persistent as water leeches." He veered right; they steadied the collision course again. His smile widened. "And they've got a torch."

"Torch?"

"They intend bellying up and torching my sail. No sail, this girl's dead in the water. They assume we boosted the rest of the rum stock, and they've come back for it."

"Let them know we didn't," exclaimed Nita.

"Ah, my dear, but we did." He kicked a huge mound of beautifully coiled rope, the sound of bottles rattled within.

He grabbed up a shotgun and scrambled to the prow, just as the pirates hoisted their torch, aimed at our sail. I wondered at Roddy's choice of weapon until I saw where he fired — three shots at the water line. The pirates swung hard, but not quick or hard enough. The boat now had a splintering hole too big to patch, they were too far out of range to use the torch, and they were taking on water.

"You see? I'm a kind man. It's a slow leak. They'll make it halfway to shore and swim the rest, work off those rummy bellies." He laughed large.

A quick movement to my right, and Handlebar almost had his chain around Nita's neck. She kicked at him just as I cracked him in the head with an oar.

"Try that again I deliver you dead!" bellowed Captain Roddy. Handlebar just smiled through the blood that now ran down his face, painting his mustache crimson.

Roddy settled down to sail, a fat pink sun sinking to his left. He took out a small radio and listened to static while he sailed smack into a dense dusk fog. I couldn't see my own hand, but the Captain was calm. He listened to something in the distance, noted a few murky flashes of light, adjusted his course.

"How can you see?" inquired Nita.

"I don't really," replied the Captain, as if surprised at such a question. "I listen for the occasional clang of a metal buoy and know how far out we are, and know the shore by the sound of waves hitting it. Those lights in the fog are signals from local fisherman and coppers, hired to steer rum boats out on bad weather nights."

"Police? Helping with the rum?"

Roddy laughed. "Of course. No one's behind this law, we all hate Carry Nation and her hatchet. Only the dries like her, a few dry agents, and Ness." He lowered his voice. "This is a pirate corridor we're crossing now. The mob runs rum right through it."

"What's the static all about?" I ask.

"Inside it is a word or two, that's all I need. I been sittin' on the wire for years. You learn the codes faster than they can switch 'em up."

"Codes?"

"Yeah. Somebody says 'apples,' I know it's safe to come ashore. 'Bluebird,' and I know what load and the course of the punt. Say 'dog' and I know tide's right to send a load out. There's steamers and schooners and dredgers and tugs anchored out there in rum row, waiting till it's safe to load up and head back to Miami. Racketeers got speedboats waiting in the shallows on the wire. Pirates hijack many a load, then run distractions... send out a few zippy skiffs with fake cargo so the lugnuts don't know which boat to chase." He cackled in appreciation. "Gotta love it, how those leeches can outplay all the heat. Pirates think their right to plunder is ancient, older than the mob's. The mob thinks they own everything that's beyond the law, so they've a right to kill you for anything more than a gutrot bathtub batch. It's rummy law seen from two sides. See that buoy?" He pointed to a buoy none of us could see. "That's a lobster trap. Pull it up, there'll be a hootch order in it. Lotta fishermen out here not fishin' for fish," he said, with that self-amused cackle of his. "We're on the dark of the moon. Rummies everywhere."

"Dark of the....?" Nita asked.

"Dark of the moon. You run rum when there's no moon."

We all glanced up at the dense black sky.

"Perfect time for drops and offloads," continued Roddy. "We're lucky this fog rolled in, or we'd never a' made it through rum row on a moonless night."

I watched the Captain steer without fear through a blackness filled with clues only he could see. Bolt was wrong. This was the Captain's world, and we were helpless in it. While we drifted in blindness, the Captain was calm. He wasn't some dinosaur lumbering into the horizon just yet. His time wasn't past and the seas were still grand for those that could navigate it.

We sailed into Delectable Bay in the dead turn of night, and tied up. We trudged a ways through some sandy, thin woods, heading toward a distant glow, and stepped into a clearing with a crude hut surrounded by torches. Roddy chained Handlebar to a tree like common livestock.

"What will you do with him?" Nita asked.

"Perhaps I'll rat him to the mob, let him take the heat for the rum boost," mused Roddy. "Or perhaps I'll hire him to sling drinks in my bar and drunks out of it. We'll see."

After a brief negotiation at the door that seemed to involve Roddy handing over a torn half of a dollar bill and a search for its match in a box of torn dollars, and we were in.

The game at Delectable Bay was a dodgy affair. Low rent and high stakes. Splendid little hellhouse: dirt floor, thatched roof, no doors. Light from the outside torches streamed in between the horizontal bamboo, creating criss-crossing patterns of flickering light across the table. The bar just an oak plank on two barrels, now well stocked thanks to Roddy. A few gilded night lilies drifted about, hoping to suck cash out of the winners later. As for the game, it was the usual. A bunch of guys shoving cash at each other all night. More sharps and blacklegs than pigeons to pluck. Just as I like it, down to business, no showboating. Draw poker, a little stud, nothing fancy. None of those dese-crations of this and that wild that usually tarnished poker. The kind of serious players that barely glanced up when Nita walked into the room, all leg and lip. Which was to my liking, as the general disregard for women among gamers serious about their game was to my advantage. It'd never occur to them that her slow turns around the table were rife with signals. Her tongue wetting her upper lip told me to raise, her hand fluttering to throat and I'd fold.

I'd been stealing pots for about an hour, tossing back just enough coin to give the fish some hope. The biggest pots I took were from Bolt, a pre-arranged sideshow. He made demonstrative displays of disgust at the rags he was dealt and the desertion of that bitch luck. That way, he was in first position to hate me, letting the real suckers feel some relief from humiliation for the beating I was giving them, instead of an itch to reach for their guns. I'd just bullied the lot with a monster hand; a queen-high straight, when the pirate walked in with his henchmen, stewed in rum and baked in rage.

It was the Dandy, Red Slash's second in command. Now he wore the red sash. His eyes darted from me to my huge cash stack. I could see his lip twitch slightly as he controlled his rage. As delicate as his features were, there was strength to his gait and stance and his first words again revealed his blunt style.

"You killed Red Slash," he said.

"It seems to have worked out well for you. You inherited his color. And position."

"Nothing I didn't already have. I am Red Slash. And you killed me," he said illogically.

"You killed my friend Miles," I countered, but mostly just to cover my confusion.

Red Slash spit. "I told you. I don't kill my own kind."

I stood. "That's not what I heard." The other players backed away from the table.

Red Slash slipped a knife out of his boot and leapt at me. I slammed his arm, twisted him round and had his head locked in the crook of my arm. But he chopped at my knee with his boot heel, slipped my grip, and we hit dirt. I was the better, but the dance took a few more turns. I soon had him dominated, and this time he wasn't twisting out. He had my hair in his painful grip but I put a fist to his belly and he fell apart. In close, he wasn't as strong as I expected him to be, and didn't smell as nasty either.

"You killed me!" he yelled. That annoying pirate persistence again.

"Killed you? You've alive, I didn't kill you."

"I'm the real Red Slash. You can't kill the Red Slash and live!"

"I killed someone I thought was Red Slash."

"You killed *me*!"

It's then that it clicked. This was not conversation between men. The illogic of his outrage, his absurd insistence that I'd killed him, could only mean one thing. I was talking to a woman.

I ripped off what I now knew to be a fake mustache and tore off the pirate's hat. A cascade of red hair tumbled out. Not just a woman, but a spectacular one. I was so shocked, it gave him…. *her*, time to scramble up. She screamed and ran outside, where I saw Roddy ready to grab her.

As I followed, I turned back once to point at my stack of green and said to the stunned players, "Divide it up, men. I filched it off you. Not a regular racket for me, I'm no sharp, but I wasn't playing fair either." Their stares remained blank. "On a higher mission," Nita added with a smile. They nodded. When they weren't playing, gamers finally did notice women. And something about the way Nita sauntered out the door melted any remnant of anger. You don't question a walk like that.

Outside, I squared off with Red Slash. Her minions backed off in deference. Roddy, Nita and Bolt did the same. It was between the two of us, and it could go either way.

"You've been used. Set as bait by the mob," she snarled. "It's the mob that's been killing the poker winners, and blaming it on us to incite others to kill pirates. You kill us, you work for the Gambinos. We both run rum, and plenty of it, but they want it all for themselves. That's why we're hijacking each others' loads."

I glanced over to the tree where we'd left Handlebar and saw an empty chain. He'd shed his shackles.

"I agree with her," Roddy was saying. "The mob's bunch is a lazy lot. If they can find anyone at all to do their killing for them, they'll roll back to sleep and let you. You kill off the pirates, you do it for the mob, same bunch that must have murdered your friend. Pick a side, Richard, or you'll just be caught in the crossfire."

"You murdered me for nothing," said Red Slash.

I still had no clue about that one.

"She's right," said Nita.

"What?" I looked to Nita. Not her too.

I looked to Roddy, then Bolt. They both shrugged. It was hopeless to argue with two determined women.

"You owe me," said Red Slash.

"You owe her," agreed Nita.

"For what?" I venture to ask.

"For killing her," insisted Nita.

I gave up.

"Help me stick it to the mob. Do it to avenge your friend," said Red Slash. "Let's hurt them just enough that they back down from this bootleg war. There's enough rum to run for the both of us. We'll stop hijacking theirs if they'll let us run ours." I wasn't sure if it was her beauty that was compelling me or my conscience, but she did seem to know how to stoke my fanatical drive for justice, not to mention my chivalrous and otherwise appointed ardor.

"Okay," I agree. "But how?"

"The big mob house is on Cable Beach," said Bolt. "And I happen to know where there's a stable of fast thoroughbreds. And where the trails are that miss the lazy lugs leaning on cars around the house."

A torch blazed and toppled next to Bolt. The next ping came when a bullet hit a stone at my feet. I was yanking Nita behind one tree just as the branch of another cracked and fell, splintering as Roddy ducked lead and wood.

Handlebar. He'd gotten the goon squad. We traded shots while dirt spit around us, but not for long. Every clip joint comes with protection, and soon the game's muscle drove back the mooks while we ran for our boat.

We hit the Cable Beach racetrack at dawn. Roddy and Nita went into the clubhouse, and I used the moment to slip them both. I grabbed Bolt and told him to ready one horse only, and draw me a map to the mob's lair.

"I'm going solo," I told him.

"Okay, tough guy," said Bolt. But he didn't budge.

"Just give me a damn horse, draw me that map, and be quick about it."

"There are two kinds of people in the world," said Bolt. "Those that enjoy life and those that don't. Doing it alone, without back-up, this your idea of a good time?"

"I don't read your pal Hemingway, if that's what you're asking. And I don't enjoy violence or think it's at the heart of life or any other crap," I told him. "I just don't want Nita along, and no way I can stop her. I don't want anyone along, for what I've got to do. No witnesses. You get it yet?"

Bolt drew the map. When he was done, he got me a horse and said, "Nice to have such a devoted woman…"

I cut him off with a snarl. "Achilles' heel more like it."

He handed me the reins. I had a lot of killing to do.

They say the devil's in the details, so I don't remember them. My fury at Handlebar's eyes on Nita and his two attempts on her life narrowed my vision to a pinprick of rage. Vengeance burned me like a fever. The rest of the night had aspects of a force of nature, a typhoon with me at the center of it. I'm told I'm handsome, but as the *Spider*, rage transforms my visage into something unpleasantly close to a death skull. I remembered my promise to Nita, but even without the mask of the *Spider* and how it escalates my mood, I was filled with the *Spider*'s passion. I raced with the devil on my tail, through some kind of hell made of masks and burning men. Later I was told I charged right through a Guy Fawkes parade. It was that night of the year when Bahamians burn him in effigy. Ever been to a Guy Fawkes parade? Like any other bacchanal. I didn't stop for a drink.

With Bolt's map branded in my brain, I rode that beautiful racehorse down twisty trails. Just as Bolt predicted, I ended up right at a vulnerable spot at the mob house: a back door to the open kitchen where the fat lunks were caught belching in their underwear. I entered as a wraith. A bitter silk cord embraced one neck, a fingerjab thrust into throat kissed another. I remember a sharp punch that, when I pulled back my fist there were bits of teeth in my knuckles. I ruined the kitchen party. Fear rippled upstairs and gripped the entire house. The night spit with sparks and flames of gunfire. I followed that narrow burning vision of light as described by Reverend Ezekiel. He was right, I knew the way. I went into still water and let myself get sucked into the very whirlpool I was spinning.

Finally, I found Handlebar cowering in the attic. Just for him, I decided to give my fists another workout. I pocketed my guns and tenderized his flesh, then bounced him down thirty steep steps, bashing his head on each one, dragged him by the hair in the direction of cigar smoke. Follow the smell of a cigar, at the other end is usually a bigshot. I entered a den, and there was the fat boss of operations, dressed just like the rest on this sweltering night; in underwear and sweat. But something about the way he sat in his underwear, ignored his sweat, calmly sipped his drink and sucked his stogie — I knew he was the kingpin.

"Quit the beef with the pirates," I told him. "Toss them a bone of a share in the rum running, and stop the bloodshed."

"Who the hell are you and why should I listen to you?" Rage was making his cheeks quiver and putting the red in his vicehound face, but his voice was steady.

"Within a year hootch'll be legal again and the marauding seadogs will slink back under rocks. Fighting pirates is a waste of time for a businessman like you. Work the inside for the next year, and you'll have a stake in every legal bar before they even open. Stop thinking with your muscle."

The fat man nodded, liking the way it played. Not that he'd admit it. "I already thoughta all that," he lied.

"And he's mine," I said, kicking Handlebar.

Another fat nod. The fatman then looked at Handlebar and said to me, "Do it now. I wanna watch this ugly piker die."

I shot Handlebar, but not before he slipped a Derringer smaller than Nita's out of his pocket and sent a bullet to my chest. I was slammed to the wall. I watched Handlebar die, then reached to stop the flow of liquid now pouring out of my chest.

Something didn't feel right. I raised my hand to my eyes and saw my blood was running yellow. I smelled it. Rum.

I reached into my breast pocket to find the bullet hole and instead pulled out the Bible the Preacher had slipped there. I opened up the good book and saw it'd been hollowed out to make room for a silver flask. I shook it. A bullet now clanked around inside the flask, rum running out the hole it'd made on its way in.

The fatman leaned back and watched me like this was all just a bit of theater for his private pleasure. I decided to oblige him and deliver a few lines. I smiled a thin-lipped grimace that must have sent a shiver down even this hardened bossman's spine. I toasted him, tilted back the flask and downed the rest of the lead-flavored rum.

"Praise the Lord for his good book and its life-saving ways," I said, and was gone.

As I raced back, I thought of that Preacher with a gun and his words of following the narrow light that was the wrong path. I thought of Bolt's words of men that live as if violence was at the heart of life, and how their time was past. I decided they were both full of bunk. But I wasn't sure, and I had someone far wiser than them to put that question to.

Back at the stable I searched out the only thing that could calm my murderous state. Nita's eyes. A woman stood with her back to me, and when she turned, I found those eyes, and they did what they did best: melt away all remnants of the *Spider*.

Then I saw what Nita was doing. She was brushing the cascading hair of the Red Slash. I now saw the pirate's eyes too, and paused. I'd seen this before, this thing that happens sometimes between two women that believe themselves to be rivals, until they meet and talk. Give them a minute together, and they realize they like each other, often the glue of the bond being complaints about the very man they thought they were rivals over. "She waited for you," said Nita. "She wants to say goodbye." Nita let the pirate come to me first.

Red Slash handed me something small and heavy. A gem, wound in copper wire and tied in a strip of her trademark red silk. "It's a free pass," she said. "Any seadog respects it. For your safe passage home."

I tucked it away and it rattled against something in my pocket. I realized I still had a hunk of Monopoly metal. I tossed it to her and graced her with what for me passes as a smile. "Safe passage if you're ever in New York. Show it to a muck that runs a shoeshine stand on Bowery and Bond Streets. He'll always know how to find me."

She slipped it in a pouch on a string that she dropped down her shirt, flicked back her red hair, and let her black eyes do the rest.

Most men would contemplate a little redheaded piracy, but for me it was easy to walk away from temptation. I knew something most men didn't: Too much of a good thing can leave a man with too little of anything.

I went to Nita. She was distant. She didn't like being left out of the action.

"Go play a game of pool," she said. I didn't ask why. When I entered the clubhouse poolroom I got it.

There was Miles, stacks of money, a woman glued to hip and a whiskey glass to lip. He turned, saw me and raised his glass in toast.

"What are you doing here?" he asked.

"Avenging your death," I snarled.

"Oh, that. I wanted to 'die' for a stretch. You know, business," he said lightly. "I'll be 'alive' and back in New York next week."

"That'll teach me to follow every rumor." Lucky for him I was too tired to punch him. And irony is wasted on Miles, but I tried a bit anyway. "You appreciate the thought, though?"

"Sure, thanks. Hey, you wanna little of this action? Big money in pool games."

My eyes were wandering over the money, the whiskey, the curves of the women in the room, just as Nita walked in, ready to save me from myself again.

"She gone?" I ask.

"Yes," says Nita.

"You liked the lady pirate?"

"She's a woman who lives like a man," said Nita casually, but looking in my eyes with the opposite feeling. "Double life so deep she doesn't know who she is."

"'Sounds familiar,' is what I'm supposed to say?"

"Something like that. And well... let's just say I guess it makes her my type."

I arched an eyebrow at Nita. She was full of surprises. Then I remembered that burning question that still needed a wise answer.

"Darling," I said, "What if I were to give up all the nasty fisticuffs and bloodshed, and take up, say, gardening. A quiet life of quiet things. Would you go for that?"

Nita smiled, calling my bluff. "Not as long as the real thing is still up for grabs."

We gazed at each other a moment, then she grabbed my arm said, "Come on, handsome. Let's take the slow boat home."

illustration by Tom Floyd

Chapter Fourteen

THE INVISIBLE GANG

by RON FORTIER

One-Eye Purtis came out of the cellar beneath Conklin's Eatery a little after nine o'clock. In his rough, leathery hands he clutched sacks of money, the night's take from the illegal betting parlor operated in the greasy spoon. The restaurant was one of six owned by Boss Malone in the Bowery section of the great city. Purtis was his number one collection runner.

He really didn't have only one eye. He'd collected an ugly knife scar over his right orb that had nearly blinded him years earlier. The resulting slice of dead white skin over the eye onto his flat cheek often presented the illusion that the ball in the socket was no longer working, thus the nickname, One-Eye.

It worked just fine and One-Eye had no trouble making his way through the rat's maze of back alleys that was his normal route back to Malone's head-quarters. He was a big, dangerous man, and armed to the teeth. There was never any worry that he wouldn't complete his nightly run. No one would ever be stupid enough to go up against a bruiser like Purtis, never mind the fact that such an action would be considered a personal assault on Malone's mob.

Chewing on a toothpick, One-Eye strolled along the almost completely darkened byways of trash and filth as if he didn't have a care in the world. That is until he heard scuffling footsteps behind him. He stopped in mid-step and looked over his right shoulder, his felt cap raised a notch over his wide forehead. Whatever light penetrated the gloom of these narrow lanes came from the apartments overhead to either side whose windows were uncovered. It was enough for One-Eye, he had excellent night vision. There was no one behind him. Just the usual trash cans standing like silent sentinels of rusted steel. All were overflowing with refuse and he could make out scurrying rats as they searched for tasty morsels. No one could hide behind those cans, they were too small.

One-Eye shrugged and continued on his way. That's when he heard the noise above him. His free hand slid over the grip of his shoulder-rigged automatic while he looked upward at the fire-escapes affixed to the brick walls. He picked out a figure leaning over the closest railing just as something was hurled at him. Too late to dodge, the object smacked into his head with a loud crack and One-Eye screamed in excruciating pain. Gone was any thought of his gun, who was following him, or what had been thrown. Instead his world became one of hurt as he dropped to his knees, his hands reaching for the spot on his forehead now bleeding.

Through the tears, his vision cleared enough so that the brick on the ground before him was perfectly recognizable. "What dah hell?" he mumbled trying to make sense of what had just happened. Somebody had just beaned him on the head with a brick! One-Eye shook his head like a lion about to roar when a second brick slammed into his back, below the neck.

"OW!" His body arched in a curve. Then another brick caught him in the ribs. One-Eye clawed for his pistol. Unless he took action quick, he was going to die. Of that there was no doubt. More bricks began raining down and he tried to move, still on the pavement. But he couldn't dodge all of them. He managed to get his gun out and fired off a single round into the blackness above. He was rewarded with hearing a high pitched cry before a brick smashed into his wrist causing him to lose the weapon. His mind, confused and awash with pain, realized the cry was not a man's cry. But what?

One-Eye never did figure it out. Another dozen bricks found him and laid him out. They did not stop coming until he was dead. Small figures emerged from the shadows and approached his body. They were giggling.

The next morning, the alley was the scene of frantic activity as the city's finest set about determining the identity and cause of the death of the recently discovered, battered corpse. A police photographer kept snapping pictures, his pop flash causing those around him, including the Medical Examiner, to blink in annoyance. Running roughshod over the entire circus was a tall, lean man with soft brown hair and quiet blue eyes visible beneath the brim of his gray fedora. Police Commissioner Stanley Kirkpatrick surveyed the scene, as his men went about their duties. At the entrance of the alley, a thick rope had been set on stanchions to keep out the curious onlookers. Cops were stationed there to make sure they, and the ever-present reporters, were kept at bay while the on-site investigation proceeded.

Kirkpatrick, impeccably dressed in a three-piece suit and overcoat, jerked up the collar to protect his neck from the light rain that had started to fall. It was a gloomy, fall day in the city. He moved about the alley closely scrutinizing the murder scene, attempting to imagine how the ambush had played out.

"It's One-Eye Purtis," police sergeant Donald O'Malley offered, as he walked a few steps behind the Commissioner. "Although it's hard to recognize his face in that mess."

"Are you sure, O'Malley?" Kirkpatrick had made the same identification upon seeing the body, but was appreciative of O'Malley's confirmation. He was also very, very nervous about the implications inherent with Purtis' murder.

"You bet, Commissioner. We've had him in the South Street station enough times to consider the fellow almost family." O'Malley tipped back his cap, scratched his temple and said, "He was one of Malacai Malone's runners."

Kirkpatrick felt his stomach sour. If someone had killed Purtis to steal his money bags, then it wouldn't take Malone long to retaliate. Mob bosses lived and died on their reputations. If Malone did not find the people responsible and make them pay, he would be looked upon as weak by the other bosses. Something he could not allow if he wanted to stay in business.

Kirkpatrick sensed the M.E.'s approach and turned to him. Ambulance attendants were lifting the body onto a stretcher. "He was battered to death," the M.E. said flatly, adjusting his wire-rimmed glasses. "Pretty much like an Old Testament execution. I counted over forty bricks on and around his body. A couple hitting the right parts of his body would have been sufficient."

"So, whoever did this wanted to make sure he was dead." Kirkpatrick has seen his share of brutal killings. This was one that had a new twist, but no more violent than many others he had witnessed in his long career.

"An understatement indeed," the M.E. concurred. "And from the positions of those bricks, I'd guess that they were thrown by at least a half dozen men."

"In this tight alley?" Kirkpatrick put his hands on his hips and turned around slowly, eyeing the two facing walls, the rows of garbage cans and the overhead fire escapes. "How the hell could six men hide in this place so that Purtis didn't see them until it was too late?"

"Geez, I don't know, Commissioner. Maybe they were invisible?"

Mother Mayhem stood in front of her charges in the basement room of the old brownstone and tapped her foot on the cement floor. They were all cringing, dirty and sniffling little toads beneath her contempt; these unwanted ragamuffins. It was a bloody miracle they had actually carried out her orders and brought back the bags of cash.

They had also brought back the dead boy. What was his name again? Tony... Anthony something or other. What the hell did it matter? He was dead and required no further attention. That had been part of the plan as well. Leave no one behind. Ever. If her mad scheme was going to work, it was vital that they remain unseen and undiscovered. That way the mobs would eventually start pointing fingers at each other and she and her little brood of snot-nosed waifs could clean up big.

Her real name was Gladys Mayhewn. The Mother Mayhem was a street tag she had earned years ago in some long forgotten brothel. That had been a rough time in Gladys' life, scrimping like all those other girls for a small piece of the Big Apples' pie.

Twenty years later, and saddled with two idiot sons; she had wandered from one crooked scam to another until this sweet deal fell into her lap. Seems the city was desperate for people to manage their over-crowded orphanages. With newspaper and radio ads clearly indicating that they, the government fathers, would not scrutinize too closely any civic-minded applicants willing to assume the positions. It took Gladys all of one afternoon to get bogus documents made up declaring her a high school graduate with a gift for organization and discipline; the last two were true, regardless of the fact they were self-taught talents. As for her formal education, she'd run away from home at twelve and never looked back.

"We did what you asked," a dirty-faced thirteen year old Mickey Carter spoke up. He was the oldest of her charges and clearly the most competent. "Now can we get our reward?" The others, all trembled, their big, hungry eyes watching to see her response.

The rotund matron lashed out with her beefy right hand and smacked the boy across the face. The slap resounded like a gunshot in the confines of the old cellar and his head rocked back, his face twisted in a grimace of pain.

"You dare question my word?" she yelled in her high, mousy voice that was so out-of-place in her huge, fat body. "Mother Mayhem always keeps her promises!"

Keeping them scared was the trick. Put the fear of God into the snot-nosed brats and they were as compliant as puppies. Mother Mayhem motioned for Mickey to step forward. He did so warily, his hands twisting his black woolen cap they were holding.

Under the bare light bulb hanging overhead, a red welt was rising on the boy's left cheek. She reached out and patted his other cheek, a dark smile covering her puffy face. "You must never question my word, boy. That's not being respectful. Do you understand me, boy?"

His eyes cast downward to avoid making contact, the orphan nodded. "Yes, ma'am. I do."

"That's better. Now you did do exactly as Mother ordered. You brought back the money and you also didn't leave anyone behind." She indicated the pitiful corpse on the floor. "You must never, ever, leave anyone behind!"

"For being such good boys, you have earned your reward."

Mickey looked up at her, his face emotionless. "Thank you, ma'am."

The lad had spunk. Then again that very backbone might some day rebel. She made a mental note to keep an eye on this one.

"Elliot," she called over to the oldest of her sons. Sipping a beer, he was leaning against the chalkboard she had used to plan the ambush on the bag runner. He was tall and muscular, his massive biceps visible through his worn, cotton shirt.

"Yeah, Ma?"

"After you finish your beer, take these boys upstairs and feed them. Anything they want. Chicken, bologna, cheese, cake... whatever. I promised them a feast and a feast they'll get."

She turned to Bruno, her youngest at twenty-three. He was short and squat like a bulldog, with a square, unshaven face and thick, bushy eyebrows. "Want I should take care of the body, Ma?"

"Yes, my dear. Put him in a laundry bag, weigh it down with rocks and dump it in the river. But wait until dark. I don't want anyone seeing you. Is that clear?"

"Yes, Ma. I'll take care of it."

With that she dismissed them all. Elliot leading the group up the stairs to the main hall, and Bruno off to the laundry room to fetch a bag. Alone with the money bag, Mother Mayhem dumped its contents on the old school desk behind her and set about counting it. It looked to be a very tidy sum. She took one last look at the tiny cold figure on the cement floor. Poor little tyke, he was probably better off. After all, it really was a cold, cruel world.

She started counting the rubber-banded stacks of greenbacks.

Later, huddled under the thick woolen blankets of his bed, Mickey Carter fed his seven year old brother, Danny, chunks of salami and cheese. He'd stuffed his pants pockets with food from the icebox, before leaving the kitchen with the others, under the watchful eye of Big E, the children's name for Elliot. Elliot, although as cruel as his mother, was also on the lazy side and if you stayed out of his way, he pretty much left you alone. So Mickey, and some of the others who'd been in on the ambush, took extra victuals up to other children on the third floor.

Although Big E had ignored this pilfering of the supplies, he was not one to breech his mother's rules. Once back on their beds, it was lights out and quiet. So as long as the boys, like Mickey, made no audible disturbances, they were free to dole out their bounty to their friends or brothers and sisters. Mickey and Danny weren't the only siblings in the place.

In the dark, Mickey heard his brother gulping down chunks of the greasy meat roll. It had been days since either of them had eaten anything but lumpy gruel and stale bread. "Go easy," he whispered, touching his brother's bony arm. "Or you'll choke."

"Okay, Mickey," came the soft response. "I'm just so hungry, is all."

The words echoed his own feelings. He hated what he and the others had been forced to do. He also hated what had happened to Tony Mustani and how Mother Mayhem had him tossed away like so much garbage. But what else could he do? Who on the outside would help a bunch of unattached orphans? No one cared if they were mistreated, starved and abused all the time. The rest of the world had chosen to forget they even existed. Survival, in the end, was left in their own, small, dirty hands. Mickey knew he had to do whatever it took to keep them alive. No matter how wrong it was.

Within the next five days, three other gang messengers were waylaid and robbed, their battered bodies discovered in dirty alleys. Soon the street bosses were arming their forces and closing up ranks. The police were baffled and none of their usual informers could provide them with anything helpful.

One day, six gunmen working for Boss Malone attacked a gambling parlor owned by Shifty Slick Williams. A drunken snitch had told one of Malone's boys that he had heard, from a friend of a friend, that Slick was behind the carrier heists. It was all the proof a madman like Malone needed. His goons went in with guns blazing and when the smoke had cleared, seven men were dead and another five wounded.

The Gang Wars had begun.

"Oh my God, he's got a bomb!" Nita Van Sloan cried, bringing her gloved hand up to her mouth in horrid anticipation of what was about to happen.

She was all dolled up and seated in the back seat of playboy Richard Wentworth's sleek black sedan being driven by his chauffeur, Ronald Jackson. The debonair Wentworth was himself leaning forward between the shoulders of his driver and the big, tall, turbaned Sikh who was his personal valet, Ram Singh. All of them, mouths agape, watched in horror as the man in the back seat of the convertible roadster stood up and hurled the bundle of dynamite through the night air towards the front entrance of the Saucy Lady Nightclub.

Dapper men in tuxedos, with their lovely ladies on their arms, were milling about under the red velvet awning, waiting to be admitted into the posh nightspot. None of them saw the lethal missile as it dropped into their midst. The bomb exploded with savage intensity and bodies were torn asunder amidst blood-curling screams of terror and pain. A pall of smoke enveloped the wreckage, as bodies lay strewn about the ruined front steps, cracked sidewalk, and demolished front doors. It was like a scene from a hellish nightmare.

But the bomb thrower and his two pals in the roadster's front seat weren't sticking around to witness the death and destruction they had caused. Once the explosion had done its work, the fellow, garbed in a dark brown suit and fedora, fell back onto his seat urging the driver to, "Get the hell out of here, Vinnie!"

A stamp on the gas pedal and the auto shot down the boulevard lit by street lamps and gaudy neon signs; straight past Richard Wentworth's Daimler.

"Nita, you and Ram Singh get out and see what you can do for those poor souls!" Wentworth ordered, as he watched the trio of killers go by. Jackson had hit the brakes upon seeing the assault.

Both the lovely socialite and the giant, bearded Indian from Punjab were on the sidewalk before the words were fully out of his mouth, so attuned were they to his wishes. Loyal and trusted allies, both Nita and Ram Singh served their leader well.

"Be careful," Nita admonished as Jackson yanked the wheel hard, put the big car into a tight U-turn and shot off down the street in pursuit of the deadly bombers. It was all the thought she would spare Wentworth and Jackson as she followed Singh's lead and started across the street. She knew with confidence that the evil men in the fleeing roadster were about to meet their doom.

"Don't lose them!" Wentworth commanded, as Jackson propelled their car down the nearly empty street. The hour was late and the theater crowd hadn't let out yet. Thank God for small favors, he thought as he twisted about and pulled a box from beneath the back seat. In the flickering light, he opened it and began removing the items stored within the secret container. A well worn slouch hat, a black cloak and a face mask all were set side by side as Wentworth unknotted his tie with his other free hand. He was about to don the regalia of the *Spider*.

Gripping the steering wheel with determined resolve, Ronald Jackson weaved past several checkered cabs as he continued to accelerate their speed. The back end of the getaway roadster was coming up fast. He watched it reach a familiar intersection and veer off to the right, ignoring a red light.

"They're turning onto 5th Avenue, Major," he related at the same time stomping the breaks and making the same turn in a loud, reckless swing that almost brought them up on two wheels.

Looking into the rear-view mirror for a second, Jackson saw the gruesome visage of the Master of Men, the *Spider*. "Take to the center of the road and pull up alongside of them!" came the deep, cold voice.

"You got it, major."

At the same time the ex-soldier was complying with his boss's order, the driver of the speeding roadster, a tough mug with a broken nose and cauliflower ears, had become all too aware of their presence. "Hey!" he yelled over the roar of the motor engine to his two companions; a wiry character with short blonde hair and glasses sitting beside him and the swarthy bomb thrower in the back, "Somebody's tailing us!"

Jake Walters, twisted about in the back seat and rose up to get a good look at the fast, oncoming sedan. "I'll take care of those clowns, Vinnie. You just keep driving and get us to the hideout!"

From a case on the floor at his feet, the heartless gangster produced a Thompson submachine gun, which he lovingly referred to as his Baby. He slapped a round bullet canister into the feed slot, chambered the first round and then came up again with the death dealer clutched firmly in his hands. Laughing crazily, Walters fired off a long burst that chewed up the road behind them before finding the grill and hood of the sleek, expensive limousine.

"Holy moley!" Jackson exclaimed, "That guy's got a machine-gun!"

Bullets hit the Daimler's hood like metal hornets before pinging off into space; barely leaving a scratch. Those that found the windshield did the same after producing several minor cracks in the glass. Early in his crusade against crime, the *Spider* had seen to the customizing of his many automobiles. All of them featured bullet-proof glass and a light-weight steel armor capable of withstanding a bazooka round. Now, Ronald Jackson was extremely glad of that foresight.

Not so Jake Walters, who looked from the still threatening sedan to his smoking machine-gun in puzzlement. "What dah hell?"

Then he heard a weird, mocking laugh like nothing he'd ever experienced before. As he looked up again, he beheld a startling, unimaginable sight. Leaning out the back window of the speeding limo was a figure draped in black and brandishing two silver-plated automatics. He looked up over the pistols into the shadowy visage of a nightmare and screamed.

The *Spider*'s automatics spat out round after round, as the wind buffeted his torso. He was leaning out of the open window with total disregard for his own safety. So enraptured was he by the thrill of battle, this primal warrior of modern times, nothing mattered in his fevered mind but the fight and ultimate victory over his foes.

As the two cars drove through the heart of the city, bullets criss-crossed the space between them. Walters, having bit down on his lower lip to quell his fears, had resumed firing the Thompson but somehow he couldn't steady his aim and his bullets missed the dark avenger by a wide margin.

Finally one of the *Spider*'s slugs caught the getaway driver in the head, tearing off half his scalp as it plowed on through the front windshield. Dead hands fell from the wheel and the roadster cut right crashing into a street-lamp at fifty-five-miles-an-hour. A few pedestrians coming out of a cigar store frantically dived out of the way. The impact was brutal, the entire front end of the roadster folded like an accordion. The man in the passenger side went through the smashed windshield and Walters was sent hurtling into the street. The street-lamp buckled and fell across the ruined car, its glass casing shattering into thousands of pieces over the sidewalk and street.

With a loud screech of brakes being jammed, Jackson brought his car to a swerving stop only yards from the crumbled roadster. The *Spider* was out the back door and moving before the sedan was completely stopped, his twin automatics at hip level, as his intense blue-gray eyes took in the aftermath of their chase. In a crouch, he made his way around the damaged vehicle to where the passenger had collided head first into the building's brick front. The fellow lay face first on the cement, his head twisted about in an impossible angle, his eyes wide and dull in death.

Bullets hit the toppled lamp post sounding a loud, angry rat-tat-tat. The *Spider* spun around while ducking. Over the mangled hood of the roadster he saw hatless Jake Walters, a thin line of blood lining his angry, battered face firing his submachine gun wildly at anything that moved.

"Come on, Spider!" the killer dared. "Come out and meet Baby!"

Realizing instantly that the indiscriminate barrage endangered innocent civilians, the *Spider* did not hesitate to come out into the open. "Here I am!"

Walters saw him and reacted fast, the barrel of his machine gun rising like the head of a snake But the *Spider* was faster, his right hand extending even as he fired a single shot that hit the crazed shooter right between the eyes. His head snapped backward, his throat uttered a gurgling cry and he collapsed, his barking weapon silenced.

Guns at the ready, the *Spider* stood over his fallen adversary and laughed. The sound traveled up and down the famous avenue and New Yorkers, upon hearing it, huddled back into their shops and alleyways It was the sound of blood vengeance.

"What now?" Ronald Jackson asked as his employer slid into the back seat while in the distance police sirens wailed.

"To West 33rd street!" the *Spider* replied. "Those were Boss Malone's men. I'm going to visit Malacai Malone and end this madness now!"

The black car backed up a few yards, turned its front end in the opposite direction and sped off into the cool, starlit night.

Malacai Malone splashed the stingy aftershave lotion over his fleshy, pink face and admired himself in the bathroom mirror. Not bad, for a fifty year old crime lord, he mused, giving his graying temples a smoothing.

Dressed in a satin housecoat, pajama bottoms and cotton slippers, Malone was a pudgy fellow standing just shy of five feet, six inches tall. He was carrying a spare tire around his middle and it might have appeared to others that he was starting to go soft. But looks could be deceptive. He was a cruel and vicious man with uncanny strength and vitality.

More than enough to satisfy the redheaded floozy waiting for him in the living room of his penthouse apartment. Her name was Trixie. She was a dancer in one of his downtown clubs. She wasn't particularly bright, but she had a chassis on her that made men's eyes widen and their mouths drool. Tonight Malone was going to discover if the pleasures promised were as real as he imagined.

He was still admiring his reflection when Trixie screamed. Malone jumped and without thinking, ran out into the spacious living area to see what had happened. Awaiting him was a tableau that brought him up short and instantly froze the blood in his veins.

Trixie was out cold, her nubile form stretched on the thick green carpet in front of the sofa where he had left her sipping a Tom Collins. Standing over her, in a twisted crouch was the most repulsive, horrible creature Malone had ever seen.

Draped in black, the gruesome looking invader wore a wide brim slouch hat. When he lifted his head, Malone's gut tightened. The intruder wore a black mask to hide the top half of his misshapen face. Visible beneath it was sallow tinted skin around a curled mouth from which fangs protruded.

"THE SPIDER!"

"I've come to put an end to your war, Malone. Not another innocent soul will suffer because of the insanity you've unleashed on the streets."

"Nobody tells me what I can or can't do," the crook retorted, starting to get some of his nerve back. The sight of the gruesome *Spider* had shocked him, but now his mind was quickly assessing the situation; to his advantage.

The apartment was on the forty-second floor. How the devil had this fiend managed to get in? Malone always kept his two toughest bruisers on guard duty outside in the hall. Certainly he would have heard some sort of a fight had the black avenger entered through the front door. Surreptitiously, Malone gave it a quick glance. It appeared locked and secure. Were Max and Eddie still out there? How quickly would it take them to come through that door?

The *Spider* pointed his twin .45s at Malone. "You don't understand. Only one of us will leave this room alive."

"But I don't even have a gun," Malone pleaded, holding up his palms. "You gonna shoot an unarmed man? That'd be murder and then you'd be no better than me, Spider!"

The *Spider* laughed and Malone felt his heart start to race. The masked man tossed the automatic in his left hand and it landed on the floor inches from Malone's feet.

"Pick it up."

"Huh, uh," Malone shook his head. "No freaking way. You won't give…"

BANG! The *Spider*'s bullet hit him in the right leg just above the knee and Malone collapsed on the carpet.

"Aaghh," He lay on his side, clutching his wounded leg, blood tainting his fingers. "You shot me!"

Outside, Max was yelling through the door. "Boss? What happened? Boss?"

The *Spider* pointed to the pistol on the floor. "I'm going to count to three. If you don't pick it up, I'm going to put the next one between your eyes."

Malacai Malone understood pain. He had dispensed enough of it in his long and notorious rise to underworld power. Now, the throbbing in his leg made it all too clear that this masked ghoul wasn't bluffing.

"One."

Malone looked from the gun to the front door. There was banging against it and more shouts from his bodyguards. "Boss! Open up!"

"Two."

Malone grabbed the automatic and whipped his arm up, firing at the same time. But unlike the *Spider*'s shot that came next, his was spoiled by fear. It ripped through the cloak over the *Spider*'s left shoulder and he cried out, his body spinning around. But Malone never got to enjoy the accuracy of it because he was dead, the *Spider*'s slug having hit him in the middle of the forehead. Malone flat on his back, his eyes dulled by death, seemed annoyed by this ignominious end.

In the corridor, Max and Eddie, upon hearing more gunshots, renewed their efforts to break down the door. Both were big men and after only a few solid whacks, the door knob tore free from its hinges and they fell into the apartment, almost losing their footing.

Their boss was on the floor with a hole in his head. On his naked chest was the vermilion symbol of a spider.

"There!" Eddie pointed. "On the balcony! He's getting away!"

Drawing their pistols, the two hoods raced for the open French doors, their guns firing wildly at the cloaked figure leaping onto the iron railing.

The *Spider* spun about and returned fire with his twin automatics. Max ducked out of the way while firing off two more rounds. He was rewarded to see one of them hit the *Spider* in the chest. Then the macabre crime-fighter seemed to fall away into space, laughing all the while.

"I got him!" Max shouted to Eddie, now crouched on the other side of the open doors. "Come on!"

Both men charged onto the balcony. A cold wind from the East met them as they leaned over the balustrade and looked downward at the street below. There was nothing there. Not a body to be seen anywhere. The pair stood in silent wonderment until big Max leaned back scratching the top of his head. "I got him, I tell you! I'm sure of it!"

"So?" his pal snapped, indicating the sidewalk beneath them. "Where's the body, if yah hit him?"

Max continued scratching until a queer look covered his visage. "But geez, Eddie, even if I didn't hit him, where'd he go?"

Had either bothered to turn and look up, the answer to this mystery would have been revealed to them. For at that very moment the *Spider* was climbing up the face of the building, his gloved hands clasping a thin gossamer line. This was the *Spider*'s special Web, a chemically treated silken rope that was as strong as any boat's rigging, but nearly invisible to the human eye.

Reaching the roof, a strong pair of hands grasped his shoulders and aided him over the ledge. "I heard shots," Jackson said, as he watched the *Spider* straighten up and begin removing his disguise.

Minus his fangs and face mask, Richard Wentworth grinned at his former sergeant. "It was a close one, alright." He dropped his heavy cloak, unbuttoned his jacket and revealed the bullet-proof vest beneath. There was a bullet-hole dead center.

"Let's go home. The *Spider*'s done all he can for now."

The first purple-orange rays of the new day were painting the top of Sutton Place as Richard Wentworth and his chauffeur entered the luxurious suite that was his inner city headquarters. Nita Van Sloan and Ram Singh awaited them, exhausted from their own ordeal at the bombed-out night club. Nita rose up from the sofa where she'd been reclining. Wentworth noticed her evening gown was spotted with soot and dried blood.

"Oh, Dick," she ran into his arms and laid her head on his chest.

"Darling, it's alright," he comforted. "It's over, for the time being. The *Spider* saw to that."

With chestnut curls dangling over her forehead, she looked up. "It was just so horrible. All those poor people. They filled four ambulances with the injured. Ram Singh and I did all we could for them."

"I'm sure you did, dear," Richard Wentworth never ceased to be amazed by the courage of the woman he loved. Nita was truly one in a million.

Ram Singh, his jacket off and sleeves rolled up, handed Wentworth and Jackson each a cup of hot coffee. "You have dealt with the cowards responsible, Master?"

"Thank you, Ram Singh," Wentworth disengaged himself from Nita and took the offered hot brew. "Yes. And their leader, Malacai Malone. Hopefully that will cool things down for a while."

"But it really doesn't solve the mystery of the Invisible Gang, does it?" Jackson stated. "We're still no closer to solving this than we were before."

"I'm afraid you're right," Wentworth agreed sadly. "For all the recent violence and blood-letting, whoever ambushed those runners is still at large."

"I am reminded of my homeland in this matter," the bearded Punjabi remarked.

"How so, Ram Singh?"

"Centuries ago an evil madman organized the destitute and homeless of my country into a ragtag army of thieves and murderers. They called themselves the Thugees."

"But what's the connection?" Nita asked, returning to the sofa. "How were they invisible?"

"Because they were all of the lower caste," the imposing Indian explained. "No one, including the authorities of the time, gave them any notice. They moved about the country committing their nefarious deeds as if they actually were invisible."

"Wow," Ronald Jackson said. "That's a pretty wild story my friend. But there aren't folks like that around these days. Right, major?"

Richard Wentworth was about to answer when Jenkyns, his white-haired butler appeared. "Excuse me, sir, but you have a caller?"

"At this hour? Who is it?"

The butler made a wry face. "The young gentleman says his name is Mickey Carter and that you know him."

"Interesting." Wentworth placed his empty cup on the coffee table. "Alright, Jenkyns. Show him in."

Nita scrunched her pretty face. "Mickey Carter. Where do I know that name from?"

"Hi, Mr. Wentworth," Mickey said entering the room behind the butler. He took off his black woolen cap, went up to Wentworth and extended his hand. "I used to hawk papers on the street in front of the Chrysler building."

Recognition dawned on Wentworth as he shook the boy's hand. "Of course, Mickey. Now I remember. But what happened, lad? There's another boy on that corner now."

"Yes, sir," the lad's eyes fell. "About six months ago my ma died of pneumonia."

"I'm sorry to hear that. It must have been rough on your father and the rest of your family."

"My pa ran off when we were babies, sir," Mickey explained. "Me and Danny, that's my kid brother, we don't have any family, so we ended up at the Charles Street Orphan House."

"I see. So what brings you here, Mickey?"

"Well, sir, I remember reading in the papers how you was always helping the police. You know, fighting crime and all. And since I don't know any coppers, I thought I'd come to you instead."

"And you want to report a crime. Is that it?"

The boy began fidgeting with his cap and Wentworth saw he was becoming nervous.

"It's alright, Mickey. What is it you want to tell me?"

"Well, sir, I know who's been stealing the money from the gang runners."

Everyone in the room became instantly attentive. Wentworth and Nita exchanged silent looks.

"Go on, Mickey," Wentworth prodded. "Who is it?"

"Well, sir, it's us."

"Excuse me? What did you say?"

"Us kids, sir. Mother Mayhem, she runs the orphanage. She's the one making us rob and kill those men."

Nita's shocked expression represented all their reactions. "That's unbelievable!"

"But it's the truth, lady," Mickey argued. "I swear it is. That's why I come here. Before she makes us do it again. I was scared before, but now I just want to stop her before she does something bad to my little brother, Danny."

Wentworth put a gentle hand on the boy's arm and led him to the sofa to sit beside Nita.

"Jenkyns."

"Sir?"

"Go to the kitchen and get some milk and cookies for our guest."

"Yes, sir."

As the butler did an about-face and marched off, Wentworth pulled up a stuffed chair and sat facing the anxious lad. "Now, Mickey, tell us the entire story. Right from the start, and don't leave anything out."

"Yes, sir, Mr. Wentworth. I'll try," Mickey nodded gravely. "It was about two months ago when Mother Mayhem first...."

The *Spider* jumped from roof to roof with relative ease thanks to the proximity of the buildings adjoining the Charles Street Orphanage. As much as he hated to operate in daylight, he had no other option. If Mickey Carter's confession was true, and it certainly fitted the details of the unsolved crimes, then he had no time to lose. The boy's very absence would alarm Mother Mayhem and her stooge sons. Maybe enough to pack it in and run.

And there were all those children to consider.

The cloaked vigilante still could not comprehend the depravity of the entire affair. In his career of battling villainy, the *Spider* had confronted evildoers of every conceivable shape and demeanor. Yet to abuse and corrupt innocent children into committing brutal murders was beyond even his hardened sensibilities to understand.

Landing like a cat on the orphanage's tar-paper roof, the *Spider* moved directly to the trap door that led down into the attic. Mickey had drawn him a crude but detailed blueprint of the entire house from top to bottom which he had committed to memory.

Using the collapsible ladder to drop into the dusty, cluttered attic, the *Spider*'s senses were alert for any signs of trouble. Happy to be out of the light, he made his way to the stairwell and descended, again moving slowly on the balls of his feet. According to the daily routine of the facility, it was still too early for the children to be up and about, which was another reason for expedient action.

Coming out into the third floor, the *Spider* filled his right hand with one of his .45 automatics. Where stealth was the order of attack, he was not about to enter any confrontation with guns blasting. Especially surrounded by dozens of sleeping babes. It would only take one stray bullet to hurt those he had come to rescue. Golden dust motes floated through rays of sunlight coming through the windows over the landing to the stairs. He stopped there, carefully eyeing the second floor before proceeding.

There was a muffled slap followed a shrill cry of pain.

"Where the hell is he?" voiced an angry, male inquisitor. "Answer me or I'll give you another taste of my belt, you little brat!"

The *Spider* glided down the loose, rickety stairs and moved to where he'd heard the threat coming from. According to Mickey, part of the second floor was used as a dispensary to quarantine children when they were ill. It was located at the end of the second floor hallway. He reached it just in time to hear another loud whack and another piercing cry. Taking the door knob in his empty hand, the hideously disguised figure carefully turned it and opened the door slowly.

The tableau before him confirmed young Mickey Carter's testimony. Two men, one tall and one short, were taking turns whipping a little boy who was bound to an examination table. The lad was naked except for torn pajama bottoms. His emaciated, white body was laying face down on the white sheeted pad, his wrist and ankles bound by leather straps. The boy's bare back was rosy red from several long welts raised up from his flesh. His tormentors were holding their belts folded in their hands eager to inflict more pain.

"Look, kid," said the tallest of the two torturers, "we don't want to keep hurting you, but Ma wants know where your brother ran off to."

"I don't know," the tyke answered through thick sobs. "Mickey was just gone when I woke up. I thought he'd gone to the bathroom."

"Not good enough, Danny," decreed the shorter of the two men. He was the one across the table and had a view of the entrance. "Guess he needs some more persuading, huh, Elliot."

Bruno brought up his belt over his head, a sadistic glimmer in his eyes.

"That will be enough," commanded the Master of Men.

Bruno's arm froze in position over his head. He looked at the *Spider* and his eyes went wide with surprise.

"Who the hell are you?" Elliot demanded, after quickly turning around.

"I am the hand of justice," the *Spider* announced as he approached, his gun steady on the tall man's chest. "Both of you toss aside your belts. Now!"

"Sure thing," Elliot agreed, fear written across his face. "Just don't shoot. Okay? See, I'm doing just what you said."

Even the biggest rat will fight back when cornered and the *Spider* was an expert on human vermin. Thus when the elder Mayhewn sibling suddenly hurled the belt at his head, the grim avenger reacted with lightning reflexes. He twisted backward a half-step at the same time firing from the hip. Elliot Mayhewn fell back clutching his bloody stomach and then sank to the hardwood floor. His expression of befuddlement was matched only by the look on his brother's face.

"NO!" Bruno screamed, seeing his brother shot. Outraged, he pushed aside the examination table and launched himself at the masked avenger.

Caught momentarily off guard by the assault, the *Spider* fired a second round only to have it miss the shorter man by inches. Before he could readjust his aim, the bulldozer-built attacker slammed into him like a steamroller and both went down. Entangled on the floor, Bruno was relentlessly throwing punches at the gruesome masked face. The *Spider*, trying to protect his head, swung the automatic up only to have it knocked out of his hand. Clenching his hand into a hard fist, he punched it into Bruno's temple, temporarily stunning him. The two rolled away from each other and hastily got to their feet, all the while eyeing each other.

"I'm gonna beat you into hamburger," Bruno spat, wiping blood from his lower lip.

The *Spider* tore off his slouch hat, and raised his fists, taking a boxer's stance. "Let's see how tough you are fighting a man instead of tied-up little boys."

Like a mad dog, Bruno growled and attacked.

Mother Mayhem was belting down a gin and tonic when the gunshot rang out. She sat up stiff behind her desk and dropped her empty glass. She pulled her heavy girth out of the chair and ran as fast as she could to the main entrance vestibule.

There she stopped at the stairs to the second floor and called out. "Boys, what's the matter? Who fired that shot?" Through her alcoholic haze she realized that neither Elliot nor Bruno owned a gun. The only one in the house was the .38 revolver she kept in her old handbag back in her office.

"Elliot? Bruno? You boys answer your mama!"

There was a loud crash and then another as if the two of them were fighting up there, which wouldn't be the first time they had gone at each other for some ridiculous reason. She grabbed the handrail cursing. If she was forced to climb those stairs, she would make both of them pay for it.

Just then there Bruno came into sight, his body flying backwards to hit the landing above her. She watched as her son raised up his head and she saw it was badly battered. Her eyes went to the corner fully expecting to see Elliot appear, equally roughed up. Instead she reeled back when the black-clad *Spider* emerged, going after her fallen son.

Gladys shrieked at the sight of him and raced back into her office. Frantically she tore open the utility closet behind her desk and grabbed a gray leather satchel. In it was the tidy sum of eighty-five thousand dollars. She then threw her handbag over her left shoulder and pulled out her gun. She cocked it and wiped her mouth with the back of her hand. She had to run; to get away while she still could. It was too bad about the boys, but what else could she do? Sticking around and going to jail wouldn't change their fates, only condemn hers. She wasn't about to let that happen.

Coming out of the office, she fired off a quick shot at the top of the stairs. The *Spider*, kneeling over the comatose Bruno Mayhewn, barely had time to dive for cover behind the corner wall. The bullet chipped plaster where his head had been.

The shot was a diversion, Gladys could care less if she hit him or not. She needed the time to get out the front door and make good her escape. On the cement steps, she was momentarily blinded by the sun and had to shield her eyes. Half way down the six steps, she heard the police sirens. They were coming up the street fast. Gladys shoved the .38 back into her purse and started across the street heading in the opposite direction.

She never saw the milk truck until it hit her. Her last sight was of a startled milkman. The truck knocked her twenty feet into the air. She came down in the middle of the road, her back and neck broken.

The first of the two radio cars stopped only a few feet in front of her body. Sgt. O'Malley, the driver, and Commissioner Kirkpatrick leaped out at the same time the agitated milkman came racing over.

"It wasn't my fault!" he cried. "She just came running out of nowhere!"

"Relax!" the commissioner snapped. "We saw it all. Just go back to your truck and catch your breath. Someone will get your statement in a minute."

"Commissioner, you'd better come see this," O'Malley advised, pointing to the satchel on the ground beside the fat woman's body.

Kirkpatrick hustled past the other uniformed officers converging on the scene. The satchel's clasp had popped open and dollar bills were spilling out. The boss cop whistled and tipped his fedora back. It appeared the anonymous female caller had been legit. That unknown citizen had said the now-deceased Gladys Mayhewn was behind the so-called Invisible Gang. The suitcase full of money certainly added validity to that claim.

He had no idea what else they would find within the orphanage itself.

"Saints preserve us!," O'Malley suddenly blurted. "It's the black devil himself!" He pointed to the roof.

Kirkpatrick looked up and felt his intestines tighten. Why me, he thought in a flash of self-pity. Why does every case I touch have to be resolved by him? But there was no answer other than the whim of the fates.

The *Spider*, slouch hat pulled down, gave Kirkpatrick a flamboyant salute and then was gone. Pigeons suddenly exploded into the sky as a loud, mocking laughter rang down upon them.

illustration by Tom Floyd

Chapter Fifteen

THE DEVILS DRUGGIST

by ROBERT WEINBERG

"Extra! Extra!" the newsboy's voice rang out like a siren. "Read all about it! Another victim killed by poisoned aspirin! Getcha' papers here! Read all about it!"

"I'll take one of those, son," said Richard Wentworth, grabbing a paper off the just-delivered stack and handing the news urchin a quarter. "Keep the change."

"Wow! A twenty-cent tip!" the kid exclaimed. "Thanks, mister!"

Wentworth grinned at the boy's enthusiasm, but the smile disappeared as soon as he read the tabloid's lead headline.

"ASPIRIN CLAIMS TENTH VICTIM!" blared the forty-point type plastered across the front page of the newspaper's early evening edition. Beneath the bold words was the picture of a young man, a college student, spread eagle on the floor of the City College cafeteria. Both of the victim's hands were stretched over his head, his fingers curled like claws, tearing at the air around him. His face was contorted in agony, his eyes popped wide open in death. On the floor nearby was a bottle of Bayside aspirin, a half-dozen white tablets spread about like bullets. Bullets in the shape of life-saving medication! Here was another victim of the aspirin killer.

Walking in ground-eating strides down Fifty-Fourth Street towards the East River, Wentworth scanned the inside pages of the news rag for the crime details. The death followed the same pattern as all the rest. Ten people had died during the past week and the police were baffled by not only the crimes but how they had been committed. Wentworth could sympathize. These crimes made no sense. The victims were young and old, men and women, rich and poor. As far as the police could tell, they shared nothing in common. Their killer made no demands and left no clues to his methods. The only thing linking the crimes was that each victim had died after taking aspirin. And, making matters worse, they hadn't even all ingested the same brand!

Police chemists were baffled. None of the other tablets in the aspirin bottles contained any traces of poison. Evidently, the master criminal placed the deadly tablets right at the top of the containers, so that they were the first ones used after the bottle top was opened. It seemed impossible but there was no other explanation that made sense.

The murders were outrageous, seemingly random, totally illogical, and yet they kept on happening.

The young man's name was Tom Robbins. Along with a group of friends, he had stayed up late the night before finishing a report due for social studies. At lunch, he'd complained of a headache from lack of sleep. No one had thought anything of him opening a small bottle of Bayside aspirin and taking two pills with a glass of milk. It wasn't until a few minutes later, when Tom had lurched up from his chair, his face twisted in terrible pain, his arms thrashing about wildly, did someone remember the warnings about aspirin. By then, it was too late, much too late.

Tom was from Philadelphia, and from all reports had been well liked and admired on campus. He kept away from illegal booze and had too little cash to gamble. Not the type to get involved with gangsters or thugs. None of his friends could think of anyone in the world who would want to harm their classmate. Yet, he was dead.

The next few paragraphs of the news story summarized the circumstances of the earlier killings. First to die had been a retired judge, leading the police to think maybe it was a mob rubout. Until the second killing had taken place, that of a junior nurse in a children's hospital. Then there had been the deaths of an elderly matron, an airplane pilot, a shoe salesman, and all the rest. Every one of them dead with their throats constricted as if being choked, unable to breath, having taken two aspirin.

There had been raids on pharmacies and midnight questioning of druggists in a wild attempt to locate a possible madman, all without results. The president of Bayside Drugs had posted a ten thousand dollar reward leading to the capture of the culprit, leading nowhere. People switched from the popular aspirin brands to lesser-known companies. But the killings continued.

The story concluded with a statement that the police were pursuing several "hot" leads and that Commissioner Stanley Kilpatrick expected a break in the case shortly. In the meantime, he advised people with headaches to put cold compresses on their foreheads and at all cost avoid taking aspirin.

Wentworth grimaced in annoyance and tossed the newspaper into a nearby trash can. Hot leads indeed! He had talked to his friend, Kirkpatrick, earlier that afternoon about the murders and the Commissioner had admitted that the police were baffled. All of the Bayside employees in the city had checked out and not a trace of poison had been found at the local bottling plant. So far, the aspirin killer had not left a single clue.

Entering the lobby of his Sutton Place apartment building, Wentworth punched the button for the penthouse. Once in the apartment, he headed directly for the music lounge and the case holding his priceless Stradivarius violin. A few quick warm up trills, and he was ready to play. Letting his emotions run wild, Wentworth launched into a passionate rendition of "Danse Macabre."

So caught up was he in the music that he didn't notice five minutes later when the door of the penthouse swung open and a lithe, attractive young woman with short brown hair glided in. She stared for a moment at Wentworth, in a near hypnotic trance as he played, and then with a slight shrug of her shoulders, dropped down to the plush cushions of the parlor sofa. Wealthy young woman of the world and Wentworth's soul mate, Nita Van Sloan, she was used to waiting.

Five minutes more passed until Wentworth, his anger and annoyance gone, put down the violin. He smiled at the sight of Nita sitting patiently in the other room. "Nita," he said, stepping out of the music lounge and into the parlor, "you should have interrupted."

"Nonsense, Dick," she answered smiling. "I know how much you value your time with your violin. Besides," she laughed, "it's the one female whose competition I don't mind."

"As if I could love anyone but you," said Wentworth. Walking to the bar in the corner, he fixed each of them a drink. As he handed one to Nita, the phone rang.

"Excuse me, my love," said Wentworth, reaching for the receiver. "Maybe it's Ram Singh or Jackson calling. I sent them upstate to do some investigating. I was hoping to hear from them by evening."

Wentworth picked up the phone and listened intently. His features hardened, his eyes narrowed. His fingers holding the receiver turned white.

"Yes, I'll tell her, Kirk. We'll be right there. I promise."

"Dick?" said Nita, rising to her feet, alarmed. "Was that Kirkpatrick? What's wrong?"

"It was Kirk all right," said Wentworth. His body was electric with tension, as if ready to explode. "He was calling from Lilly Hapshaw's apartment. Kirk thought he might find you here."

"Lily?" repeated Nita. She and Lillian Hapshaw had been roommates at Vassar and had remained close friends ever since. She clasped her hands in front of her face as tears filled her eyes. "You don't mean——"

"I'm sorry, Nita," said Wentworth, "but Lily's been found dead on the floor of her apartment, yet another victim of the aspirin killer. Kirk wants us to rush right over and take a look around. He's hoping that you, as one of Lily's closest friends, might spot something out of the ordinary. Are you up for it?"

For a second, a mask of tears blurred Nita's beautiful features. Then, as if switching from one emotion to another, her face hardened and turned into a steely mask of resolve. No tears for anyone from this version of Nita Van Sloan. This was the dark side of Nita that only Dick Wentworth and a few other companions knew existed.

She leaned forward and stared Wentworth directly in the eyes. Her voice never rose above that of a whisper. "I went to Vassar with Lily Hapshaw, Dick. She was a friend of mine. As sweet and pleasant a girl as you can imagine. I can't understand who would want to kill her, and I don't care why. What I do know, is that I want that person *to die*. To die like Lily, gasping desperately for air. Is that understood? There should be no mercy for Lily's killer. None at all."

"As you wish, so shall it be," murmured Wentworth, his mouth close to one of her ears. Not a trusting man, he knew the range of modern listening devices. He kept his conversations short and to the point. "The *Spider* guarantees it."

Nita, along with Wentworth's assistants Ram Singh and Jackson, were the only people who knew that wealthy man-about-town and amateur sleuth, Dick Wentworth was also the *Spider*, Master of Men. It was in this alternate identity that Wentworth dealt out permanent bullet-justice to those fiends who might otherwise escape the long hand of the law. A ruthless vigilante feared by the Underworld, hunted by the police, the *Spider* acted as judge, jury and executioner in regards to those who broke the law. The most dangerous man alive, when the *Spider* promised no mercy, he meant it.

Together, the two hurried down to the huge underground garage beneath the apartment building. "I sent Jackson and Ram to upstate New York to check out the companies supplying the chemicals used to make aspirin in the city. So far, they've found nothing unusual. They won't be back until tomorrow. So tonight it's just you and me hunting for this crazy aspirin killer."

Wentworth slammed on the gas pedal of the huge Daimler, sending it spinning onto late afternoon Manhattan Streets. Next stop, the apartment of Nita's college chum, Lily Hapshaw.

Lily Hapshaw lived in a classy apartment building for single young ladies on the city's upper West Side Drive. It was one of those fancy Riverside Drive addresses with a doorman at the front for privacy and you had to be buzzed in from an apartment upstairs. When Wentworth and Nita finally got to Lily's suite, the police had already rearranged the furniture and kitchen looking for clues. The body had been removed, taken to the city morgue for further examination. From the angry expression on the face of his friend, Police Commissioner Stanley Kirkpatrick, Wentworth knew that so far the cops had not found anything of interest.

"As much a puzzle as the earlier crimes?" asked Wentworth as he briefly shook hands with Kirkpatrick. "Another dead end?"

"You nailed it on the head, Dick," said Kirkpatrick. Though the Commissioner suspected his friend was the armed vigilante known as the *Spider*, he also knew that Wentworth had one of the best crime-solving minds in the city. More than once, Dick Wentworth had helped Stanley Kirkpatrick crack a difficult case. His advice was always welcome.

"Miss Hapshaw came home early from a charity auction at the World History Museum. We're trying to locate the cab she took but I doubt if it matters. When she arrived in her apartment, she told her maid, Angela Torres, she had a splitting headache and asked the girl to bring her a glass of water. Torres was in the kitchen for less than a minute, but when she returned, Hapshaw was already on the ground, gasping for air. As per usual, there was a newly opened bottle of aspirin at her side. Torres summoned a doctor – one lives in the building - but by the time he arrived, it was too late. Miss Hapshaw was dead, suffocated from lack of air, just like all the others."

"Where's the maid now?" Wentworth queried.

"In the parlor," said Kirkpatrick. "Sgt. Muldoon is questioning her, going over her story. I'm having the doctor interviewed as well. I doubt either one is involved, but it never hurts to double check the evidence."

Kirkpatrick was a hard-working, nose-to-the-grindstone cop. Wentworth knew that if there was a clue to be found in the apartment, his friend would find it. The problem was that so far in all of these murders, not a shred of evidence had turned up.

"The maid was sure no one entered or left the apartment while she was in the kitchen?" asked Wentworth.

"Impossible," replied Kirkpatrick. "The door was locked and bolted from inside. The aspirin killed her, Dick. The lab boys are analyzing the contents of the bottle while we speak. Maybe this time we'll get lucky and find traces of the poison."

"Oh, Dick," said Nita, who had been staring at the chalk outline where the body had fallen. "There's nothing out of place here. And Angela has been with Lily for years."

Nita looked flustered. "Being in this apartment, knowing Lily died here, gives me the shivers. Dick, would you mind if we left? I'm sorry to get so emotional, but Lily and I were very close."

"I understand, Nita," said Wentworth. He nodded to Kirkpatrick. "You seem to have the matter well in hand here, Kirk. I should have realized how much of a shock Lily's death would be to Nita. Let me take her home. I'll talk to you again in the morning."

"We'll catch this madman, Nita," said Kirkpatrick. "The whole force is working on finding Lily's killer."

Nita smiled wanly at the Commissioner. "I'm counting on you, Stanley. I know you're doing your best."

Back in the car, Wentworth looked at Nita with the faintest of smiles on his lips. "Getting the shivers, my dear? You, who has personally stared in death's face more times than I like to think about?"

"I needed to tell you something immediately without Stanley around," said Nita. She blushed. "I would have been a star on the stage."

"No doubt about that," said Wentworth. He steered the Daimler into traffic. "Now talk."

"Stanley's account of Lily's death stirred my memory, Dick," said Nita. "I remembered her telling me once in college that she couldn't swallow pills without washing them down with a full glass of water. That otherwise she choked violently on the tablets."

"Then, if Angela was telling the truth and she was just returning with some water from the kitchen, Lily couldn't have taken those aspirin in the meantime," said Wentworth.

"Angela has been Lily's maid for years," said Nita. "I'm sure she would-n't lie about anything."

Wentworth's fingers tightened on the Daimler's steering wheel. "Knowing that one fact puts a whole new spin on the murders. If we assume Lily wasn't poisoned by the aspirin, then what actually did kill her? It couldn't have been the bottle. Too many people handle it during a sale. Then what?"

Wentworth suddenly slammed on the brakes. "Damn!" he exclaimed. "It was right in front of my eyes."

Behind him, several drivers honked their car horns in annoyance. Shifting gears, Wentworth guided the touring car into a nearby parking space. Eyes blazing, he turned to Nita.

"No wonder the police could never find any other poisoned aspirin in the bottles," he explained, his voice filled with fury. "That's because *none* of the tablets contained anything lethal. The poison was in the *cotton swab* lodged in the top of the container to keep the pills from being exposed to moisture. That's the one thing all these victims had in common. They opened new bottles of aspirin, removing the cotton packing seal to reach the pills. Not knowing that by touching the seemingly innocent material, they were absorbing the poison."

"Then the criminal committed his crimes by removing the original cotton swabs from every aspirin bottle in a store and replacing them with poison-tainted ones," said Nita. "That means he had to have access to the store stock before anyone came in. Making him either a sales person or a manager. But, Dick, what sort of devilish brew kills on contact with the skin?"

"A certain deadly mixture of South American plant leaves and roots known as curare," said Wentworth. "I read about the brew in a book about the Amazon jungle last year.

"The poison is used by natives in South America to coat the points of their blowgun darts. The toxin is absorbed through the victim's fingers into their bloodstream. Minutes later, it paralyzes the muscles in the victim's face, then their throat, then their lungs, causing them to die soon afterwards from respiratory failure. It's a horrible, painful way to die."

"How terrible," said Nita.

"There's talk of using extremely low doses of the concoction as an anesthetic during major operations," said Wentworth. "So, some good might come of it in years to come. But, at present, the poison is so rare outside of the jungles of Brazil that it's not surprising that the police chemists didn't recognize its effects."

"Dick," said Nita, "Angela mentioned that Lily had just returned from a charity auction at the World History Museum."

"My thoughts exactly," said Wentworth. "If I remember correctly, there's a gift shop inside the museum. Most likely they sell bottles of aspirin there."

"The museum?" repeated Nita. "The killer is targeting patrons of a world history museum?"

"Strange as it seems, the location makes perfect sense," said Wentworth. "I should have realized it sooner. It's the *one* place where students and retirees and people with time on their hands often visit in these tough times. The museum is open for free to rich and poor, young and old, men and women. I'm still not sure of the killer's motive, my dear, but I feel certain that's where we'll find our murderer. At the World History Museum."

It took all of Wentworth's considerable persuasive skills to convince Nita not to accompany him on his midnight mission to the World History Museum. Instead, she was stationed at Sutton Place apartment with a stop-watch, with strict instructions to call Stanley Kirkpatrick with all the information they had deduced earlier that evening, if Wentworth didn't return home safe within two hours. "I know you can take care of yourself under most circumstances," said Wentworth, standing in front of a mirror as he adjusted a black slouch hat on his head. "And in most circumstances I'd be happy to have you accompany me. But tonight's different. We don't know who we are fighting, how many of them are waiting for us, and worse, how many of them are armed with curare, one single touch of which can kill."

Wentworth fastened on the yellow vampire fangs that gave his already ghastly made-up features a horrific tint. "*My life* I'm willing to risk catching this madman. *Your life* I'm not. So no more arguments, Nita. You stay here and watch the clock. If I'm not back in two hours, alert Kirkpatrick to our deductions. And leave the gun work to him."

"I don't like it," said Nita, angrily, "but I'm not a fool." She reached up and kissed the face of the ugliest man in the world, at least as achieved through the liberal use of Hollywood makeup, directly on his bloodless lips. "Find and kill this madman, Dick. Vengeance for Lily! Make him pay."

"That I will," said Wentworth, and with a flick of a thick black cape, he was gone.

No longer did tall debonair Richard Wentworth walk the streets of Manhattan. Instead, a masked man with piercing grey eyes darted from shadow to shadow. He stayed well out of the sight of ordinary people. This figure wore old dark clothes, with a jet black cloak across his shoulders, and a large slouch hat hanging in front of his face. He moved through the streets with astonishing speed. He was heading directly for the Museum of World History and no thug or cheap floozy thought to stop him for a light or beg for a quarter. There was something about the cloaked figure in black that inspired fear. Some inner sense warned them that this was a man to be left alone.

Wentworth reached the museum a little after 10 p.m. The place was locked and closed down for the night, but for one with his lock-picking skills, that was a minor inconvenience. The halls were dim, with only a few small lights shining in the gloom. According to the newspaper, budget measures had cut the number of guards patrolling the huge place down to two, and at this time of the evening, they were off on the other side of the building.

Not exactly sure whom or what he was waiting for, Wentworth perched himself in the midst of a full figure diorama celebrating the French Revolution. With his grotesque features, long stringy hair, intense grey eyes, and ragged clothes, he seemed to melt into the exhibit. Certain that something would happen sooner or later, Wentworth settled down for a long wait.

Twenty minutes later, a dark skinned man with jet black hair, dressed in ordinary street clothes but wearing neither shoes nor socks came trotting along the hallway. Wentworth recognized the native as a Jibaro tribesman from far up the Amazon River. The man was carrying a two-foot long blowgun made from a bamboo branch across his back. Proof positive to Wentworth that the aspirin killer was headquartered somewhere in the museum. The tribesman disappeared down a stairway leading to the museum basement.

Another ten minutes passed before a second Jibaro Indian, a near exact match to the first, followed his fellow tribesman down the stairs. From below came the sound of several men speaking.

Carefully, the *Spider* waited for another fifteen minutes but no other native appeared. Finally deciding that the criminal mastermind only employed two henchmen, Wentworth slid off his perch in the diorama and slipped through the shadows to the open doorway. The steps led to a landing ten feet below. From there, another ten feet of stairs descended to the museum's huge basement.

Most of the lower level was shrouded in darkness, but the area closest to the stairs was well lit by several camp lights. Three men sat busy working at a wide table. Two of them were the Indians who had passed Wentworth upstairs. The third was a middle-aged man with bushy black hair, thick eyebrows, and deeply tanned skin. Wentworth recognized him immediately. It was Damon Jones, the assistant-curator of the museum. Here was the mastermind behind the aspirin killings. But why? Wentworth wanted to know Jones' motive and there was only one sure way of finding out.

Effortlessly, he slid the twin .45 automatics out of their sheaths in his cloak. Leaning on the steel railing of the landing, Wentworth aimed his guns at the two Indians. If there was going to be trouble, they would be the ones he needed to eliminate first. Ready for any possible disaster, Wentworth spoke.

The words, due to the vampire fangs he wore in his mouth, came out harsh, distorted, barely recognizable. But, when the *Spider*, Master of Men spoke, people listened.

"Damon Jones!" cried the *Spider*. Instantly, the assistant curator was on his feet, staring upward with crazed eyes at the menacing figure standing a dozen feet over his head. At Jones' right and left rose the two South American Indians. Their hands were flat at their sides. Evidently, they realized that any move to reach for their blowguns would be met with a curtain of lead.

"You're guilty of killing ten innocent people during the past week in Manhattan," said the *Spider*. "The guilty must be punished and in your case, the punishment is death! Can you give me one reason not to blast you down where you stand?"

"Yes!" cried Jones. "I can."

A wild, insane grin spread across the curator's face, and he gestured dramatically with both hands at the stacks of open boxes on the table. "The cotton in the aspirin bottle was merely an experiment to see if the curare would kill effectively. I only murdered a dozen or so using that method. Now, we've been using the poison in an entirely new way. Next weekend, thousands will die. Thousands!"

"For what reason?" asked the *Spider*, encouraging the madman to continue speaking.

"The fickle public stopped visiting my exhibit on the Amazon jungle," declared Jones, his voice calming. "They thought it was boring. *Boring*? After I made two trips up the river to guarantee the display's accuracy? I even brought some native tribesmen back with me to perform at the museum. I destroyed my health, suffered through malaria, and for what? The director planned to close the exhibit. Because, he told me, the public was no longer interested in the jungle. Well, I got my revenge on the public! Just as I will have my revenge on you, Spider!"

With a swoosh, the twelve inch blade of a steel machete swept across the spot where the *Spider*'s head had been an instant before. If Jones hadn't gloated, the killing blow might have caught the crime-fighter by surprise. As it was, the *Spider* jerked to the left and then down, avoiding the deadly blade by tenths of inches. With a growl of fury, the *third* native, a latecomer to the scene, tried to swing the huge knife around, aiming to catch Wentworth in the shoulder. But now the *Spider* was prepared.

Twin guns barked as if in sequence. One, two, three, four slugs slammed into the Jibaro tribesman with the force of a ten-ton sledge. With a high-pitched scream, the native flew back off the landing and dropped with a loud splat on the concrete floor below.

Still, the distraction provided enough time for the three men behind the table to scatter. Like angry bumblebees, a swarm of darts flicked by Wentworth's right ear. Extraordinary reflexes took control. Not even focusing on his target, the *Spider* swung around one revolver and fired. Another native screamed something in an unknown language and instants later, his lifeless body hit the floor.

Wentworth snarled in delight, the kill-crazy laughter of the *Spider*, the man who knew no fear. A laugh that had sent more than one crook scrambling for an exit. Not tonight.

With a *thwump*, a tiny blowgun dart slammed into the *Spider*'s forehead, catching him right below the brim of his slouch hat. Without a sound, the masked crimefighter dropped to his knees, his hands still holding his two guns limply looping on the steel bars of the railing. The *Spider*'s eyes fluttered as if desperately trying to remain conscious, then closed. A shudder of pain ran through his body, then stopped.

"Death to the Spider!" crowed Damon Jones, rising up from behind the overturned table. Beside him, the remaining Jibaro Indian straightened, his blowgun clutched in one hand. It had been his dart that had laid the *Spider* low.

"Too bad you're dying, Spider," said Jones, gnashing his teeth together like some hungry animal. "Otherwise you could have attended the free concert the museum is planning for next weekend in the park. You would have loved the main event. Death and destruction entertain thousands."

"That's all I needed to know," said the *Spider*, his eyes opening, his lips twisting into a nightmarish grin. With a shake of his head, he dislodged the poisonous dart trapped in the thick theatrical black wig that he wore beneath his slouch hat. The twin automatics in his hands, which had never dropped to the cement, rose, and roared. Jones and the lone Jibaro crumpled to the floor, dead.

In the distance, Wentworth could hear the sound of sirens. The police, summoned by Nita at exactly ten o'clock. Hurriedly, the crimefighter pulled out his cigarette lighter and exposed the seal of the *Spider*. There was one last task to be done.

When Kirkpatrick and his team of detectives arrived five minutes later, they found four dead bodies – Damon Jones and his three Jibaro assistants – all killed by the bullets of a .45, and all with the mark of the *Spider* on their foreheads. Scattered around them were thousands and thousands of pairs of earplugs. When tested at the police crime lab, all of them were found to be coated with a thin but deadly layer of curare. Kirkpatrick wondered for weeks exactly how Jones planned to use the earplugs, but that was a question he never answered.

"I wish I had been there," said Nita, later that night as Wentworth related the events that had taken place in the museum. There was the echo of a leopard's snarl in her voice. "I would have enjoyed firing the bullet that ended Jones' life."

"It was your clue that put me on the madman's path," replied Wentworth. "Without your quick thinking, he might have managed to kill thousands more."

"I still don't understand Jones' plot, my darling," said Nita, "Why earplugs?"

"Jones was in charge of the outdoor concert the museum had planned for the following week," said Wentworth. "A few phone calls confirmed that instead of some pleasant summer music featuring a string quartet, the assistant-curator had booked a loud, raucous hillbilly band known as the Arkansas Three."

"Whose sound would have driven all lovers of good music in the park to distraction," said Nita. "Or resort to earplugs—"

"Provided free by the museum," said Wentworth. "Killing everyone who used them."

"What a diabolical scheme," said Nita. "Jones was truly a madman. Can you imagine anyone enjoying such country music?"

"Unbelievable," said Wentworth. "Absolutely unbelievable."

illustration by Tom Floyd

Chapter Sixteen

THE MAD GASSER OF MANTOON

by JOE GENTILE

Paralysis had him pinned down like an anvil to the chest, and it was unrelenting. His borrowed time had elapsed. The Spider was unable to even flinch, as a couple of the more courageous men from Mantoon came right up to him with no fear and pushed. They rolled him right into a large hole in the ground that was mere feet away. The Spider landed with a dull thud, and all he could think about in the beckoning dark was Nita. He was not afraid of death by any means, for there were times he would have embraced it, but being helpless was not how he imagined things would end. Maybe there still was enough time, he thought…as they shoveled dirt onto his face and his world dimmed.

It was August 31st, Thursday night, when Hell first came to a little town in Illinois known as Mantoon.

In the twilight hours, the Raef residence became the first of many homes hit with this unusual brand of terror. The bedroom window was raised from the outside in the pitch black night. Nothing could be seen until a small dark metallic hose rested on the window sill. A sleeping Mr. and Mrs. Raef did not stir right away, as the gas filtered into the room.

Urban Raef woke first, and then in turn, woke his wife. A heavy sweet odor made him feel nauseous. Mrs. Raef smelled it to, and they both became scared stiff…as all feeling left their limbs.

Something was wrong. She just knew it. Nita Van Sloan was wound tight like a spring as she sat with her legs tucked under her on a very cushy maroon easy chair in Wentworth's penthouse suite. She just couldn't get it out of her mind that Richard was in danger. She had no proof of this, of course, just her intuition. Too much time had passed since his phone call. Shaking her smooth chestnut hair left and right, she tried to snap herself out of it.

"I feel it too, *missie sahib*." Ram Singh said in his soft smooth baritone.

The big turbaned Sikh was looking at Nita, nodding in agreement, as she fidgeted in her chair. He palmed the handle of the big knife that was always tucked in his sash at his chest, for it never failed to reassure him.

"Ram, you too?"

With a glint in his eye that took her breath away, Ram looked at Nita with a chilling calm.

"It would be my honor to serve by your side, for it has been too long since my blade has tasted blood."

"Oh Ram, you charmer, you know just the right thing to say to a girl." Nita smiled coyly at Ram, knowing that he would be good as his word and then some, for Ram would fight to the death for either her or Richard without hesitation.

Nita was about to get up from her chair when there came a cavernous bark followed by excitable running footsteps from down the hall. Her Harlequin Great Dane "Apollo" bounded into the room. He ran to Nita, and put his big black and white head right in her lap. His tongue was hanging out as he panted, giving him dimples, which made it look like he was smiling. He was a huge beast, trained since a puppy by Wentworth to be Nita's companion in his absence. Now, he was fully grown, and close to five feet tall when standing on four paws. He looked up at her with his big pleading dark eyes.

"Apollo, you silly boy, you want to come too, don't you? What do you think, Ram?"

"It will be a long trip- "Ram started to say as the big dog raised his eyebrows and turned his head around to look at him.

With a smirk and a bow, the muscled dark warrior said: "I can think of no finer companion for battle."

That brought on another loud bark, which brought a small smile to Ram's lips and a laugh from Nita.

Richard Wentworth, aka the *Spider*, was in Chicago on business, when he espied a copy of The *Chicago Herald-American* newspaper at a newsstand at the airport. One of the headlines caught his attention:

"Mad Gasser on the Loose in Mantoon!"

The article stated how this small Midwestern town was being terrorized by a madman. The townspeople were being gassed in their own homes, falling to paralysis and then left for dead! Local police referred to the attacks having "no motive". There's always a reason, Wentworth said to himself, as he felt that unmistakable anger of his rise up, as innocents were being trampled upon. His eyes blurred with the thought that there was much more to this than what has been reported. He immediately rented a car, bought a map, called Nita to let her know that he would be gone for a while more, and was on his way to Mantoon.

When Wentworth arrived, the paranoia had already settled in like a suffocating rolling fog. Everywhere he went, people were talking about the gassings. Folks were afraid to leave their homes at night, and stayed with friends to increase their safety. Up until now, the police had very little to go on.

Every night of this hot month, the gasser would approach the houses silently, place the end of some kind of nozzle near a partially open window or door, and let the gas take its course. A dark mysterious figure, all in black and wearing a knit hat of some kind had been spotted on more than one occasion leaving the scene, but had not been apprehended.

The gas, which was not visible to the naked eye and had a very sweet odor, left its victims at first nauseous and then paralyzed. A few had recovered the next day, but some were hospitalized. Others weren't so lucky. It appeared the whole point was fear, and Wentworth knew *many* madmen who traded heavily in such a commodity.

Richard Wentworth was known all over the country as a wealthy entrepreneur, philanthropist, and amateur criminologist. To those who knew him, it would be no surprise that Mantoon caught his interest. And although he had been of service to many police departments in this regard, this was his first time in Mantoon, where they weren't exactly welcoming him with open arms:

"It's just a random attack. Someone different every time", said the apathetic loose-jowled Chief Cole of the Mantoon Police.

"How do you explain the same woman getting hit four times? Coincidence?"

"See here, Mister Wentworth, I don't care who you are, because to me you're just a nobody. You're not police, not the FBI, not even a reporter. As far as I'm concerned, you are obstructing justice-"and on and on it went.

That night, the *Spider* waited right outside the police department. He stood in the dark very near the front door, almost invisible amidst a few trees, for his black cloak seemed to envelope and dissipate any light near it.

His patience was rewarded as a lone policeman exited the station. The man was approaching his own car, and the *Spider* materialized in front of him, or at least that's what the cop would say the next day.

"There has to be a suspect, Officer Danning."

The friendly-faced policeman stared at the *Spider's* masked face full of pointed teeth, and stopped breathing, but just for second. The *Spider* liked that. The world needed more police with guts.

"Who are you?"

"I am the *Spider*, and I will bring all of this nonsense to a close and leave your city tonight if you will help me."

"The *Spider*? Thought you were a myth."

"Yet here I stand. Now…"

"Yes, we had a suspect."

"Had?"

"Look, we are not even supposed to mention him, for the family is fairly a strong one here…connected to all kinds of the wrong people, you know. Even the FBI don't seem to really care-"

"Give me his name."

"…How can I know that I can trust you?"

"Trust your instincts."

Just then, there was a shout from nearer the station. It was two FBI men running to them.

"Hey there!"

The *Spider* held a low whisper one sentence exchange with the policeman, and then was gone like a shot.

The FBI men ran up to Danning.

"Who the hell was that?"

"Calls himself the *Spider*."

"The Spider!"

"Yeah, what, does that mean something to- "Danning turned to say, but the federal agents were already running back to the station at full speed. Danning stared for some time, as he tried to fit some pieces together in his mind. Something was not right, besides being told to not make an arrest in the gassing case. He then got in his car and drove home.

He didn't get far before he heard the police radio screech about the complaints of another possible gasser victim. Then heard something else. It was a description of who was being chased at the scene of the crime. He turned the car around without braking.

The *Spider* had also heard the broadcast from his own car, as he had his police radio tuned in. He was very close to the latest gasser victim's location when he saw him…a figure dressed all in black, running away through the wooded farmland behind the small brick house.

Stopping his sleek Hispano-Suiza, the *Spider* glided silently into the night like a wraith. His figure looked like a black flag that was floating towards the fugitive. In less than five seconds, the *Spider's* superior speed brought him almost on top of the black-clad gasser. The *Spider* was about to tackle the figure, when he noticed something in the air around him. It was a scent. It smelled sweet. It had its effect almost immediately, as the *Spider's* legs stopped working, and he fell. He shook it off, and managed to get back on his feet, but the gasser was not to be seen.

Before the *Spider* could determine his best course of action, a black sedan squealed into the farm house, spitting up gravel and a cloud of dust. Four men exited the vehicle with guns drawn and took off in the *Spider's* direction.

"FBI! Stop or we'll shoot!"

The *Spider* knew there was no way the G-men would believe him, and the real culprit had disappeared, so he had no choice. He tried to run, limping along at first through the brush. He eventually re-gained his ability to run, but for how long? He had no time to ponder, as another car sped into the farmland between the *Spider* and the four men.

A single man got out, and was positioning himself between the predators and the prey. He had his hands out in front of him pleading for the men to hear him out. They rushed right through him, knocking the late-comer to the ground.

The *Spider* was looking over his shoulder at this, but had no choice but to keep running, and circle around to get back to his vehicle. Then, he heard a shout from the man on the ground, telling the *Spider* to be careful for the word was out, and soon the town would think he was the gasser! That voice belonged to Officer Danning! The *Spider* couldn't help but smile knowing that there was at least one man in law enforcement in this town who was interested in justice. Barely had that information been shouted, when there came a roar of gunfire. The *Spider* was shell shocked with horror as the body of Officer Danning twitched and jumped with each bullet that pierced the honest cop's form. He was tempted to stay back and make those fools pay, but again, he could not raise his guns against the police, no matter how much he seethed to do so.

Turning his back with distaste, he ran on. He was about to turn in between two houses, when their lights went up, and people came running from the house…with actual torches!

The *Spider* kept going straight instead, not wanting to hurt innocent townspeople either.

But the more he ran, the more people started to chase him. He was living his worst nightmare as he could not kill a single enemy, for they were all innocent.

The *Spider* knew it was only a matter of minutes before he would succumb fully to the effects of the gas. He ran at a speed in which few Olympic athletes could match, for few had honed their physical skills to the degree of what the *Spider* had done.

If he was right, he needed time and space to let the effects pass, but that was a luxury he might not get any time soon, as the good citizens of Mantoon, Illinois were taking justice into their own hands, along with rifles, clubs, and shovels too. Who could blame them, really, thought The *Spider*. Their friends and neighbors were being terrorized by some black clad villain, and the police had proven ineffectual.

The nausea had started to kick in. *Blast it*, all he needed was a minute to clear his head!

It was the *Spider's* intention not to hurt any of the innocent crowd, but that was becoming increasingly difficult, as the people lined the streets of the main business strip in town. Here there were storefronts on both sides, but all the stores were deserted now, because no one felt safe to go out at night anymore.

Now his legs were getting weak, and it wasn't because of running. Even draining his deep reservoir of strength couldn't stop him from a step. No way to know how much further he could go.

Shots were fired as he ran, but the *Spider* knew those shots were coming from above, and not from the residents. Snipers on the store roofs tried to pour lead rain on him. They missed…again and again. And it was on purpose. They weren't trying to kill him, those on the roof, they were just trying to steer him, but where? His stomach was churning, as the chemical reaction kicked into overdrive, so the *Spider* did the only thing that presented itself.

He cannon-balled into a storefront window with such propulsion, that barely any glass beside the hole his form made fell from the window. It gained him a couple of seconds, but would that be enough to distance himself from his bulldog pursuers? Forcing himself up with sheer will power, The *Spider* bolted for the rear door of what appeared to be a small town tavern. All of Mantoon was barking at his heels.

He threw open the door with abandon, and ran into the grassy knoll behind the tavern.

His leg muscle synapses were protesting his every command, as he kept pushing himself forward.

They were waiting for him. The *Spider* was not surprised. Then the paralysis took a hold of his legs. It was all he could do to stand upright, with his guns drawn. The sweat was dripping through his black face mask, and he could feel it coagulate around the rim of his wide-brimmed hat, but you could never tell that from looking at him. With his "color of the night" cloak enveloping him like a shroud, all you could really see of the *Spider* was his sharp pointed teeth, his piercing eyes, and the glint of steel from his two 45's.

Until the searchlight hit him square in the face that is.

"So *you're* the monster that's been running riot through this peaceful little town", said a voice in a megaphone that the *Spider* knew belonged to Dom

Caperno, rat-like henchman of Chicago Outfit boss Tommy Accardo.

The *Spider* could sense that many of Caperno's men were around him, even though he couldn't see much of anything.

"Vermin, the *Spider* will leave your entrails for the vultures to feast on." With every ounce of will he could muster, the *Spider* leveled his wrist upward and blasted the search light with one shot. Then he let out a rumbling, almost tumbling laugh that seemed to come form everywhere…all at once.

It had the effect the *Spider* was hoping for, as Caperno quieted, and no one approached. The crowd from the streets found their way to the rear door of the tavern, and were now spilling out onto the knoll, but they too stopped at the sound of that living-in-the-asylum laugh.

The *Spider* fell to the ground with a purpose. Using his elbows, he shimmied his way deeper into the dark, as Caperno's men rushed him. He could still knock off more than a few even from his vantage point of being prone. But then, the paralysis was complete. He literally could not move, not one muscle.

The crowd was panicking, and Caperno's men were running around with guns drawn.

"Everyone just relax. Your FBI has this all under control." FBI, thought the *Spider*, would these people really fall for that? The ensuing calm answered his question.

A flashlight beam fell across the *Spider's* face.

"Hello, *Spider*, thanks for being convenient."

Caperno's narrow unshaven face was right against the *Spider's*. The stench of unrelenting evil oozed from Caperno's pores like a cheap aftershave. "What's wrong, can't move? Yeah, we've heard that's no fun. Do stick around for the last act in your miserable life, courtesy of Tommy Arccado, and of course, the god-fearing people of Mantoon."

"Ok, everyone, here is the Mad Gasser!" Caperno roared through the megaphone, as a cheer went through the throng of onlookers.

"We give him unto you."

The *Spider* was unable to resist in anyway, as a couple of the more courageous men from Mantoon came right up to him and they pushed. The rolled him right into a large hole in the ground that was a mere feet away. The *Spider* landed with a thud, and all he could think about was Nita. He was not afraid of death by any means, for there were times he would have embraced it. Maybe there still was enough time…

The big roadster crunched gravel as it came to a rolling stop under the streetlight at the edge of Mantoon. The streets ahead were deserted. There was no one anywhere braving this night. Nita was in the backseat with Apollo, as she leaned to the front seat to where the ever vigilant Ram Singh was scanning the surroundings.

"Ram-"

"Yes, it is too quiet. There was terror here."

"We need to find Dick before it's too late."

With that, the big Sikh exited the car.

"I will not fail."

"Now wait a minute, Ram- *Ram look out!*" yelled Nita, but not before Ram sensed something amiss, and fell to the ground with a roll. A round of automatic gunfire laced the side of the car where Ram was once standing. At this, Apollo's eyes lit up with excitement and anticipation, as his feet anxiously skated back and forth on the floor of the back seat

"FBI!" came a cry from the men after the gunfire had ceased, "Give it up!"

FBI? Shooting first and asking for surrender second? Not likely, thought Nita.

Outside the great car were a half dozen armed men, who had opened fire on Ram and Nita. They had just exited a dull black car that was sitting alongside a series of trees, where they were hidden from view of the road. With one quick move of her hand, she slid open a small slat within the car door that faced the men. The door opened a gun port where she placed her gun and waited.

She saw Ram then, as he snaked silently from one tree to the next.One moment he was visible in half shadow, and the next, there was nothing there. One of the men leaped sideways into a tree, smashing his head into the trunk with a dull ripe melon sound. Then there was an array of gunfire and smoke as the armed assailants opened fire in the vicinity of where Ram could have been. Nita was not going to let anyone gun down her friends, so she too started shooting, taking specific aim at the FBI agents when she saw one through the trees. The men scurried for cover, but continued shooting. Another gunman went down silently, as a bloody gash appeared in his chest, courtesy of Ram.

Spider webs appeared on the bullet proof glass of the Chrysler as the men continued their assault. Nita ran out of ammunition.

"Damn!"

She tried to reload, as two FBI men walked calmly toward the car, lining it with lead. They grabbed a hold of the car and shook it, rocking it, guns still in their hands.

Having a difficult time just staying in her seat amidst what felt like an earthquake, Nita looked directly at the two men outside.

"Hey, how can a girl be expected to gunfight under these conditions?"

The men outside chuckled to themselves over the "dizzy" dame.

Looking at the expecting Great Dane, Nita quieted him with a glance.

"Yes, Apollo, I know. Stay down. Wait for it."

The two men scraped a slim metal bar in between the car window and the window frame, which forced open Nita's door.

She was cool and calm, giving a disarming smile right to the thugs.

Upon a snap of Nita's fingers, Apollo let loose a ferocious, drool-dripping teeth-baring growl. As opposed to a canine growl, the sound was more like a roar from a pit beast in hell.

The gunman, whose eyes were on the gorgeous Nita, didn't even see the massive pup at first. In his shock and fear, the sound of Apollo's demonic taunt literally made his gun fly out of his hands.

Apollo wasted no time after his lion's roar warning, and leapt over Nita at the first man, knocking him flat to the ground, with Apollo literally standing on top of him.

"Get him offa me...can't breathe."

"Holy-! What is that?" yelled the second gunman, completely frozen in fear looking at Apollo.

Apollo gave her the time she needed to reload, so Nita exited the car holding her gun casually, stepping on the pinned man's chest with her spiked heel.

"Let me introduce Apollo. He likes to play with his food." She turned to the frozen gunman, and pistol whipped him across the mouth with her automatic. The man almost fell to the ground, but stopped himself with his hands, so he was in a low crouch looking up at Nita.

"Lady, I don't know who the hell you think you are-"

He didn't finish his sentence, as Nita's spiked shoe steel toe met his chin with a *thunk*.

"No one knows how to talk to a lady anymore."

The remaining armed men were running towards the car, gun drawn. With a calming breath, Nita aimed her weapon The men spotted her and Apollo, skidded to a stop, and took off the other way at full tilt.

"That's my good boy. You can get down now." Nita said, patting Apollo's massive head. The Great Dane slowly walked off the man's chest, as Nita bent down to look for any kind of identification on the squashed man. She found none.

"What self respecting FBI man is going to leave the house without his badge?"

Ram Singh approached so silently, that Nita was inwardly startled as he said:

"Not FBI, *missie sahib*, demons without a conscience."

The *Spider* lay inert, but alive, in his tomb. His breathing was methodically slow, as he reserved his strength. What little air that was left would be gone in a matter of minutes. He made every effort to calm his screaming mind which demanded freedom, for with any lesser concentration of intellect, he would have collapsed and given in to the voices. But there was hell to pay yet. Justice remained undone. So he sucked on the sweet nectar of revenge, and that sustained his desire to go on.

A chatty gas station attendant told Nita that the Mad Gasser had just been captured by the FBI. Since they had already run into what was being called FBI, she was suspicious, and asked where that took place. After that, it was up to Apollo's nose.

All of them searched behind the tavern.

Nita was on all fours sifting through the loose ground, not caring about anything else but finding Dick. Apollo was sniffing with his nose pressed against the dirt. Ram Singh was carefully searching the grounds with a flashlight, hoping to find something, anything, that would point him to his master.

The *Spider* felt it then. He smiled, even though no one could see it, and even though he tasted dirt. It was just a tingle in his hand, but he knew that the paralysis was beginning to wear off. He knew there wasn't enough time for nature to take its course, so he put his iron-clad will to the test. His brain was sending an emphatic command to his muscles, and it would not be denied. Slowly at first, but then with strength, the *Spider* began to make a swimming motion, as if to go upstream. He knew that the pressure and the lack of oxygen would kill him in a matter of minutes, maybe even seconds, but he moved with calm, for panic would only make things worse. So slowly, inexorably, he swam up through the ground.

Just then, a fist shot up through the dirt.
Then another.
Apollo barked, and Nita and Ram ran towards it.

The *Spider* felt a strong sinewy hand meet one of his own, as it tried to lift him.

There were many muffled sounds from above. Some talking, and some other sounds as well…digging…barking?

The *Spider* was brought forth through the dirt like a raised submarine through the ocean. Ram and Nita were desperately pulling him up, as well as Apollo who had his mouth gripped tight on the *Spider's* cloak. When the *Spider* was completely out of his grave, he fell to the ground coughing, as Nita fell down with him almost in tears.

"Dick? Tell me you're okay."

.The *Spider* looked through her, and a chill sizzled along her nerves, as she could see that all was indeed well, for the *Spider* was still in residence.

"We can kill two birds with one stone, now that we're all here."

"I prefer whetting my blade to a stoning, but as always, *sahib*, at your service." Ram said with a bow.

The *Spider* grinned, but with the sharp pointed teeth, the sight was not unlike a hungry denizen of the netherworld about to feed. He and Ram pushed the dirt back into the hole that was to serve as his grave.

"Nita, take Apollo, and get me some neighborly gossip on a loner high school kid named Farley. A good man paid with his life to give me that name, so let's make it count. Talk to some of the victim's families. Try to find a connection. I have already reserved a couple of rooms at the Inn. We'll talk at there tomorrow evening. Ram, you're with me. We have take care of some unfinished business."

"Death to the mice who think they are men?"

"Oh, I think that is definitely on tonight's agenda."

"Then by the grace of the Guru I continue to be blessed with good fortune."

The two men tracked back to the *Spider's* car, which still lay abandoned where he left it. Within the confines of the Hispano-Suiza, the *Spider* and Ram felt the town's silence close in on them like a tomb. They had found one of the black sedans that chased the *Spider* earlier, and sped off in hot pursuit. It was all rather fortuitous…too lucky, but there was no reason to stop.

They reached a clearing between two small flat-top buildings, but the car they had been chasing had just vanished. There were tire tracks that ran right past there, but the tracks stopped and started again. Both men caught site of that, as their big car rolled to a stop. It was too obvious that these two flat-top buildings housed a trap.

"They will be waiting for us." The *Spider* said nodding towards the doorway of the nearest building.

"It is my most fervent wish that there are at least a dozen." Ram softly said.

"I'll take those odds every time, my friend."

Ram stood at one side of the door with his knife at the ready. With his guns drawn, the *Spider* kicked down the door and then swiftly dove to the opposite side of the door as Ram. The doorway then erupted in a storm of smoke and bullets, which lasted a full 30 seconds.

The first brave soul who jutted his neck out through the smoke met Ram's blade immediately. At the same time, the *Spider* dove low through the entryway, guns firing rounds of death in front of him. There were an even dozen of Caperno's men with surprise on their face and guns in their hands. With only the dim moonlight from the outside illuminating the room, the real fun began.

Ram had quickly followed the *Spider's* lead into the room of doom. He grabbed the first thing he came into contact with, which was an arm. Ram's iron grip caused a snap of tendons and a cry of anguish. Ram promptly lopped off the arm.

Two men leaped from each side of Ram, taking him down to the cement floor hard. One man had Ram's turban, smashing his face into the ground, while the other man had pinned both arms behind his back trying to wrest the big knife away. That knife was much more than just a knife to the big Sikh, and getting it away from him was like separating Siamese twins without a scalpel. Ram managed to catch one man in the eye with the pommel of his sword, but a third man joined the rugby scrum, and kicked Ram hard in the face. Ram spat out a tooth, but kept on fighting. One man was kneeling on his arm, pinning it and the knife to the ground. Another was sitting on his legs, while the third had free reign to punch Ram repeatedly. Ram did not let out any sound.

The *Spider's* initial volley dropped a pair of gunmen like marionettes that just had their strings cut. The dark, as well as the *Spider's* speed and ferocity, was hampering some of the gunplay from the men. The ambushers weren't prepared for the *Spider* and Ram to survive long. Two of the men went down by "friendly fire".

"Stop shooting unless you are right on top of them! Get them! There's just two of them!"

The *Spider's* 45's were barking every few seconds. The dim light only heightened his hunter's senses. The *Spider* sniffed out the criminals like a dog loose in a butcher shop. When he grabbed one, he would raise a gun to the man's face, and shoot point blank. It was the quickest death dealing these hardened gangsters had ever been party to. The *Spider's* laugh was everywhere, as he reared back his head like a wild animal. With his black coat pulled around him, and moving at almost superhuman speed, the *Spider* was practically unseen, as enemy bullets missed their marks time and time again.

The *Spider* knew something was amiss, even through his full-bodied berserker enjoyment of the proceedings. His steel grey eyes tracked through the darkness like a heat seeking missile, and his acute hearing listened for the familiar sounds of Ram's knife rending flesh. Nothing.

He pressed forward with no regard for himself, as bullets, knives, and chairs came at him from all sides. The *Spider* blurred through the assault unscathed, as if protected by some unseen force. He reached the wall where he had last seen Ram, and found a group of men. He didn't hesitate. He grabbed one man up by his shirt, pressed a gun to the man's head and fired, and then heaved the dead carcass out of the way like a rag doll. The next man had started to go after the *Spider* upon hearing the gunshot. The man leaped, but was stopped short as the *Spider* deftly side-stepped, and brought all of his considerable strength into one punch downward. The blow landed square between the shoulder blades, and the man's body slammed straight down to the floor. He would never get up again. A gun was pressed to the *Spider's* head from his right side. The *Spider* grinned maniacally at this mistake, for the attacker should have just fired, but he hesitated. That's all it took. In that split second, the *Spider* had shot up his right arm, like lifting a dumbbell, and punched away the gun. And then, with his other hand, he put a .45 into the attacker's face and fired. Brain matter sprayed over the *Spider's* gloved hand.

"Die, dog, die!" came the familiar battle cry of Ram Singh. The *Spider* grinned, knowing that it meant Ram was still alive. There was a swoosh through the air, a soft ripping of fabric, and then a heavy thud as a body fell to the floor. Ram, literally shaking with a combination of anger and fatigue, stood over his prey with his knife darkened with blood. The *Spider* put his hand on Ram's shoulder.

"Warrior?"

"I am more than fine, *sahib*. A few teeth are replaceable. They must have thought me an old woman, if they thought that would stop me."

The next evening, Nita and Apollo met up with Ram and Wentworth at the Inn. She told him of Farley: the boy who was an outcast at his local high school, the boy who was spoken about in whispers, the boy who possessed a near genius brain for chemistry. He kept to himself mostly, but a neighbor did speak of something that happened there recently. There was some kind of small explosion that was heard coming from the house, but there was no explanation given. The police had repeatedly told them that Farley was proven to not be the Gasser."

"Simple, my darling, they were pressured not to by the Chicago Outfit."

"So, the police will just let this kid continue gassing the entire town? What kind of sense does that make?"

"It doesn't. So, it's up to the *Spider* to relieve the pressure by ripping the Outfit apart, which has already begun. What is the connection of the victims to Farley?"

"I'll know that later this evening, as I have made arrangements for Ram and I to meet with some of them."

"Excellent. In the meantime, the *Spider* will pay a call on the boy."

The address that Nita had given him, at first glance, didn't look right. A grand house, sure, but not what he was expecting. Circling around back, the *Spider* found a little metal trailer parked in the back yard. One inside lamp shown down on a small work table. It was the perfect place for a teenager to experiment with things and not be a danger to anyone else. The *Spider* peered through the lone window, and it didn't take long for his intellect to grasp what was going on there. There were few men alive who knew more about poisonous chemical concoctions than the *Spider*. He would wait for the boy to return, and put an end to this little charade.

The *Spider* perched atop the small trailer, hidden in shifting shadows of the moving tree branches nearby, and waited. Just then, from the rear of the house, a door creaked open, and a small shaft of light stretched across the grass, and then disappeared just as quickly. Soft footsteps came towards the trailer in the dark. A thin white hand reached for the small brass doorknob. The *Spider*, leering over the side of the roof, looked down and laughed maniacally. There was a musical crescendo to it, as it came on slowly and then faded until you weren't sure you even heard it at all.

"Who-who's there?" stammered the young man at the door.

"I know your secret. The *Spider* knows all."

The young man looked up, and looked right into the moon lit face of the *Spider!* The fangs, the mask, the wiry hair, the dark cloak...

The boy was literally shaking in his boots, which the *Spider* loved to see.

"Why doesn't it explode? The chemical you've been concocting is supposed to be an explosive as well as a paralyzing agent. You failed, didn't you boy?"

"I- I don't know what you're talking about. Leave me alone."

"No, I don't think I will."

"The *Spider!*" came a yell from close to the house, which was then followed by bullets. With the first sound of the yell, the *Spider* was moving. He had dropped flat on the roof, drawing out his pair of 45's with one smooth move.

He saw the silhouettes of men coming towards the trailer. That was more than enough for the *Spider*, as he fired off his twin cannons, knocking off three of the men before they took another step! The boy was huddled against the door in a fetal position.

The *Spider* had the advantage, as the men couldn't get a level bead on him atop the trailer. They all fell to his unerring aim, just like ducks in a shooting gallery. The *Spider* was enjoying himself, as his wicked grin would attest.

"I will ask you one more time, mortal. The gas was supposed to explode, wasn't it?"

"I-I-I don't-" The boy was close to in shock, and Wentworth noticed something in his eyes, or more precise, the absence of something. The boy was somewhere else mentally, and the *Spider* was unsure if he could reach him at all.

"Why?" The *Spider* said almost softly. He looked directly at the boy with his penetrating grey eyes that few could resist a command from.

In that moment, the clouds had parted, as the boy looked at *Spider* like he was doing so for the first time.

"They were helping me to make it more powerful. They like to give out fear, they said."

"HEY! You on the roof!"

The *Spider* looked past the boy and saw the flashlights of a couple policemen. He refused to fight the police, for that was a fine line he didn't want to cross.

"Walk towards them slowly." The *Spider* commanded, and the boy obeyed.

By the time the police ran to the trailer, the *Spider* was gone.

"C'mon, son, you need to come with us now."

And then they put the boy in a white jacket and lead him away to an awaiting white van, destined to deposit the boy in a place where his sanity could be tortured and locked away forever. Not quite what the watching *Spider* was hoping for, but it would do…for now.

At least some of the police were doing what they felt they could do to protect the town. If they weren't allowed to arrest the boy, at least he was somewhere where he couldn't continue his terror.

After receiving a very telling report from Nita ,Wentworth strode into Chief Cole's office unannounced, and sat himself on the corner of the Chief's desk. Cole, who was on the phone, put the receiver down, and kept his mouth open at the audacity of Wentworth.

"What in tarnation-?"

"Chief," said Wentworth charmingly, "tonight it's over. I don't have the time it would take to explain all of this to you, but it's over. There will be no more gassing. No more Chicago boys masquerading as FBI-"

"My turn, Mister Wentworth, so you listen up. We're not some country hicks here, for we saw through those FBI men early on-"

"Good for you, Chief, good for you. But here's the rub. Farley, the Mad Gasser, has been taken away, so that should alleviate at least one of your worries. After tonight, you can gather up the entire Chicago Outfit at dawn, and not be concerned about any reprisals. Plus, you have to know that the victims weren't random, right? They all were connected to Farley's high school, whether they be teachers of his past or present, parents of his classmates, workers at the school, etc. High school just isn't kind to some."

"What? And how would you know all that?"

"I just do. Don't be afraid anymore, Chief, justice is in town."

He kept to the darkened alleyways, as he knew he would be a target, and hoped to avoid any innocents getting caught in the crossfire. It would only be a matter of minutes probably, before the rats scurried out from their holes. There wasn't much left of the Outfit, but what was left, wouldn't let the *Spider* leave unscathed, of that he was sure. So, if he could draw the criminals out, the town would be rid of them once and for all...even if the town was completely unaware that they were being saved by the *Spider*.

It didn't take long. Gunfire riddled the side of the building The *Spider* was walking next to, as small shrapnel-like pieces of wood and stucco shot past him. With the first shot, the *Spider* dropped and rolled and was returning fire upwards at a window in the rear of the bank across the alley. As the sound of gunfire ended, the *Spider* raced back to some cover inside the darkened doorway of an old wooden shed.

A car with its headlights turned off slowly drove down the alley toward the *Spider*. As it approached, the *Spider's* heart sank, as he recognized the automobile. It was the Chrysler...*his* Chrysler...although its windows were smashed, and it was caked with dirt.

It pulled to a stop just a few feet away from where he was standing. The passenger door opened, and Nita and Ram were pushed out! They fell to the street with an awful thud. Nita looked beaten and unconscious at best with her hands tied behind her, while Ram was bound and gagged like a prize dinner ham, bruises and bloody cuts all over his body. The *Spider* had told them to wait at the Inn for him. He should have known better.

"Look at what we found, *Spider*." The voice came from the car. It belonged to Caperno. "Throw your weapons into the street, and come out with your hands up."

"That will be your final mistake, cretin. You will die, just like the rest of your men whose decaying corpses litter the streets of this town." The *Spider* said between clenched teeth.

"If you do *anything*, I guarantee that your friends will be shot and killed where they lie."

The *Spider* couldn't tell how many men were in the car, or how many were in that window across the street. Initially he thought there were just three men left in Caperno's gang, including Caperno. Was there just one in the window and two in the car?

"Perhaps you would like a little show first?" said Caperno, as he came from the car, holding a gun in the *Spider's* general direction.

Caperno, standing right in front of Nita looked her up and down, licking his lips.

"Your boy genius has been removed." The *Spider* shouted.

"Makes no difference to us. We got the formula, and I must say the test trials were quite successful, wouldn't you say? Think of how much fun a big city like Chicago will be when we set this loose."

The *Spider* went in for the distraction. Just keep him talking, he thought. "Little man, you have failed. The formula was NOT successful, for the gas was supposed to do more than paralyze, wasn't it?"

"Maybe so, maybe no…"

"And without the kid's brains, you have nothing." The *Spider* seethed.

"I can't hear you anymore, *Spider*. Something else is taking all of my concentration, so if you'll excuse me."

"Mmmm, look at you…delicious." Caperno salivated to Nita.

At that last comment he moved even closer to Nita, where she felt his hot breath on her face. Waiting for when Caperno would be at his closest, Nita went into action! She was only feigning being knocked out! The *Spider's* heart leapt! She flung her head forwards as hard as she could. Blood spurted from Caperno's nose, as he swore loudly.

"Damned dame!"

She dove for Ram's trussed up form, trying to nudge him to cover, as the *Spider* leapt into the street guns a-blazing! He fired numerous rounds into the upstairs window across the alley. Caperno was holding his bloody nose, waving his gun around like a blind man, but he couldn't see too well through the blood. Nita managed to kick a leg out at Caperno, and he crumpled to the street. The *Spider* stopped firing, and waited…there was no return fire. No one was trying to gun them down while they were so vulnerable in the street. He moved to where Nita and Ram were, untied Nita's hands, but all the while holding his guns ready, one pointed towards the bank window, while the other was aimed at Caperno. A figure did appear in the window. Its shape was that of a man, but where its stomach should be, was just a big hole. You could see the curtains right through it. The man fell out of the window, end over end like a thrown tomahawk.

The *Spider* put his guns away, turned to Caperno, and shoved him hard into the ground…over and over, until the man's face was just a pulp of flesh, unrecognizable to any who knew him.

"There is no reason a creature like you should live!"

The *Spider* pressed his cigarette lighter to the man's wrist which left a bloody spider imprint. Just in case any Chicago folks wanted to know who was responsible for all of this.

"Nita…darling…?" The *Spider* said, as he slowly turned to her, cocking his head to one side with his eyes glazed over.

"I-I'm fine, Dick, thank you." The two looked at each other, as if they weren't surrounded by dead bodies.

"You are a woman after my own heart, love." He said, as his eyes returned to the eyes of Richard Wentworth.

"But see what I have to do to get it?" she said, brushing herself off, and seeing to Ram, who's breathing was slow, but steady.

The *Spider* bent down to join Nita at Ram's side.

"Oh, Dick…" she said, untying him.

"He'll be ok, Nita, don't worry, it looks worse than it is. He is the strongest most stubborn man I know. We will get him medical attention as soon as we're out of here."

He said this with calming ease, although his face bore grim concern for his friend. With effort akin to lifting a bag of groceries, the *Spider* lifted Ram and put him over his shoulder.

"The terror gas formula dies here. But, I could have sworn there was yet one more member of the Outfit-"

"Apollo!" Nita yelled, cupping her hands for directional volume.

Both he and Nita stared off into the night waiting. At first there was no sound, but then they heard it. Feet. Running. Four feet.

Apollo rounded the corner still sprinting. Upon seeing his masters, he crinkled up his mouth in what only can be described as a smile, and skidded to a stop by the *Spider* and Nita.

Nita noticed Apollo had something in his mouth. "What does he have?"

The *Spider* motioned, and the big dog dropped something fleshy to the ground. It looked like a mangled hand that was still attached to a wooden baseball bat.

"And that, I take it, was the missing man who beat Ram?"

"After they drove us off the road, the car rolled, and we were knocked out. At some point, I dimly remember a couple of men with bats smashing the windows and taking us. One of them was chased away by Apollo. I'm sure that was a short chase."

"Good boy." The *Spider* said, patting the dog on the head, and Apollo lapped up the gratitude like it was a juicy beef bone.

illustration by Tom Floyd

Chapter Seventeen

THE CALLING OF THE SPIDER

by MORT CASTLE

The time is well past midnight and still so long before dawn. The city sleeps and in his study, Richard Wentworth gazes down upon it.

Then he strides to the RCA Victor Tru-Tone phonograph by the bookcase. There is a click, and the promising hum of warming tubes. Wentworth studies the revolving record's label:

COMMANDER RECORDS/SEPIA STARS:

Angel Valentine

"Lost and Lonely Blues"

Blues Ballad w /Guitar Acc.
by Lerone Preston

Something quick and regretful flickers in Richard Wentworth's eye as a diamond needle hisses in the opening grooves of the 78.

Voice pinched and aching and true, Angel Valentine sings:
Someone can save you from hunger
Save you from the cold,
But no one can save you
From the lonely in your soul
You got the lonely blues
You got the lonely blues ...

A DARK NIGHT: LATE SPRING

Ended. Sixty hours of unceasing pursuit, no sleep or nourishment, driven on only by obsession and the miracle-like, energy inducing pills of Professor Brownlee, but now, he had them. The final three. The highest ranking of the Mad Mullah's crazed army. And the most trusted and cunning.

The *Spider* had them!

An effervescence that might have been exhaustion and exhilaration seemed to fill Richard Wentworth's mind as he burst into the dimly lit room, blue steeled automatics instinctively taking certain aim. Nor was Wentworth truly conscious of the thrumming growl emitted from deep within his chest until it metamorphosed into a triumphant roar.

The three Levantines had been studying a map of New York's subway system, and now, fitting the occasion, they froze in fearful surprise, then attempted to scatter, to arm themselves, to fight ...

"No!" Wentworth snarled. "Not a movement, fools!" He flourished his guns with seemingly mechanical, yet fluid precision, and not one of the trio doubted that a shot fired would find its target. "Keep your hands on the table! Do not let me see an eyelid flutter or an Adam's apple bob. Keep silence now"- Wentworth laughed-"and hear me!"

"I am the *Spider*," Wentworth said, "and I am"-he paused as though making the simplest of declarations—"The Master of Men!"

The center figure, younger than the other two villains, could not help blurting, "But the Mullah ..."

Wentworth understood the man's confusion-and hope. After all, when these three had last seen their divine dictator, Ahmed Faraz, the Spider had been the prisoner of the "Mad Mullah."

Wentworth sneered. "Ahmed Faraz burns in Hell!" Wentworth brandished his guns. "And I am the one who dispatched him to that locale."

He stood before them, in freakish disguise, with celluloid fangs making him a vampiric demon and flyaway wig making him a gibbering lunatic, but the eyes behind the domino mask burned the truthful intensity of Richard Wentworth's eyes.

"You are," Wentworth said, "the last of the minions of the 'Mad Mullah,' and now"-Wentworth laughed-"you will join him."

"No," said the young man in the middle. "Spare us. I beg you ... "

They begged, all right, the three of them. With prayerful hands, and ululating, whimpering voices, they pleaded and groveled and wept.

Could he not find a hint of Mercy, of forgiveness, deep somewhere deep within his soul?

Wentworth seemed to consider it.

"No," he said, calmly.

Then his guns roared. In the flashing explosions, Richard Wentworth stood serene as two ruthless .45 caliber bullets apiece shattered the chests of the men and sent them flying.

It was not quite finished, this night of Justice and Death. Before he slipped into the darkness, Richard Wentworth drew out a cigarette lighter and pressed its base to the brows of the slain men. On each dark forehead, a red spot glowed, a red spot that had hairy, ugly legs.

It was Wentworth's calling card of death: the Seal of the *Spider*!

EARLY SUMMER, THREE WEEKS LATER

The woodlands gleamed in silver-golden moonlight. It was "Rather a splendid night for a country drive, my dear," Richard Wentworth remarked to Nita Van Sloan, as his hands confidently gripped the steering wheel of the sleek black vehicle that hugged the curves and blazed down the straight-aways of the quiet country road. Though the car's hood ornament identified it as a Buick, and a casual observer would likely say, "Sure looks like a Buick to me," the automobile was nothing that had ever rolled off a Detroit assembly line-or ever would. The eight cylinder engine effortlessly cranked 310 horsepower, the windows were all bulletproof glass, and, upon the touch of a steering column button, pitch-black smoke clouds would spew from the exhaust. Most important, as Richard Wentworth had pointed out to Nita, the transmission was based on a GM prototype that the manufacturer planned to incorporate in production models in a few years. Professor Brownlee, scientist, engineer, inventor, and ally of the *Spider* had-*acquired*-the plans, modified them, and improved the design for the specific needs of the vigilante. The car Richard Wentworth drove smoothly shifted *automatically* with need for neither clutch or gearshift lever. Why, Richard Wentworth said enthusiastically, think how helpful that would prove when the *Spider* had to fire his automatic out the window while driving ...

"A full moon," Nita Van Sloan said. "So perfect. So lovely." Her voice became wistful. "So romantic."

"Why, yes," Richard Wentworth said, "I suppose so." He smiled at her, and said, "I love you, my dear."

Nita Van Sloan raised her head of clustering curls and her eyes were questioning. She had only just managed to stop herself, to forbid her red lips to shape the words that used to come so naturally to her-*I love you, Richard*-because there were times, *too many times*, that the man she had known, the man with whom she had fallen in love, her fiancé, Richard Wentworth, Esq., no longer seemed to exist.

Rather there was an *impostor*, an actor, an assumed alter ego, who had taken the name Richard Wentworth. Yes, he had the noble brow, the aristocratic, refined features of one whose ancestors were counted among the nobility of Europe, the thoughtfulness of word and manner, leavened by a jovial, if occasionally tart, insouciance suiting a gentleman of leisure ...

But the Richard Wentworth with whom she had fallen desperately and wholly in love? Where was *he* to be found? Now, when Richard held her, even at moments that should have been most intimate, it was somehow as though he were not truly present, but had sent an automaton to act his part: Richard Wentworth, *doppelganger*!

Adieu, auf Wiedersehen, and fare thee well, Richard Wentworth. In your stead, we have the *Spider*.

The fake fangs highlight your *true* smile as you laugh that joyful and cruel laugh. Leaden vengeance blazes from your .45 caliber automatics. You exult. You toss your head, that fright wig bobbling, and you laugh and laugh ...

I am the Victor.

I am The Master of Men.

I am what I am.

I am The Spider!

Even in the persona of Crimedom's Blinky McQuaid (itchy-twitchy Blinky!) or the street corner beggar-violinist, Tito Caliepi, his appearance as grotesque as his name, or any of the other half dozen disguises Richard Wentworth had created or would creaas you laugh that joyful and cruel laugh. Leaden vengeance blazes from your .45 caliber automatics. You exult. You toss te, there resided a certain core of *truthfulness* that was apparent to Nita Van Sloan.

But where was the truth to Richard Wentworth?

Where was *Richard Wentworth?*

What if "Dr. Jekyll" were the assumed identity, and "Mr. Hyde" the true self-only this Mr. Hyde proclaimed his allegiance to Justice, if not to Law and Order!

"Something on your mind, my dear?" Richard Wentworth asked.

The Spider's brilliant deductive reasoning at work, thought Nita Van Sloan. Oh, she was being petty and selfish, Nita chided herself.

"It's nothing," she said, as she reached out to click on the radio. She prayed she had not tuned in a police band or a secret emergency shortwave broadcast to the *Spider* from Ram Singh or Professor Brownlee, but no ... It was, thankfully, lilting music: " ... *Take It Easy*, by Orville Knapp and His Orchestra, with the lovely Edith Caldwell on vocals. We'll hear Knapp's haunting theme song, *Accent on Youth,* in just a little while, but now, let's have a song for this special time, the time that is the very heart of the night."

The announcer spoke in seeming baritone reverence over an introductory piano glissando, "This is Angel Valentine and her unforgettable *Solitary Soul.*"

Richard Wentworth snapped off the radio. Though Wentworth always—*always!*—maintained his composure, Nita Van Sloan thought she saw something flash across his face, an emotion that was an inexplicable combination of sorrow and fury.

"Richard," Nita Van Sloan started.

"No," Richard Wentworth interrupted brusquely. "That is not a song we need to hear. Not now."

Nita Van Sloan heard his words. She understood the literal meaning and what had not been expressed.

Richard Wentworth was leaving her. He was already gone. Oh, he would continue to drive along the road, chatting and smiling perfunctorily. But Richard Wentworth was somewhere far away, a place deep within himself.

A realm of memory and, there are some who would say, *soul* ...

SOME YEARS AGO: A NIGHT IN HARLEM

Cafe society swells flocked to Darktown not only to have a good time but to be seen having a good time. The rounds began for Nita Van Sloan and Richard Wentworth at The Cotton Club, where, as always, Duke Ellington and his band personified exotic elegance. Then they left the "only whites admitted" club for some of the salt and pepper cabarets just off Lenox.

It was here, Richard Wentworth maintained, that the best music and dance could be found; this was where the European tradition became infused with the wilder rhythmic influences of the descendant of Africa.

Richard Wentworth was a Renaissance man: a musician of considerable skill, a near virtuoso violinist and mandolin player. Richard Wentworth raced cars. Richard Wentworth played tennis, polo, and was a crack shot with pistol and rifle, as well as being a not unskilled archer. For charity, Richard Wentworth had sparred three "exhibition rounds" with James J. Braddock, forcing the future champion to clinch on three occasions. He had wrestled Ed "Strangler" Lewis to a 20 minute draw.

And much of the time, Richard Wentworth went through life feigning interests and enthusiasms.

Richard Wentworth was bored as hell.

Oh, Richard Wentworth had had occasion to call himself the *Spider*, but he was not yet The Master of Men, not yet the hardened and tenacious foe of all that was evil. He was a man who had known action in the Great War, who had done his patriotic duty, but who had felt himself come keenly alive, *truly* alive!

—when the foe man's bullets plucked at his uniform and the copper stench of blood and battle was a swirling miasma all around ...

—and a steel resolve burned away any fear he might have harbored or any feeling akin to fear ...

—and his own weapons tolled blazing death notes!

For such a man who'd passed the test of battle with the highest grades, a man who'd learned in combat his unmistakable calling, a humdrum civilian life became near unthinkable. And so, from time to time, he'd become a self-styled (and "ahem" not ineffectual) "amateur detective," solving crimes, matching wits with criminals who thought themselves somewhat above the law and far above other men.

Tonight, however, Richard Wentworth intended to be only Richard Wentworth, and it was none other who directed his turbaned Sikh servant and friend, Ram Singh, at the wheel of the limousine, to take Nita Van Sloan and him to the High Note.

"As you will, Sahib," the bearded, swarthy man said.

It was at the High Note's gaudy neon entrance that Richard Wentworth saw something. Three colored men, well dressed but brutishly large and rough, were "escorting" another Negro, a tall, slim, light skinned man, from the club; they were giving him the bum's rush. They forced their obviously frightened charge into an alleyway.

Nita Van Sloan did not appear to notice, but Ram Singh did. "Sahib," said the Sikh, in a voice that indicated he was ready for anything. On more than one occasion, Ram Singh had proven that the case with deadly knives and near super-human strength.

Richard Wentworth tossed his "special" walking stick from left to right hand, pushed back his topper, and said, "Ram, if you might accompany Miss Van Sloan ..."

"Home," Nita Van Sloan said curtly.

Richard Wentworth scarcely seemed to hear.

He strode into the alley.

He saw, beneath a dim bulb near a basement stairwell, the slim man slammed against the bricks and held there by two of the three captors. Their comrade reached into his trousers pocket and, with a gleaming smile, pulled out a straight razor that he snapped open so that the blade shone even more brightly than his grin.

"Country boy," he said, "you causin' annoyances with your obstreperousness. Mister Z do not want that, no, he do not."

"I come for Angel," the slender Negro said. He added, "Ain't afraid of you."

The man with the razor said, "Country, you be fearless like Dan'l in a lions' den, I'se still gonna cut you. Gonna cut your throat from ear to ear."

"I think not," said Richard Wentworth, as he stepped into the pool of murky light. "I'm sorry to interrupt your fun, gentlemen, but let's all be off and about our business now, shall we."

Four pairs of eyes fell on Richard Wentworth. The man with the razor faced him directly. Though his tone was obsequious, he did not sound as though he meant to be deterred. "Suh," he said, "beggin' yoah pardon, but this is a minuscule *small* matter jes' 'mongst colored folk. No need to be troublin' yourself, suh."

"No trouble," Richard Wentworth said, and without hesitation or indication, he sprang forward, Holding the shaft of his walking stick with his left hand, he yanked the handle and shining Toledo steel gleamed in the murky corridor.

"Was it 'Cut your ear from throat to throat ...'" Wentworth asked, brandishing the sword cane. "Is that what you said?"

A straight razor fell to the pavement as the man who'd wielded it shrieked as the razor tip of the blade chicked a sliver of flesh from his right ear and then the left. Blood snaked down the man's face, scarlet on ebony.

The other two hooligans released their prisoner. One drew out a slapjack, the other a .32 caliber snub nose revolver.

But by then Richard Wentworth had dropped his sword. His right hand held a blue steeled .45 caliber automatic, the gun designed to knock down the enemy—and to make sure he did not get up. Wentworth laughed. It was as much the sound of that laughter as Richard Wentworth's actions that froze the men in place—and that froze the blood in their veins.

"Why, is this to be a gunfight at the ofay corral?" Wentworth said. There was a hint of hopeful bloodlust and barely controlled rage in his mocking laughter.

"Go on now, lads, " Richard Wentworth said. In a sleepy minstrel show drawl, he commanded, "Scoot. Time for dem feets to do they stuff."

The trio did indeed scoot off on stuff-doing feet.

"Thank you, sir," said the man Richard Wentworth had rescued. The man seemed relieved Richard Wentworth thought, putting away his gun and sheathing his sword in the cane scabbard. But there was an puzzling tone in his voice as well. If there were one truth his studies of psychology had taught Wentworth, it was that very few people were what they seemed; everyone was an enigma.

"You're welcome, my friend," Richard Wentworth.

"Now, pardon me, sir," the man said, "I'm goin' back to the High Note."

"Hmm, what's that?" Richard Wentworth arched an eyebrow. "I *think* I recall your encountering some difficulty there."

"They not stoppin' me," the man said. "Mr. Z, he cain't put me off. I takin' my Angel outta that den of iniquity and ..."

"A moment," Richard Wentworth said, interrupting with an open palm. "I think we should talk."

Oh, yes, there was mystery here, Richard Wentworth thought, something that intrigued him ... him or the *Spider!*

The man was obviously not from the city. His suit was clean but antiquated blue serge, tight in the shoulders with the narrowest lapel; his polka dot tie might have been fashionable when Teddy Roosevelt organized the Rough Riders. Hatless, when any smooth-moving Harlemite prided himself on his "lid," the man's tightly curled hair was cleft down the middle, a backwoods bumpkin look.

"I'm Richard Wentworth," Wentworth said, offering his hand.

The man hesitated, and then, unsmiling, shook Richard Wentworth's hand. He said, "Lerone Preston."

LATER THAT NIGHT: RICHARD WENTWORTH'S PENTHOUSE APARTMENT

This is the story Lerone Preston told Richard Wentworth.

It was Angel Valentine who had brought him to New York. He loved her. The Valentine Family sang gospel. Though not as well known as the Gospel Trumpets or the Sutch Sisters, they were able to get by, traveling the roads of Glory throughout the South. It was Pops Valentine on piano, with a low rumbling bass voice, and Mama on tambourine, but it was the voice of the Valentines' only child, Angel, that brought people swaying to their feet, raising their arms in praise, that brought sinners to redemption and ever-lasting life.

You understood the ethereal when you heard Angel Valentine. She had a voice that speared into the loneliness we all carried within us—and then filled that aching vacancy with the promise of hope.

You might have had thoughts other than spiritual when you gazed upon Angel Valentine. She had light skin, so light she could no doubt pass if she chose to, and high cheekbones and wide-set eyes that made her look exotic if not exactly Oriental. Or perhaps you might have religious thoughts after all, remembering the "Song of Songs" of King Solomon and its mention of "breasts like towers."

Lerone Preston had been a carpenter and a good one, doing quick, clean quality work. Black and white alike trusted Lerone Preston, and with the Depression being so bad, why those as couldn't pay money had eggs and side meat or perhaps a lamp or not so old pair of shoes to offer. That was how he got the guitar. It was a Stella, and, what happened then was ... well, what it was was *strange*, to tell the short and tall of it.

See, from the first, holding that guitar, there was no learning nor practicing nor anything like it had to happen. Lerone Preston just *knew*— Presto! Alakazam! Lerone Preston heard a song on the radio or the Victorola, he could play it. Didn't matter if it was Scrapper Blackwell playing piano and singing "Your Picture's Faded" or Eddie Lang doing the guitar solo on "Someday Sweetheart." Didn't matter if it was a passin' through rough blues man like Charlie Patton or Hi-de-Ho Cab Calloway and all the orchestra on the big screen. Lerone Preston could take a song—*any* song—put it into and down and around his guitar, and just like that and ain't you well told, it was *his* song.

The carpenter man became a music man. Copasetic to say, Mr. Lerone Preston suddenly had himself many, many, many people who highly valued his company. Many of those people just happened to indulge in *spiritus frumemti*. A number of those people, say, a nice *round* number, happened to be female, and Lerone Preston, now a guitar ace and wizard and an all around player most serious, found himself well suited to strumming all sorts of strings..rm65

Truth: Lerone Preston played the Devil's Music and the Devil's Games and was well on the way to having Old Nick as crap-shootin' comrade, mighty hot rhythm section, and full time landlord.

Did not happen. No. What happened then was Angel Valentine.

There he is, Lerone Preston, juking and jiving and getting him some serious ground rations from the trimmest trim and the rightest and tightest, and he hears of this Valentine Family, which has a pert l'il thing therein, and he shows his seriously hanging over self up to a church service so far back in the woods you had to ask permission of two possums and Captain Cracker to get to it. See, it was about the music, which had in manner most serious by then.

But then he saw Angel Valentine.

Then he heard Angel Valentine. She sang "Jesus is Tenderly Calling You Home."

She sang, "I Am So Happy in Him."

And Lerone Preston felt the love of God Almighty Jesus My Savior Blessed Be His Name rock him and shake him and seize him up and hurl him down.

And Lerone Preston was saved, praised be!

He was also in love with Angel Valentine.

He joined the Valentine family, his guitar accompanying the singers and praising God's holy name. It was agreed, then, that after a suitable period of courtship, a chaste courtship conducted under the vigilant eyes of Pops and

Mama Valentine, that Lerone and Angel would wed.

Then something—*untoward*—happened.

Fate, or perhaps the Devil, intervened in the plans of man.

They were playing a revival in Bolton when an A and R crew from King-Tone Records set up recording equipment in a vacant storefront. The Valentines earned twenty dollars a side for six sides. But the King-Tone Records men made it clear that, "Angel, you should be singing blues. You should be singing jazz. You should be ... Look at Ma Rainey. Look at Ethel Waters. That girl comin' up, that Billie Holiday ... "

Say-hey, baby, you got star *quality*."

Why, thank you, sir, responds Angel Valentine, but she is meant to do the Lord's work and that was that.

Except Lerone could see that was *not* that, because there was a look in Angel Valentine's eyes that was faraway dreamy and yet glinting and hard.

One day not long after, she was gone.

Tonight, Lerone Preston had found her, found the woman he loved. No need to tell you, Mr. Wentworth, sir, about what all he had to do to find her, but find her he did.

And he sneaked into the High Note where Angel Valentine was head-lining. He told her, "I'm here to take you home again."

She told him, "I don't even know you. Not anymore. Broom off, Country Boy."

Then a white man—*it was that Mr. Z*—showed up and he snapped his fingers and three big colored bruisers showed up and ...

Mr. Wentworth knew the rest.

DURING THE NEXT MONTH

At first, Richard Wentworth thought it would prove a simple task to reunite Lerone Preston with his beloved Angel Valentine. Wentworth had little need of detective skills to learn matters of public record: One "Mr. Z," born Lester Zweigel, was the High Note's owner of record, and, as was the case for so many New York night spots, there were *allegations* the proprietor was Mob connected. The musician's union gave Wentworth the singer's telephone number and address, a nondescript hotel off 123rd.

But for a week straight, her telephone went unanswered and round the clock surveillance of her residence provided not even a glimpse of her.

Richard Wentworth met his friend, Police Commissioner Stanley Kirkpatrick, for lunch at the Toreador on 55th Street in Manhattan. Over cigars and Beefeater martinis, Wentworth said with seeming casualness, "Is there anything you could tell me about the High Note Club in Harlem and the fellow who runs it—what is his name again—Oh ... Yes, the chap known as 'Mr. Z.'"

"Mr. Z," Kirkpatrick answered. "Could also call himself 'Mr. C,' as in *Criminal* or Mr. H, for ... Well, never mind."

Kirkpatrick raised an eyebrow, and said with all innocence through a plume of smoke, "Why might Mr. Z interest you, Richard? Do you think there might be a certain *web* of intrigue surrounding the man?"

Richard Wentworth laughed. Though the *Spider* had crossed Kirkpatrick's path only a few times, the veteran lawman had his suspicions; he also had principles and would not act without convincing evidence.

Wentworth explained, "One of my investment groups is interested in purchasing the High Note; we might retain this Mr. Z as day to day manager of operations."

Stanley Kirkpatrick shook his head. "You do not want anything to do with the High Note. Nor with Mr. Z."

"Pray tell, why might that be?"

"There's a drug problem in Harlem. Unless the government takes heed of Harry Anslinger, who's with the newly formed Federal Bureau of Narcotics, marijuana will remain legal, cheaper than even rot-gut hooch, and far easier to obtain. Harlem's the holy grail for grasshoppers, Richard, and marijuana leads them to need something stronger, something far worse ..."

Kirkpatrick lowered his voice. "And it's *coming*, Richard. Heroin will invade Harlem. China used to supply the nation's underworld. Now it seems the Corsicans and Hondurans own the narco game. Your Mr. Z did some traveling last year. Corsica. Honduras."

"It's coming and Harlem is going to be Hell."

NIGHT: A WEEK LATER

In the High Note's locked basement, she lay on the cot in only her dirty slip. Oh, Lord. Lord, lord ... And why was she callin' on Him? She had pushed God out of her life; no place for Him. Didn't take God with her to the city when she come up here. Didn't give Him prayer nor praise when she was waxing sides with those sharp dressing, low living, drinkers and dopers. Didn't have her biggity self no need for God, did not. She had Mr. Z looking out for her, getting her a recording contract on the *Commander Sepia Stars* label, setting her up as leading blues chanteuse at the High Note, giving her just a little something new, something you will like, sugar-cookie, just a little something to take you *waaaaay* out there ...

Just a little something to turn Angel Valentine into Mr. Z's slave.

I am dying, Angel Valentine thought. I am dying and going to Hell and the sooner it happens, the better. Eight hours since the last fix. Her muscles were tied in knots, she was simultaneously freezing and burning up, she couldn't breathe with the air itself pressing down on her, and her heart jolted and sputtered and blasted like an old Tin Lizzy on a drizzling morning.

Angel Valentine had ceased to be a living human being; she was nothing but total and all consuming need masked in a human shell.

She needed junk.

"Oh, God," she groaned, "save me." A wave of belly cramps made her draw up her legs.

She did not expect God to come a rescuing like Ronald Coleman with wings. She had chosen Sin. She had permitted Sin to choose her.

Lerone? Thought he had ... Couldn't be sure. Thought he had been here and she told him to go away. Maybe she didn't want him to get hurt. Maybe she was feelin' good then, feelin' fine like that first 15 seconds when the rush hits you so hard that it takes you off the Earth and it's better than love and better than anything and you don't need anyone because you are all the Universe, or at least all that matters in it.

Then she heard a squeak and there was a slant of light. There was Mr. Z. There was the gleaming needle.

"Angel, my dear." Heavy pink wet lips in a meaty white face shaped the words. "Is this what you want?"

It was what she wanted.

It was all she wanted.

THE NEXT NIGHT

He seemed not in the least disturbed by the patdown his host deemed necessary. "Thank you for seeing me, old chap. The name is Lawson Bisping," Richard Wentworth said, his voice that of an Eton-educated Englishman. His appearance, however, spoke of another education entirely: skin wrinkled and unhealthy, aquiline nose bearing the telltale blush of gin berries, hair more white than gray but all totally lifeless. Seeming to be caving in on himself, he appeared a model of middle-age dissipation, a testament to a life given to vice.

Richard Wentworth sat on one side of the desk. Alongside him stood a tall, turban wearing man with an abundant black beard. "My servant, Sanjeev Patel," Richard Wentworth had introduced him, with the turban dipping in an obeisant nod. Utterly expressionless, one of Mr. Z's brutish black bodyguards stood watch, arms folded, by the office door.

Across the desk, Mr. Z said, "So, Bisping, what can I do for you?" He chuckled greedily. "You got money, there's not much I *can't* do for you."

"In my journeys 'round the globe," Wentworth said, waving a languid wrist, "I've made pleasurable use of a somewhat exotic stimulant. I'm an old China hand, and in Hong Kong, Shanghai, and Peking, I have found certain, shall we say, 'refinements' of the pretty poppy to be to my taste. Nor did I encounter difficulty procuring similar substances in Afghanistan or Morrocco, or during more recent travels in Corsica and Honduras."

Mr. Z smiled.

"Yet," said Wentworth with a shrug, "though I've been told I might find that which I seek here in Harlem, I've discovered to my consternation that I am not sufficiently fluent in the indigenous language to do so. The local dialect is called 'hep' or 'jive,' I've been given to understand, but it's beyond me. To these ears, it's all mumbo-jumbo tick-a-tee-floo-barb. I am therefore hopeful, Mr. Z, that you have rapport with the Harlem wogs and can provide me what I seek."

"You pay, I provide," said Mr. Z, gluttony transfiguring his visage. "How large an amount are we talking?"

The amount Wentworth stated was rather large.

The price Mr. Z stated was rather large.

An open palms gesture indicated monetary concerns were not a concern for Lawson Bisping, then Wentworth said, "Oh, one other purchase ... the girl, the one we heard, that Angel Valentine ... "

"Not for sale," Mr. Z said.

Richard Wentworth chortled lasciviously. "*Rental*, then. I've promised my man servant, Sanjeev"—Wentworth gestured with a condescending laugh—"a *reward* for his vigilance and that bit of flash will quite fit the bill. Perhaps watching representatives of such diverse cultures get to know one another might entertain *us* as well."

Made sense, Mr. Z decided when he heard the price "Bisping" would pay.

A very few minutes later, a big Negro (and one Wentworth had previously encountered!) brought in Angel Valentine. She looked neither surprised nor frightened nor wary nor interested. She was glazed over. She had the look of the prisoner or the slave.

"This should prove amusing," Wentworth said, rising. Casually, he turned, put a cigarette in his mouth, made as if to light it and puffed through the cigarette. The black bodyguard at the door slapped at his face, took a blundering step, and crumpled.

At the same moment, the man in the turban swung. His perfect upper-cut landed on the jaw of the Negro who had his hand on Angel Valentine's elbow.

"Hey!" Mr. Z was trying to rise, trying to claw open the top drawer of his desk.

Richard Wentworth puffed through the cigarette, and there was a tick of light as a sliver of steel flew through the air. Professor Brownlee's narcotized dart caught Mr. Z on the tip of the nose. "Ah," he yelled at the sting, swatting at it. He did not get full dosage, but it was as though he were instantly drunk. He fell back into his chair, mouth open, eyes wide.

Richard Wentworth laughed triumphantly.

"Lerone?" Angel Valentine gasped in amazement as she recognized the marise, trying to claw open the top drawer of his desk.

"Yeah, baby," said Lerone Preston, who in his disguise might well have been Ram Singh's *near* identical twin brother. "I gonna save you. Take you from here. We goin' home. You be all right ..."

He could not move, but Mr. Z could speak. His tongue was thick and the words came slow, but he said bitterly, "No, no one saves anybody. Not the way it works. No one gets saved. No one."

Richard Wentworth looked at the bloated man who, even near unconscious, was spewing the poison that had made him what he was. And in his mind, Richard Wentworth was saying, *I have saved these two people. And Lerone Preston will save his Angel. They will be all right. She is freed and they are redeemed.*

Lerone Preston and Angel Valentine were *saved*.

Something that felt *good* glowed within Richard Wentworth, him, something that made him feel *alive*.

The *Spider* had saved them.

Richard Wentworth, "amateur detective," thrill seeking adventurer, or knight errant seeking a crusade, no, that was not the *Spider*.

The *Spider* had a higher calling.

A LITTLE MORE THAN A YEAR LATER

The news did not make the headlines.

It was on page six of the *Entertainment and Amusements* section, afternoon edition.

GOSPEL SINGERS ARRESTED FOR POSSESSION OF NARCOTICS

The gospel singers were one Angel Valentine, Negro, and her accompanist (also Negro), Lerone Preston. Both were charged with possession of heroin and drug paraphernalia. Police claimed that the popular gospel musicians had sold drugs to others, some as young as 13 years of age.

Richard Wentworth studied the photographs of Angel Valentine and Lerone Preston. Then he made a telephone call to Police Commissioner Stanley

Kirkpatrick. No, no possibility of any mistake, no police frame or bungling; Valentine and Preston had been caught dead to rights and were going away for a long time.

"I see," Wentworth said.

Later, he went out alone.

Mr. Z died that night. Just before a .45 caliber bullet exploded his heart, Mr. Z thought he heard the masked gunman softly say, "You were right." Mr. Z thought it unfair that he had not a clue what that meant. Mr. Z's corpulent body bore a mark seared onto his brow: the seal of the *Spider*!

Not long after, not far from the docks, a warehouse burned to the ground. It was owned by an American branch of the Cavallari family who had roots and relatives in Corsica. Firemen arriving to battle the blaze thought they heard fiendish laughter in the air as they fitted their hose couplings to hydrants while flames scratched the doors of heaven.

Two hours later, a Honduran freighter failed to dock in New York; instead, at sea, it mysteriously exploded. Rescue teams found few to rescue, but did turn over to police several crates of a chemical substance thought to be narcotic in nature.

And still later, so late that night, and so late in the dark heart of so many nights that came after, Richard Wentworth gravely and silently pronounced the vow of his truest self:

Because I cannot save anyone from evil ...
I will destroy *Evil.*

It was the vow of the Master of Men.

It was his destiny.

It was the calling of the *Spider*.

illustration by Tom Floyd

Chapter Eighteen

THE SPIDER AND THE MONSTER MAKERS

by CHRISTOPHER MILLS

As Mickey "No-Nose" Norton plunged from the 31st floor of the Belmont Towers with the scarlet likeness of an eight-limbed arachnid seared on his forehead, it was not his short, sordid, and utterly misspent life of petty larceny and craven violence that flashed before his gaping, mud-brown eyes.

No, in those last scant moments of awareness before his mortal existence came to an abrupt conclusion on the concrete sidewalk that bordered bustling Broad Street, all that occupied the pitiable hood's consciousness was the grotesque, leering face of the cloaked apparition known as the *Spider*. The blazing demonic eyes gleaming behind a black domino mask and grinning, fang-filled maw of the Master of Men filled Norton's brief final thoughts, dominating them completely.

Even the roaring wind in "No-Nose's" ears could not compete with the *Spider*'s hellish laughter, a mirthless, soul-shattering cackle that drowned out Norton's own screams and echoed thunderingly within his skull.

The *Spider* perched precariously on the narrow ledge and watched with grim amusement as the flat-faced felon splattered scarlet on the sidewalk thirty-one floors below. Pulling his black cloak tightly around himself, he turned to the sheer brick face of the building and began to ascend as effortlessly as the arachnid that was his namesake, his strong, deft fingers snagging purchase in the slightest of recesses.

There was some irony, the darkling figure mused, in "No-Nose's" unfortunate plummet, as the case which currently consumed the *Spider* had begun with a different fatal plunge, just weeks before.

A tragic young woman had thrown herself from her own balcony, driven to suicide by one of the most fiendish villains the *Spider* had ever known.

The unfortunate soul in question had been Elizabeth Frances Cameron, the beautiful teenaged daughter of Carl J. Cameron, one of the city's most-respected financiers. Pretty Elizabeth had only recently returned to her family's uptown apartments from her final term at Vassar, her mind and heart filled only with her imminent marriage to Victor Pryce, the dashing young scion of one of New England's more prominent families. Her fiancé was but twenty- three, darkly handsome and already beginning to forge what all expected to be a historic career in politics, while she was just nineteen, slight and fair, with auburn locks and a sprinkle of faint, tasteful freckles across the bridge of her upturned nose.

The families were thrilled at the upcoming union.

The bride and groom were very much in love.

But in the pre-dawn hours of her wedding day, Elizabeth awoke from a terrible nightmare in agonizing, body-wracking pain. What felt like lances of liquid fire shot down the length of her spine, and the pounding in her skull suggested that it might explode. Her limbs were leaden and seemed unwilling to work properly. She tried to cry out, but her throat would emit nothing but a rasping croak. In agony, the stout hearted girl dragged herself from her bed and crawled to the vanity. Laboriously, she raised her heavy head to peer into the glass...

When her body was discovered, some minutes later, sprawled broken on the concrete twenty floors below her bedroom window, she was not immediately identified. It was only after the girl's maid, roused by the commotion in the street below, checked her mistress' boudoir and found the youthful bride missing, that anyone considered that the misshapen corpse on the gore-splattered pavement might be that of Elizabeth Frances Cameron.

For only one with the most morbid of imaginations could have possibly conceived that that freakish figure draped in tattered, bloody silk had once been a beautiful girl.

Her arms were twisted, deformed, and of different lengths. The right hand had swollen to the size and approximate shape of a catcher's mitt; and on the left, the fingers had fused together into a bony club. The legs, too, once long and sleek, were stretched and distorted, with kneecaps the size of saucers. Her fair, freckled skin had become leathery; her very head enlarged to nearly twice its proper size, with a jutting jawbone and bulging, crooked brow.

The bride had become a brute... overnight!

Three days later, a second young girl, the sixteen year-old heiress to a copper fortune, took a ragged shard of a broken mirror into her distended digits and plunged the silvered glass deeply into her own breast... on the eve of her society debut.

Law enforcement officials were baffled.

The ravenous press cried, "plague!"

The devastated families mourned their losses.

And the next day, the first ransom note was received.

When James William Reynard, sixty-five, the city's most prominent real estate developer, opened his morning mail, he found the scrawled letter – a document that demanded a "ransom" of twenty-five thousand dollars. If he refused to pay, his twenty-six year-old second wife, Amanda Reynard, would find her beauty pageant-winning looks stolen in the night, leaving her a living grotesquerie, fit only for a Cony Island freak show.

The note was signed: *"Proteus."*

Reynard had not acquired a third of Manhattan Island (and a sizeable portion of New Jersey) by being a fool.

He paid.

Stockbroker Alexander Waltham, however, did not. The Wall Street wizard was a practical man of facts and figures, bereft of imagination. He refused to believe that any human agency, however diabolical, could possibly have been responsible for the deformities that had stricken the first two girls. Surely, it had been a macabre coincidence, a tragic but freak occurrence. Food poisoning, perhaps.

Within a week, his daughter Helene became the third victim – and was quickly committed to a private sanitarium and placed under heavy sedation. The poor girl now faced an agonizing existence behind closed doors, the twisted, silently suffering shade of a once vivacious and compassionate young woman.

It was at this point that the *Spider* became involved.

After finishing a late breakfast on the terrace of his Sutton Place penthouse overlooking the Manhattan skyline, millionaire Richard Wentworth sipped strong black coffee and intently studied the open newspaper spread on the table before him. Sitting across from him in the bright morning sunlight was his lovely fiancée, Nita Van Sloan. Nita's patrician features were uncharacteristically pale and drawn, her warm, violet eyes moist with emotion as she regarded her companion.

"It's like a nightmare, Dick. We knew these girls! You and I were invited to Elizabeth Cameron's wedding!" Nita pointed a delicate finger at the newspaper. "And Helene Waltham was a friend, a lovely, talented young woman with her whole life ahead of her. Now, she's…confined to an institution – *a monster!*"

Wentworth's eyes were cold, his expression grim. "No, Nita. The true monster is the villain that wrought this evil upon her."

Wentworth paused, his brow furrowed. "According to the papers, he calls himself *Proteus*. In myth, Proteus was the son of the sea god, Neptune. He had the power to see the future and change his shape at will. Obviously, *this* Proteus can somehow change the shapes of *others*. He is a ruthless defiler of beauty with neither conscience nor soul. He must be stopped!"

Nita recognized the ring of steel in his voice. "Dick! You're going –"

"Yes, my darling," the handsome tycoon said, his voice dropping an octave. "The *Spider* will prowl the streets of this city tonight!"

But before the *Spider* could bring justice into the night, he needed information, more information than could be gained from the ink-stained minions of the Fourth Estate. Richard Wentworth reached for the small silver bell beside his coffee cup, and rang it lightly. Its peal was faint and seemed to be immediately lost in the breeze that softly traversed the terrace, yet within moments, the millionaire's Indian manservant, the loyal Ram Singh, appeared at his master's right hand.

"Get Commissioner Kirkpatrick on the phone, Ram Singh," Wentworth commanded, "and see if he's available to join me for lunch at my Club."

The imposing Sikh nodded once, turned on his heel and silently departed to see to his master's will.

"But Dick," Nita exclaimed, "you've only just eaten breakfast!"

"This luncheon will be to feed the mind, not the body, darling. I'm certain that the police have withheld some vital facts of this case from the press. With luck, perhaps I'll be able to persuade Stanley Kirkpatrick to share some of those official secrets with the *Spider*!"

Less than an hour later, Wentworth sat at yet another table with coffee in hand, this time at his private club. Across from him, impatiently perched in his chair, was a stocky, ruddily complexioned man — Wentworth's devoted friend and the *Spider's* determined nemesis, New York Police Commissioner Stanley Kirkpatrick.

For several years, the city's top law enforcement official had waged a relentless crusade against the *Spider*, without knowing that the masked vigilante with the blazing automatics was, in fact, his friend and confidante, Richard Wentworth. As a sworn servant of the peace, Kirkpatrick hated with all his lawman's heart the unorthodox methods that the *Spider* ruthlessly employed against the evils of the underworld. In fact, Dick Wentworth was fully aware that, despite their close and long-standing friendship, if the Commissioner ever obtained definitive proof that Wentworth and the *Spider* were one and the same man, he could expect no mercy from the peace officer.

Indeed, on more than one occasion, the Commissioner had reason to suspect that his friend was truly the notorious *Spider*. Fortunately, so far, Wentworth had always successfully deflected those dangerous suspicions elsewhere.

"It's terrible, what's happened to these young women," Wentworth said, after formalities had been satisfied. "Nita and I knew a couple of them, you know."

"I'd be surprised if you hadn't. That's your social circle, after all." The Commissioner waved for a waiter. "I don't know why you eat here. The service is terrible."

"You must remember, Kirk, most of this club's patrons are dilettantes, men of leisure. We don't have the same sort of busy schedules that our prominent civil servants do, and thus, are allowed the luxury of patience."

"Hmmph."

"Relax, Kirk, drink your cocktail and tell me more about this morbid case."

Kirkpatrick paused. It was police business, after all. But, despite his secret suspicions, Dick Wentworth was a good friend with a sharp mind, and his insights had often proved valuable in the past. "Have you heard of *acromegaly*?"

"Can't say that I have," Wentworth admitted. "What is it?"

"It's a rare disorder of the pituitary gland. According to the doctors, it usually affects middle-aged adults and can result in the abnormal growth of extremities."

"Is that what has happened to these girls?"

"That's what the doctors tell me.'

"How terrible. But it seems rather unlikely that several young women would develop the same unusual affliction all at once."

"That's just half of it. Not only is it very rare, but usually, the symptoms of acromegaly develop gradually, over many months and years. One might notice a ring fitting too tightly, or shoes being too small long before any effects are visible. But in each of these cases, the condition proceeded to an advanced state literally *overnight*."

"Is that possible?"

"Despite what all the experts say, the evidence at hand insists that it is. Nothing else could have caused the extreme deformities that these poor girls have suffered.   And suffered is the word for it! The Waltham girl – the only survivor so far – must be kept constantly under anesthetic, otherwise she'd go mad from the pain! Is it no wonder the others took their own lives?"

Wentworth's handsome features had taken on a grim cast. "There's a fiendish agency behind this, Kirk."

"Fiendish, and cunning. Those letters – literally ransoming these girls' very *beauty* – why, it's a scheme worthy of the devil himself!"

"What are you doing to find him, Kirk?"

"Everything we can, of course. But it's difficult. Normally, we'd start by looking for similarities – find out what the victims may have in common, and proceed from there. But in this case, all of the girls traveled in the same circles, visited the same places, and attended the same events. There's almost *too much* to tie them together! Where do we begin?"

"There must be something," Wentworth muttered.

"And we'll find it, Dick, rest assured. We have the finest detectives in the country on the city's payroll. It's only a matter of time."

"But in that time, how many more girls will be disfigured, their lives destroyed?"

The Commissioner shook his head sadly. "I don't know, Dick. I just don't know."

Suddenly, a thought occurred to the handsome millionaire: "There's been another note, hasn't there, Kirk?"

Kirkpatrick nodded grimly. "Yes. Received it this morning. Another demand for twenty-five thousand dollars."

"Who?"

"Sandra Blaine, the twenty year-old daughter of Adrian Blaine, the Deputy Mayor!"

Shortly after dusk that evening the *Spider* perched, like a grim gargoyle, on a narrow ledge across the street from the Deputy Mayor's lavish Park Avenue apartments, his Stygian cloak pulled tightly around his lithe, athletic frame. Commissioner Kirkpatrick, determined to take no chances with the Deputy Mayor's daughter, had placed uniformed police officers in the street in front of the Belmont Towers, as well as in the building lobby, outside the apartment's doors, and within the suite itself. But the *Spider* took no chances, either; he was prepared to watch young Sandra Blaine's 31st floor window throughout the cold, bitter night, the only egress inaccessible to and unprotected by the police.

Long, cold hours slowly ticked by as the *Spider* tirelessly observed the young woman's window, until, shortly after midnight, the stoic sentinel caught a slight movement out of the corner of his eye. Like a predatory raptor, he cocked his head slightly, zeroing in on the source of the distraction: a single human figure slowly but steadily scaling the sheer marble façade of the luxury apartment house several floors below the Blaine apartment. Even the *Spider* was impressed by this gravity-defying display of physical prowess. But the ascending man's skill identified him as surely as a police mugshot or file fingerprint – only one man in the city could climb such an edifice with the evident speed and facility – the notorious cat burglar, *Mickey "No-Nose" Norton!*

Across the bustling boulevard, the petty criminal notorious for his fist-flattened facial features soon reached the ledge just outside Sandra Blaine's boudoir. He rested there briefly and then, with dexterous, practiced fingers, produced a diamond-tipped glasscutter from the pocket of his dark trousers. In just a few seconds, the intruder had unlatched the window, silently raised the sill and slipped silently into the room beyond.

The bedroom was richly furnished and decidedly feminine. In the large, canopied bed, the svelte form of young Sandra Blaine restlessly slumbered, delicate hands clutching the blankets tightly against the sudden inrush of crisp autumn air. Norton unbuttoned a small, padded pouch attached to his belt, and carefully withdrew a hypodermic needle. In the dim light from the street outside, he raised it to confirm that its contents of amber fluid was intact and, reassured, crept slowly toward the sleeping girl, careful not to make any sound that might disturb her sleep or draw the attention of the police guard outside her door.

As he stood over the woman, Norton hesitated. He knew that thE hypo in his hand delivered deformity and death, and the girl before him was very beautiful, indeed. He thought of the substantial cash payment he had been promised, but knew that it wasn't the money that had brought him to this young beauty's bedside. No, it was pure, abject fear — fear of the terrible vengeance his employer would visit upon him should he fail in his appointed task.

Norton took a deep breath, and steeling himself, bent over the girl. He placed the needle against the pulsing jugular vein within her pale, slender neck...

...then a thousand sticks of TNT exploded violently behind his eyes, and he was plunged suddenly into darkness.

When "No-Nose" Norton snapped abruptly awake a few minutes later, his head pounding like a bass drum, he found himself once again on the narrow window ledge, 31 stories above Broad Street, his arms and legs tightly bound. The only thing between him and a fatal plummet to the hard concrete below was the strong, iron grip of the black-cloaked figure firmly rooted to the sliver of cold marble beside him. He turned his head toward his captor and immediately regretted it as cold fear embraced him.

It was the *Spider!*

Satan's own eyes smoldered behind the *Spider's* domino mask, and Norton recoiled as the nocturnal avenger's lips slowly curled back to reveal glistening, pointed fangs. "Easy, Norton," the *Spider* hissed in a sepulchral whisper. "You wouldn't want to fall now, would you? What would *that* do for your reputation?"

"Dear Lord..." Norton whined. "Please..."

The *Spider* chuckled mirthlessly. "You surprise me, Norton. I thought you made of sterner stuff. How can a man so brave as to climb a building like this, in this wind, in darkness, be afraid of... *me?*"

"Don't kill me, please!"

With his free hand, the *Spider* held the gleaming hypodermic before the burglar's bulging eyes. "What does this syringe contain, Norton?"

"I don't know!"

"I will ask you only once more, Norton – then I will let you fall and seek my answers elsewhere. What is in this hypodermic?"

"Wait! I really don't know! It was given to me by the guy who hired me!"

"Who is your employer, then?" The hoodlum hesitated a moment, and the *Spider* gave him a violent shake. *"Tell me."*

Norton gulped. "The doc! He gave me the stuff – and the names of the girls!"

Wentworth's gray eyes narrowed behind the mask. "A doctor?"

"Yeah! A doctor! His name's Hoxton! Doctor Ivan Hoxton!"

The *Spider* grinned, ivory stilettos shimmering in the moonlight. "Thank you, Mickey. That's all I need."

The *Spider* released his grip.

Richard Wentworth had met Doctor Ivan Hoxton on several occasions. A young physician from a prominent family with a successful practice and a promising future, Hoxton's fortunes had taken a downward turn of late, with rumors of disastrous investments or some sort of scandal which had, it was said, all but depleted the hereditary Hoxton coffers. As a result, the handsome doctor had all but disappeared from public life, despite previously being prominent in society affairs.

It was nearly sunrise by the time the *Spider* arrived at the Hoxton family's Long Island estate. The vast grounds were untended and overgrown, and the main house itself, while still somewhat grand, had a tired, rundown appearance, looking all but abandoned in the dim false dawn. The mansion's many windows were dark and empty, giving no hint of life within. Quickly concealing his sedan beneath a copse of cedars, the *Spider* sprinted silently across the shaggy lawn through the thick morning fog, seemingly chasing his own shadow in the waning moonlight.

Producing a slim leather case from somewhere within his folds of his billowing cloak, the *Spider* set to work on the locked back door. In his nimble fingers, the custom made lock picks (one did not fight crime as long as the *Spider* had without mastering many of the tricks of the felonious trade) made short work of the expensive tumbler and bolt. Within moments, the cloaked

Wentworth had entered the Hoxton home and begun his search.

The first floor was vacant, save for sheet-covered furnishings and a light coating of dust. But there were signs of recent activity in the kitchen – dishes unwashed in the basin and fresh produce and milk in the large icebox – so the estate was not completely abandoned. The *Spider* quickly ascended to the second floor of the manse and found it also unlived in... but while inspecting a dusty bedroom in the South wing, Wentworth paused briefly at the window. He let out a soft exclamation of surprise and smiled grimly, for the estate's old carriage house was visible from that window, and a soft light could clearly be seen flickering within.

Cape fluttering behind him like great, menacing wings, the *Spider* all but ran through the dark, empty house. Outside, the moon had set and the sun was beginning to show through the trees. His warm breath was a misty vapor as he padded across the wide gravel drive to the old carriage house and peered through a small, dusty window.

Along the walls of the old carriage house's interior were long neglected, cobwebbed leather horse collars, bridles, reins, blankets and other tack unused since the coming of the automobile. But, in the middle of the room, several long, narrow worktables had been erected, covered with the glassware and other accoutrements of a chemist. Beakers, vials, Bunsen burners, rubber and glass tubing, a microscope and more filled every available inch of the table surfaces. The light the *Spider* had viewed from the main house shone from a large oil-burning hurricane lamp resting on a small stool next to a metal cot. On the cot a single human figure could be seen, tightly wrapped in a gray wool blanket against the morning chill, to all appearances, restlessly asleep.

The *Spider* found an unlocked door and entered the cold, drafty building. Careful not to wake the slumbering man – no doubt Doctor Ivan Hoxton himself – the *Spider* quickly inspected the makeshift chemical laboratory and soon found several prepared hypodermic needles, all filled with what looked like the same ochre liquid contained in the syringe he had confiscated from the late "No-Nose" Norton. Not far away, Wentworth also discovered a small pad of ruled note paper with a list of scrawled names – names familiar to the masked millionaire from his own personal acquaintances and the society columns. From Elizabeth Cameron to Sandra Blaine, all of Proteus' victims were there, along with names and addresses of at least a dozen other potential prey. Most blood curdling of all was the very next name on the fiendish list.

The *Spider* smoothly eased his two identical, blue-steel automatics from their concealed, soft leather holsters and trained them on the prostrate form on the cot. Then, he laughed – a ghastly cacophony that echoed eerily off the walls of the old carriage house.

Doctor Ivan Hoxton – for it was indeed he – bolted upright, eyes wide with terror. The once-handsome physician and highly desirable bachelor was all but unrecognizable. His hair was unfashionably long and unkempt, and he sported several days' worth of dark stubble upon his hollow cheeks and pointed chin. At the sight of the looming, masked creature above him, his mouth dropped open and a feeble cry of surprise and shock came forth. "Who–?"

"You know who I am, monster," the *Spider* hissed.

"The Spider!" exclaimed the disheveled doctor as he slowly disentangled himself from the blanket. "I didn't believe you existed!"

"You'll soon come to wish I did not, Doctor Hoxton… or should I say, 'Proteus?'"

"No! You don't understand! I am *not* Proteus!"

The *Spider* scowled. "Don't lie to me, Hoxton! The proof of your wicked handiwork is all around you. *You* are the mad sculptor in whose evil hands three young women were brutally reshaped into living horrors!"

"No! I am merely the instrument! It is Proteus who is the mastermind of these crimes! It is he you want!"

"And who is Proteus, then, doctor, if not you?"

The doctor buried his unshaven face in his hands. When he spoke again, his voice was but a whisper: "My brother! *Xander Hoxton!*"

"Your brother?"

"All my life, Xander has brought dishonor to the Hoxton name. As a youth, he set fires and delighted in the torture of small, helpless animals. As an adult, he was worse – a gambler, blackmailer and thief. About ten years ago, tired of cleaning up after my brother's crimes and covering for his worst excesses, my father finally disowned him, and Xander left the country. First he was spotted in South America, and later the Orient. We occasionally heard stories, almost unbelievable stories, about his escapades and criminal activities. Then, a few years ago, we were told that Xander had perished, somewhere in the Far East, gunned down by… competitors.

"But two years ago, shortly after my parents died in an automobile accident, Xander reappeared. He came to my clinic in the city and bullied his way in, and, as always, I was unable to stand up to him. No matter how miserable an example of humanity he may be, he's still my older brother. The only family I have left – and he needed my help…!"

Suddenly, two gargantuan hands came down on the *Spider's* broad shoulders with such tremendous force that the cloaked avenger staggered beneath the heavy, unexpected blows and nearly lost his grip on his weapons! Absorbed by Hoxton's story, the impossible had occurred: *someone had crept up on the Master of Men unnoticed!*

Recovering immediately, the *Spider* spun around, raising his blue-steel pistols, only to find himself face-to-face with a towering, hulking grotesquerie.

Nearly seven feet tall, the brute was hideous in the pale morning sunlight that penetrated the dirty windows, a grossly misshapen mockery of humanity with a hairless skull, jutting jaw, protruding brow and flared, bulbous nose. Crimson-shot, deep-set eyes blazed as the twisted giant raised one of his massive fists to deliver a devastating blow, and, without hesitation, the *Spider* fired his trusty automatics, filling the laboratory with smoke and thunder.

The molten slugs caught the ghastly brute squarely in his massive barrel chest, but did not knock him down. Nor did they stop him from completing his blow, which lifted the *Spider's* heels completely from the ground and sent the cloaked crime fighter through the air to crash violently into one of the lab tables, which splintered under the impact. Beakers and vials shattered, scattering shards of glass across the dirty floor, and the *Spider* found himself momentarily stunned, his body wracked with pain, gasping for air to fill his empty lungs.

Seemingly unconcerned by both the dazed vigilante and the bullets in his chest, the furious giant turned on Hoxton, his gravelly voice a harsh, menacing whisper. "What are you doing, you fool?"

"I had no choice, Xander – he had those guns..."

"Coward! You've always been weak, Van – gutless and soft!"

The doctor hid his face and stammered out an unintelligible reply.

The *Spider* slowly and unsteadily climbed to his feet, and Xander Hoxton, the depraved, deformed demon who had taken the mythological name of Proteus for his own, turned to face him. He smiled. "And who – or what – might you be?"

Wentworth matched the brute's grin with an insolent smirk of his own. "Men call me the *Spider!*"

Proteus shrugged his massive shoulders. "Never heard of you. But that won't stop me from crushing you beneath my heel like any other insect that might get in my way!"

"Perhaps! But before you try, tell me this, Hoxton! Why have you infected those poor girls with your own affliction? What possible reason could you have?"

Xander Hoxton gestured toward his gibbering sibling. "For two long years, this fool – this alleged medical genius! – has been trying to devise a cure! Some way to reverse my condition, to make me normal again! But all he's accomplished in that time is to drain the family coffers and create a serum that can artificially stimulate the pituitary gland and duplicate the disease!

"He insists he needs more time and money! So I thought of all the pretty, pampered women; all the spoiled lovelies with doting fathers and loyal husbands reeking of wealth and privilege."

Proteus continued, clearly taking a perverse pride in his fiendish scheme and relishing the opportunity to gloat. "I knew that those powerful, wealthy men would pay to keep their ladies beautiful once it was demonstrated beyond any doubt that I could take that beauty away... and they have! *And they will keep on paying!*"

"And Norton?" the *Spider* asked.

"I suppose you caught the little weasel, and he told you how to find us. It doesn't matter. There are plenty of others like him for hire. The city practically crawls with the vermin!"

The two bullets lodged in the man monster's chest didn't seem to bother him in the least as he began to advance upon the *Spider*. Wentworth stood his ground and raised his automatics again. "Stay where you are, Proteus!"

Proteus chuckled: "Those pitiful bean shooters won't stop me, *Spider*! During my years in the East, I made many enemies and outlasted them all! I've been stabbed, shot, and even poisoned... and yet I still live!"

"Nobody lives forever, Proteus!" cried the determined *Spider* as he once again unleashed the full fury of his twin .45s. Sizzling lead tore through the air and ripped through Proteus' shirt, the wounds gouting blood. The grotesque behemoth staggered slightly as the slugs hit, but still would not fall!

Enraged by the pain, however, Xander Hoxton lunged forward, his massive arms and slab-like hands reaching menacingly for the masked Wentworth. The *Spider* attempted to evade the oncoming behemoth, but Proteus' speed belied his great bulk, and Wentworth was dragged helplessly into the deadly embrace of those mighty arms!

Proteus laughed with depraved pleasure as he tightened his death grip on the trapped *Spider*, his thickly thewed limbs contracting around Wentworth's arms and torso, slowly forcing the air from his lungs. "I'm going to crush the very life from you, *Spider*," Hoxton snarled. "Your spine will snap like kindling and your ribs will be ground to dust!"

The *Spider* struggled frantically, gasping, his guns forgotten, gloved fingers clawing desperately at the fiend's powerful forearms. He felt his ribs bend and snap under the tremendous pressure, and a crimson haze flooded his frantic mind. Phantom fireworks exploded before his eyes, and as his vision blurred, he felt the icy hand of fate descending upon him...

Suddenly, the crushing pressure was gone, and the *Spider* collapsed heavily to the floor. As his vision cleared, he was shocked to see Doctor Ivan Hoxton clinging to his malformed brother's broad back, brandishing a leg from the shattered lab table. The physician was violently striking his sinister sibling with the improvised club, and although it did not appear to hurt the brute, the distraction had saved the *Spider's* life.

Despite his aching back and the pain from his broken ribs, the gasping *Spider* urgently scanned the carriage house in search of a suitable weapon to bring to bear on the bestial Proteus. Then his eyes came to rest on the still-blazing hurricane lamp and its large glass reservoir of thick, golden oil.

Without hesitation, the *Spider* seized the heavy lantern from the table beside the cot, discarded the hot, curved glass chimney, and hurled it with all of his remaining strength at the struggling Hoxton brothers.

"Death to the bringers of death!"

The lamp hit Xander Hoxton high on his chest and shattered, the viscous oil immediately saturating his clothing. The voracious flames spread quickly, and the devil called Proteus whirled about wildly, howling in agony as his tough, leathery skin bubbled and boiled. The entangled brothers crashed together into the remaining worktable, sending bottles and vials flying into the air, and spilling volatile chemicals all over. Some combustible liquid in a smashed beaker caught a fluttering spark and erupted into bright blue flames, which quickly and uncontrollably spread. Chemicals, scattered papers, and the dry, antique timber of the old building itself were soon engulfed in purifying hellfire.

Both Ivan and Xander Hoxton were now screaming and flailing about, their flesh and clothing ablaze, futilely attempting to extinguish the surging, searing furies. Acrid, sulphurous smoke quickly filled the air, and the *Spider's* eyes burned painfully as he stumbled unsteadily towards the door and away from the raging inferno.

At the threshold the *Spider* paused and glanced back briefly, bearing grim, satisfied witness to the Hoxton brothers' final, agonizing moments. Justice had been served.

The *Spider's* justice.

The old building burned quickly and completely. Wentworth watched from the concealment of a grove of evergreen trees as the firefighters fought a losing battle against the blaze, and felt content, despite the pain of his injuries and smoke in his lungs. The brothers Hoxton were dead, their diabolical serum lost to the merciless flames of their personal hell. Their sick extortion scheme was ended, and the girls whose names had been scrawled on Proteus' list of future victims would be able to sleep soundly that night. No woman would ever again know the agonies of their disfiguring disease.

Wentworth made his way back to his hidden sedan. Evil had been punished; the monster makers had suffered for their heinous crimes. But as the weary avenger began the journey back to the city, the sanctuary of his Sutton Place penthouse and the ministering attentions of his lovely fiancée, he could not help but wonder what would have happened if he had waited but one more day before beginning his hunt for Proteus.

For the very next name on Hoxton's list of the damned was none other than *his own, beloved Nita Van Sloan!*

illustration by Tom Floyd

Chapter Nineteen

BANQUETS FOR THE DAMNED

by JOHN JAKES

Author's Note

I grew up a fan of the Spider. I bought every issue, and collected old issues published before I discovered the Master of Men. I loved the unforgettably lurid covers, the outsized villains, the breathless, end-of-the-world tone of each novel - and the way Wentworth and his brave companions managed to save civilization yet one more time. So I was happy to write this new Spider adventure, a tribute to my favorite pulp magazine hero.

- John Jakes

Below 59th Street, Fifth Avenue was burning. The fiery destruction wasn't limited to the swank midtown area. Far down the canyon, the sky glimmered a lurid red, indicating more fires, more destruction in Herald Square, and beyond - Wall Street, the Battery.

An army of looters paraded in and out of Fifth Avenue shops and department stores not yet touched by fire. Men and women, shabby but strangely confident,smashed showcases, scooped up diamond necklaces, wielded weapons indiscriminately to shoot or stab or decapitate New Yorkers unfortunate enough to be caught on the street on this night of city-wide carnage. The looters had left their bread lines, their Hoovervilles, their little stands where they offered old apples for a nickel, and were finding a new path to prosperity.

"Step on it, Jackson," Richard Wentworth cracked from the back seat of the Daimler. "Break the speed limit."

Stolid Jackson maneuvered the expensive auto through an obstacle course of over-turned taxis, flaming jitneys, a city bus stranded on the curbing while hysterical passengers beat on the glass to find a way out. Wentworth saw a looter turn a shotgun on the bus and blow a huge hole in a window, spattering it with the blood of an elderly woman inside.

Smoke made driving difficult, as did the geysers of water from damaged fire plugs. Even inside the super-quiet Daimler Wentworth heard the wail of police sirens. How could the beleaguered men of New York's finest prevail against hundreds, not to say thousands of zombielike predators roaming the streets on this Walpurgisnacht of crime? The predators who ran in and out of burning stores had no sense of morality - that had been wiped away by what- ever madman was responsible for their rampage. As Wentworth opened the concealed box in the Daimler's jump seat he glimpsed a young woman with a long knife resembling a machete. An elderly gentleman tried to outrun her. She caught him easily and, laughing, lopped off his head.

Broken stop lights flashed red and green and yellow every few seconds, a bizarre palette of colors. Desperately Wentworth took what he needed from the concealed box: the black domino, the fearsome pointed teeth, the lanky wig. A lift-up panel in the seat beside him yielded more: the dark slouch hat, the cape, and, most precious of all, the twin .45-caliber automatics that were the tools of the Master of Men ... the *Spider*.

A gasoline tanker truck ran out of a cross street, plowing through the corner display window of the great Saks store where it blew up, incinerating the lower stories in a sheet of flame. At the next corner, a small brightly lit tourist bureau was curiously untouched; Wentworth saw bright posters of Rhine Castles, and a placard in English offering INFORMATIVE LITERATURE about the German-American Bund.

Further on, in a dark street in the 40's just off the Avenue, a small band of ragged men and women were tearing down and spitting on old election posters bearing the familiar visage of FDR. A fat woman lifted her skirt and danced on the torn half of a smiling FDR.

Wentworth was no longer the Daimler's passenger; a fearsome snaggle-toothed creature in a cloak rode there. "Take 35th Street," the *Spider* snarled. He prayed to the Almighty that he would be in time to save his beloved Nita, and perhaps the city itself ...

It had begun innocently enough, several days ago, at Café Old Heidelberg, a new, very small and deluxe eatery recently opened, and declared "hot" by the city's food columnists. Only two dozen tables fitted inside the confined space in the West 40's, far from the regular German section up in Yorkville. There were no electric fixtures visible, only candles, on tables and in sconces. Red-flocked walls darkened the scene further, lending an almost Satanic atmosphere to the establishment. Definitely not your typical beer-and-gemutlichkeit rathskeller.

Still, Richard Wentworth and Nita Van Sloan, celebrating one of their rare free evenings together, had to agree the cuisine was outstanding.

"I've never had such delicious schnitzel, darling," Nita said. The glowing candles enhanced her brunette beauty, and burnished the triple strand of pearls Wentworth had given her for her birthday. In a secluded front foyer, a muted phone seldom stopped ringing; Wentworth heard a vaguely foreign voice say from there, "Madam, we cannot possibly accommodate you until three months from now, August ninth, nine-thirty p.m.. If you arrive more than fifteen minutes late we cannot hold your reservation. Everyone wants to taste the creations of Chef Teufel."

"Phony name, I'll wager," Wentworth said, sipping more of his crisp Montrachet. "I suppose it doesn't matter if he can cook."

"Where did he come from, do you know?" Nita asked.

"I heard it was Berlin, though no one's sure. This place just appeared. It's the way with restaurants in Manhattan. Hundreds open, hundreds close every year."

The kitchen doors opened. A grossly fat man in chef's whites and a jaunty toque emerged to visit at the tables, shaking hands, accepting compliments. His luxuriant mustaches and chin beard glistened with pomade of some kind. The man had a jolly Kris Kringle look about him, except for his eyes, which Wentworth thought feral. Wentworth didn't like those eyes one bit.

Eventually the big-bellied man worked his way to their table. He spoke thickly accented English. "Good evening, I trust the meal has been satisfactory?"

"Absolutely wonderful," Nita enthused. "The creme brulee is the best I've ever tasted."

"So glad you enjoyed it, Fraulein," the fat man said. "And you, mein herr? Did Chef Teufel's creations live up to your expectations?"

"Certainly." More guarded than Nita, Wentworth flicked a gold lighter, exhaled smoke. "You have an unusual name."

The chef shrugged. "A little conceit for the restaurant business. My given name you would find virtually unpronounceable."

"You're German, then?" asked Nita.

"Ja, a small town in Swabia unfamiliar to Americans. I learned my art at many of the finest hotels in Zurich and Paris and Berlin." A small, pink, almost adder-like tongue licked out to wet the chef's lips. "I also spent time at the Von Horingen School of Special Culinary Studies in Dresden."

"Don't believe I know that one," Wentworth said cooly.

Someone at the kitchen door motioned to the chef.

"Come again, I will tell you about it. I opened this small establishment to finance the good works of a larger one, the Angel of Mercy Free Kitchen. It's on Ninth Avenue and 34th."

"You serve the poor?" Nita asked.

"Any who are in need. Poverty knows no race nor creed nor political affiliation. Drop in some time, I will be delighted to show you around. You as well, sir," he added in a belated aside to Wentworth. Clearly he didn't like the handsome guest. For some reason Wentworth couldn't clearly explain, he reciprocated the hostility.

When the chef had waddled away, Nita said, "I'd love to see that kind of charitable place at work. Times are so depressing, so many people out of work and starving, everyone speculating about the possibility of war, it's very good to hear about the chef's program."

Wentworth directed a thoughtful look at the kitchen doors. "Before you visit, I think someone else had better precede you."

"The Spider?"

"An alter ego," Wentworth said with a smile.

"More coffee, darling?"

Next day, while the stolid Jackson waxed the Daimler and Ram Singh tinkered with the engine, tuning it to even higher performance, Wentworth taxied to the glorious New York Public Library on Fifth Avenue. He tipped his hat to the guardian lions outside, as he always did.

His mood darkened when he scanned old newspaper files for information about the Von Horingen School of Special Culinary Studies. Rolond Von Horingen, a German-Swiss neurologist, had given up his medical practice without explanation, to open the Dresden school which taught a limited number of students the doctor's esoteric theories of nutrition and food preparation. The American papers were sketchy about it, but apparently Von Horingen believed that certain foods, in the proper combination, could block traditional morality and overcome inhibitions, so that the person who consumed those foods became, literally, amoral, willing to do anyone's bidding so long as the rewards were satisfactory. The European medical community had jeered at Von Horigen, ostracized him and driven him out of business. He was shot to death on the bank of Lake Como by police as he ran naked through the streets with strings of garlics and onions trailing from his long-nailed hands.

Wentworth discounted most of it, but his lingering impression of a shrewd, diabolical brain lurking behind the facade of the genial chef prompted him to do some further investigation.

Later that night, Wentworth's friend Police Commissioner Stanley Kirkpatrick broke a long-standing date for dinner, calling Wentworth on the phone:

"Sorry, Dick, but apparently we've got a new crime wave building. Seventeen armed robberies, nine unpre-meditated murders, forty cases of arson, so many complaints of assault and battery we can't count 'em, not to mention an outbreak of rape, and vandalism of every description. All in the last twenty-four hours."

"Committed by whom?"

"Derelicts. Floaters. People ground down by this damn Depression. Four of the culprits, one a woman of seventy, were shot for resisting arrest. They all seem to have one curious thing in common. They flop in, squat in, or have recently passed through one rather limited neighborhood on the island."

"And that is?"

Richard Wentworth shivered unaccountably when his friend said, "Hell's Kitchen."

Slouching down Ninth Avenue, the bum saw derelicts huddled around a fire built in an old oil barrel. A block on, two roughnecks mercilessly beat and kicked a sailor, then stripped him of his valuables.

Arriving at 34th Street, the bum saw a man and woman emerge from a brightly lit doorway with a sign beside it.

ANGEL OF MERCY FREE KITCHEN, ALL WELCOME.

Almost immediately, the man began tearing at the woman's clothing. The bum passed by them as they engaged in frenzied sexual congress beneath a street light.

Several of the dispossessed hurried by the bum in a race to beat him to the free food presumably waiting inside a dilapidated three-story brick building whose faded facade bore the faded words Ace High Tire Warehouse. The bum shambled behind the others into a large, high-ceilinged room where two hundred or more victims of the Depression waited for food at a double line of steam tables. A squat man with an eye-patch occupied a table by the door.

He looked the new arrival up and down: an unshaven bum with a gimpy leg, wearing a striped jersey under his threadbare coat, a thrift store homburg, and pebbled glasses. The squat man shoved a ledger at the bum.

"You get one meal a day, mein herr, that's all. What's your name?"

"McQuade. Blinky McQuade. I come from - "

"We don' care whether you come from Hades or Hackensack. Sign your name, make your mark, get in line."

Wentworth, disguised, did his best to nod humbly. He shuffled to the nearest line and from there observed the charity kitchen. Each person took a tin plate and utensils, then stepped forward to receive a mound of mashed potatoes and some kind of yellowish gravy-like substance with chunks of meat in it. The diners took their plates to trestle tables. Wentworth quickly saw that after a few spoonfuls, the demeanor of the diners changed subtly. Grins appeared; eyes glittered and darted about. Wentworth heard arrogant, boastful remarks; cursing. The charity recipients seemed to eat and then to... change.

"Eat up, hurry up" - another thug-like individual roamed among the trestles, prodding the slowest - "get back in the streets, we got plenty others waiting." All at once Wentworth realized he'd better forego the special cuisine this place was offering. How fitting, how macabre, that this front for a criminal scheme had opened in Hell's Kitchen.

He clasped his hands over his belly and groaned. One of the servers, a lout with a stub of a cigarette dangling off his lower lip, glared at him. "Whassa matter, buddy?"

"Sick. All of a sudden sick to my stomach."

"C'mon, this'll fix you up." The server slopped a ladle of the yellowish concoction onto Wentworth's tin plate. "Nobody leaves the Angel of Mercy without eating."

Wentworth pushed the tin plate away. "No, I can't, thanks, but - "

"Hold that fellow. I want to speak to him," bellowed a voice Wentworth thought all too familiar. A massive shadow-shape had been standing well behind the steam tables, in semi-darkness, arms folded, watching the dispensing of the free dinners. Now he heaved himself forward, spotlessly white in his chef's clothing. Teufel's pomaded hair gleamed. Wentworth wanted no conversation with him. He pivoted and came shockingly close to the barrels of two revolvers in the grimy hands of a pair of thugs.

"Pull off his glasses," Teufel ordered loudly. Which the first thug did. Wentworth, as Blinky, never carried anything more dangerous than a clasp knife.

"Let me see him."

They seized Wentworth's shoulders, spun him about.

Chef Teufel stalked behind the nearest steam table. One of the thugs knocked Wentworth's stained homburg off his head.

"I thought I recognized him, sooty cheeks and all. Bring him to the kitchen."

Imperiously, Teufel turned away, expecting his orders to be carried out.

Wentworth was faster. He stamped on the foot of the hooligan on his left, grabbed him by his lapels and threw him against his companion. Both men reeled into a trestle table still occupied by diners. All went down in a shouting tangle of arms and legs.

Spinning around, Wentworth seized the edge of the nearest steam table and tilted it backward. Scalding yellow fluid caught the servers and, from the waist down, the evil boss of the kitchen. One of the servers shrieked like a baby. Teufel pivoted, his fine white trousers ruined, his eyes fixed on Wentworth with a hellfire of hatred. All at once Blinky McQuade wasn't gimpy; he dashed to the door like a marathon runner on his last quarter mile, and out into the dark.

To the east, the Manhattan skyline shimmered with a dull redness. Gunshots, screams, squealing tires, the crash and rend of metal seemed to assault him from the north, the east, the south, everywhere except the Hudson River a short way west.

Wentworth began to run northward, to the rendezvous with Ram Singh and the Daimler. To his amazement, then his consternation, he heard no pursuit, no oaths, no shots to bring him down. What was the matter with the crazed Teufel? Certainly he wasn't a coward.

Madmen were seldom cowards ...

Wentworth ran on into the night.

Next day the crime wave spread.

Newspaper pundits speculated. FOOD POISONING LINKED TO CRIMINAL RAMPAGE? At four in the afternoon, still disturbed by the fact that he'd been   recognized but not pursued, Wentworth called at Nita's building on Park Avenue. They had a date for cocktails at the Pierre.

No familiar voice answered when he buzzed. The doorman appeared.

"Help you, Mr. Wentworth?"

"Miss Van Sloan, please."

"Oh, she went out about a half hour ago.

Something about a visit to a charity that serves free food down in Hell's Kitchen. A polite gentleman brought a special invitation."

So that's why Teufel had let him go - to lure him back. Punish two instead of one...?

He rushed from the hotel lobby. The early darkness of autumn had come. To his left, a horrific glare showed him something he could hardly believe.

Below 59th Street, Fifth Avenue was burning ...

The *Spider* crept noiselessly through the fetid alley behind the Ace High Tire Warehouse. A starved cat yowled at him and jumped off a garbage can; the lid flew to the bricks and clanged. Rats with ruby eyes scurried away from the sound.

Cautiously, the *Spider* waited until sure the disturbance would not bring a watchman or beat cop. He flexed his hands, leaped high, caught the swing-down fire escape which luckily wasn't too noisy from rust. He crouched on the level platform at the second floor. A large opaqued window resisted every effort to pry it open. From his tool belt the *Spider* brought a highstrength line attached to a three-prong grapple. A small gas cylinder at the end of the line fired at the touch of a button. The grapple soared to the coping above the third floor, lodged there with a soft chunk. The *Spider*'s lips peeled back from his fanged teeth, the closest he could come to a smile.

He tested the line, found it secure, stepped up on the fire escape rail, swung outward, raised his heels and completed the swing feet first, shattering the window. Plummeting through, he saw a metal catwalk limned by dim wall fixtures in the abandoned warehouse. He balanced himself to keep from falling, listened to the broken glass tinkling on the cement floor a story below.

When he deemed it safe, he skulked along the catwalk and down to the ground floor. The steam tables had been emptied and cleaned, the trestle tables washed and made ready for the next recruits who would eagerly consume one of Chef TEFL's hellish meals, then go abroad to rob, pillage, and burn. If such an army of mindless anti-social criminals continued to grow, unchecked, another week or two would bring New York to its knees.

The *Spider*'s eyes adjusted to the lower light levels in the warehouse. He spied a rivet-studded iron door in the wall opposite the Ninth Avenue side. A bolt thick as a man's wrist secured the door on this side, but the bolt wasn't slid home. The *Spider* presumed a similar, interior bolt was in place.

He padded across the cement floor. A metal door beside the much larger one opened suddenly. Two hulks in brown shirts and twill jodhpurs strode into the warehouse. The *Spider* heard a guttural word in German, which translated as window.

The hulk in the lead pointed to the scattered glass. His companion stared, then caught on. For a moment neither saw the *Spider* running at them in a crouch. Then one of the burly men spotted him, cried a warning in a foreign tongue. Lugers in the hands of the brown shirts began to spit and blaze. The *Spider* was already rolling behind one of the trestle tables, which he tipped forward, a barricade instantly hit by slugs from the attackers. Chips of wood flew; bullets ricocheted and buzzed away.

The *Spider* waited for a pause, one or both of the gunmen jamming in new magazines. When it came, he flung his hands over the edge of the trestle table and pumped .45 rounds one after another.

The first guard dropped as though pole-axed. The second began firing again, even as his eyes blanked and his polished boots began to kick and jerk in a mad rigadoon of death. The *Spider* fired relentlessly, splattering the killer's bloody brain matter on the cement wall behind him.

Echoes of the thunderous fusillade died away. Cordite reeked throughout the warehouse. The *Spider* padded forward, knelt to press a small round tube to the center of the first man's forehead, leaving the mark of a crimson spider above the bridge of the corpse's nose ...

Re-loading for his next assault - .45's blasting away at the exterior bolt to destroy the one on the other side - the *Spider* was caught short by the sudden creak of the right-hand door, the spill of light from the room beyond. A ghastly kind of fluctuating yellow-orange radiance - the light seemed to illumine the whole chamber beyond the door. The *Spider* saw a huge hanging banner, red as poppies, a circular white field in the center bearing a familiar mythological sign already loathed by millions of Americans because the Nazis had adopted the ancient swastika as their own ...

"I would enter with great care," boomed a voice from an invisible source; the *Spider* recognized it all too clearly. "I have my hand on a lever which I need only to trip to add a delicious final ingredient to my beautiful new recipe. I call it - " The guttural voice of Chef TEFL milked the moment for all of its sinister content.

"Bisque Van Sloan."

The *Spider*'s nerves froze. He crossed his hands, slid both still-hot .45s into holsters. Then he raised his hands. "I'm coming in."

"That, I believe, is the voice of my former café customer, *Herr* Wentworth."

The *Spider* stepped into the inner chamber, hands high. Light fell across his flopping hat brim, the ends of his lank hair where it brushed his collar. The *Spider* was thunderstruck by one of the most ghastly, macabre scenes he had ever witnessed in his many confrontations with masters of villainy.

Toque jauntily in place, Chef TEFL crouched on a platform raised some ten feet off the floor. In front of him, emitting low, ugly gurgles as bubbles burst, a viscous liquid in a brimming ladle emanated that yelloworange light. Slowly, the surface currents eddied; slowly, the glow transitioned from a blood-orange to a sickly yellow and back; slowly, surface bubbles popped with ugly gaseous sounds.

The *Spider* saw three huge Nazi banners, one on each wall. Three more brown-shirted hulks armed with, respectively, a rifle, a double-barrel revolver, and a sub-machine gun with an enlarged drum, menaced him from firing positions around the ladle. And - *God help us*, the *Spider* thought - suspended from stout leather cuffs at the end of a heavy chain, Nita Van Sloan rotated slowly, her bare feet scarcely a yard above the crust of Teufel's hellish soup. The chef's white-gloved hand hovered near the release lever. The *Spider* had no illusions about what it would release.

Poor Nita's hair hung loosely around her bare shoulders. Her outer garments had been torn away, leaving only tatters of lingerie that barely concealed her supple body. Long vicious scratches and large bruises marred her exposed flesh. She turned slowly over the ladle, her eyes slitted, drowsy ..

"So"—Chef TEFL said it so that it came out zo, with a protracted, hissing "oh" sound—"I recognize the voice but not the face. Mr. Wentworth the man of leisure has turned into some Halloween grotesque."

"Get down from there, you Nazi filth."

"Why? Do you propose to bargain with me? Somehow I feel that you have no chips to place on the table. Am I in error, *Herr* Wentworth?"

The repetition of the name made Nita's eyes fluttered. "Dick?" she whispered, her bosom beginning to heave within the ragged confines of her torn slip. "Oh, dear heaven, is it you??"

"I have this to bargain with," the *Spider* said. "Myself. My life for hers."

Chef TEFL laughed, a high, screeching mockery.

"And I should surrender one verdammt Amerikaner when I already have two in my possession? Not likely, mein freund."

He pumped the lever; hidden gears and ratchets clanked and squealed. The chain jerked and dropped Nita a foot closer to the bubbling liquid.

The most aggressive of Teufel's henchmen, the one with the large-drum subma-chine gun, spoke impatiently. "I say boil 'em both and be done with it, kommandant."

Teufel screamed apoplectically. "But you are not in charge. You have nothing to say. You are cogs in the magnificent machine, nothing more." While Teufel's attention was diverted during the outburst, the *Spider* reached behind his collar and drew a spring knife from its concealed sheath. The man with the rifle shrieked and clutched his throat when the *Spider*'s silver death-dart struck.

"Kill him, kill him," screamed the chef.

The *Spider*'s .45s leaped into his hands. Cataclysmic crashes and sizzling spurts of fire tore the sub-machine gunner's face apart. The double-barrel revolver fired a round an instant before the *Spider* blasted its owner to oblivion; a spasmodic reaction discharged the other barrel, pointing downward now. It blew off the gunman's left foot, though he was slowly sagging, too dead to feel it.

The few seconds of intense gunplay had galvanized Chef TEFL into action. Panting, he pulled on the control lever. The chain bucked and jerked. Nita dropped again. The *Spider* flung both automatics behind him, caught the searing-hot rim of the ladle and, like a circus performer taking the maximum risk, teetered to his feet on the rim, flailing the air for balance.

Chef TEFL screamed obscenities in German and worked the lever yet again. The *Spider* leaped, all the force of his powerful legs propelling him through the air. He struck Nita like a football tackler, driving her backward to the edge. Simultaneously, TEFL threw off the chain's locking brake, allowing Nita to fly beyond the ladle's rim as the chain unreeled.

Nita struck the hard floor, crying out. The *Spider* seized the dangling chain, kicked high and wide like a champion gymnast, and let go, momentum hurling him over Teufel's hell-brew. He narrowly missed the ladle's far rim as he crashed to the cement.

The *Spider* raised his head groggily. The chain was still unreeling from its ceiling drum. Somehow Teufel's left ankle and calf had tangled in the iron links. Unreeling and unreeling with enormous noise, the chain yanked him from the platform and dragged him cursing and screaming in German under the suddenlyagitated yellow-orange surface of his finest culinary creation ...

A knock at the door of the hospital room sent Wentworth to answer. The nurse had no time to utter an apology before Commissioner Kirkpatrick bowled into the softly lit private suite.

"Kirk," Wentworth said, pumping his hand. "Good of you to come."

"How is she?"

"Recovering. Slowly. Shock, mostly."

Nita heard their quiet voices, turned her head toward them, her eyelids fluttering. Wentworth drew his friend aside.

"How is it outside?"

"Under control, thank the Lord. With that free kitchen shut down, and no more unwilling soldiers created by his damned food, we've been rounding up the others by the dozens. Finally I think we're on top of it."

He stepped forward, holding out a fragrant bouquet of roses. "I brought these for you, Nita. And these - "

"Kirk, I wouldn't," Wentworth began as his friend proffered two conveniences cartons.

"*Coq au vin* from the Pierre - your favorite. And some nourishing soup from the deli." The soup carton exuded an aroma that quickly filled the room.

Nita blanched and clutched Wentworth's sleeve.

"Would you call the nurse, darling? I think I'm going to be ill."

ABOUT OUR CONTRIBUTORS

➤ **MORT CASTLE's** most recent publications include the reprint of the novel *Cursed be the Child*, deemed "a classic of its kind" by RAVE REVIEWS, from Overlook Connection Press, and *On Writing Horror: Second Revised Edition*, by the Horror Writers Association, which he edited, from Writer's Digest Books. The Tim O'Rawe penned screenplay based on Castle's novel *The Strangers* has been optioned by Whitewater Films. A writer for four decades, Castle has seen more than 500 publications in many venues, including TWILIGHT ZONE MAGAZINE, WRITER'S DIGEST, and HOG FARM MANAGEMENT. He teaches in the fiction writing department at Columbia College Chicago and is considered one of the world's leading 5 string banjo players among fiction writers in his height, age, weight, and mental health divisions.

➤ **BILL CRIDER** is the author of fifty published novels and numerous short stories. He won the Anthony Award for best first mystery novel in 1987 for *Too Late to Die For* and was nominated for the Shamus Award for best first private-eye novel for *Dead on the Island*. He won the Golden Duck award for "best juvenile science fiction novel" for *Mike Gonzo and the UFO Terror*. He and his wife, Judy, won the best short story Anthony in 2002 for their story "Chocolate Moose." His latest novel is *Murder among the O.W.L.S.* Check out his homepage at www.billcrider.com

➤ **SHANNON ERIC DENTON**: A veteran storyteller who worked as a storyboard artist on numerous projects including Paramount Pictures OSCAR NOMINATED feature *"Jimmy Neutron: Boy Genius"*. Shannon directed the original commercial animations for the movie marketing campaign. From 1995-1999 he contributed to the design and development of almost every animated action adventure show produced by the Fox Kids Network including the *"X-Men"*, *"Spider-Man"* and the Annie nominated *"Silver Surfer"* series as well as doing comic work for Marvel, DC, Dark Horse, Tokyopop, and Image. Shannon is featured in a section of the Watson-Guptill book Toon Art: The Graphic Art of Digital Cartooning and his artwork graces the cover. Shannon's writing has been seen on Cartoon Network and has been covered in Entertainment Weekly. Shannon is partners in the online website, *Komikwerks* which has an alliance with AOL and Stan Lee and is also publishing a line of illustrated prose novels under the imprint of *Actionopolis*.

➤ **CHUCK DIXON** is perhaps best know for his lengthy run on various *Batman*-related comic titles comprising hundreds of scripts. His greatest recommendation for writing the *Spider* is that he has actually fired a matched pair of automatic pistols simultaneously. He did this, however, without hitting a damned thing.

➤ **STEVE ENGLEHART** has written pretty much every comic you've ever heard of. All *Batman* film and animation for the last 30 years comes from his conception, but there's also the *Green Lantern Corps, Silver Surfer, Doctor Strange, and Coyote*. He created the *Night Man* comic and wrote for its television incarnation. He wrote the story for the *Tron 2.0* video game and worked on *Bard's Tale IV*. NASA chose his biography of the Wright Brothers for their school curricula. Currently, he's writing *The Long Man*, a sequel to his novel *The Point Man*, about an immortal vs. the neocons.

THOMAS FLOYD, an ex-soldier, adventurer, demolitions man, roustabout, roughneck, and mechanic, who has settled for a simpler life on the Great Plains. Now only interested in producing illustrations that harken back to the day when magazine racks were a feast for a young artist's eye, and when heroes and adventure flooded magazines, the airwaves, and film. He relives the thrilling days of yesteryear with his webcomic at www.captainspectre.com. You can also view his art at www.thomasfloyd.com.

RON FORTIER has been writing comics and adventure fiction for the past thirty-five years. He is most known for his work on Now Comics' the *Green Hornet* and *Terminator-The Burning Earth* with Alex Ross. Recently Ron has revived the classic pulp hero, *Captain Hazzard* in a brand new series of pulp novels published by Wild Cat Books. www.lulu.com/wildcatbooks You can catch up with him at www.Airship27.com

JOE GENTILE, Co-Publisher of Moonstone, keeps pretty busy, but in his spare moments, has written many graphic novels as well as other fiction: *The Phantom, Buckaroo Banzai, Kolchak the Night Stalker, Sherlock Holmes, Werewolf the Apocalypse, The Mysterious Traveler, The Spider*, etc. Be on the look out for his new novel: "*Sherlock Holmes & Kolchak the Night Stalker: Cry of Thunder*". When he's not writing, editing, publishing, or trying to sleep, Joe also plays bass guitar, and enjoys a good life with his wife Kathy and their two personality-ridden dogs Apollo and Artemis. More of Joe's work can be found at: www.moonstonebooks.com

JOHN HELFERS is an author and editor currently living in Green Bay, Wisconsin. He has published more than thirty short stories in anthologies such as *If I Were An Evil Overlord, Time Twisters*, and *Places to Be, People to Kill*. His media tie-in fiction has appeared in anthologies for the *Dragonlance®* and *Transformers®* universes, among others. He has written both fiction and nonfiction books, including the third novel in the first authorized trilogy based on *The Twilight Zone™* television series, the YA novel *Tom Clancy's Net Force Explorers: Cloak and Dagger*, and a history of the United States Navy. His most recent novels are *Shadowrun: Aftershock*, co-authored by Jean Rabe and the ACTIONOPOLIS book *Thunder Riders*.

C.J. HENDERSON is the creator of both the *Jack Hagee* hardboiled PI series and the *Teddy London* supernatural detective series. He is the author of some 40 books, including such diverse titles as *The Encyclopedia of Science Fiction Movies* and *Black Sabbath: The Ozzy Osbourne Years*. He has written thousands of non-fiction articles and hundreds of short stories. He has also done a great amount of work in the wonderful world of comics where he has handled characters from *Batman* to *Kolchak: the Nightstalker* and from *Archie* to *Cherry Poptart*. For more information about this talented writer and winner of The Sunniest Smile in Town award five years running, go to www.cjhenderson.com for free short stories and endless shenanigans.

HOWARD HOPKINS is the author of twenty-seven western novels under the penname Lance Howard, along five horror novels and one young adult novel under his own. His most recent western, *Nightmare Pass*, was published in December of 2006, with the next in the series, *Hell Pass*, due in April, 2007. His recent comic horror work was turned into a mini movie for DVD and his cheerful tale of Christmas serial killing, "Slay Bells", appeared in a short story anthology titled *The Holiday Mixer*. A long time pulp hero fan, he has published forty issues of the pulp journal *Golden Perils* and written a history of The Avenger titled *"The Gray Nemesis"*, which is now available again in electronic format www.howardhopkins.com/page4.htm. He lives in a small Maine seacoast town and plays mandolin, guitar, piano, sax and lead sings for a quartet that volunteers at local nursing homes. Website:www.howardhopkins.com

JOHN JAKES sold his first short story at 18 and has written professionally ever since. His multi-volume sagas, *The Kent Family Chronicles* and *The North and South Trilogy* won him international fame, and he continues as one of today's best-selling historical novelists. His latest work, *The Gods of Newport*, was published in 2006. He grew up reading the popular literature of the 1930's and 1940's, naming *The Spider* tales as particular favorites.

Award winning illustrator, **DOUGLAS KLAUBA** was born in Chicago with a pencil and a paintbrush always in hand. His work is instantly recognizable by its pulp magazine and retro movie poster influences, blended to create what Klauba calls his "Heroic Deco" style. Doug's paintings have been included in the art annuals of Spectrum: The Best in Contemporary Fantastic Art and the Society of Illustrators. His painting *Mercury Jack* has exhibited in the Spectrum Show at the Museum of American Illustration and his painting *da Vinci's Dream* was awarded Best in Show at the 2005 World's Fantasy Convention. www.douglasklauba.com

JAMES ANTHONY KUHORIC is the 2006 Spike TV Scream Award winning author of the *Army of Darkness* comic book series (Best Movie to Comic Book honors) and is a veteran writer of horror and sci-fi comic books. 2007 marks a decade of telling tales in comics, the sequential art form he fell in love with as a youth. His work includes script and prose contributions to the sci-fi and horror classics *Battlestar Galactica, First Wave, Stargate SG-1, Kolchak the Night Stalker, Lexx,* and *Army of Darkness*. This year he unveils his darkest work yet with the brutal undead western saga, *Dead Irons*. His biggest joy in life is watching his two sons grow and experience the wonders of reading. Look for more *Army of Darkness* insanity from Ash Williams as he returns from the *Marvel Zombies* crossover and is launched into a post apocalyptic world where the Deadites rule and mankind is on the brink of extinction. For more information on James and his projects, visit http://www.dynamiteentertainment.com/htmlfiles/.

ELIZABETH MASSIE is a two-time Bram Stoker Award-winning author of horror/suspense fiction. Her books include *Sineater, Welcome Back to the Night, Wire Mesh Mothers, Dark Shadows: Dreams of the Dark* (co-authored with Stephen Mark Rainey), *Shadow Dreams, Power of Persuasion, The Fear Report, Twisted Branch: A Novel of the Abbadon Inn* (written as "Chris Blaine"), and more. Her next novel, *Homeplace*, will be released from Berkley in August 2007. Elizabeth is also the creator of "Skeeryvilletown," a cartoon community of monsters and freaks. She lives in the Shenandoah Valley with illustrator Cortney Skinner and can be reached at www.elizabethmassie.com .

CHRISTOPHER MILLS is a freelance writer, editor and graphic artist with over two decades of experience in the publishing industry, working primarily for newspapers and comic book publishers. A professional writer since 1990, he's scripted numerous independent comic books in a variety of genres, including *Leonard Nimoy's Primortals*, Shadow House, The Night Driver and the critically-acclaimed crime thriller,

GraveDigger: The Scavengers. He's also authored a handful of published short stories, with more in the works. Currently, he's writing several comic books for various publishers, a regular online DVD review column, and a bunch of other projects. His website is www.atomicpulp.com.

WILL MURRAY may be uniquely qualified to write *The Spider.* As a child, he suffered from arachnophobia, but loved *Spider-Man.* The author of scores of novels and short stories featuring *Doc Savage, The Destroyer, Spider-Man, The Phantom, Superman and Batman,* he is a recognized authority on 1930s pulp heroes. Murray boasts of having read nearly every *Spider* novel written by Norvell Page, and once dated his great grand niece, surviving both experiences for the most part. He wrote "March of the Murder Mummy" because he felt Richard Wentworth battled far too few Egyptian enemies, especially after the Living Pharoah debacle.

MARTIN POWELL has been a professional writer since 1986 and is perhaps best known for *SCARLET IN GASLIGHT,* the Eisner nominated graphic novel featuring *Sherlock Holmes* and *Count Dracula.* Martin's unique style of comic book scripting has also been showcased at *The International Museum of Cartoon Art* at Boca Raton, Florida, in a special celebrated exhibit. He lives in a creepy one hundred twelve year old haunted house in Minneapolis, with artist Lisa Bandemer, their two nearly human dogs and five diabolical cats. He enthusiastically lists *THE SPIDER* as one of his all-time favorite characters. **http://www.myspace.com/martinpowellphantomshadow**

ANNIE NOCENTI is a journalist, photographer and screenwriter. Her work has appeared in *Prison Life, Filmmaker, Utne, The New York Times, High Times, Heeb, Scenario* and many other publications. She is a writer and editor at large at *Stop Smiling* magazine www.stopsmilingonline.com. Her feature film script *"Patriotville,"* starring Justin Long, is in post-production. She is currently working on a documentary about Baluchistan. (see the Dec/Jan issue of *BrooklynRail.org* for that story) She has written many comic books, including *Daredevil, Typhoid Mary, Spiderman, Batman and Longshot.*

DENNIS O' NEIL is an award-winning writer, editor, lecturer, and teacher who has worked in comics for over 40 years. He lives with his wife, Marifran, in Nyack, New York.

BOB WEINBERG is the author of 16 novels, 2 short story collections and 16 non-fiction books. He's also scripted comics for Marvel, DC, and Moonstone comics. Bob's probably best known as the author of *The Masquerade of the Red Death.* trilogy he wrote for White Wolf Games. His work has been

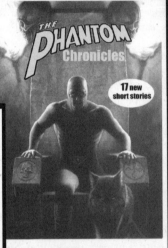